EDGE OF THE ENFORCER

Cherise Sinclair

LooseId®

ISBN 13: 978-1-62300-411-8
EDGE OF THE ENFORCER
Copyright © May 2014 by Cherise Sinclair
Originally released in e-book format in May 2014

Cover Art by April Martinez
Cover Layout and Design by April Martinez

Image/art disclaimer: Licensed material is being used for illustrative purposes only. Any person depicted in the licensed material is a model.

DISCLAIMER: Many of the acts described in our BDSM/fetish titles can be dangerous. Please do not try any new sexual practice, whether it be fire, rope, or whip play, without the guidance of an experienced practitioner. Neither Loose Id nor its authors will be responsible for any loss, harm, injury or death resulting from use of the information contained in any of its titles.

This book is an original publication of Loose Id. Each individual story herein was previously published in e-book format only by Loose Id and is a work of fiction. Any similarity to actual persons, events or existing locations is entirely coincidental.

Printed in the U.S.A. by
Lightning Source, Inc.
1246 Heil Quaker Blvd
La Vergne TN 37086
www.lightningsource.com

AUTHOR'S NOTE

To my readers,

The books I write are fiction, not reality, and as in most romantic fiction, the romance is compressed into a very, very short time period.

You, my darlings, live in the real world, and I want you to take a little more time in your relationships. Good Doms don't grow on trees, and there are some strange people out there. So while you're looking for that special Dom, please, be careful.

When you find him, realize he can't read your mind. Yes, frightening as it might be, you're going to have to open up and talk to him. And you listen to him in return. Share your hopes and fears, what you want from him, what scares you spitless. Okay, he may try to push your boundaries a little—he's a Dom, after all—but you will have your safe word. You will have a safe word, am I clear? Use protection. Have a backup person. Communicate.

Remember: safe, sane, and consensual.

Know that I'm hoping you find that special, loving person who will understand your needs and hold you close.

And while you're looking or even if you've already found your dearheart, come and hang out with the Doms of Dark Haven.

Love,
Cherise

ACKNOWLEDGMENT

Thanks to you all for talking me into writing about deVries. (And although he won't say as much, he's grateful too.)

Kisses to Suede and Phantom for answering questions about the sadistic mindset.

My gratitude to Leagh Christensen, my personal assistant, for shouldering an amazing amount of thankless tasks, and blessings upon Lisa Simo-Kinzer, gracious Mistress of my street team and discussion group.

Thanks to my beloved ShadowKitten's street team for enthusiastically pouncing upon potential new readers and for help with story questions.

Where would I be without my evil beta readers—Bianca Sommerland with her love of darkness and heightened emotions, Fiona Archer who likes balance and romance, and Monette Michaels who expects consistency (sheesh!) and intense action. Sweet Liz Berry kept deVries from stepping out of line, and Molly Daniels added a keen eye—and lively discussions on weaponry. Thank you all!

A big shout-out goes to my editor, Maryam, and the awesome copy, line, and proof-editors at Loose Id. Their passion for turning a manuscript into something y'all would want to read is so, so appreciated.

I'm sending big hugs to all of you who come and play on my Facebook pages and in the new Discussion Group. My days are brightened by cat jokes, heated discussions about the Masters, eye-candy, and your enthusiasm for answering odd questions.

As always, my love and appreciation to my Dearheart, who ruthlessly drags me out of the cave and reminds me that life is meant to be lived.

CHAPTER ONE

N o moon. Beneath the cold stars, the pickup bumped over the rutted road, tossing the mercenaries around like fired shells from an M-4.

"Fuck," deVries growled under his breath. He resumed his kneeling position and braced himself on the wooden side slats. Grasping Harris's shoulder, he used his free hand to apply pressure to the young man's belly below his bulletproof vest. Blood poured out, warm over his fingers. The new merc wouldn't live. They'd put dressings on the leg wounds, but from the amount of bleeding, the bullet in his pelvis had ripped up his insides.

Medical care was too far away.

"I-I'm cold," Harris whispered. The kid was in his midtwenties.

Too fucking young to die.

"Hey, Iceman. Here."

DeVries caught the jacket a teammate tossed over and added it to the others on Harris. Poor bastard. Last one to join the team. First one to go.

"You got anyone back home?" deVries asked.

A convulsive tremor shook the kid. His systems were shutting down, one by one, no matter how hard his body fought. "Uh-uh. Wife left me." Another shiver. He sucked air. "She d-didn't like being poor. Want her back so signed on here. Pay's good."

Yeah, mercenary work paid top dollar.

"Got no one," the broken whisper continued. "You?"

"Nah." No one to go home to. No one to talk to about his job or his merc work. No one to mourn if he didn't return. Missions like this made for a fine adrenaline zing. Didn't make for a long life.

The kid had screwed up. Tripped and alerted the perimeter guards. A nice clean extraction had turned into a goat fuck. DeVries's armor had stopped one bullet; the next one had ripped a chunk of meat from above his hip. His jeans were already soaked with blood. Couple inches over and he'd have been lying beside Harris.

"We get the guy out?" Harris whispered.

"Affirmative. You did good"—what was Harris's first name?—"Luke. The man'll be reunited with his family by tomorrow." But it sucked that the asshole they'd rescued wasn't worth someone's life.

"Won't see it."

Grief and anger twisted in deVries's gut. Dammit. Wasn't fair.

In the faint moonlight shining down into the bed of the farm truck, Harris's eyes were dull but level.

"No, you won't." DeVries wouldn't lie. If a man could face the question, he deserved an honest answer. DeVries closed his hand over Harris's chill one. Squeezed. "I'm sorry. You have anything you need done?"

"Buy the boys a round for me."

His throat tightened. "You got it."

Harris's eyelids drooped, and his breathing turned shallow.

DeVries settled in beside him. A man shouldn't die alone. Each time the truck hit a bump, pain stabbed into deVries's side, reminding him he was alive. One day, he'd be the poor bastard lying there. No pretty woman to cry for him and make him fight to survive. Only a teammate to keep vigil.

And he'd die...for what? To save a dirty politician from his well-deserved desserts? To get a few extra bucks in the bank?

He'd turned down money before. His mouth tightened, remembering his fucked-up childhood and how his mother's pimp had yelled at her. "...good-looking boy. The little shit could fill his pockets with big bills, and he says no? You got the stupidest kid in Chicago."

But deVries hadn't wanted to be a whore. To sell himself for money. He'd craved a real home. Someone to love him. Right. Now here he was, a mercenary and alone. God had a fucking good sense of irony.

⟨⟨⟩⟩

A week later, deVries walked through the chill autumn air up to the door of Dark Haven—the notorious San Francisco BDSM club. As he entered, he found a line of members waiting in front of the reception desk.

Fine with him. He could use the time to get his head into the right space for the night. With a sigh, he leaned on the wall, feeling the drag of exhaustion like he wore diving weights on his belt.

Damn fucked-up mission. The throb of grief was more painful than the wound in his side. Harris had died before they'd reached the pickup point. Hadn't even had anyone to notify. Because his wife didn't want to be poor. Yeah, some bitches could be greedier than any soldier for hire.

With an effort, deVries sidestepped old dark memories. He was in enough of a crappy mood. The healing gash along his hip still hurt like hell, and ripping the stitches open would be stupid, so using his favorite flogger was out. But, damn, he wanted a good, long session. The need to inflict pain was a low hum in his bones.

The pretty receptionist named Lindsey smiled at the next person in the line.

"Hi, HurtMe," she said in her soft Texas drawl, taking the membership card from the young man. "Are your classes going well?" Despite the leisurely, warm river of her voice, Lindsey had a personality that danced like a sunlit fountain.

Under her attention, the masochist glowed as he told her about his exams.

DeVries shook his head. Lindsey was the reason the line moved so slowly. The girl liked people and had the ability to talk with anyone about anything.

Too lively to sit, she stood behind the reception desk. Her

wavy brown hair, streaked with red-and-gold highlights, had grown over the summer to her bra line. Quite a bra it was too. The club owner, Xavier, had decreed an animal theme for the night, and Lindsey wore a fur leopard-printed bra. Be nice to see what covered her ass, since the girl didn't lack imagination.

Rather a shame she never stripped naked, though. She had a sweet little body—one designed to be used well and often. Unfortunately she didn't enjoy the harder forms of kink.

"Have a good night, sweetie." Turning, she looked at deVries and held her hand out. "Sir, may I take your card?"

He handed it over to put through the card reader.

"Thank you."

He noticed how she averted her big brown eyes, and her mouth tightened. Apparently, what he'd told her a while back had hurt her feelings. She needed to get over it.

"Lindsey," he growled.

Her gaze flashed up to his.

"Better."

She gave him a puzzled blink, and hell, he wanted her under him, giving him that confused look as he started doing everything he'd imagined to her.

But he wasn't going to go there, even if she did still owe him a blowjob and anal sex from a paintball party last July. Sadly, he'd been called away on a mission and hadn't collected. Pissed him off at the time. Just as well—fucking her would have been a piss-poor move. Lindsey was a sweet submissive, and he had no use for niceness in his life.

"You look tired." She handed his card back. "Are you all right?"

Yeah. Warmhearted as could be.

"No." With a brusque nod, he turned away. Tonight he'd delve into the darker side, indulge his need to give pain, erase the bitterness of the last mission. This one couldn't take what he needed to dish out. Few women could.

Only males held up well when deVries got this needy.

As he walked into the club, he glanced back and saw Ethan

Worthington lean over the desk and run his finger over Lindsey's play collar.

Not surprising she smiled a welcome. The Dom was intelligent. Well-liked. And had more money than God.

Looked like the lucky bastard would be the one to enjoy the sweetie. Well, more power to him.

Jaw tight, deVries shoved through into the main clubroom, feeling as if he'd like to kill someone. Again.

"I DON'T ENJOY a lot of pain," Lindsey said to Sir Ethan, trying to concentrate on the conversation and not watch deVries stalk through the door. God, the way he moved was like a timber wolf on the hunt. Powerful and deadly.

Sexy as hell.

And he didn't like her. Oh, she had thought different at the Fourth of July games. He'd sure acted growly when he'd been called away. But later, back in San Francisco, when she reminded him of her debt, he said he'd collect her ass *if* he wanted. His dismissive attitude showed he had no interest in her whatsoever.

Way to make a girl feel like a scrawny chicken not even good enough for the stew pot. He hadn't even noticed her sexy costume sewn from less than a yard of furry fabric.

"Lindsey." With one finger on her chin, Sir Ethan drew her attention back. His clear blue gaze was perceptive...and understanding. "Do you really want to play with a sadist?"

"I... No." God no. Especially not one like deVries...who didn't want *her*.

An hour later, Xavier strolled out of the main clubroom into the reception area. Several inches over six feet, with Native American dark coloring, black eyes, and black hair in a braid down his back, the owner of Dark Haven never failed to make Lindsey sit up straight and lower her gaze. Somehow, he gave a whole new meaning to the word dominant.

A step behind him, his wife, Abby, had flushed cheeks,

swollen lips, and reddened skin around her wrists. Obviously they'd already had a scene.

Xavier smiled at Lindsey. "Work time is over, pet. Go find someone to play with."

As he picked up the new member applications, Lindsey stood up and stretched. "Sounds good. Thank you, my liege."

Sitting down in the chair Lindsey had vacated, Abby tilted her head. "How are you doing? Are you ready for a girl's night soon?"

"I'd love it." She'd have to skip lunch for a day or two to afford it, but girlfriends came far, far higher in the priority scheme than food. "Next weekend?"

"Rona said she was busy on Friday. Can you do Saturday?"

Lindsey nodded.

Abby patted Xavier's bottom. "Your receptionists are going to be on strike next Saturday."

He raised an intimidating eyebrow. "That means Dixon will have to take the desk for a shift."

"Well, I'm sure he'll leave us a mess. Nonetheless, we're still taking the night off."

"You're definitely a stubborn little fluff." Xavier bent to capture his wife's lips.

Lindsey smothered a sigh of envy. Once upon a time, she'd thought she'd have a loving husband, a family. A home.

As Xavier headed back into his club and Abby turned to greet an entering member, Lindsey glanced at the desk. She'd left it bare except for one stack of papers. If Dixon took reception, disaster would ensue. The cutest submissive in Dark Haven, Dixon considered himself a lover, not a secretary, and never filed anything.

However, huge paper piles were a piddly price to pay for a weekend night off and a chance to drink without having to work the next day. Abby was a professor at a small college, and Rona did hospital administration.

Back before her life had gone to hell in a handbasket, Lindsey had been a social worker. And had loved it.

Now she was a receptionist—and her temp job would end this week. Job hunting wasn't easy, even though the fake ID she'd bought last spring passed muster. But when she'd fled Texas, she realized what the lack of her college transcripts and past employment recommendations would mean.

She was stuck in minimum-wage jobs despite her years of education.

Come to think of it, education sure hadn't helped her pick a good husband. He'd taken her in completely. She closed her eyes at the memory of Victor's sneer. *"Why would I want a cunt like you when I can fuck sweeter meat?"*

God, she'd been blind. She remembered her daddy's John Wayne quote. *"Life's hard. It's even harder when you're stupid."*

Wasn't that the truth? Now she had a warrant out for her arrest and cops who would kill her before she ever made it to jail. Who had already tried. She glanced at the long scar on the back of her wrist.

Abby returned a man's membership card. "Have a great night." As he walked into the main room, she turned to Lindsey, and her forehead creased. "Are you okay?"

No. "Sure." Lindsey gave her an only slightly twisted smile. "Saturday it is. Party time!"

After sharing a high five, Lindsey headed into the club.

On the main floor, tables filled the center of the room between the two stages. Members in leather and latex, corsets and chains, naked or fully covered, were socializing, dancing, drinking, and watching demonstrations. The dark wave music of Anders Manga reverberated through the huge room, keeping the dancers at the far end moving.

At one time, she'd loved to dance. Two-step. Line dancing. But that time was over. She stood for a moment, hobbled by despair. She couldn't go home to Texas. Not when the head of her husband's smuggling operation had turned out to be his brother, Travis—the police chief. Not when the corruption extended into other law enforcement agencies like the border patrol.

She exhaled slowly.

If she couldn't go back, she had to move forward. If nothing else, the police officer's death—as well as her husband's—had taught her how short life could be and to fully live in what remained to her.

Here in San Francisco, she'd embraced that philosophy. Joined Dark Haven. Turned long-held fantasies into reality. She was no longer a novice in the BDSM lifestyle.

So where was Sir Ethan? Mistress Tara was demonstrating wax play on the right stage. On the left one, a Dom and his submissive were setting up equipment for their upcoming scene. Sir Ethan wasn't at a table watching or at the bar near the far end. Or on the dance floor.

He'd probably gone downstairs.

She took the stairs down into the more intense environment of the dungeon. Here the music was punctuated by the sounds of impact toys like floggers and paddles, by groans and moans, harsh breathing, an occasional shriek.

To her disappointment, when she spotted Sir Ethan, he wore a dungeon monitor's badge. He wouldn't be able to play until he was off duty.

He gave her a wave and mouthed the word *later*. Oh well, he was worth waiting for. He was one of the best Doms in the club. Although he read her so easily it was scary, he hadn't pushed when she'd said she didn't want anything serious.

Too many of the Doms seemed to want to form a relationship—and what was with that? Didn't they realize men were supposed to prefer keeping things light?

Shaking her head, she walked past a suspension scene where the Dom had flipped the submissive into head-down position to give him a blowjob. Lindsey bit her lip. Hanging in the air really took a sub's control away. Adding oral sex into such a mix might be a bit much, and yet there was something wonderful about being able to please a Dom that way.

Farther down, a needle-play scene made Lindsey wince. The Domme had created a needle design on the submissive's back that looked like fairy wings. Really painful ones.

Next, a gay Master was flogging two of his slaves, one and the other, working them both with an amazing skill, especially since one was obviously a needier masochist. But the Master seemed to be enjoying each.

At the end of the room was...deVries. Hell, she shouldn't stop, but the sadist did such fantastic scenes that she loved to watch him, although the thought of taking so much pain made her sweat—and not in a good way.

As always, he'd attracted a number of observers, so she quietly positioned herself at the rear.

For some reason, his usual flogger was still in the bag, and he was using a violet wand instead. The male bottom, johnboy, was strapped down on the bondage table. Leather had been wrapped around his exposed testicles.

DeVries applied the wand here and there, obviously testing the bottom's tolerance for electrical stimulation...and pain. After a few minutes, he used a cane on johnboy's thighs, stomach, and chest, occasionally adding some light whacks to his penis and balls.

Lindsey realized her legs were clamped together in sympathy.

DeVries returned to the wand. Gradually, the bottom's muscles grew rigid. He was groaning. Fighting. Sweating. Then as johnboy slid into subspace, his eyes glazed and his lips curved up, despite the way his body shook.

DeVries played him like a musical instrument, dropping the intensity before deliberately bringing him up to even more pain, over and over.

Heat curled low in Lindsey's belly. Holy shit, she never, ever wanted pain like that, and yet she'd never seen anything so erotic in her life.

The audience grew. Conversations were kept to a whisper to avoid disturbing the scene. With a shock, Lindsey realized the man next to her was the bottom's Master—and partner. She frowned and glanced at deVries.

As if understanding her unspoken question, Master Rock said, "Johnboy needs more pain than I'm willing to dish out. So occasionally, I hook him up with a sadist." As his partner groaned, Rock watched with an indulgent expression. "I asked deVries not to let johnboy get off; I intend to reap the benefits."

Well. That was different. Lindsey turned back to the scene.

The expression on deVries's face was akin to the submissive's. Intent, completely focused, showing both satisfaction and pleasure.

What would it be like to have all that attention focused on her? She actually felt her heart skip a beat at the thought.

Acting as if he had eternity to play, deVries switched to the cane again. The whapping sounds were drowned out by johnboy's gut-wrenching groans. Faster. Harder.

At last deVries stopped and waved a hand at Master Rock. "All yours. Primed for action."

And God, johnboy really was. He was so hard his cock pulsed with each heartbeat.

From the mouthwatering bulge barely contained inside deVries's worn-soft leathers, he was in equal discomfort. Lindsey's brows drew together. The arrangement was all good for the two gay guys, and yet, what about the sadist? He didn't get relief?

Come to think of it, she rarely saw him fuck anyone here. And she'd watched him. Ever since she'd joined the club last spring, he'd fascinated her. Damned if she was sure why.

Tilting her head, she studied him as he cleaned his equipment and stowed it away. His hair was military short, his face lean with a strong jaw and well-formed hard lips. A frown line showed between his eyebrows. No laugh lines; he didn't often smile. He wasn't quite as tall as Xavier, but God, his broad shoulders and muscular chest under a black T-shirt made saliva pool in her mouth.

And the way he walked was simply deadly...as if it wouldn't bother him at all to turn someone into a pile of bones and blood. Knowing how much deVries enjoyed dispensing pain, Xavier often asked him to administer punishment to unruly submissives—who'd nicknamed him the Enforcer.

Lindsey bit her lip. Why the hell did she have to be attracted to a sadist?

Now he was done with the heavy scene, what would he do? She felt a smidgen of pity as she watched him pack his toy bag, leaving the submissive tied to the table for Rock to enjoy. No one was there for deVries.

However, though most of the observers had left, several still waited, attention focused so intently on deVries they reminded her of sheep at feeding time. As he slung his bag over his shoulder and picked up his wand case, the submissives—male and female— went to their knees. Offering themselves. In the very front was HurtMe— one of the masochists he often played with. When the blond touched his forehead to the ground, Lindsey snorted. Obviously deVries would have no problem scratching his itch after a scene.

She started to leave and paused, wondering which he'd choose. Sub gossip hadn't made mention of a favorite, which might simply mean the Enforcer was exceedingly private in who he was screwing.

At least, since she wasn't kneeling, he wouldn't think she was one of the applicants for his favor. She couldn't take another insult.

When he assessed the offerings indifferently, her mood lightened. It was reassuring to know she wasn't the only sub he'd ever rejected.

Without picking anyone, he headed for the stairs. As he neared Lindsey, she caught his tantalizing scent, wild and musky with a hint of clean masculine sweat.

He stopped in front of her. His gaze was hotter than a Texas summer sun as it swept over her feline costume—cat ears, furry bra, and leopard-fur boy shorts. Violence lurked in his eyes.

And the growl in his voice was unyielding. "Changed my mind. I could use some sweet wildcat pussy, and you're up. I'm calling in my debt."

"Wh-what?" The explosion of air from her lungs made his lips tilt...slightly. She shook off the disbelief. "You said no."

"I said when I wanted. Choose—do I fuck you here or at your house?"

Oh my effing God. Only a sneaky weasel-dog like him would pull such a stunt. She'd hankered after him forever, and yet the thought of being with him dried the spit in her mouth.

She jerked her gaze from his intent one and saw Sir Ethan

behind him. Watching. As a dungeon monitor, he could tell deVries to go jump in a lake. He lifted one eyebrow.

But...she'd participated in the games last summer. And lost. There hadn't been any time limit on collecting the prize.

DeVries stood silently, letting her think. His gray-green eyes showed no expression.

Under Dark Haven's rules, she could safeword if she was really scared...only it would be a cheat. She wasn't past her limit. He hadn't done anything yet. But under his hard gaze, she sure felt like a newborn calf trapped by a wolf.

She shook her head at Sir Ethan and said to deVries, "Fine."

"Where?"

Heavens. Let him take her here—where all those submissives would watch? Uh-uh. Home? Unease made her bite her lip. What could he learn about her there? Not much, actually. Thank goodness it wasn't really her place. "Home."

He looked a little surprised, then nodded.

Aw heck, she was going to have sex with the Enforcer. Maybe it was only for an hour or so, but...*he wants* me. A thrill shot through her and made her quiver.

And lit his eyes with amusement.

CHAPTER TWO

H er Pacific Heights place was fairly close, and yet she always felt nervous when outside in the open. *What if Travis finds me and sets someone up with a rifle?* She never managed to relax until she was out of the parking garage and safe in the secured building.

Her heart rate was still elevated when the doorman greeted her with his usual *Miss Lindsey*, and she led deVries into the elevator.

On the way up to her floor, he frowned at her and tilted her face up. "If you're this scared, maybe you should back out."

"Huh?" God, he thought she was afraid of him. "Oh. Right. Parking garages make me jumpy."

After a long regard, he nodded. The elevator doors opened. As they walked down the hall to the overly ornate, very gorgeous condo, he set his hand on her lower back. The warmth of his palm went right through the denim wraparound dress to sear her skin, blasting away any thought of fear. The knowledge his powerful hands would restrain her body in a few minutes made the very air of the hallway shimmer with heat.

After she ushered him in, he strolled across the living room and silently took in the view of the Ferry Building and the Bay Bridge. Down below, the city sparkled with lights. "Pretty pricy digs, little girl."

"I like them," she said lightly. It had been an unanticipated dream when a rich friend of Xavier's left for Europe and needed a condo-sitter. Although the Italianate décor was stuffy—at least to her mind—everything was oh, so luxurious. Even the fancy house Victor had owned in San Antonio didn't compare.

Abandoning the view, deVries turned. Utterly confident and masculine, he looked at her, taking her in at his leisure, until she could almost feel his attention stroking against her skin. "Lose the dress." His voice was level. Unreadable. "Kneel there and wait for me."

Oh. Man. Her fingers fumbled with the dress's ties as every nerve in her body started to dance.

The surroundings didn't please deVries. Cold and formal—very different from the warm little submissive kneeling in the living room. But the view over the Bay was a plus. Maybe he'd do her there, looking down at the lights of the city.

He studied her for a minute.

Fast, shallow breathing. The flush on her lightly tanned cheeks deepened with his perusal. He could see her nipples were hard under the fuzzy bra. Her hands on her thighs weren't palm up as he liked, but were turned over, her fingers digging into the skin. Nervous. Excited. Maybe a little scared.

She should be.

"What the hell were you thinking letting a stranger into your home?"

Her startled gaze met his. "You're not a stranger. I know you."

"Hardly. I could break your pretty neck."

Her lips curved slightly. "Bless your heart; you're worried about me, aren't you?"

"About your common sense."

"I've never brought... I mean, I'm careful. Abby was on reception and knows you're here...so Xavier will also know." Her smile disappeared. "I'm not completely stupid. Xavier and Simon are your friends."

"You're smarter than you look."

Her glare was pretty ineffective considering her cat ears

had slid sideways. "If you're through insulting me, how about I give you a blowjob and we call this quits?"

Fuck, she was cute when steamed. His hard-on had returned; his cock was past ready for relief. Pity that, since he had no intention of rushing. Not with this little submissive. However, she needed to learn that snark didn't win a reward. Not in his universe. "If you're so eager, you can *start* with a blowjob." He stepped in front of her. "Go on."

Her flush was more from anger now than arousal, but her gaze lowered. And she leaned away from him.

Hell. Even for him, he was being an asshole. He dropped to one knee and lifted her chin. Confused brown eyes met his. Setting his hand on her shoulder, he bent and kissed her gently. Pulled back an inch. "Check the attitude, baby, yeah?"

She gave a tiny sigh and nodded. Her eyes were liquid and soft—anger gone. There it was...she wanted him.

He ran his tongue over her lips, felt them part, and took her mouth. Jesus Christ, she had soft lips. Her body was vibrating with anticipation. Nice.

This time when he rose to his feet, she leaned forward. Her eager, graceful hands undid the buttons of his leathers, releasing him. Fuck, the freedom felt good.

She started to take him in her mouth, and he made a reproving noise. "Tongue first. Hands on my thighs."

Gripping his legs, she licked around his dick, tracing the veins, teasing the head, the slit. Pink heightened the color in her cheeks, and her knees squeezed together. Nice. She liked giving blowjobs. "Take me in your mouth."

Her annoyed look at his direction was totally bogus. She moved one hand to direct his cock toward her.

"Hands stay on my legs."

"Sheesh," she said under her breath. After some awkward fumbling, she got his cock in her mouth, and damn, the feeling of being engulfed in steamy softness almost made him lose control. A tiny purr vibrated through her throat and into his dick. She bobbed her head up and down, her little tongue swirling, taking her time. Trying to tease him.

Uh-uh. Letting her have too much control wasn't good for either of them.

So he leaned forward and bracketed her head with his hands. His slightly bent position tilted his shaft in a better angle for her throat, and he used her hair to guide her. He slowed so his control couldn't get fucked up, then went faster.

When her fingernails dug into his legs despite the leather, he grinned. She appeared submissive enough in the club—however, he'd only seen her in lightweight scenes. He wondered how much she really surrendered.

By the time he was through with her tonight, she'd give him everything.

LINDSEY HELD ON to Devries's legs, trying to think. Couldn't. Her mouth was filled with his cock. His ruthless fist in her hair took all control from her, and every thought in her brain kept swirling away.

He thrust harder, pulling her head down on him, hitting the back of her throat. She struggled to suppress her gag reflex and swallowed to increase his pleasure. His guttural groan sent a shiver of delight through her. He wouldn't let her offer him less than he wanted—and God, she loved knowing that. And loved trying to give him more than he thought he could get.

To her dismay, he set her back on her heels and buttoned himself away.

When she pouted, he traced his finger over her wet lips. "Very nice, babe." His half smile streamed into her, warming her. "Stand up."

With a hand under her arm, he helped her up and moved closer. His lean fingers were teasingly rough as they glided over her collarbone around to the back of her neck. She shivered. When he gripped her nape, her knees almost buckled. Holding her still, he ran his other hand over her torso.

He lifted her hand and kissed her fingers—lips unexpectedly gentle. The hold on her nape was unyielding.

After removing her bra, he stroked his finger around her breasts. Between them. Across her stomach. Her ribs. One finger above her mound. As his hand played over her body, his gaze stayed on her face. Learning her. Her hot zones, her triggers.

His fingers brushed down her spine and reached the ever-so-sensitive hollow at the base.

Her toes curled into the carpet. Jeez, he hadn't even touched her pussy, and she was ready to come.

He lingered there, one finger circling right where her buttocks joined her back, dipping down into the crease, and finally, finally farther. His big hand cupped one buttock, and he gave a grunt. "You got a nice ass, girl."

Standing at her side, he pushed her briefs down to tangle around her ankles, and she tensed. All of her body seemed to be pulsating, begging for more. Growing increasingly sensitive the longer he touched her.

She could feel him watching her. Waiting...for something. With an effort, she controlled her breathing, tried to act like a good submissive and be patient—even though she wanted to grab his T-shirt and demand he take her.

Now, dammit.

He made a huffing sound—a laugh—and smacked her ass, hard and stinging.

The shockwave blasted into her, swirling like water down the drain and right to her clit. "Criminy!" Her fingers curled into fists as her need yanked at her like a bull in breeding season.

"Enjoy that, do you?" His voice was a low growl. Releasing her neck, he set his palm on her stomach to brace her and spanked her. The sound of his palm slapping her bottom rang through the room, each blow an explosion of bright fire sliding into a deep pool of molten sensation.

The blows lightened. He slowed, stopped, and tipped her face up with steely fingers under her chin.

Tears had filled her eyes, and yet her skin burned with a tantalizing heat. And she wanted more. More and more and more.

"Step out of the briefs." He waited while she forced her shaking legs to obey. "Thighs wide, pet."

Oh God. She widened her stance, biting her lip against the moan when he cupped her mound, his fingers skating over her labia. "Drenched." He gave a grunt of approval. "We're going to get along well."

The thought was terrifying. Appalling.

Horribly exciting.

His fingers spread the wetness up over her clit before he teased it. When he bit her neck, she couldn't keep the moan back. His chuckle vibrated the delicate skin under her ear.

But when he ran a wet finger around one nipple, she suppressed a frustrated sigh. Typical guy. Her nipples weren't sensitive; touching them affected her as much as playing with her knees. Men never understood that, though.

His gaze intensified as he switched to the other nipple, flicking it lightly.

She shifted, feeling as if she was letting him down. As if she should react. Act pleased or something. "Uh—"

"Don't talk, pet." His face in the faint light was hard, his lips almost cruel, his focus totally on her. No one had ever watched her so closely. The knowledge was heady, yet sent a curl of anxiety pricking up her spine.

He pinched her right nipple lightly, and his fingers implacably, bit by bit, pressed together.

She grabbed his arm, yet her clenching hand made no impression on his thickly muscled forearm. As the increasing pain in her nipple tangled with her nerves, biting into her, the pressure seemed to be on her clit as well. Her breathing caught, sped, caught.

"Oh yeah," he muttered. "You were designed for clamps, baby. And electricity."

What?

He released her, and his palm engulfed her breast completely. She had a moment to wish she were bigger before he angled his hand so he could pull her breast outward and *squeeze.*

Hurting her. Smothering a cry, she felt her back arch as the inferno of need rolled through her.

"Fucking beautiful." He moved to her other breast, tormenting it until it swelled with pain, until her pussy throbbed in demand.

"Oh criminy." She'd never felt like this, her senses conflicting. Raw.

His dimple showed before he wrapped her hair around one hand, holding her as his demanding lips moved over hers, his tongue plunging within, taking and taking. As he squeezed her breast again, his mouth drank in her cry of pain.

He lifted his head, and his gaze burned over her face, before his mouth descended on hers again. Each time he hurt her, his hand tightened in her hair, his lips forcing her to respond. The ground swayed beneath her as her bones turned to rubber.

When his cheek brushed hers, his jaw was scratchy with stubble and his whisper hot against her ear. "Fuck, you're sweet."

He drew her closer, kneading her ass with a powerful hand. As he rubbed his chest against her acutely sensitive, abused breasts, she felt trapped, engulfed by hardness. Her entire body melted down into a puddle.

"We're going to have fun." He kissed her lightly, chucked her under her chin as if she were a child. From his bag, he removed a towel, putting it over the arm of the sofa. He picked up a glass anal plug as thick as a cock. "Bend over there, pet."

She swayed, almost dizzy, but not so much she couldn't fear. "Too big," she whispered. "Please…"

"You think?" He glanced down at it and chose one more slender. His nod toward the couch was implacable as he took lube from his bag.

Her asshole was already puckering as she bent. The towel was scratchy against her mound. God, although she'd given anal sex a fair shot in the past, the activity simply wasn't one of her favorites. Why had she agreed to it? She gritted her teeth. *Dummy, don't ever play war games with Dominants.*

After pulling her cheeks apart, he unhurriedly worked the plug in. Cool and slick and still…too damn big. When she tightened against it, he smacked her butt hard enough to make her yelp. He paused and started again.

Burn, stretch, burn, stretch. The plug pushed her open to the widest point, and she whimpered.

"Fuck, I love that sound." And he continued until it plopped into place. "You can wear this for a bit; my cock will widen you some more."

Oh no. No, no, no. Her fingernails were permanently dug into the sofa cushions, her body totally stiff.

"Easy, pet." The growl of his voice softened. "You'll be able to take me." He stroked her bottom in relaxing circles, and the aching in her asshole eased. "Safeword's red," he said. "Same as at the club. You're experienced enough to use it if you need to, girl."

His raspy baritone was oddly soothing, and his leisurely intimate caresses slowed her stampeding heart, guiding her away from fear as if he'd taken the reins from her hands. She dropped her head to rest on her forearms. Surrendering. He'd do to her what he wanted to do.

And she'd let him.

"Good girl." A minute passed. Another. Only the measured stroke of his callused hand marked the passing of time.

Eventually he hauled her to her feet and tossed the towel onto the center cushion. "Sit on the sofa."

When she sat, the scratchy terry cloth rubbed against her tender bottom. As the plug pushed higher inside her, she shifted, trying to find a place that didn't put pressure on it. There wasn't one.

"Don't worry; you won't be thinking about it soon." DeVries gave her the ominous statement as he set bandage scissors on the coffee table. He wound rope around her wrist and paused. "Your file showed no medical concerns. Are marks a problem?"

Not in San Francisco, where everyone wore a sweater or a suit. "No, Sir."

"Good."

He ran the ropes over the sofa ends and down to the wooden legs, pulling her arms out to each side. As he finished the knots, she looked at the leather wrist and ankle cuffs in his toy bag. Why was he using rope?

He followed her gaze. "Metal and electricity don't mix well."

Electricity. Oh God.

After positioning her with her ass on the edge of the bottom cushion and her shoulders against the sofa back, he tied each ankle to a sofa leg. Her knees were widely apart, her pussy open and…way too accessible. To *electricity*.

As he set up the violet wand equipment, she looked up into his tanned face. In the dim light, she couldn't read his eyes. "I'm not a masochist," she whispered. "I'm—"

"I know." He squeezed her shoulder. "I won't hurt you past what you can take."

Oh God, he wasn't very reassuring. There was a wide gap between *take* and *enjoy*. She closed her eyes and concentrated on regulating her breathing.

"Eyes on me, pet." He stepped on the foot pedal, and the wand came to life with an ominous crackling. Inside the mushroom-headed, transparent tube, the gas turned a glowing violet color.

The mushroom top approached her arm, making a bacon-in-the-frying-pan sound. She tensed. But for nothing. In fact, she didn't feel a thing.

He studied her face before adjusting the setting. She felt a slight tingle. Another adjustment. The sound grew louder.

This time, as he ran the wand up her arm, a quarter inch from the skin, she bit her lip. The tingling had changed to an odd sparky feeling, not…quite…painful.

His lips tipped up slightly. "About right." He moved the tube over her upper arm, hovering above the skin. Fine sparks hit her, and her arm twitched, pulling on the rope.

Over her shoulder. Downward. Oh God.

She shivered as he circled one breast, and the other, the tingling like a myriad of tiny bites. Her nipples bunched until they ached.

"Nice." His voice was husky.

"DeVries," she whispered, not sure what she wanted to say. "I—"

His foot came off the pedal, and he leaned forward to kiss her, sweetly and slowly. His mouth traced over the curve of her neck and down.

He took one nipple in his mouth—typical man, going for the breasts—and sucked hard. His teeth pinched the peak painfully.

She gasped, sensation bursting through her.

He sucked on the other peak, nipped, straightened, and smiled into her eyes. The hint of a dimple appeared in his right cheek. "Now, we'll play."

After changing the attachment on the wand to a long metal-tipped cord he tucked under his belt, he stepped on the foot pedal. Sparks flew from his fingertips, tingling over her.

He moved one hand up, always less than an inch from her skin, and one finger circled her breast. Angled in toward her right nipple.

She tensed. Bit her lip against the need to yell *no*.

His gaze made a circuit, checking her face, her muscles, the position of his hand. He circled the areola, almost touching, and the arcing electricity felt like bubbly water. Pleasant.

All too soon he widened the gap between his finger and her skin, and the bubbles turned to needlelike sparks. *Painful* sparks. She jumped, tugged on the ropes, yet could feel her body responding, wanting more as arousal bloomed with liquid heat inside her.

He did her other breast, creating a stream of sensation to her lower half, until her pussy was throbbing. She shifted position, shifted again, and couldn't even get her legs together to try to ease the urgency.

His chuckle was a wolflike growl. "Squirmy little girl. Pretty." He shut the wand off and leaned forward, taking her nipple in his mouth, sucking on the abused tissue until she arched. He switched to the other one, and his tongue was enticingly wet and hot and smooth after the tormenting sparks.

The next time he turned the electricity on, he used his finger to make sizzling circles over her stomach, up her arms, and across her armpits. She giggled and wiggled...and gasped when her movements drove the anal plug deeper.

He moved down her thighs, teasing her with forays toward her mound. And each time the lightly painful sparks grew close, her hips rose upward to get touched *there*. And yet the idea was terrifying.

When the wand turned off, she moaned. Her pussy was so

swollen, aching. She was dying here. "Sir," she whispered. "Please."

His eyes were half-lidded as he regarded her, "We can stop. I don't know you well enough to push you."

But... She didn't wish for him to stop. Not really. "I meant— I want—"

"I know what you want, little girl." His half smile was affectionate. Cruel.

Her insides clenched.

He went down on one knee between her legs, positioning himself so his wide shoulders avoided her knees and thighs.

What was he going to do? The Enforcer didn't do oral—at least he never had in the club. To her surprise, he licked over her pussy, and his stiff tongue circled the entrance.

She was so needy and swollen, and the feeling of his mouth was totally lush, everything she wanted...yet not quite enough.

He swept his tongue over her clit, teased at the hood, and all her nerve endings seemed to focus on that spot.

And then he put his knee on the foot control, turning on the power. Bit by bit, he moved his head toward her thigh. Sparks leaped from his cheek, and her muscles jumped with the jolt of electricity. He tantalized her other leg with his face. And moved closer.

His nose almost touched her outer labia, and it felt like being in a Jacuzzi with the jets pointing directly at her. "Oh God!"

He pulled back, increasing the sparking until it was edged toward pain, as if the tingles were pushing through her skin and going deeper.

As he shifted upward, the muscles of her inner thighs tightened, trying to squeeze her legs together. God, she wasn't sure she could take the feeling directly on her—

His tongue hovered over her clit, and electricity zipped from it to the exposed nub with an exquisitely painful burst of pleasure. "Aaah!" The pressure low in her core tightened.

He backed off and released the power.

As she sank back against the cushions, he nuzzled her. His

beard stubble scraped over her shaved outer labia, over her mound. His tongue ran over her like hot, wet silk. The pressure inside her coiled fiercely.

His lips closed around her clit, and he sucked lightly. *More, more, more.* Each tiny suck lured her closer. Her hands fisted as her thighs trembled. Her moan was long and shaky and made him laugh.

He lifted his head and, oh God, turned the electricity on again. The tiny zipping sounds increased as he leaned forward.

The shock struck a second before he closed his lips around the button of nerves. She was so swollen, so exposed that the bare touch of his tongue was almost too much. He sucked, and her hips bucked.

Immediately, he opened his mouth, and sparks flew in the tiny gap between his lips and her pussy. The tingles hit her from all sides, like bubbles hitting her at highway speeds.

Too much. Heat washed over her. She shuddered, pulling at the restraints, needing more, needing less.

A chuckle rumbled from him. He licked over her clit, easing the sensation, before opening his lips around her. The sparks struck her again.

"Oh God, oh God, oh God!" Her whole body went rigid as her center clenched, as her orgasm surged upward, hit the top, and there was no stopping. The devastating sensations exploded outward like a fireball of pleasure, out of control, consuming everything in its path. She gasped for air as the room went brilliant with light.

After a second, she opened her eyes and—

He licked over her again, and she was so, so sensitive, each light abrasion sent more waves blasting through her, taking her air with it.

"Noooo." Sweat trickled down her back. Her whole body was trembling. "No more. Pleaaase."

"You think?" His eyes glinted with pleasure.

As she panted, trying to regain her breath and keep her heart from pounding out of her chest, the ropes came off her wrists and ankles. Her arms flopped to her sides. Someday, maybe in a year, she'd try to move.

Her eyes shot open when hard hands closed around her waist. He picked her up, ignoring her squeak. Once again, he bent her over the arm of the couch. The coarse towel rubbed her mound. A lube packet dropped onto the cushion beside her shoulder.

Oh no. No, no, no.

"Time for my second prize, pet." He smoothly removed the glass anal plug, leaving her empty inside. She heard a condom wrapper.

She wasn't *ready*. Couldn't think. "Wait. Just..."

To her relief, he pressed into her pussy, filling her. Her insides clenched around his hot, thick shaft as he slid smoothly in and out.

But just as she was starting to really enjoy the sensations, he withdrew. And picked up the lube. A few seconds later, he pulled her buttocks open, and his cock probed her already tender anus.

Oh. Damn.

As he pushed in, her neck arched, bringing her head up. *Ow, ow, ow.* She attempted to stand.

His hand in the middle of her back kept her right there, positioned for his ruthless advance. "Don't worry; this won't hurt...too much." And his voice was amused—and pleased.

Holy shit.

Slick with lube, he pressed and retreated, gradually working his way in.

Her tight ring of muscle burned and stretched, trying to adjust to his size—he was huge!—and it hurt. Yet, even as he advanced, her whole lower half seemed to flare awake, like the lighting of the giant Christmas tree in San Antonio.

"That's right," he murmured. "You can take me." He forged in, relentless as only the Enforcer could be, doing what he wanted for his own pleasure.

Yet the knowledge he'd cared enough to satisfy her first was intensely erotic.

Cheek rubbing the cushions, she whined and squirmed as he impaled her. His hand on her back held her down, and she whimpered.

She could feel his thighs burn hot against hers. He was all the way in.

"Hurt, baby?" he asked.

"Yessssss." Her answer came out a moan.

"Perfect." His laugh was deep and gruff. He controlled her hips with an unyielding grip as he drew back unhurriedly and surged in. Over and over. When he halted and added more lube, the coldness of the liquid around the heat of his shaft made her tremble.

He thrust harder and faster until the *slap, slap, slap* of skin against skin, and the alternating full-to-empty sensations dominated her world. Dragged her back into need.

Her breathing changed. Her hips tilted up slightly.

And he paused...and chuckled. "Greedy little Texan."

His boot between her feet pushed her legs so far apart that with every thrust, her clit rubbed the towel. Over and over.

Oh God, oh God. As if caught in a blender, her entire lower half spiraled up and up into soaring pleasure. She mewed, clawing at the cushions, as the world dissolved around her.

"That's the spirit." With a rough, guttural growl, deVries plunged into her so deeply she felt his groin grind against her bottom before he released.

Sometime later, she realized she was in a blanket, lying on the couch. Dizzy as a drunken coyote. She rose up on an elbow.

On one knee, deVries was cleaning off his equipment and packing it away in his terrifying-looking metal case. He glanced at her, assessed, clasped her shoulders, and moved her to a sitting position.

As he held her there, her world spun for a second before righting. Once her eyes uncrossed, she gave him a nod.

He handed her the glass of water on the coffee table. When

had he gotten that? "Drink up, pet."

Her hand shook only slightly as she took a sip and felt her desert-dry mouth absorb the liquid. She chugged most of the rest.

His lips quirked before he turned back to his packing.

When he was finished, he rose and took her glass to the kitchen. "Need more?"

She shook her head, not finding any words coming to mind. *Thank you* didn't seem adequate. Sure, he was here because he wanted to collect on his prize from shooting her during war games; nevertheless, he'd also...well, okay, gifted her with an amazing orgasm with his violet wand toys. And again with anal sex.

He'd *hurt* her and liked it. But she'd liked it too. How did a person talk to someone she really didn't know after having been so...intimate in such a strange way?

"First time I've ever seen you tongue-tied." He squatted in front of her and tucked a strand of hair behind her ear. "You look befuddled."

Good word for how she felt.

The living room lamps lightened the green flecks in his gray pupils, turning his eyes the color of a forest mist. She traced her fingers over the sun lines at the corners of his eyes, the strong angle of his jaw, his corded neck. Satisfaction lurked in the heaviness of his lids.

The knowledge she'd pleased him was a low hum in her veins.

"Let's get you cleaned up." To her surprise, he scooped her up and carried her into the bathroom. He stood her on her feet outside the shower, turned on the water, and waited for it to warm. After setting her inside, he stripped and joined her.

The water felt wonderful on her sweaty body—and stung on a few of the more tender areas, so she turned around.

Oh wow, just look at him. The brighter bathroom lights played over deVries's body. Totally, devastatingly gorgeous. All muscle. Leaner than a weight lifter, and somehow more dangerous. A purple bruise marred his forearm, mottled black-and-green bruises covered his hip, and above was a row of stitches. "What—"

When she looked up, his gaze was cold. Deadly.

Her mouth closed on the rest of the question.

As if she hadn't spoken, he squirted some soap into his hand and scrubbed her down.

Eventually the chill disappeared from his eyes, letting her breathe.

When he stroked up her right forearm, he stopped and turned her arm toward the light. The long white-pink scar ran from her elbow to the back of her hand. Another, smaller one was on her left arm. So ugly. All the same, the window glass had cut her arms instead of her face; she wouldn't complain.

Gray-green eyes narrowed, and his brows rose slightly.

No. She tilted her head toward his bruises and cuts. If he didn't have to answer, neither did she.

After an uncomfortable moment, he gave her a raised eyebrow of acknowledgment and continued washing. Accepting her reticence.

Her breath eased out. Lying to him, right here, right now, after what they'd shared would have been unbearable.

His silence was a balm after the intensity before. With surprisingly gentle hands, he washed her efficiently, not lingering over anything, and merely the touch of his callused fingers made heat sweep through her.

God, she'd gladly mess around again. What was wrong with her?

But, once finished, he set her outside the shower and handed her a towel. "Go to bed, babe."

She stared at him, unable to think of what to say. Drops of water glinted in the light furring on his chest, trickled down the line of hair to his cock. Made her want to follow it with her tongue.

His eyes crinkled. "You're definitely befuddled." Leaning down, he gave her a light kiss, turned her, and swatted her ass to move her out of the room.

In the doorway, she glanced over her shoulder. He'd stepped back under the water to finish washing. *What a strange man.* Shaking her head, she donned a T-shirt and pair of panties. Should she wait for him?

Her wobbly legs answered the question by taking her to the bed. Her mama would be horrified at the discourtesy of not seeing a visitor to the door, but deVries was fully capable of letting himself out when he left.

She slid into her bed. The thousand-thread-count, Egyptian cotton sheets whispered sweetly against her sensitized skin as she sank down into the mattress.

A few drowsy minutes later, she watched deVries walk out. Beautifully naked. Holy God in heaven, he was ripped, from the hard curves of his biceps to the deep valleys carved between his pectorals. The line of black stitches above his left hip didn't seem to affect him, whereas if her flesh had been slashed, she'd consider it an excellent idea to take a pain med, lounge around, and watch TV all day.

Bet the man had never lounged a day in his life.

When he walked past and into the living room, she sighed. He hadn't said a word. Sure, he'd gotten what he wanted; even so, she'd thought he'd at least say good-bye.

To her surprise, he came back in, dumped his bag and case by the nightstand, and tossed his clothes on top.

"What are you doing?" she asked, sitting up in the bed.

He ignored her and went back out, returning a few minutes later with the rope restraints from the couch. He tossed them on the pile of clothes. "Almost forgot these. Might have scared your guests."

She choked at the thought. Not that she'd ever invited anyone here—it wasn't really her place, after all—but still. "Discovery could be bad. So thanks."

After he looked around the room, he ran his finger over the silvery silk quilt and cocked an eyebrow. "Doesn't seem like your style or color, babe."

She shrugged. What could she say—it wasn't.

The light from the living room cast shadows on his hard face as he stared down at her. She watched him. Why wasn't he patting her on the ass and leaving? Everyone said the Enforcer was a fuck-'em and forget-'em sort of guy. To her surprise, he crawled under the covers with her.

"What are you *doing*?"

"Sleeping. I'm wiped. Not safe to drive."

"Oh." Sleep with deVries? She swallowed hard. Before she could figure out how to say *I'll call you a taxi*, he rolled her onto her right side and spooned behind her. Her bottom rubbed against his groin. His rock-hard arm over her waist pinned her down as he curved his left hand over her breast.

He wanted to cuddle? The Enforcer? "But—"

"Go to sleep, or you'll spend the night gagged."

Well. Yet, even as she searched for the answer to his obnoxious threat, her heart quickened. His gravelly voice alone could carbonate seawater—and when he exerted his will? She simply fizzed.

Unfortunately, all those hot, hot bubbles flowed straight to her pussy. She rubbed her thighs together, trying to still the throbbing. She wanted him again. Criminy, what was wrong with her?

His hand flattened between her breasts, and he snorted. "With a pulse like that, either you're scared or you're horny." He slid his palm over her panties, ascertaining for himself exactly which it was. "Soaked."

The touch of his firm fingers made her quiver. "I'm sorry. I'm fine. Don't—"

"Shut it." With pitiless hands, he tossed away the covers and flattened her onto her back. "Just as well. I didn't get enough of a taste."

"But—"

The warning in his narrowed eyes froze her vocal cords.

He stripped her panties off, baring her. Pushing her legs apart, he knelt between them. His gaze moved over her opened pussy...looking at her there.

As her cheeks flared with heat, she slid her hands over her mound to cover herself.

"You don't wear underwear if you're with me," he growled. "And you don't withhold something I want." Ruthlessly he positioned her fingers to keep her labia open.

"What are you—"

"You put your hands down here, I use them." He nudged her fingers outward, forcing her to hold her folds more widely apart. "Hold yourself open for me, and don't move."

"But—"

"And don't speak." He licked over her, his tongue stopping to wiggle right on top of her clit.

So wet. So hot. Her back arched as heat blossomed in her core.

He watched her with a slight smile. "Screaming is okay."

Propped up on one elbow, sprawled between her legs, he lowered his head. His tongue worked her hard and fast, impossibly effective with her clit so totally exposed. With his free hand, he slid two fingers inside her, thrusting rhythmically—hard and fast.

Her pussy clamped down on him, and he laughed, closed his lips around her clit, and sucked.

Good thing he'd given her permission to scream.

CHAPTER THREE

DeVries woke, lying still as he assessed his surroundings. Kitchen appliances hummed. Someone in the condo above had heavy feet. The woman tucked against his side breathed softly.

Normal sounds. Normal scents. Nothing burning. No stink of ordnance or gunpowder. No stench of fear or blood or sweat. Only the faint fragrance of a cinnamon candle. Laundered linens.

But the citrusy shower soap on Lindsey's body and the scent of sex affected him like a female in heat must a wolf. He hardened. *Jesus, again?*

In the middle of the night, he'd realized she'd rolled away from him. He rarely slept with a woman and never fucking *cuddled*, but...for some reason, he'd tugged her back. When his arm had grazed over her small breasts, her nipples contracted to press into his skin. Still she hadn't woken.

His cock damn well had. Swearing under his breath, he'd donned a condom, then used his hands and mouth to bring her to the brink even before she wakened. When her eyes opened, he'd held her in place and thrust in. She'd gone rigid, and damned if she hadn't come immediately, her cunt pulsing around his cock. *Fucking satisfying.*

And now he wanted her *again*. The girl definitely cranked his engine.

He looked down at her. Curled against his side, head on his shoulder, one leg over his thighs. Her cheeks and chin were reddened from his beard stubble, her pink lips swollen. She knew how to use her soft mouth. And she'd enjoyed sucking his dick, giving as generously as she received.

Like he'd figured, she was a sweetheart. A nice woman. Submissive. Gentle. Fun. The type of woman he envied his friends for having. Simon's Rona was smart and organized and bighearted. She adored her kids and her husband; hell, she cared for an entire hospital.

Xavier's Abby was a genius, terrifyingly literate, and a nurturer down to her bones.

No surprise this little Texan made up the third woman in their girl-gang.

Using one finger, he stroked over his bite mark on her shoulder. Felt like he'd branded her. *DeVries was here—no trespassing.*

Not that he had any intention of ever scening with her again. One night had been folly; two would be insanity.

But he hadn't left yet, and he had an urge to have her one more time. A pity she'd be too sore to take him anally again. *No.* Although he didn't mind hurting her for their mutual pleasure, turning her off anal sports would be a shame. He owed it to other ass-players not to screw it up for them.

Besides, he was in the mood for a basic missionary position.

He'd fuck her and leave right after. Best to keep it light. Simple. Especially with this little sweetie who'd lured him into spending the night. Give her a chance, and she'd get her hooks into him. A woman could be more dangerous than any snake-infested jungle.

So after donning a condom, he tipped her onto her back, ignoring her murmur of protest, and used the rope from last night to secure her wrists over her head.

She blinked sleepily at him, rousing sluggishly. Heavy sleeper, wasn't she? In his business, her habit would get her dead. The thought of anyone hurting her sent an iron jolt of protectiveness through him. He hauled in a breath and kissed her lightly.

Her lips softened immediately, giving him what he wanted.

"Morning, baby." Hooking his leg over her left ankle, using

his other foot to push her right leg out, he opened her to his hand. "Very nice. You're already getting wet."

She flushed a deep pink, her legs trying to close, the rope sawing on the headboard at her thwarted effort to—to cover herself. When taken by surprise, she was a modest little thing. Be fun to keep working on her reaction until it went away.

No. One more fuck and I'm done.

He propped himself up on his elbow, deliberately taking a look. Moving her folds to one side. Lifting her clit hood. Chuckling as she flared redder.

And got wetter. The girl roused to his hand as quickly as any woman he'd taken, despite her embarrassment.

Her pussy was fucking beautiful. Puffy outer labia, slick inner. Clit starting to protrude. Using his legs to keep her open, he played for a while, enjoying her responsiveness. She was silky hot inside. Tight. Her cunt muscles tried to suck in his finger. Be fun to do some dildo play with her—how wide of one could she take before begging for mercy?

Her nipples weren't a hot spot for her, but her little knot of nerves was pleasingly sensitive. A brush would make her tremble. A light pinch made her flinch, and a protracted one sent blood rushing to her cheeks and her legs trying to close. *Oh yeah.* What he could do with that bundle of nerves for fun.

Hell, why not? "Look at me, little girl."

Her gaze came to him, biggest fucking brown eyes he'd ever seen. She knew she was defenseless; she wanted to be that way.

He liked her that way. His cock turned rock hard in agreement.

As he trapped her gaze, he captured her clit between thumb and fingers, squeezed, and held. Hearing her heels scraping on the sheet, feeling the trembling of her body, he drank in the gift of her surrender.

Seconds passed. Eyes holding hers, he released her.

As the blood surged back into her mistreated flesh, as she sucked in air, he topped her and sheathed his cock in to the hilt.

Damned if she didn't fucking come...and keep coming as he hammered into her.

LINDSEY FELT USED. Abused. Taken. And she'd climaxed so hard her heart had left bruises on the inside of her ribs.

On top of her, deVries was thrusting, hitting deep, connected to her on the most intimate of levels. With his arms braced on each side of her shoulders, he lifted his hips to watch his shaft slide in and out of her. His smoke-green eyes glinted with satisfaction. "Put your legs around my waist."

She brought her knees up, letting him drive deeper.

With the next stroke, he ground his pelvis against her poor mistreated clit, deliberately making her hurt.

And somehow the pain danced along her nerve endings, sparking off desire again. Her vagina tightened around him.

His rare grin flashed at her. "Damn, girl, you're a treat."

If he thought she'd get off a second time, he was sadly mistaken. She wasn't even close.

"Got toys in your nightstand?"

"Wh-what?" He did *not* ask that. No way.

"Damn straight, you do." He reached a long arm out, yanked open the drawer, and stilled as his fingers undoubtedly found her stash. "Like a variety, do you?" Rocking his hips against her in gentle thrusts, he fumbled in her drawer, picking up one vibrator after another, finally settling on the one with the forked design.

Holy shit, of all the ones to pick. She thought of it as a sadistic mini-tuning fork. Even worse, it had the most intense vibrations, and she was already sore. "No, not that. It's too much."

His head dipped, and he kissed her, long and slow, before whispering against her lips, "I know."

In a smooth movement, he released her wrists from the ropes, withdrew, and stood at the foot of the bed, leaving her quivering. A hard yank downward positioned her with her butt on the mattress edge.

As her right leg dangled off the bed, he cradled her left knee in his elbow, and he thrust back inside her. The position let him go deep, penetrating her so fully she wiggled in halfhearted protest. Making him smile.

He reached to one side, and she heard a low hum. A second later, he laid the vibrator on her mound, thankfully high, and secured it there with his palm.

It wasn't as bad as she'd feared, but the distant vibrations kept ramping up her arousal until she was angling her hips to press his hand firmly onto the device.

"Want more?"

"God." She couldn't possibly come again, and yet the erotic sensation shivered over her skin, settling like a heavy weight in her pelvis.

"Thought so," he murmured. After moving the vibe down until the ends barely bracketed her clit, he drove into her hard. Mercilessly. Over and over.

The vibrator buzzed on her even as his cock pounded from inside. She tightened, tightened.

"Lindsey," he growled.

She raised heavy lids, seeing his intent face.

"Come for me now." He moved the toy so the brutal vibrations hit her clit fully on both sides. His hips rotated, mercilessly grinding into new places inside her.

Her breathing stopped as every...single...nerve in her whole body fired simultaneously. A massive outburst of sensation broke over her, twirling her in pleasure, tumbling her away.

She gasped right before another hit. And another. One tornado after another.

Little by little, the convulsions eased. When she managed to pry her eyelids open, he was staring at her, his gaze intimate. Perceptive.

"Nice." As she shuddered under him, he set the vibrator aside, put an elbow under her other knee so her legs were lifted into the air. He drew out and plunged deep, pumping fast and long, followed by shorter shocking stabs. When he sheathed himself completely, he was so huge and hard, she could feel every pulse of his shaft as he released inside her.

Risking a reprimand, she ran her hands over his shoulders, the velvet skin stretched tight over bunched muscles, a tactile symphony of sex.

With a measured breath, he eased his cock in and out, like a sweet farewell. His lips curved as her vagina clenched around him in tiny after-tremors before he pulled out. "You're a treat, all right," he rasped.

She wouldn't be calling him a treat—he was more like the iceberg that sank the *Titanic*.

After giving her a brief hard kiss, he headed for the bathroom, and she managed to turn her head to watch. The man was simply gorgeous. He always wore a shirt at the club; naked, his shoulders seemed even broader. The line down his spine to his ass was bounded by muscle, and his butt was world-class. He was even tanned, despite the overcast San Francisco skies.

With a frown, she realized white lines of scars marred his smooth skin. She'd felt the tiny ridges while they were making love. And he had a long, stitched-up gash. Jeez, she didn't even know what he did in real life. Maybe a cop? Her stomach clenched at the thought.

Hearing the shower come on, she considered joining him for one more wonderful chance to watch water flow down the valleys created by his bunching muscles. To run her fingers over his tight, tanned skin. She giggled as she rolled out of bed. She sure couldn't see him in a tanning salon. He didn't seem to have an ounce of self-consciousness or conceit.

Not like me. She donned the cheap terrycloth robe with the fraying hem. A secondhand purchase. Not pretty. Not sexy. But hey, it was what she had.

Her mouth turned down. Before she'd married Miguel, she'd felt pretty. Before she'd married Victor, she'd felt sexy. Neither feeling had lasted very far into either marriage. Experience had taught her a guy would say anything and act any way to get what he wanted. Intellectually she knew she was pretty enough; unfortunately, her subconscious still heeded Victor's and Miguel's opinions.

At least deVries had honestly found her sexy to desire. Had liked her enough to want to be with her. Totally awesome. *He likes me.*

She tied the robe closed. Didn't it just figure that now she had someone over who might appreciate hot lingerie, she couldn't afford any? Her life sure had changed in the blink of an eye—from a Texas ranch, to college, to Victor's fancy San Antonio house, to being on the run and broke.

She bit her lip. She couldn't live like this the rest of her life. Not only for herself, but for everyone else being hurt. Victor's brother, Travis, wouldn't have shut down the smuggling operation. Guns, drugs, slavery. Travis had to be stopped. Somehow.

The last time she'd talked to a cop, she'd almost died.

Her cheerful mood was broken as a chill swept over her. She'd slept like an exhausted puppy with deVries in her bed. Not worrying about whether Travis Parnell might have found her and sent someone to silence her.

She glanced back at the shower and headed for the kitchen.

A few minutes later, she set the small café table in front of the bay window. Pretty convenient she'd baked quiche the day before—it made a great ready-made breakfast. He'd probably think her an idiot to feed him, but Mama had exacting notions about hospitality.

Of course, her mama would consider deVries more of a devil than a guest, and she'd be right. Be that as it may, if Lindsey fed the man, maybe he'd mellow and actually talk to her. *Breakfast with the Enforcer. God.*

On the way back to the kitchen, her gaze fell on the antique rolltop desk. And the newspaper clippings showing Craig's body, his police uniform stained with blood. More articles were there about the hunt for Lindsey Rayburn Parnell who had apparently shot her husband, Victor, then murdered a cop to escape. *Lies, damn them.*

Footsteps reminded her of her guest. Breath catching, she shoved the rolltop down to cover everything even as deVries walked out of the bedroom. Her voice shook as she said, "Good morning."

"Morning." His gaze ran from the desk up to her face.

"I have some breakfast for you." She hurried over to the kitchen island, picked up the plates, and carried them to the table. *Be cool. Be cool.* After a calming breath, she turned and gave him a bright smile. "I hope you like quiche."

He hesitated, obviously surprised. "Long as eggs are cooked, I'm good." He joined her, nodding when she lifted the coffeepot. "Thanks."

While he ate, she burbled about the weather, the club, anything she could think of. She'd never had trouble talking with people. Psychology and social work degrees had perfected her ability to plow through the most awkward of moments.

If only he would stop looking around the room. The worry she might have left something else out made her squirm. Even worse, every time his eyes met hers, her brain emptied of thoughts like water swirling down the drain.

As he took his last bite and leaned back with coffee in hand, she finally asked, "So, what do you do for a living?" Aw heck, she sounded dumb. Nonetheless, she was dying to know where those scars came from. "Are you a cop?" Her fingers tensed on her cup.

His eyes were more green than gray in the morning light, and she could have sworn amusement lurked in the depths. "I work for Simon."

Right. Rona's husband owned a security and investigations firm. "Is it *that* dangerous?" Oh shit, she'd blurted her question out.

"What?" He paused with his cup halfway to his mouth.

Her gaze dropped to where his leathers covered the stitches on his hip.

"Happened during my time off. A buddy tripped—the clumsy bastard—and I ended up with this."

Jeez, was his buddy playing with a knife or something? "Oh. That's a crappy thing to happen on a holiday."

"Guess so." Although his eyes had somehow darkened, his lips twitched.

She eyed him suspiciously. Sometimes she got the definite impression he thought she was funny, even that he was teasing her—but surely not. Honestly, as a social worker, she had awesome instincts about people. Normally. However, the Enforcer somehow managed to wipe her mind as if she were a computer and someone hit *Delete File.*

"So where in Texas were you raised?" he asked.

"Um. Did I say I was from Texas?" Why had she been stupid enough to ask him questions?

"Got the accent, babe."

"Oh." Here she'd thought it wasn't very noticeable. *Where in Texas...* Hmm, she sure wouldn't mention her town on the Mexican border where everyone knew Lindsey Rayburn. "A-around Dallas. How about you?"

His gaze was on her fingers...and the napkin she was crumpling. "Born in Chicago." He glanced around the room. "Guess you don't have to do anything to make a living."

At least she could tell the truth for this one. "Oh, but I do. I work as a receptionist." Well, she would work for another day or so until the woman whose position she'd filled returned from maternity leave.

"Receptionist?" He straightened. "Right. Bullshit."

WHEN THE PRETTY submissive's gaze jerked up, deVries almost winced at his rude statement. Still—no receptionist could afford this place. The table where they sat would take a year's salary. The rest of the furniture was of the same pricey level. Not possible.

He'd already been annoyed over her *"raised around Dallas"* bullshit. She was a piss-poor liar. "Did you inherit money or something?" Like this condo.

She gave him an incredulous look. "I wish."

Curiosity drove him on. He'd never been able to release a question once his teeth were dug in. "Guess you must have married for money, huh?"

"I—" Red swept into her face, one shoulder went up, and damned if her head didn't give an unconscious affirmative. "I—" She picked up her cup as if it could provide a shield.

Married for money. One major kick to the gut. It brought a partnering thought. "You telling me I fucked a married woman?"

"No. No, I don't have a husband."

That, at least, looked honest. "Divorced, huh?" Was that how she'd ended up rich? His mouth tightened.

When her cup shook, she set it down. "Why all the questions?"

Receptionist married a wealthy man only to divorce him. The guy had probably owned the condo before she took it and everything else the poor bastard had. She sure as fuck wasn't paying the mortgage on her salary. "Bet you didn't have a friendly divorce, did you?"

Even as she flinched, she averted her gaze, confirming his suspicions.

Goddamn women. The guy probably worked his ass off; then wifey decided she was entitled to everything he'd earned. *"Sorry, Mr. deVries, your account is overdrawn."* He'd never forget the bank teller's voice when he'd asked why his debit card hadn't worked. A decade later, the memory still kicked him in the gut. Nothing like having a "loving" wife clean out the account while he served his country in hell. *Yeah, thanks, Tamara.*

He inhaled deliberately and tried to control his temper.

"Um. More coffee?" Lindsey ventured, lifting the pot.

Such big brown eyes. He felt as if he'd kicked a puppy. Maybe he was wrong. Maybe she hadn't cleaned the guy out. "I guess your ex is living in ritzy shit like this too?"

The coffeepot thumped onto the table as she paled. He saw guilt on her face, plain as hell.

He didn't need an answer. A muscle twitched in his jaw. "I got to be going."

She rose as he did, silently watched him retrieve his toy bag and electro-case.

When he glanced at her, she took a step back, and her arms wrapped around her torso. All big eyes, innocent as a baby. Damned if she wasn't even smoother than his ex. Lindsey's poor bastard of a husband probably hadn't seen the viper beneath that smooth skin until the poison flooded his veins.

He yanked open the apartment door.

"DeVries?" Even her voice sounded sweet.

Made him want to puke. Before the door closed behind him, he looked back. "Debt's paid."

LINDSEY FELT HER knees buckle. She dropped down into the chair, staring at nothing.

What did I do? Everything had been going fine. Last night, he'd actually smiled at her a couple of times. The sex had been rough, yet somehow gentle. He'd even kissed her as if he liked her. Not sexual kisses—friendly ones.

Yet the minute she'd told him what she did, he'd turned all cold. And his face... He looked at her as if she was a-a slut or something.

Her heart was shriveling up like a winter-blasted weed.

What had gotten his panties all in a wad? Because he didn't like her job or didn't approve of divorce? Seriously?

Indignation flickered to life, attempting to overcome the empty feeling inside her. What a jerk. He'd deliberately made her feel like a whore. *"Debt's paid."*

Well, he'd sure gotten everything she'd owed him. Her face heated as she remembered what all she'd let him do. How crazy he'd driven her. She'd let him face-fuck her. Take her anally. Laugh at her and call her greedy.

Now he acted as if she was a slut. Her lips trembled.

I'm not a whore.

He'd *used her* like a whore, hadn't he? When would she learn?

Miguel hadn't desired her—he'd needed to marry her so he could get a green card. Victor had wanted her ranchland that bordered Mexico, not her. She drew in a shaky breath.

She'd thought maybe here, away from everything, she could get herself back together. Dark Haven had been a refuge, a place to swim free, to rediscover who she was.

At least until now.

She drew the robe tighter, covering her legs. Maybe she *had* acted like a slut. After all, she'd known her time with deVries would be a one-night stand. Just sex.

She'd told herself it was okay for a girl to have fun as the men did, without obligation or guilt. Surely no one in the lifestyle would disagree.

But to find out deVries hadn't even liked her when he...fucked...her. As with her husbands, she'd been something to be used. And once he'd finished, he'd tossed her away like garbage.

Her hand shook as she forced herself to drink the coffee. He was wrong. She was a good woman. A fine person. Not a slut.

Oh God, I'll never be able to face him again.

At least she could avoid Dark Haven for a while since Saturday would be her time with Rona and Abby. She squeezed her eyes shut. If enough time passed, she'd find the courage to share with them what had happened. Surely they'd have some insights.

She'd known he was a weasel. She'd *known*.

CHAPTER FOUR

"I love girls' night out." The next Saturday, Lindsey popped a stuffed mushroom in her mouth, smiled at Rona and Abby, and checked out the room. The place was one step up from a fern bar, with great appetizers, strong drinks, and lots of good-looking men. Yet no matter how good-looking, no male was going to tempt her for a long time.

Maybe a lifetime.

"Agreed," Abby said. Her tailored shirt and dark slacks were balanced out by the pale yellow hair curling in a froth around her face. "I've missed you both."

Rona's blue-green boatneck dress matched her eyes and enhanced her curves. She pushed her wavy blonde hair back. "Me too."

"Me three," Lindsey finished. With Abby's new marriage and college job, the women hadn't been able to get together often.

Abby looked Lindsey over. "What happened to the red-and-gold streaks in your hair? You look so sedate."

Trust a sociologist to be observant. "I'm job hunting." Lindsey's mood took a dive. "And was apartment searching for a couple of days too."

"Is the condo-sitting over? I thought Xavier's friend wouldn't return for another month," Rona said.

"She wasn't supposed to, except she got homesick and asked if I could move out early." Lindsey shrugged casually. She'd had a signed agreement, but the woman had cried on the phone, and Lindsey hadn't had the heart to say no. She knew what homesickness felt like. "I found a new place easy enough."

Probably because no smart person would live there. Nonetheless, she had no job and couldn't afford anything nicer. San Francisco rental prices were outrageous, which was why she'd jumped on condo-sitting. Sure, her friends would put her up, but she followed her daddy's philosophy—don't borrow what you can't pay back.

"What day do you want us to show up to help you move?" Rona asked.

"No need. I've got it covered." When she'd taken the condo, they'd helped move her newly acquired furniture into storage. Her stuff could stay there; she didn't want her property in the dive. And no way would she let her friends visit her either. Shoot, there were fist-size holes in the living room walls. Outside, every corner had gangbangers and drug deals and hookers.

Neither Abby nor Rona would think the little mouse who scavenged in her kitchen was cute—although he kinda was.

"Lindsey," Abby said. "You know we're happy to—"

"Look. My hair still has some color," Lindsey interrupted. She lifted her long hair, showing the purple underlayer. "See? It only shows if I put my hair up."

"That's quite a dark purple," Rona said. "Are you in mourning for the job or the condo?"

Mostly for the wretched memory of a sweet night gone bad. "Neither. The condo was lush but awfully fancy for my comfort." And too much like Victor's carefully decorated house, where everything had been bought to impress. Lindsey swirled the remnants of her drink in her glass. "And the temporary receptionist position wasn't a great job, even though the people were nice."

"You always think people are nice," Abby commented absentmindedly as she waved to get the attention of their waitress.

Rona turned, lifted a hand, and the waitress trotted over. "Another round, please, and the check," Rona said.

Abby glared. "I don't know why waitstaff will respond to you and not me."

"Charge nurse, nursing supervisor, hospital administration," Rona said. "I'm always giving orders. You have no idea how wonderful it is to sometimes hand all decisions and control over to Simon."

Abby smiled. "Actually, I have a rather good idea."

For one whole night, Lindsey had felt that wonder. Had wanted to give deVries anything he asked for. With a sigh, she lifted her glass and finished off the watered-down cosmopolitan. The alcohol hummed in her blood, making her feel sentimental. And glum.

"Sweetie, you weren't at the club last night." Abby tilted her head. "I saw you leave with Zander last weekend. I've been waiting to hear how it went."

Even as Lindsey's mouth flattened at the jerk's name, she felt a flush heat her cheeks. "Not much to say." *Best sex of my life, worst putdown of my life.*

"Not a good evening?" Abby didn't sound surprised.

Everyone knew the hard-core sadist never stayed with a submissive.

I knew he didn't. And his spending the night had seemed...wonderful. Special. *Yay me.* "His jets were revved after a scene with johnboy, so he called in my debt from last summer. He just wanted to...to get off."

"That's damned cold." Rona curled her hand around Lindsey's.

Lindsey's eyes burned with tears. As the eldest, she'd always watched out for her two sisters and flighty mom. How strange—and wonderful—to be on the receiving end.

"Here you go, ladies." The waitress handed out the drinks and gave the check to Rona.

When Lindsey dug in her purse for money, Rona shook her head. "My treat tonight."

"You paid last time."

"After you land a job, you can take us out to celebrate. All right?"

Pride warred with practicality before she nodded. "I guess so."

"You sure had a wretched week." Abby's face filled with sympathy.

"At least the week is over." Her smile felt a bit twisted. "And I'll stay away from deVries."

Rona straightened. "Did he hurt you?"

Oh spit, her declaration hadn't come out right. "Just my feelings. Physically, he pushed my limits some, but"—and wasn't it hard to admit?—"I liked it."

"I know how that can be," Abby said.

Rona nodded. "All right, then." She picked up her drink in a toast. "Here's to Lindsey finding a fantastic job." As the glasses clinked together, Rona added, "Take your time finishing your drinks. I'm going to text Simon not to pick us up for a while."

Close to an hour later, Rona's husband appeared, striding across the room as if he owned the place. He didn't, did he? Her head a bit muddled, Lindsey tried to remember. No, he had an international security business. No bars.

Of course, Abby's husband, Xavier, probably owned some bars, and he'd look right at home in this swank establishment.

DeVries wouldn't. Considering the faded leathers he wore, the bouncers might not even let him in. Nope. He was a total loser. *Jerk. Asshole.* She took another sip of her drink. No more thinking about the creep.

When Simon reached the table, he slid his fingers into Rona's hair, tugged her head back, and the possessive kiss he gave her made Lindsey's chest ache.

She loved knowing her friend had such an affectionate, territorial husband, even if it emphasized how alone Lindsey was. Yanking her gaze away, she bent over, looking for her purse. They shouldn't keep their designated driver waiting, especially since he'd been nice enough to come inside to get them.

To her surprise, Simon dragged a chair from the next table and sat between her and Rona. He lifted Rona's glass. "Should I even ask how many of those drinks you've had—let alone what they are?"

Rona smiled. "I think it's best you don't know."

Simon took a sip and winced. "You have a point, lass." His

laugh was dark and easy, like a smooth scotch as opposed to deVries's rotgut, harsh laugh.

So why did Lindsey crave deVries's?

Simon set the drink down with a thump and turned to Lindsey.

She flushed as she was treated to the intent regard of one of Dark Haven's most experienced Doms. "Rona says you're job hunting," Simon said.

Lindsey couldn't help the accusing look she sent her friend. Discussions between the women were supposed to be secret. Well, okay, job hunting wasn't particularly confidential, but still...

Simon's lips quirked. "Maybe I can help your search, since Xavier and I know quite a few business owners. Have you attended college or taken any training?"

God, how could she explain? Her thoughts tangled as she backtracked through the lies she'd used. Should use. Had she told Rona—

"Lindsey?"

Under his dark, intimidating gaze, she blurted out the truth. "I have a master's degree in social work."

Abby gasped.

"I'd only been working for a couple of months when"— *when I fled, leaving everything behind*—"when I left Texas." Just ahead of being arrested for murder.

Simon frowned. "With that kind of background, why are you a receptionist?"

"I...I don't want to be found."

"The divorce was bad? Did he try to hurt you?"

Divorce. Abby and Rona must have disclosed her lies. If only an angry ex-husband was all she was running from. She shivered. "Oh yes."

Simon's eyes narrowed...as did Rona's.

Abby put a warm hand on Lindsey's forearm.

Aw heck, she was making a hash of this. Lying wasn't in her skill set. "I think eventually he'll forget about me." Her assumption was valid...since he was dead. Regrettably Victor's brother was the police chief; he'd never forget. "Meantime, I'm playing it safe"—real safe. Even her name and social security number were falsified—"and not leaving a trail by requesting school records or résumés. Instead, I take crummy jobs."

After another moment of study, Simon moved his chair, positioning himself knee to knee with Lindsey. He took her hands in his heavily callused ones. His eyes were steady. "Tell me about your work experience."

She glared at Rona. "Next time you arrange an interview, would you set it up for *before* I've been drinking?"

Rona and Abby burst out laughing.

Simon's fingers tightened. "Answer me."

God, the low command sent a quiver down her to her toes. His gaze stayed on her face as she swallowed against the sudden dryness.

Be honest. Don't put him on the spot with his friends. "Okay, it's like this. I think I'm good at counseling, and people who worked with me said I was great." On the other hand, she'd only had a couple of months' experience. "As a receptionist, I did well enough, even though I hadn't used some of the software. My boss says she'll be happy to give me a reference."

Her sister had scolded her before for being too modest. Had said she should never run herself down.

Someone else had no problem making her feel like scum. *"Debt paid."* Damn deVries.

"I might not have much office experience; however, I learn quickly, I'm smart, I'm organized, and I'm good with people." There, that sounded nice. Maybe too boastful?

Simon squeezed her fingers and let her go. "Very well laid out. I've seen how easily you handle the desk at Dark Haven." His measured gaze moved over her, as if weighing her in his mind. "Let's try this. My executive assistant needs to work part-time for a couple of weeks. She hasn't found anyone in-house to assist her—at least not one she likes. Possibly she'd get along better with a smarter, less experienced person. Would you like a crack at it?"

Her ears followed his words; her brain lagged behind. The

fact her lungs ceased working didn't help. After a second, she wheezed, "Did you just offer me a job?"

"This is the first time I've interviewed someone in a bar, let alone an applicant who wasn't remotely sober." His mouth curved up. "Yes, Lindsey, I offered you the chance to see if you can impress my admin. If you can't, no harm done. Either way, I'll help find you something. However, this would bring you in some money while you're searching for a better match."

"It'll work," she promised him and a smiling Rona. *It will damn well work.*

Two hours later, a horrifying thought brought her upright in bed.

DeVries worked for Simon.

CHAPTER FIVE

On Friday, deVries stepped off the elevator at the eleventh floor and walked around the corner. He'd gone straight to the Demakis offices after a long week of bodyguarding the prissiest, bitchiest movie star he'd ever met. And he'd met quite a few. He'd thought he was fairly easygoing, well, not really—but Jesus, by the time the week ended, he'd considered paying her stalker to take her out.

To top it off, she'd thrown a tantrum at his announcement he was leaving. When his replacement, Marley, looked as if she were considering walking out, damned if he hadn't fled like a wimp.

As he shoved open the door to the offices of Demakis International Security, he shook off his irritation. At least he'd be in San Francisco for a while. He could visit Dark Haven tonight and find someone to play with. Maybe johnboy or HurtMe. Or Dixon might be available, even if the submissive couldn't take as much pain.

After a good S/M session, deVries could fuck his brains out with a willing female.

His mouth tightened as he remembered the previous week. The innocent-looking, cute...*money-grubbing*...submissive. Been years since a woman had taken him in so thoroughly. Yeah, she was *good*. Might even have a bit of a conscience left, considering the guilt on her face when he'd asked if her ex was in a ritzy place like hers.

Did some women have a biological glitch making them more mercenary than men? They might appear loyal at first, but wave a wad of cash in front of them and some would sell out their own kin.

Or, in the case of his mother, her son.

As he stepped into the reception area, he stopped abruptly. "What the fuck?"

Lindsey, the Texan with a calculator for a heart, sat at the admin's desk. "Mr. deVries." Expressionless, no light in her wide brown eyes. Her voice was icy. "Mr. Demakis said you were to go straight in when you arrived."

"What the hell are you doing here?"

"Working. Do you have a problem with that?"

"Guess so." He set his hands palm-down on the desk and leaned into Lindsey's space. "I don't like you."

The tiny lines around her eyes flinched, but she didn't move. Didn't evade his gaze. Didn't display fear, and he had to give her props for that. A pity she'd be afraid very shortly when he—

"Zander, I'm glad you're back," Simon said from behind him. "How did you enjoy Los Angeles?"

DeVries turned, and his boss's knowing smile pissed him off good. "Did you know what a bitch your so-called star is?"

"Of course." Simon motioned him into his office and said to the Texan, "Take an hour for lunch. Mrs. Martinez is on her way up."

"Yes, sir."

Without looking at deVries once, she bent over, digging in a drawer in her desk. Her desk.

DeVries dropped into a chair in Simon's office and glanced around. Creamy carpet. Off-white walls. Yet the mahogany desk, leather furniture, and colorful abstract art kept the place from the frozen feeling of the Texan's fancy condo. "You hiring Dark Haven subbies now?"

Simon's gaze cooled. "Mrs. Martinez's daughter is getting married, and she requested help for a couple of weeks. Rona suggested I hire Lindsey."

And Simon gave his wife just about anything she wanted.

DeVries considered mentioning Lindsey's past. Unfortunately, what she'd done to an ex-husband had little bearing on her performance as a secretary. Odd she was working at all, but perhaps an upscale office was the perfect hunting ground for her next sucker.

"Do you have a concern with Lindsey?" Simon asked evenly.

Fuck. "Nothing related to work. Won't be a problem."

"Good enough." Simon flipped open a folder on the desk. "Now debrief me on Los Angeles. I also want your input on security for the Scofield's residence."

DeVries turned his attention to the matters at hand. The Texan would undoubtedly stay out of his path, both here and at Dark Haven. She didn't strike him as suicidal.

For over an hour, they tossed ideas back and forth, and finally Simon nodded. "Looks workable." He glanced down at the notes he'd jotted. "Give this to Lindsey to type up, would you, please?"

DeVries took the papers. At the door, he stopped. "How's she working out?"

Simon's level look made him feel like a fool. "Very nicely. Her degree is in social work, and she lacks office experience; however, sheer doggedness gets her past that. I'll keep her as long as she wants to stay."

Social work? *Jesus.* "Why the fuck would a rich girl major in social work?"

"Rich girl?" Simon gave him a quizzical glance. "Where'd you get such an idea?"

"Saw her condo. Pacific Heights."

With a disgusted sound, Simon leaned back in his chair. "Someday you might want to *talk* to the woman you're fucking."

Unable to think of a response, he closed the door. Simon's reaction implied Lindsey wasn't rich, and deVries was off base.

Or Simon had been taken in by someone's puppy-dog eyes and an oh-pitiful-me story.

DeVries crossed the hallway to the reception area. Lindsey was behind the desk, sitting beside Mrs. Martinez.

The gray-haired secretary's tailored silvery suit hinted at her impressive efficiency; her pleased smile showed her true nature. Sweetest woman on the planet.

"Zander, it's wonderful you're back." She held her hand out to him and accepted a kiss on her cheek as her due. "If you'll be here a few days, I'll make you an apple pie."

His mouth watered. The woman knew how to cook. "If I'm out of town, I'll fly back."

Her laugh was delighted. Still smiling, she turned to the silent little Texan. "Lindsey, do you know Alexander deVries? He's Simon's best operative."

"Yes, we've met." Lindsey tilted her head stiffly. "Mr. deVries."

Well, if that was the way she wanted to play it, fine. He gave her a nod and handed Mrs. Martinez the papers. "Simon needed these typed up."

In his office, he dropped into his chair. As one of Simon's three lead security agents, he rated his own space rather than a cubicle. Not high on his list of priorities, but he liked the privacy. Leaning back, he stared out the window where the Bay sparkled in an undoubtedly short interlude of sunshine.

Quite the puzzle. A pretty divorcee who ended up well-off enough to live in Pacific Heights—yet worked as a receptionist.

She'd dressed...comfortably. Not rich. Black jeans and boots, silky red shirt. A black jacket dressed her outfit up adequately for an office.

Mrs. Martinez dressed fancier.

Lindsey had a degree in social work—or so she'd told Simon. Social workers and con artists didn't belong in the same box.

He scowled. Although she'd lied to him last weekend, he hadn't noticed any dishonesty before that. However, he'd been played for a fool before. Tamara had lied to him constantly, and he hadn't caught on.

Even so, that was a decade ago. He'd been younger. Hadn't been a Dom and used to studying for small telltale signs of deception. He'd never have thought to distrust his wife.

The sound of Lindsey's giggles came through the closed

door. Sweet. Open. Her apparent sincerity was one of her traits he'd found compelling.

Simon knew about her ritzy condo, yet didn't think she was rich. Had he checked her references? Seen her college transcripts? He wasn't an idiot, after all.

"I'm missing something," deVries muttered. As a kid, he had never been able to step away from a puzzle. Got into fixing computers for the sheer fun of figuring out how they worked. As a SEAL, he'd specialized in surveillance, surreptitious entry, and breaching. Now, as a trained investigator, he should be able to unravel the puzzle of Lindsey.

He leaned forward and brought up the first search program.

⟺⟒⟺

Why couldn't the man go do his investigating and bodyguarding somewhere else? Like maybe New York? Late that afternoon, Lindsey walked past deVries's office. Door closed. Through the smoky glass, she could see him at his desk. Having him in the same building made her more nervous than her resident rodent on cleaning day. Little Mouse Francois had the right idea—jump in a hidey-hole until it was safe to come out.

What kind of a man could be so nice to her all night and zip straight into disliking her? That was just...wrong. Made her feel as if every certainty was gone.

When he'd said, "*I don't like you,*" she'd almost started to cry.

Behind her, in reception, the phone rang, and Mrs. Martinez answered.

Lindsey wanted to help, but she'd been told to enjoy a break before the admin left.

The break room was tiny, with a small table, fridge, sink, and microwave. The new coffeemaker obviously got the most use. Lindsey put a clean cup under the spout and inserted a hazelnut-flavored pod. As she waited, she called her sister.

"Hey, it's Lindsey."

"Sissie!" Amanda's high voice was delighted. "Changed phones again?"

"You betcha." The better to make sure her number never got in the wrong hands.

Her little sister gave an unhappy sigh. "I wish—"

"Me too." She forced cheerfulness into her voice.

"Well, I'm glad you called. I wanted to talk to you."

Worry tightened Lindsey's throat. "What's wrong? Have you been to the doctor?"

"Criminy, relax!" Her baby sister heaved an exasperated groan. "I'm fine. The last scan showed I'm clear. It's all good, Linnie."

"Oh." Lindsey's shoulders slumped with relief. The cancer hadn't come back. "Okay. Sorry."

"You worry more than Mama and Melissa combined."

"I know." Hearing Amanda's giggle, Lindsey felt her spirit soar. *Just listen to her. Alive. Laughing.* So different from three years ago, when she'd been diagnosed with cancer and was well on her way to dying. She'd been losing weight, her face drawn tight with pain. Now she sounded as she had before—Mandy had laughed all through childhood. "So what's up?"

"Texas A&M accepted me. I'm going to be an Aggie!"

"Really? When did you get old enough to go to college?"

"Linnie!" The reprimanding tone made Lindsey chuckle and tear up at the same time.

"S-sorry." She cleared her throat. It had been worth it. Sure, if Victor hadn't offered to pay for Amanda's treatment, Lindsey wouldn't have rushed into marrying him. Maybe she'd have had a chance to learn what an evil person he was or even why he'd been so eager to get married.

She curled her lip. At a guess, he'd needed only one smuggling trip to reimburse him for everything spent on Mandy's treatment. Yet the past didn't matter. Her sister was alive, laughing, and planning her future. That was what counted. "Congratulations, Mandy. Seriously. That's awesome."

"I know, right? I can't believe I actually caught up on all those classes I missed. And Mom's giving me a birthday party next week." A pause and smaller voice. "I wish you could come."

The thought of setting foot in Parnell's jurisdiction, of what might happen to her... Lindsey's stomach twisted painfully. *Relax.* She was far, far from Texas. "Sorry, sissie." Would she ever be able to go home? "Are y'all doing okay?"

"The cops swing by every couple of weeks to see if you're hiding under the couch or something." She snickered.

"You're not telling them anything, right?"

"Nah, we only say we don't know where you are. I'm glad you don't tell us, so I don't feel like a liar." She hesitated. "Chief Parnell is...kinda scary, though."

Lindsey stiffened, remembering the twisted hatred in the police chief's eyes. *I shot his brother.* And Parnell liked to kill. Thank goodness Mandy would soon be leaving town. "You never see him alone, you understand me? Never."

"I'm not stupid. If Mama's not home, I go out the back door and over the fence." Mandy giggled. "But it's fun when she's there. She knows she can't lie worth a darn, so she just goes into a crying fit whenever the chief mentions your name. And he gets all disgusted and leaves."

Even as guilt settled in Lindsey's stomach, she grinned. She could see her mama doing excellent hysterics. With proper Southern gentility, of course.

"Melissa came over for supper last night. She's getting the day off to come to my party!"

"Good."

"And she says she's still keeping the cattle and the hands away from your property."

"Even better." Thank God for Melissa. The two of them had always taken care of Mama and Mandy. Like when Amanda got sick, Lindsey had obtained the money for the experimental treatment, Melissa provided the support, and Mama had— Lindsey rolled her eyes—Mama had cried. They all loved their mother, despite the fact that in an emergency, she was as much use as tits on a boar. "Now tell me about what you're going to take the first semester."

After her sister finished with the local news, Lindsey dumped her coffee into the sink and went back to the reception room.

"I'm off to help my baby with her flower arrangements," Mrs. Martinez said and pointed to a pile of papers on the desk. "If you have time, can you file those away?"

"You bet."

Lindsey stood and watched the short woman hurry out of the office. After a minute, she recognized the feeling welling inside her as grief. She'd been a bride twice now. Even with Victor and having a few qualms, she'd thought there was love. She'd looked forward to children.

Surely the death of dreams should have some ceremony attached.

Feeling the thickening in her throat, she shook herself.

The wagon train of destiny has passed, girl. Barking after it won't make it stop.

Carrying the papers, she went into the narrow filing room. Tucked behind the reception area, the room was isolated and perfect, since she couldn't see deVries's office.

Mood lightening, she hummed to herself, answered the phone when needed, and filed papers. As, Bs, Cs...

"You look like you know what you're doing." DeVries's gravelly voice echoed in the small room.

Lindsey spun. "Jesus, you scared the spit out of me." *God, God, God.* How could she have been so stupid as to turn her back on a door? Anyone might have walked in. Shot her dead.

Trying to regulate her heartbeat, she picked up the paper she'd dropped.

"Bit jumpy?" His gaze swept over her, sending a different type of anxiety into her.

"I drank too much coffee." She assumed a pleasant smile. "Was there something you needed, Mr. deVries?"

His face darkened. "Considering all the ways I've tasted you, fingered you, fucked you, calling me *Mister* is pretty formal."

Her spine snapped straight. "I thought formality would serve us best. After all, I don't like you, and you don't like me."

"Hell," he said under his breath before giving her a scowl. "I was out of line."

She nodded acknowledgment of his half-assed—though unexpected—apology.

"I didn't come in to apologize, though." He gave her a stare as if she were a scorpion scuttling around on an outhouse floor. "You're working under a fake ID, Miss Adair. What's your real name?"

As her hands went cold, she took a step back. The file drawer jammed into her hip, blocking her retreat. "You researched—"

"Yeah. I did. Give me a real good explanation of why, and maybe I won't tell Simon."

Her fear disintegrated as rage danced along her nerve endings. How dare he snoop? Threaten her? "Go away." Trying to block his existence from her universe, she turned and leisurely filed the paper she'd crumpled.

The air seemed to darken. What kind of man could change the very atmosphere in a room?

"I'm waiting for your explanation."

He could wait until the stars fell from the sky. "Run and tell Daddy, little boy. What are you, five?" She took a long inhalation and told her shoulders to relax. *God, I just want to go home.*

"Let's start with this: why're you working here?"

Because if I'd stayed in Texas, I'd be dead. She turned and glared at him. "Why do you think, you idiot? Because he *pays* me. You know," she said sweetly, "Simon thinks you're so clever, but I kinda figure you can't find your ass with a flashlight and a search warrant."

Silence.

Perhaps that hadn't been the smartest comment she'd ever made. Well, if he couldn't take the heat, he shouldn't have come into her filing room. She slammed the drawer shut and started on the next letter. *D.* DeVries's name was on a lot of the investigations. He was respected here. What would Simon do when his buddy outed her? Still, Simon knew she was hiding. Surely he wouldn't fire her. She felt her lower lip tremble and compressed her lips. *Leave me alone.*

He didn't leave. His voice was even raspier as he said, "I think you should—"

"Lindsey, it's five o'clock. Time for you to head on home." Simon's smooth voice hit the room like the warmth of a fire after a chill morning walk.

She turned.

DeVries still stood in the doorway, his expression unreadable.

"Okay," she said to Simon. "Thank you."

"Not a problem. You're doing an excellent job."

Pleasure swept away her worry. "Oh, that's nice to hear."

"Only the truth."

After closing the filing drawer, she left the remaining papers on the small table and headed for the door. DeVries didn't even try to get out of her way as she squeezed past him.

"Butthead," she said under her breath barely loud enough for him to hear.

DEVRIES WATCHED HER grab her purse and leave, his annoyance almost mitigated by how pretty she was when she was ticked off.

Such an easy-to-read face. She'd tried to conceal her fear and anger, and failed. He chewed on the inside of his cheek. If she couldn't hide those, she wasn't much of a con artist. Dammit, all his instincts insisted she was a nice person.

And yet, she wasn't who she said she was.

Simon gave him a level stare. "Don't screw with my staff."

DeVries considered staying silent, but his boss needed the truth. "Lindsey Adair doesn't exist—at least not prior to a few months ago."

"I already knew that." Simon leaned a hip against Mrs. Martinez's desk, which the nonexistent girl had left spotless.

"But—" Seeing the smoldering anger in Simon's eyes, deVries reconsidered. The Dom had a protective streak a mile wide. "Got it. You know, I figured she was rich."

Simon lifted an eyebrow. "I'm rich. Does that mean we can't

be friends?"

"Jesus." The next time he had Simon in the ring, he might just beat the hell out of him...or try, at least. Simon had retired from full-contact martial arts, but he hadn't lost any of his skills. "I saw her place, and no receptionist could afford that. She even admitted she married her ex for his money."

"You jumped to conclusions, Zander, which isn't like you." Simon shook his head. "You know, when I attempted to give her an advance on her salary, she said she wouldn't take something she hadn't earned. And she doesn't live in the condo anymore."

"She moved? To where?"

"None of your business, is it?"

As Simon walked away, deVries scowled after him. What a goat fuck, and he'd created it himself. Why had he assumed the worst about the girl?

Nonetheless, she was lying about who she was. Why?

Could she be in some trouble? DeVries walked into his office and booted up a different search program. Damned if he'd leave a mess like this behind him, especially if Simon sent him out of town again. People didn't always return from a mission.

CHAPTER SIX

eVries found Lindsey's apartment building without any problem except mounting disbelief. The brick structure looked like it had been built before America was discovered. What the fuck was she doing living in this rat-infested part of town?

Scowling, he circled the block looking for a place to park. No parking garage. Or lot. Only street parking. *Jesus Christ.*

The entry wasn't locked. He walked past graffiti-covered metal community mailboxes, over ripped carpet, and stopped at the elevators. One was out of service. The other... Not being stupid, he took the stairs.

On the fourth floor, he could hear the televisions from each apartment. Smelled as if someone had used the far wall for a urinal. With a grunt of disgust, he knocked on her door.

No sound from inside. He couldn't call her—she had no listed phone number. He knocked louder. Nothing. Hell.

A Goth-attired teen hurried past him down the hall. She had enough piercings he had to wonder what her parents were thinking.

"Hey, kid."

The girl skidded to a halt. "What?"

"Lindsey live here?" Assuming she wasn't using a different name here too.

Almost dancing with impatience, the girl said, "Uh-huh. Her and Francois. Only she's not there now."

Hell of a name, *Francois*. And Tex had pretty fucking bad taste in men if this was what her lover could afford. Why the step down in life? Step down? Hell, she'd fallen straight to the basement.

He was missing something here. Had to be. Annoyance turned his voice to a growl. "You know where she is?"

"Dakota got chased up a tree. Lindsey went to get him."

DeVries gave a snort of exasperation even as he mentally kicked himself. Yeah, the Texan was a real mercenary bitch—dashing off to rescue a cat. *I'm an idiot.*

The girl opened the door across from Lindsey's apartment. "Mom? Dakota needs you!" Only silence answered, and the girl kicked the frame. "Shit, she's not home yet."

"Give me some directions. Maybe I can help."

"Really?" The kid's expression of relief was unsettling. How high was the damn cat in the tree?

"Down the street toward the school." She pointed to the west. "A couple of blocks. I've gotta wait for Mom."

"Got it. Thanks."

Heart pounding painfully inside her rib cage, Lindsey stood in front of the tree, holding her tiny can of pepper spray. Excellent stuff. Good for blinding at least three big men.

And, hey, the ones facing her weren't big men. Weren't even really men.

Unhappily there were a whole lot more than three.

The cold wind off the Bay swept through the street, making the paper and cans in the gutter rustle. She shivered, wishing she had on a coat. A long-sleeved T-shirt wasn't enough.

"This is boring, guys," she said to the teens. Piercings, tattoos, oddly designed hairstyles—about what you'd expect from a gang in this neighborhood. And dirty? Sheesh. The ripe aroma of young male sweat was enough to make her eyes water. "Y'all go home. Dakota and I will do the same."

She'd already been here at least ten minutes. Why the heck

hadn't someone called the cops? But she knew. This wasn't a neighborhood where people stepped forward—even to dial the police.

The knife in her jeans pocket seemed to wiggle, begging her to pull it. Regrettably it was awfully small. And a blade would ramp up a standoff to a whole new level.

"Get your ass gone, bitch. This ain't your biz." The ugly words came from a boy with an ambitious shadow of a mustache. Her daddy would have washed his mouth out for using such language to a lady.

"He's not even close to your age. Why are you mad at him?" *Sheesh, Lindsey, as if they're going to see reason?* Logic wouldn't dent their attitudes—and yet, she couldn't help but try. The tiny canister of pepper spray was slick in her sweaty fingers. More sweat trickled down her back despite the cool autumn air.

"His bro hit me. So I'm gonna fuck his brother up."

There was logic. The gang activity in the area was the reason Dakota's family was moving. This was his last day in school. Probably the group had missed catching up with his older brother, so they'd take their anger out on the kid.

"I'm not leaving," she said. "And whoever tries to get him will have to come through me."

Oh shit, wrong thing to say!

They lunged at her from all sides.

She hosed them with the pepper spray.

Shouts of anger filled the air.

She hadn't gotten nearly enough of them.

Blinded, one ran into her, knocking her back a step. Another brought a 2x2 down on her wrist. Pain ripped through her flesh and bone. *Hell.* The spray canister dropped from her nerveless hand.

A fist slammed into her face. She shook her head, blinked back tears, and nailed the creep in the eye. A kick to the balls downed the next guy.

The one behind him knocked her sprawling onto the unforgiving concrete. A boot hit her hip. As pain blasted into her, she barely muffled a scream.

They were getting past her. *No!*

On hands and knees, she kicked at the legs bypassing her for the tree. One yelled when she got his knee. Another hit the ground. Panting, she tried to stand, failed...and someone on the sidewalk screamed. Pulling her pocketknife out, she managed to open it.

The shouting went silent as the gang around her moved back. Had the cops arrived?

With a grunt of pain, she pushed herself to her feet and retreated to defend the tree. Her eyes were blurred with tears, and she roughly wiped her hand over her face. What was everyone looking at?

Oh. My.

DeVries faced the gangbangers, and she recognized his cold, cold expression. He'd looked at her that way.

Around him, three of the mob were down—one with an obviously broken arm. The rest of the hoods were inching sideways. Away.

He didn't even seem to notice as he prowled toward her. One fool swung at him. He caught the young man's fist and yanked him forward far enough to slam an elbow into the tattooed face. The sound of the nose breaking barely preceded the wail of pain.

Like cockroaches under bright light, the gang fled in all directions.

DeVries hadn't even spoken.

He stopped in front of her, plucked the knife from her hand. "Like that'd scare someone," he said sarcastically. He closed and dropped it in her jeans pocket.

Feeling the trickle of blood running down her face, Lindsey swiped at it.

DeVries's gaze settled on her fingers, his jaw tightening. "You have to be one of the stupidest people I know," he said in a frozen tone. "Risking your life for a fucking—"

Her gratitude died—thankfully before she threw herself in his arms—and she turned away. *Got to get Dakota. Leave before the gang returned.* Grabbing a low branch, she tried to climb up, but her right hand was still half-numb from the blow to her wrist. Her fingers wouldn't close. A whine of frustration escaped.

Hard hands closed on her shoulders and pulled her back. His eyes had gone more gray than green, piercing through her as he lifted her chin, turned her face from side to side, looking at what was probably a gash and bruise. Felt like it anyway, and God knew, she'd experienced far worse at the hands of the crooked border patrol agent, Ricks.

She tamped down her anger. DeVries had risked his life to save her, after all. Some gangs carried firearms. And knives. He could have been badly hurt. "I appreciate the help. Thank you." She wrenched back and got nowhere.

"What are you doing?"

"I'm fixin' to get Dakota. You just let go of me now."

A corner of his mouth tipped up, the ice leaving his gaze. "Your accent gets thick when you're mad."

She glared.

He gave a low chuckle. "Where's the fucking cat? I'll get it."

"What cat? I'm fetching Dakota." She pointed up in the tree, where the eight-year-old boy had his little arms wrapped around the trunk. He was crying silently.

"I'll be damned."

She'd never seen him startled before. What—he'd thought Dakota was a cat? When she started to laugh, his eyes narrowed into a cynical look.

"Makes more sense, except...you'd probably have done the same thing for a cat, wouldn't you?"

Of course. She shrugged and winced at the pain.

"What I thought." He pointed at the sidewalk. "Sit there while I recover your kid."

Instead she looked up. "Dakota, this is..." She glanced at deVries. Would he kill her if she used his first name?

The dimple appeared beside his mouth. "Friends call me Zander."

Well, maybe he could consider Dakota a friend, right? "This is Zander. He saved us, sweetie. Now he's going to help you get down." She frowned. "You be gentle with him or—"

"Or you'll kick my ass, Texas?"

The affectionate half hug he gave her almost stopped her heart.

He swung easily up into the tree. Before he reached Dakota, he paused, and she could hear the rumble of his voice.

After a few seconds, the boy offered a wavering smile and let deVries haul him into his arms.

While they were occupied with climbing down, she used the bottom of her T-shirt to clean her face of blood and tears.

After deVries was down, she pulled Dakota into a hug. Tremors still shook his skinny frame. But he was safe. "Let's get you home, honeybunches."

He clung to her hand on the silent walk back to the apartment building, and she noticed with a stab of the heart that when deVries walked too far away, Dakota tucked his fingertips into the man's jeans pocket, keeping him close.

DeVries didn't say a word.

They met Dakota's frantic mother running out of the lobby, trailed by Dakota's sister. They all walked upstairs together. DeVries stayed in the hall while Lindsey went into Dakota's apartment to finish explaining to his mama what had happened—and how dangerous it was.

When she emerged, she looked around, hoping deVries had gotten bored and left.

He was still there, waiting silently by her door.

Oh. Damn. She was too tired to fight with him or answer his snoopy questions. Yes, he deserved a thanks—and it was going to be delivered in the hallway.

"Thank you again," she said, trying for warm and cool both. "Now, did you come here for a reason?"

"Yeah." He touched her chin with a light finger. "And we'll talk once you're cleaned up."

"My face will keep. What did you need?"

He held his hand out. "Keys."

"You are such a butthead," she muttered and heard him

snort. After digging her keys out of her pocket, she slapped them in his palm.

As if escorting her home from a dance, he unlocked her door, put his arm behind her back, and guided her into her apartment. "You got antibiotic ointment?"

He was past stubborn. "I can tend myself, thanks."

"Where is it?"

She huffed in exasperation. When Abby and Rona had complained about their annoyingly overprotective Doms, Lindsey had only felt envy. Now she was beginning to comprehend their feelings on the subject. "Bathroom."

"Good." He herded her like a cattle dog into her tiny bath, sat her on the toilet seat, and tipped her face up. Anger tightened his jaw as he studied the damage. "Caught yourself a good one," he said, the concern not concealing the steel beneath.

She scowled. She hadn't rolled belly up like a coward. With Ricks, she hadn't had a chance to fight; this time she'd done better. "I gave some good ones back."

The approving glint in his eyes was unexpected and made her heart jump inside her chest. "I saw that, baby. You've got a nice right hook."

Before she could recover from the compliment, he turned to rummage for a washcloth.

His hands were harder than iron yet disconcertingly gentle as he washed the blood from her cheek. He applied ointment before dealing with her scraped palms the same way. "All done."

"Thank you." The gratitude was real...as was the need to blink back tears.

"Not a problem. Let's get some ice on your face." After sitting her down on her living room couch, he sauntered into the kitchen.

The minute he disappeared, the aftermath of the fight set in. First a tightness in her throat, a flutter in her stomach. *Hold together a little longer, and he'll be gone.*

Nothing could stop it.

Coldness swept through her body, and she shivered. Huddled in a corner of the couch, she wrapped her arms around

EDGE OF THE ENFORCER | 69

her knees and shook as the sound of shouting crashed back over her, the fear, the feeling of fist meeting face. Her jaw ached from trying to keep her teeth from chattering.

Holding an ice pack, deVries appeared in front of her. "Ah hell." After setting the pack on the end table, he scooped her up and took her place, settling her on his lap.

"Don't." She retreated into herself. No matter how nice he was now, he didn't like her. She could do without his charity. "Just go. I don't want you here."

"Too bad for you that's not going to happen." His voice wasn't mean, simply matter-of-fact. Almost affectionate. Tucking her head into the hollow of his shoulder, he rubbed her neck with his free hand.

He was so warm...and she didn't want to be alone. Not now. She turned her face into him, inhaling the soap fragrance of his shirt, the underlying masculine scent. When she sighed, he hugged her closer. She'd never realized what a difference it made to feel safe.

"Did you know you have a mouse?" he asked. "I saw it run across the kitchen."

"A mouse?" She blinked. As her muscles relaxed, tiredness swept through her. Her head felt too heavy for her neck. "You mean Francois?"

There was a pause, and he burst out laughing. Rough and dark and sexy. She wasn't sure she'd ever heard him really laugh before. Hadn't thought he knew how.

She drank in the sound like parched soil in an autumn rain. "Hey, only the finest of apartment rentals provide a ready-made pet."

He grinned at her.

She grinned back...until she remembered he didn't like her. How he'd treated her like a whore. *"Debt paid."* She stiffened.

"Lindsey." He shifted her to a more upright position and looked straight at her. "I screwed up. I'm sorry."

Whoa, little doggies. "Huh?"

His dimple appeared, disappeared. "I thought you'd taken your ex for everything he owned to get your fancy condo. You looked guilty when I asked if you married for money. And you did say it was a bad breakup and he isn't living in a ritzy place."

Her mouth dropped open, and her irritation slid right down the banks into a river of rage. "I was condo-sitting for a friend of Xavier's."

WHEN THE LITTLE Texan's face turned red, deVries knew he was in deep shit. Her hand slapped his chest to push him away.

He didn't relax his grip. She was going to hear him out—before she kicked him out.

Assuming he could stand to leave her in this dump.

A shame it looked as if he needed to explain further—which was like gutting himself. He cupped her stubborn little chin, stroked his thumb over her lips. She shoved at his wrist without effect. He saw her consider biting him.

Damn, he liked her. "Tex." He softened his voice. "I was married before. It ended badly."

The pushing stopped as her gaze met his. "*You* were married?"

The incredulity was humorous. And insulting. She figured he was too much of a bastard to catch a woman? "When I was your age." Stupid twenties.

"You're divorced?" she asked carefully.

He had her attention. Good. Unable to resist, he ran his fingers through her wavy hair and discovered glints of a dark color under the mink-brown strands. *Purple?*

She tried to jerk her head away.

"When I was overseas, she screwed around," deVries said. "I got shot up and was stuck in rehab, so she emptied our bank account to have her breasts enlarged and lips puffed up. I came home to divorce papers." The taste of bitterness was still foul. "A month later, she married a rich CEO."

Lindsey's frown softened into understanding. "I'm sorry."

He'd been too fucked-up to fight her for his savings. Sure his severance pay had kept him fed, yet starting over had been...difficult. He shook his head. Dragged his thoughts back. "I

EDGE OF THE ENFORCER | 71

jumped to conclusions about you. Simon said you're not rich."

The sympathy disappeared from her face. "You talked to Simon. About me." Mouth tight, she pushed off his lap and stood. "You know, deVries, your problem isn't you jumped but that you didn't bother to talk with me at all. I was just an easy fuck."

"Lindsey." He rose. "I said I screwed up."

She retreated. "Yeppers. You did. Thank you so, so much for the rescue. Now go home."

Like hell. He curved his hand around her nape, pulled her closer. A brush over her lips, her resistance started to disappear. She had a great mouth. Soft and—

She shoved at him. "Go away."

He needed to leave; she was right. She didn't need more stress. Not now. He took a step toward the door.

A scratching sound stopped him.

The goddamned mouse. She lived in a complete dump. In a fucking bad area. Unease gripped the back of his neck coldly. The gang would return, bent on revenge. He took out his cell and hit Xavier's speed-dial number.

"Make your calls some other time. deVries..."

He eyed Lindsey. She knew his first name now and kept using his surname. Was starting to piss him off. "Call me Zander unless we're in the club. Use it there, and I'll whip your ass." And wouldn't he enjoy doing that?

Despite her obvious ire, a flush of arousal crept up her face. She liked the thought of punishment. In fact, if she were his, she'd probably call him by his last name just to see what he'd do.

She'd find out.

He'd whip her ass. Before he fucked her. Jesus, he was getting hard thinking about it.

"Problem?" Xavier's voice came over the phone.

Focus, Iceman. "Yeah. Does Abby still need a renter for her place?"

"She does. An ad goes into the paper tomorrow."

Lindsey's brows drew together. "That's not any of your busi—"

"Lindsey's new apartment is in the slums, and her building should've been condemned last century. Now she's pissed off a local gang." DeVries felt a ripple of mirth when she lunged in an attempt to swipe the phone from his hand. Fisting her hair, he held her far enough away to avoid getting kicked while he continued his conversation. Feisty, wasn't she?

"I can't afford Abby's place." Lindsey jerked on his arm. "DeVries...I can't—"

Xavier had obviously heard, since he said, "Abby would be delighted to have her there. Let's try it like this—for the first month, Lindsey can pay utilities only. If she wants to stay after that, she and Abby can work out a rent to suit them both."

"No. I won't take advantage of friends," she growled. "I don't—"

"Sounds good." DeVries smiled down at her flushed face, enjoying the hope lighting her face—as well as the dismay. Had more pride than a US Marine, didn't she? "When can she move in?"

"Get her out of there. Give me her address, and I'll send movers over tonight."

"This your stuff, babe?" DeVries motioned to the stained couch and chair.

"DeVries, I can't let Abby—"

"Not what I asked." He waited, his gaze holding hers.

"Jeez." Her clipped voice almost disguised her accent. "The place came furnished. My furniture is still in storage."

"There's a relief." He spoke into the phone. "Hear that? No movers needed. We'll pack what's here and meet you at the duplex."

"Good." Xavier's voice hardened. "Now that I know she can't be trusted to look out for herself, I'll keep a closer eye. As will Simon."

You won't be the only ones.

CHAPTER SEVEN

In the waning sunlight, Lindsey followed deVries's SUV across San Francisco to Mill Valley. He hadn't thought she should drive, but she'd won the argument. Like she wanted to be dependent on him for anything as basic as transportation?

Maybe he'd been right—she was still shaky. Hell would freeze over before she admitted it to him.

Nonetheless, she felt for him. He'd risked his life to serve his country and his wife—sheesh, someone ought to smack her into the next state. Lindsey knew how unbearable it was to be betrayed by a spouse.

Nonetheless, rescue or not, nice guy or not, he wasn't a risk she could take. When it came to him, somehow she was just plain too vulnerable. She should never have taken him back to the condo, should have continued playing lightly at Dark Haven, should never have slept with him.

She was alone, and she needed to stay alone.

When deVries pulled over to the curb, Lindsey shook off the depressing thoughts and parked behind him.

She slid out of her car—carefully. Her right wrist and hip ached, and the left side of her face really hurt. And she had one mother of a headache. Anything on her body not screaming in pain was aching. She was a mess.

Taking a minute to be sure her face didn't show her misery, she checked out the area. The Mill Valley neighborhood was an attractive, older residential street with two-story clapboard houses. The tiered yard held easy-care bushes, trees, and ground cover. It looked as if the house had been divided in half, each side having an upstairs and downstairs. Two front doors opened onto the small porch entrance.

She'd never visited Abby's duplex before. By the time they'd become friends, Abby had already moved into Xavier's home. And now Abby was stuck renting her duplex—to *me*. Guilt washed over her. Poor Abby hadn't had a chance to refuse. Dammit, this wasn't the way she treated friends. Precious friends.

"Let's move, Tex." DeVries opened the back of his SUV.

"Right." Lindsey kicked a rock off the sidewalk, winced at the pull on her sore butt, and reached in to grab a box.

"Wrong one." He tugged the heavy box from her, put it back in the vehicle, and handed her one so lightweight as to be pitiful. When she frowned at him, amusement lit his eyes again. Still, without saying anything else, he picked up her two suitcases.

As they reached the porch and saw the two doors, Lindsey hesitated.

From an upstairs window, Abby's call came. "Door on the right. It's open."

The living room was empty of furniture. Delicate floral wallpaper covered the walls, a gilded mirror hung over the white brick fireplace. Abby had left behind a worn needlepoint carpet in the center of the hardwood floor. Pretty and feminine.

A wide arch divided the space between the living area and dining area. There, a dining room table and chairs remained, which Abby probably hadn't needed in Xavier's already furnished house.

"Lindsey!" Followed by Xavier, Abby trotted down the stairs, saying, "Now, my girl, you can explain exactly why you insisted you had a great place and you didn't need—" She reached the bottom step and stared. "Oh my God, what happened to you?"

Xavier snagged his wife with a long arm. "Easy, fluff, she's not at fighting weight." With Abby pinned to his side, he put a finger under Lindsey's chin to tilt her face up. His black gaze lingered on her cheek before he glanced at deVries and lifted his eyebrows.

"Happened when Tex had a face-off with a gang," deVries

stated.

"DeVries rescued me," Lindsey said reluctantly. She certainly didn't begrudge praising him. Harder to swallow was admitting to her friends that she'd been in trouble.

"How'd you anger a gang?" Xavier asked, his deep voice carrying the hint of a growl.

DeVries put an arm around her and drew her back. "They wanted to beat up a boy." He held his free hand at his ribs to show Dakota's height. "Lindsey and her pepper spray had them stymied for a few minutes. When I got there, they'd gotten brave enough to charge."

Did he actually sound proud of her? She leaned on his warm, hard body for a second, until common sense returned. *You're wanted for murder. Lovers are not in any plan in any foreseeable future.*

She stepped out of his reach. Good thing he couldn't get all bossy with Xavier watching.

On second thought, this was deVries. He might anyway.

"What the hell!" Dixon's horrified shout came from the front entrance.

With a groan, she grabbed her forehead. Holy heck, her head was going to fall right off—and would probably bounce along the floor and trip someone. *Oops, sorry, did I just kick Lindsey's head?* Considering the way her day had gone, she wouldn't be surprised.

Dixon charged across the room. DeVries's snarl made him skid to a halt.

"She's bruised up, boy," deVries snapped. "Keep it down and take it easy, clear?"

"Yes, Sir," the young submissive whispered and held his arms out. "Linnie?"

She stepped into Dixon's embrace. His gentle sympathy was a balm for frazzled nerves. "Pretty, pretty Linnie. It's okay, girlfriend."

God, she loved her friends. After a minute of sheer self-indulgence, she stepped back. "Thanks, Dixon. I needed that."

"Anytime, sweet thing." He smirked at Abby. "I told you

she'd want to see me."

Abby rolled her eyes at Lindsey. "We were coordinating schedules at Dark Haven when Xavier called. Dix wanted to be sure you were all right."

Lindsey bit her lip. Xavier hadn't even talked to Abby before offering the duplex. "I'm really sorry Xavier just kind of dumped me on you. But I'll pay rent starting today and—"

"Oh hush. My liege has laid down a decree. Do you want to get me in trouble?"

"I—"

"Seriously, I agree with him. My liege won't let me pay for anything these days, so I'm not hurting financially. Take the duplex for a month, and we'll talk, okay?"

Charity. It rubbed on a person like a wool saddle blanket. And yet, she did need to get away from her other apartment. "Thank you."

"Now, you'd better sit down before you fall down." Abby tugged out a chair at the dining room table and motioned for her to sit. "We'll play helpless females and let the guys unload the car."

"Forget the female stuff. We'll let the *Doms* unload." Dixon sat as well, bouncing once in glee. "You two missed the fun last weekend. Like HurtMe pitching a hissy fit at johnboy. He thinks johnboy trespassed on his personal territory when he—"

Drowning out Dix's voice, Xavier and deVries clumped into the house, carrying another load. Only half listening to the gossip, Lindsey slouched in the chair and watched the men work.

On the next trip, Rona followed them in and walked through the archway to the dining area. Hands on hips, she gave Lindsey a thoughtful perusal. "The way you're moving your head says you have a headache."

"Aren't you supposed to be in administration?"

"Nurses never stop being nurses. Did you take anything?"

"Uh-uh." Lindsey shook her head...carefully. "Isn't that stupid? I can't believe I'm sitting here hurting and didn't even think of it."

Rona opened her purse. "I have ibuprofen."

Dixon jumped up. "I'll get water."

By the time she'd taken the pills and settled back, the men—who now included Simon—had finished unloading the few boxes. With every trip, she'd felt deVries's gaze land on her, as if he thought she'd drop dead if he didn't keep an eye on her.

When Simon walked over, Lindsey frowned. "I'm sure there's a rule somewhere that a boss isn't supposed to help his secretary move."

He didn't even smile. "There is. However executive administrators' assistants are in an entirely different category of regulations."

Rona snorted. "In fact, according to Simon, the rules are the boss has to order the pizza."

"I never buck the regs." Simon glanced at his watch. "Pizza and drinks should arrive any time."

Pizza? "You guys..." Lindsey's eyes filled; her shoulders began to shake. *No, no, no. No crying.* Because if she started, she'd never stop. Blinking hard, she sucked in a breath and pushed the weakness away. "Thank you, Simon."

"My pleasure, pet." He frowned as his gaze skimmed over her face; then he walked over to talk to Xavier.

Rona disappeared into the kitchen.

A clinking noise made Lindsey turn. DeVries was coming in the front, tossing his car keys from hand to hand.

Lordy, why did he have to be the one to stampede her hormones? Taken piece by piece, he didn't seem as if he should be so compelling. The cropped hair was meh. His face looked more battered than handsome. His body—well, okay, his build was even better than any superhero's. In fact, he was kind of like a really deadly Thor. She sure couldn't forget what his naked body felt like against her and exactly how rock hard each muscle was.

Gaze fixed on her, he prowled across the room, much like an Anatolian guard dog checking out a potential threat. He went down on his haunches beside her chair. "I'm going to give you some time to get settled in."

The way his thigh muscles bunched under his thin jeans was mesmerizing. "Uh-huh."

He unhurriedly ran a finger down her uninjured cheek. "Another day or so, we'll have dinner and talk."

Wait. Dinner? She snapped back to the conversation. No way. She pushed his hand away from her face. "DeVries—"

"Zander." His fingers curled around hers.

God, he was more stubborn than an oak stump. "Listen, I understand why you were unhappy with me, but it's better if we leave well enough alone."

"I'm not much on leaving well enough alone."

"I am. Friends and that's it." She gave his hand a firm shake and let go. "Thank you for the rescue."

Unreadable gray-green eyes simply looked at her for a prolonged minute. Without another word, he rose and walked out the front door.

She'd won.

So why did it feel like she'd lost?

"Holy fag-fucking-doodles," Dixon breathed. "Did the Enforcer just make a move on you?"

"No. Absolutely not."

"Mmmhmm."

Abby didn't speak, but her brows drew together as she glanced at the door.

"Well, I gotta get my ass in gear. My shift starts in an hour." Dixon kissed Lindsey's cheek and rose. "If you need anything, sweet cheeks, you give me a call."

"I will. Thank you for coming over." God, having friends was...was the best thing in the world.

As Dixon left, Simon helped Lindsey to her feet. "Rona is setting up so we can eat outside. What would you like to drink?"

Right about now, her mama would be making margaritas. The unexpected sweep of homesickness shook her. *I want to go home.* "Anything is fine."

Simon led her to the patio with Abby following. Xavier had pushed the two patio tables together and was arranging the chairs while Rona set the table.

Lindsey looked around in amazement. The backyard of this

side of the duplex was fenced-in and lush with autumn blooms. It reminded her of the gardens shown in fairy-tale books.

Abby opened the cooler set by the door. "Want a beer?"

The desire to say yes ensured her answer. "No. Not today. A diet soda, please."

Simon lifted an eyebrow. "You sure?"

"If I drink when I'm anxious, I get more scared." And since last spring, she'd rarely felt safe. She gave him a crooked smile. "It's not worth it."

With a start, she realized Xavier was watching her. "Sounds as if you've been afraid before today," he murmured. "Why is that, pet?"

Oh shit. When would she learn she couldn't blabber? Especially around men like Xavier and Simon, who actually listened. Even deVries displayed Dom-focus. "You know how it is... A nasty husband can leave bad memories."

His skeptical expression was worrisome, but at least he didn't ask more questions. Maybe because she looked so battered or maybe because she wasn't his submissive to interrogate. Either way, *thank you, little baby Jesus.*

"As long as it's only memories." Simon's dark brows were together. "If not, I expect you to call me. You'll dial 9-1-1 if you need to, correct?"

Whoa, there was the perfect lead-in to what she needed to know. "Sure. On the other hand, I've heard not all law enforcement officers are trustworthy. Of course, maybe that's only a Texas problem. Is California better?"

"Doubtful," Rona said. After serving Simon, she put a piece of pizza on a plate and set it in front of Lindsey. "They recently indicted two customs agents for taking bribes."

Dammit. "Well, there you go," she said glumly. "Can't nobody be trusted."

"It seems so, doesn't it? However some occupations are more trustworthy than others." Xavier seated his wife and sat down beside Lindsey. "Like social workers. Simon said you have an MSW in social work with a small amount of experience and no credentials."

She gave Simon a frown. "Do y'all gossip about me all the time?"

"In spare moments, child. You're too young to take up much time."

Under his amused gaze, she could only laugh and turn back to Xavier. "That's right. Why?"

"I could use someone with your background in Stella's Employment Services." Xavier leaned back in his chair, studying her. "You'd help match up women with jobs and point them toward new career choices."

She nodded. She could do that.

"There would be a small amount of travel to women's shelters for the same type of assistance. In fact, a friend has requested Stella's for a shelter she recently acquired."

"I don't have a license—"

"That's not a concern. The shelters have clinical psychologists on staff. Even so, we've found filling out applications and looking for work can be more emotional than you'd expect."

Oh, she knew all about emotional. Realizing a life was not only ripped up, but years were lost, never to be replaced. Childhood dreams didn't always make it into the future. "I understand completely."

A smile flickered on his hard lips. "I thought you might. Want the job?"

She wanted to jump all over an acceptance, but... She gave him a suspicious look. "This isn't a makeshift offer to keep Abby from nagging at you?"

"She hasn't nagged me since I hung a ball gag by the bed."

From Abby came a muttered nasty word.

After kissing the top of Abby's head, he gave Lindsey a level look. "It's not makeshift work. I can use you if you're up for it. And, quite honestly, I think you'd be excellent."

Her smile couldn't be restrained. "In that case, yes. Yes, yes, yes."

"...and then I'll cut her up so bad that even in hell, Victor will hear her screams." The knife came down on her thumb. Cut deep. The pain...

Lindsey jerked awake, hearing her screams echoing inside the room—no, not the room, inside her head. *God, God, God.*

Gasping for breath, she fumbled beside her pillow, found the lamp, and turned it on. The bare room took form around the pile of bedding she'd used for her bed. No Travis. No knife. She was in San Francisco. In Abby's duplex.

With a shuddering breath, she struggled to a sitting position and forced herself to look down. The ancient secondhand flannel shirt was white and blue and damp with only sweat—she wasn't covered in Victor's blood.

Her thumb—she flexed her fingers—was fine. *Okay. Okay. Just a dream.*

As her breath hitched, she laid her head on her knees...and cried.

Eventually, she realized light was seeping under the curtains onto the glossy hardwood floor. Dawn had arrived. *Thank you, God.* The door to the bedroom was closed, the dining room chair she'd carried upstairs was still shoved under the handle. And the idea of opening the door made fresh sweat break out on her palms.

She could almost see her daddy make a c'mon gesture with his hand. *"Courage is being scared to death but saddling up anyway,"* he'd always tell her—and she'd tease him about watching too many John Wayne movies. Except, who knew? Maybe there *was* a section of heaven for old cowboys.

Saddle up, girl. Picking up her tiny pocketknife, she rose, feeling every bruise from yesterday's fight. Her cheek hurt, her hip, her arm. Once steady on her feet, she grasped the chair and set it away from the door. Her skin prickled with nerves as she opened the door. She went through every single room in the place. And found nothing.

There was no Travis Parnell lying in wait with a knife. No Ricks hiding in a closet. No gang outside on the patio.

By the time she finished, she was trembling, her insides hollowed, her bones toothpick fragile. Sinking down on the steps, she leaned against the railing. Hell of a way to start a morning.

After a few minutes, she straightened. Time to set up her computer and make coffee. She could shower when she wasn't feeling so antsy.

Later, the movers would come. Damn and bless Xavier. She smiled ruefully. After everyone left yesterday, she'd found a note propped on the kitchen counter. *Movers are scheduled to arrive with your furniture tomorrow at ten. Don't bother to argue; I won't listen. Xavier.*

Overprotective, managing Doms were something else. She huffed in exasperation, recalling when Rona and Abby had helped transport her furniture to the storage unit, she'd given Abby the spare key...and now Xavier had it. Sneaky, wonderful friends.

The secondhand furniture she'd bought last summer would look nice here. Her white linen couch and chairs should go well with the delicate floral wallpaper, whitewashed fireplace, worn needlepoint carpet in the living room. Maybe she could bring in some houseplants. With a pang of grief, she thought of the multicolored African violets at Victor's city house, and the spider and snake plants at the ranch. *"And how are my spiders and snakes today?"* she'd ask them. Had they all died?

With a frown, she glanced at the second floor. The large bedroom up there would easily hold her rather battered bed, dresser, and nightstands. She bit her lip, remembering with what hopes she'd bought the secondhand furniture, imagining how a Dom might use the four-poster bed frame. Dreaming of deVries, actually, and totally wishing he was interested in her.

And now he was. "Pffft." She could far too easily get *involved* with him and what? He'd had a cow just finding out she was using a fake name. He'd be thrilled at learning he was dating a murderer. The leaden feeling inside grew heavier.

More importantly, if he found out, he'd be in all sorts of danger. Not only could he be arrested for aiding and abetting a fugitive, but if he did anything to help her, Travis might kill him.

She was finding it difficult enough to not tell her friends everything. DeVries would push far, far harder. And she was so damned lonely.

I want to go home. To Texas. To spend the holidays with

Mama and Mandy and Melissa.

Instead, she'd be at Xavier's house for Thanksgiving, bless Abby's heart. And before Christmas, some of the Dark Haven people were going to the Hunt brothers' wilderness lodge outside Yosemite. This time, though, there wouldn't be any *Doms versus submissives* games. She rolled her eyes, remembering how deVries had shot her with the water pistol, winning a blowjob and anal sex from her.

The mountain winter season would be quieter, she figured. She'd have time to play with Logan and Becca Hunt's baby boy who'd be a few months old now. Such a cute age. Her little niece had only been a couple months old when Lindsey had fled Texas. *I've missed nearly her whole first year.*

That was water under the bridge, right? Time to get to work. She could almost see her daddy nod approval, doing his usual John Waynism, *"When you stop fighting, that's death."*

"I know, Daddy. I'm working on it." Lindsey pushed herself off the stairs. First step as always in a new home was to set up the hiding place. She trotted into the bedroom and dug through her overnight bag for the fake smoke detector.

Victor's USB flash drives were still tucked into the empty plastic disk. She'd taken them from the ranch drive, hopeful they'd contain evidence against Victor, Travis, and Ricks. The border patrol agent had certainly wanted to get his hands on the drives. But no one really knew what Victor had stored on them—the memory on each device had been encrypted. Talk about a letdown.

So her job was to figure out the password.

After installing the smoke-detector-safe inside her bedroom door, she set up her laptop on the dining room table. She had a ton of articles to read on password cracking.

She glared at the screen for a second. Why did all those television shows make hacking look so easy? It really wasn't.

But if she opened Victor's flash drives, and *if* they held the evidence of smuggling, she could send the contents everywhere. To the police, every single Homeland Security department, and maybe even the newspapers. Someone, surely, would arrest Parnell—even if he was chief of police, and Ricks—even if he was a border patrol agent.

They didn't deserve those respectful titles. They deserved nothing good. Ever. And her mission was to send them to jail where they'd never hurt anyone again.

Maybe once they were taken care of, she could restart her life, free of fear. Free of waiting for someone to either arrest her or kill her. Or...her skin turned clammy as she thought of Travis Parnell, Victor's brother. If he caught her, he'd torture her before he murdered her.

CHAPTER EIGHT

T he afternoon sun did nothing to warm the chill air off the Bay as deVries stood outside the battered women's shelter, studying the falling-down fence, the lack of outdoor lighting, and how the encroaching bushes offered ample hiding for trespassers. What the hell were these people thinking?

After one of Xavier's rich friends bought the shelter for her charitable organization, she'd voiced some concerns, and he'd asked Simon to check out the security.

DeVries had figured he'd merely modernize the systems, but hell, there was nothing here to upgrade.

"Mr. deVries?" Mrs. Abernathy came down the front steps, the light glinting off her silver hair. At first glance, he'd figured her for a sweet old lady. One minute of talking to her and he'd discovered a shrewd personality balanced her grandmotherly kindness. "What do you think?"

He frowned down at her. "I think if someone wanted in, he wouldn't have a problem."

"Yes, such was my concern as well." She patted his arm, startling him. "The previous owners—a church—barely managed mortgage payments. All they could do was hope an abuser didn't discover the address. Of course, we do take elaborate precautions to prevent that; however, in this technological age, keeping secrets is difficult."

Which was one reason Demakis International stayed in business. "They had any problems before?"

"When Simon talked to the parson, he learned of two…I

think he called them 'breaches' in the last year." Her mouth tightened. "That is unacceptable. We offer these women safety; we must be prepared to deliver it. Do you have an idea of what we'll need?"

From what Simon had said, he and Xavier were fronting the security work, and deVries was inclined to make sure the place got the best. "Gotta see the inside before I write up an estimate."

Her lips pursed. "Some of the women are nervous around a man. Let me find you an escort." She led the way into the house.

"I'll start here." He dropped his bag beside the front door.

"Excellent. I'll be right back."

"Fine." A tap on the wood of the door showed it was too thin by far. The locks—at least it had a dead bolt. But between the wussy door and the shit frame—well it might keep a girl out. If she weighed under ninety pounds. Should have a metal grill as well. And a panic button.

Footsteps rapped across the small entry. "If you would show him around for a few minutes," Mrs. Abernathy was saying to someone, "until I find one of the staff who is free."

"No problem. Edna's busy right now filling out forms"—the woman's Texas drawl and soft voice stroked over deVries's skin like silk—"so I have a bit of time." The "I" sounded like "Ah."

DeVries grinned, pleased as hell. Lindsey hadn't been at the club last weekend, which was good, considering she'd probably felt like shit. Just the memory of her bruises had pissed him off...but had made for a nice S/M scene with HurtMe. The masochist could take anything deVries wanted to dish out.

DeVries had figured on cornering her at the office, only to find that Xavier had snatched her up for his own business, which must be why she was here at the shelter. The Stella organization specialized in helping women return to the work force. Seemed to him the Texan's warm personality would be a perfect fit.

Smiling slightly, deVries looked over his shoulder.

Same black jeans and boots and jacket, this time over a T-shirt with an armored ratlike animal and the tag: *Armadillo— Texas speed bump*. Halfway across the room, Lindsey came to a sudden halt. "You—"

"Show him whatever he needs to see." Mrs. Abernathy headed away. "Thank you, dear."

DeVries rose to his feet, trying not to crack up at the expressions chasing over the little submissive's face. Frustration and worry smoothing to an attempted nonchalance.

"Don't ever play strip poker, pet," he said. "You'd be naked within three hands."

Her irritated look was fucking adorable. "I'm supposed to be your escort. Where do you want to go?" She still stood in the center of the room.

After jotting down what would be needed for the front door, he slung his bag over his shoulder and walked over to her. Watched her hands tighten at her sides as he stepped into her personal space, and she had to look up at him. "Are you afraid of me, Lindsey?" he asked softly.

Fuck, he could almost see every single vertebra in her spine stand at attention.

"No, no. Of course not."

"And we're friends. You said we were friends, didn't you?" Damned if he could figure her out. Definitely attracted to him, yet trying to keep a distance. Why?

"I...right. You bet. How could I have forgotten?"

"Well, good. Worried me for a second."

She heaved a frustrated sigh and—okay, he was behaving badly, but he'd never seen anyone quite so much fun to tease.

"Show me the back door, please," he said. When she spun and almost trotted away, he extended his gait and caught up easily, setting his hand a few inches above her ass. In a friendly way, of course.

"You know, touching me could be considered sexual harassment," she muttered.

"Maybe. Maybe not. Saw your lips turn pink. Cheeks too. You're leaning toward me. I'd say your body wants to fuck me. 'Course, might be your brain says you should knock me into next week." He stepped in front of her and tilted her face upward. "Am I wrong, Tex?"

Was that a little growl? Definitely cute.

"I think I'd put more weight on the knocking-you-into-next-week side."

"I'll keep it in mind."

When she headed into another room at a fast pace, he followed and stopped at the sound of gasps and an actual shriek of fear. *Jesus.* One side of a wide kitchen held a large table filled with children apparently having an afternoon snack of fruit and yogurt. All staring at him as if he'd killed their pet dog.

Their caregivers weren't much better; two of them had backed against the wall. The third held her ground.

"Criminy, Mrs. Abernathy should have warned people," Lindsey muttered. "At ease, ladies. This is Zander. He's a nice—" She stopped, obviously remembering he was a sadist. "He's a good guy."

The certainty in her voice shook him.

"Why's he in here?" one of the women asked. "Did he come to get…someone?"

"Hell, no," deVries answered for himself. "I'm here to set up a security system to keep you all safe."

After studying him for a minute, two of the braver kids slid off their chairs and approached. One barely came to his thighs, looking up at him with the softest brown eyes he'd ever seen. He gave Lindsey a glance. "Bet you looked like her when you were little." He crouched down and still loomed over the mite. "You got a question for me, baby?"

"What's a scurty stem?" she asked.

Her companion—with identical brown eyes—stared at deVries. "Will it keep Mama and Jenna safe too?"

How the fuck could anyone hurt a kid? A shame he couldn't find the bastard.

Two more children approached to twine themselves around Lindsey's legs. Cute as all get-out. And the rugrats already had her pegged as a soft touch.

He turned back to the brother and sister. "I'm going to make it so no bad man can get into this house. That's my job." He dared to reach out and run his knuckles down the big-eyed girl's cheek. "You'll be safe here and your mama too."

If his own mother had had a place like this, would she have pulled herself together rather than descending into the hell of selling tricks for alcohol and drugs? He shook off the thought, managed a smile for the children, who still stared at him as if he were the Green Goblin about to kill Spider-Man. Not making any sudden moves, he walked to the door.

The back entrance had a decent door and frame with a totally shit lock. "Seen chicken coops with better protection," he muttered to Lindsey.

"People sometimes forget trouble can walk in on two legs." The arch of her brows showed she had slotted him right into the trouble category.

He barely managed to keep from laughing. She hadn't yet realized how much trouble she was going to be in.

LINDSEY WATCHED AS deVries knelt and dug into his bag. Power tools, a lockset.

"Jeremiah, come back!" Jenna tugged at her brother's hand.

Pulling his sister with him, Jeremiah inched his way closer until he was within touching distance of the big Dom. "Whatcha doing?"

The lines at the corners of deVries's eyes crinkled. "See the lock?" He twisted the door's dead bolt.

Jeremiah nodded, his sister imitating him.

"I'm going to put in a bigger one." DeVries opened the package and showed how the bolt was much longer.

"Oooh."

"You didn't change the one in front," Lindsey commented.

He glanced at her. "With the crap door frame in the front, a longer bolt would suck air. Not do any good."

"Oh." Guess he did know what he was doing. Come to think of it, anything deVries did, he'd make sure he did really, really well.

With a sigh, she took a chair and settled down with the children. Jeremiah's sister climbed into her lap. Her brother remained, watching deVries's every move.

DeVries drilled a hole and changed out the old mechanism. "Hand me the long screw, bud." He nodded at the open package.

After a worried glance, Jeremiah bent to look through the screws, checking every second to ensure the man wasn't getting angry.

DeVries waited—and Lindsey recognized the patience. He displayed it in the club—and in bed, as well. Why the heck did he have to be so appealing?

"This?" Jeremiah whispered, holding up a long screw.

"That's it. Good eye, bud." With the casual compliment, deVries turned back to the job, not apparently noticing the way Jeremiah's entire face lit as if the sun had come out from behind clouds.

But only someone who'd seen the Dom in a scene would realize he missed *nothing*. Although a muscle had tightened in his cheek, he kept working, asking Jeremiah for different items, being careful to describe them well enough no mistakes could be made.

Finally he closed the door and glanced at Jeremiah. "Why don't you check it out? See if it works." He tapped the latch. "Turn that."

Jeremiah obeyed.

"Can you get the door open now?" DeVries kept an eye on him as he put the tools away.

Jeremiah turned the doorknob and tugged. "Hunh-uh."

"Good." DeVries stood, set a light hand on the skinny shoulder. "Couldn't have done it so quickly without you, bud. You're a great assistant."

Jeremiah's expression showed wonder and dawning pride.

With a choked sob, Lindsey helped the little girl off her lap, keeping her face turned away, blinking hard. After a swallow, her voice came out fairly even. "Where to now, Mr. deVries?"

"I'd like a tour of the windows, Miss Adair," he said politely. Why did she doubt his politeness would linger once away from the observers? He ruffled Jeremiah's hair. "I'll be back in a couple of days, bud. If you're free, I could use your help."

"Okay," Jeremiah whispered. He was vibrating with urgency until they left the kitchen. His footsteps charged in the opposite direction, toward the back room where his mother was doing laundry. Even then, his voice barely rose. "Mooom, guess what?" Children with fathers like his learned to stay quiet.

"Jesus fucking Christ." DeVries's jaw was tight, his eyes cold and hard.

"What?"

"Be a downright pleasure to have a *chat* with whatever bastard knocked the kid around."

She couldn't hide her smile or the sudden wetness in her eyes.

He ran a gentle finger down her cheek. "You got a big heart, Tex."

Apparently, so did he.

Before they reached the upstairs bedroom, a staff member appeared. "Lindsey, Mrs. Abernathy sent me to show Mr. deVries around."

"Good timing. Edna's probably ready for me." With a feeling of relief—and reluctance—Lindsey nodded at deVries.

His face showed nothing; however, his words—"See you later, Tex"—set her nerves to dancing.

In the small meeting room, Edna was looking through the papers on how to write a résumé and to interview. Underweight, short hair graying, curling into herself in a slouch as if she didn't want to be noticed. The fading bruises on her face said why.

"All finished?" Lindsey asked as she sat.

Edna nodded.

Lindsey glanced over the application. Her work experience was years in the past—waitress and a hotel maid. Physical condition was good, or would be in another week. Spelling adequate. Penmanship clear. The next page was blank. "Why didn't you fill out the vocational interest form?"

"What's the point?"

Lindsey understood her meaning. Edna was forty-nine. Her children were raised. Laid off from work, the husband spent his days drinking and taking his frustrations out on his wife. She'd probably endured his abuse to keep their kids fed and housed, but now...

"Several points, actually," Lindsey answered. "First, you're liable to live to be ninety, right?"

Edna's eyes widened. "I... Maybe. My mother is still alive."

"So, working as a waitress will get tiresome. And when you retire, social security might not cover all your expenses." Lindsey waggled her eyebrows. "With four children, you're undoubtedly going to have grandchildren you'll want to gift with loud, obnoxious toys, right?"

Edna actually smiled. Even abuse didn't extinguish a sense of humor. Then she frowned. "You're saying money will always be a problem?"

"If you don't think ahead. The good news is Stella's is very keen on their clients moving past minimum-wage jobs. They hold classes at night and weekends, and if there's something you want to learn they don't offer, there's usually a way to get it." She leaned forward and took Edna's hands. "You're making a big change already, yet while you're at it, why don't you shoot for the top?"

"I..." Edna's gaze dropped to the papers.

"Besides"—Lindsey squeezed the cold fingers—"your ex can't even keep a shit-labor job. Wouldn't it be cool to have a classy one he couldn't dream of matching?"

Edna's shoulders straightened, her head lifted, and her expression changed to one of resolve. "You're right." Her lips curved. "And you are a sneaky young woman."

Wasn't it odd the entire room felt brighter? "That's me. So fill out—" Lindsey glanced at her watch. "No, you can't. Your group session starts in a few minutes. Can you complete this form later? We'll talk about it next week." She put the already completed papers into her leather satchel.

Determination had lit the older woman's expression. "I can do that."

Lindsey felt her eyes heat, and she wrapped an arm around Edna's shoulders in a brief squeeze. "You're going to do great," she whispered.

In the hallway, deVries was leaning against the wall, bag

over one shoulder. He nodded at Edna and stepped in front of Lindsey. "You all done here?"

"Uh…" Could she make up a reason to have to stay? Except every lie she told made her feel as if she were smearing dirt on her skin. She felt filthy enough already. "Guess so."

"Good." He put a hand on her shoulder. "I could hear you through the door. You're damned good at talking to people, baby."

She blinked up at him. A compliment from the Enforcer. "Um. Thanks."

"Could have used you in interrogations."

Seriously? Her stare of disbelief made a dimple appear in his cheek. Her attempt to retreat didn't work. "So what do you want?"

"I saw a grill on your back patio. Let's swing by the store, pick up some steak, and I'll cook while you make the rest of the shit."

She stopped. "Are you inviting yourself over to my place for supper?"

"That would be an affirmative, pet." He smiled down at her. "I rescued you and helped you move. Seems you owe me. Again."

"Really." Her stomach twisted as she remembered the first time she'd owed him…how it had ended. He'd explained, but if he turned cold again, how could she bear it? "So, am I going to get another *'debt paid'* from you afterward?"

"That really bothered you?" He guided her out the front door.

"Well, yes." She slapped a hand on his chest and shoved him back. "You also said you didn't like me. I know guys make lo—uh, fuck—anyone. All the same, being intimate with someone you hate is just plain downright icky."

"*Icky.*" His lips quirked. "I didn't hate you when I fucked you. It wasn't until the next morning I decided you were a mercenary bitch."

She heard Victor's voice. "*Hell, you married me for my money.*" The memory was an unexpected blow. With an effort, she kept it from her face and pushed the sickness away. In its place, she plastered on a scowl and used it on deVries. "You really do enjoy pissing me off, don't you?"

"Fuck yeah." The way his dimple came and went made her knees weak.

"So you really did like me that night?" Her question came out in a whisper.

He pushed her hand off his chest and yanked her forward into a full frontal. "You mean when my cock was buried in your pussy, or when I took your ass?" His head lowered, and his words whispered against her lips. "Or licked you until you screamed?"

Her mouth went dry, and the sound she made was simply needy.

"Oh, I liked you." He planted a kiss on her lips before giving her a level stare. "Baby, I wouldn't have fucked you otherwise."

The tornado of relief flattened her defenses and swirled them away.

As she stared up into his sage-colored eyes, she knew she was screwed every way from Sunday.

—◈◈◈—

DeVries brought the sizzling steaks from the grill to the patio. While he'd been cooking, Lindsey had covered the table with a bright yellow cloth and set out colorful stoneware dishes. He glanced at her. "I didn't see these in the dump."

"No. They were with all my stuff in storage." She looked around. "It's nice to have everything back."

Not that she had much, he thought, as he rummaged through the cupboard for steak sauce. "Got a lot of macaroni and cheese, babe."

Rather than whining about being broke, she grinned. "Hey, I love macaroni and cheese. It's comfort food."

"Mmmhmm." Sure it was—maybe once a month, not every day. Yet, she'd actually wanted to split the cost of the groceries earlier. *Jesus.*

She took a seat at the table and handed him one of the beers he'd bought.

"You gonna be okay in the duplex?" He dropped down into

the chair across from her. Taking a sip of the beer, he watched as she served him a green salad, a mound of cheesy potatoes, and one of the steaks. Graceful and smooth. Unlike him, she'd probably learned table manners from birth, rather than years later in a foster home.

"It's great." She gave him a rueful smile. "I guess I should thank you for telling Xavier about the mess I was in."

"Not a problem. Speaking of which..." He toed off his boot and unstrapped the leather sheath from his calf. "If you're going to carry a knife, wear one that will do some damage."

"But..."

He set it on the table. "Figured this might be a good size for you. One on your belt would be better—this is hard to reach in a hurry—but with the people you're around, you probably don't want to terrify them."

"I—" She stopped and said carefully, "Are you giving me your knife?"

"Yeah, Tex, I'm giving you my backup-backup-backup knife so I don't see you waving a pocketknife at someone again."

Her eyes actually lit. She unsheathed the knife. Flat handle, double-edged blade. Heavy. Smaller than he preferred. Still, it'd get the job done in a pinch.

"My daddy liked guns," she said. "Hunting. But I never learned." Her mind seemed to go elsewhere, and she shuddered.

Probably thinking about Bambi's mother. Damn cartoon. "I take it you prefer knives?"

"You bet. Every cowgirl should have a knife—even if it's only to open some beans when she can't find a can opener." She held it up, and her smile was gorgeous. "Thank you. Really."

"No problem. Really." He took a bite of the potatoes and stilled. The girl could cook. "Besides, I intend to collect."

"Doesn't that just figure?" Her scowl was definitely cute, but under it...was that surprise? "You want sex with...me?"

His eyes narrowed. "Damn straight I want sex with you. You didn't think I would?"

"I..." She shrugged and said lightly, "It's nice to be wanted."

The lightness was bullshit and contradicted by the hurt in her eyes. "Who didn't want you?"

Her mouth dropped open. "I didn't say that."

Bull's-eye. "Who didn't want you?"

"Well, jeez, I've been divorced twice. What do you think?"

He leaned back to watch her move her potatoes from one side of the plate to the other. Uh-huh. She had hurt buried in there. And despite his avoidance of relationships, he wasn't blind. Women rarely escaped a relationship with their self-confidence intact.

She'd been angry when she thought he'd fucked her without liking her. Hard to imagine a man not liking little Tex, but the world was filled with assholes. "I think both your husbands made you doubt your attractiveness."

Her pupils constricted, and the tiny muscles beside her mouth flinched down. "I forgot the salad dressing." She shoved to her feet and rummaged—pretended to—through the fridge before returning with a small bottle.

He couldn't help pushing despite the fact his fucking curiosity had led him into landmines before. However, her reaction seemed to exceed the normal bitterness from a divorce. And, he plain wanted to know... "Did you love them?"

Her muscles tensed as if she'd jump up again. Too bad for her she'd run out of culinary excuses. He put his hand over hers, a physical restraint, and pushed with his voice. "Lindsey, did you love them? Simple question."

She slumped, gaze on her plate. "I thought I did," she whispered.

"They didn't?"

She shook her head. When her hand trembled under his, he wanted to take her in his arms.

No. She wasn't ready for that kind of comfort. Not from him. By being an asshole, he'd destroyed the trust he'd earned the first night. "I'm sorry, baby," he said, releasing his hand and his dominance.

She pulled in a breath harsh enough to hear. Her shoulders straightened. "So, what's going on with the security system at the shelter?" she asked lightly.

Damn, he fucking admired her spirit. "I'll make sure they get top-of-the-line equipment." He cut a bite of his steak. Sampled. He hadn't lost his touch. "You've got a decent grill out there."

"It's Abby's." She looked around. "I really love this place already."

"Good." He damned well planned to get her to cook for him again. "No rodents here?"

Her laugh was light, cheerful, back to the Lindsey he knew and had avoided before because she was so damn appealing. "I miss Francois. He was good company."

Now that was pitiful, a fucking field mouse for companionship. Jesus, she was something. Rather than screaming when seeing a rodent, she'd named it Francois. She'd faced down a gang with pepper spray. Despite her big eyes and gentle heart, she was a strong woman. Fucking strong. "I'll keep you company tonight."

Her eyes narrowed. "Why?"

He grinned. "Because I like you?"

⋘⋙

In the kitchen, Lindsey glanced into the sink. Empty. The Enforcer had actually loaded the dishwasher and put the condiments away. Helping out was sure more than either of her husbands had done. Of course, Miguel had helped in the kitchen before they'd married. Not after he'd obtained his green card. Obviously, premarriage behavior wasn't an index of reality. *Don't get carried away, girl.*

Carrying the plate of sweets into the living room, she found him on the couch, flipping through the channels.

"Looking for a game?"

His dimple showed. "Nothing good on. Got any movies?"

With one arm propped on a plush red pillow, he looked right at home on her overstuffed white sofa. She'd chosen comfortable, practical furniture. It sure wasn't delicate—but neither was she. Good sturdy Texas stock, that was her. "Movies are in the bottom of the stand."

Grabbing a cookie as he walked past, he gave her a firm kiss and squatted down in front of the TV. Startled, she could only stare at him, then, okay, stare a little longer because the man had a really fine ass.

With a shake of her head, she set the cookies on the distressed white coffee table and snuggled into a corner of the couch. Was he seriously planning to stay and watch TV? Wasn't it a tad domestic for him?

But he inserted a DVD and joined her, dragging her over his body so she lay sprawled on top of him. Resigning herself to watch a gory movie, she blinked in surprise. "You like *Jurassic Park?*" Jeez, it had a romance and children and—

"Yeah." His dimple flashed for a second. "Not for girly love shit. I'd just rather watch dinosaurs than war."

"Oh." She frowned. DeVries's bearing, his ability to snap out orders, the careful assessment he did of his surroundings, all screamed soldier. "Were you in the military?"

"Mmmhmm." After adjusting her so her cheek rested on his shoulder, he took another cookie, eyes on the screen. "You're a great cook."

"Grandma's recipe." She lifted up to look at him. Melissa's husband had been in the Air Force. "What branch?"

His foggy-green eyes flicked down to her. "Navy SEAL." With a firm hand, he pushed her head back down.

Ooookay, guess the military wasn't going to be a topic of conversation. What the heck, she'd always enjoyed this movie, and lying on top of a muscular guy wasn't a problem. In fact, he was a pretty comfortable mattress and wonderfully warm.

"That why you took a fake name?" he asked. "A divorce?"

She stiffened and had to force herself to relax. He kept tossing unexpected questions at her. Butthead. So she used his answer, "Mmmhmm," and had to smother a snicker when his jaw tightened. But he turned back to watch the show.

As they watched, she deliberately commented on the romance which made him chuckle. In turn, he critiqued the actors' idiotic combat maneuvers. Bet he was something in the field.

WITH HER HEAD on his shoulder, the little Texan was half-asleep, draped over him like a limp kitten. He usually went for larger women, but this one was just plain cute. And when she was happy, she revved right up to totally beautiful.

His curiosity nagged at him. He still didn't know why she used a fake name. Might be a divorce. Might be scandal. Might be related to breaking the law. Or maybe she was running from someone. If some asshole was threatening her, he needed to know.

As *Jurassic Park* ended and the credits scrolled up the screen, deVries turned off the television. How sleepy was the girl? Steady, even breathing. One hand curled around the side of his neck.

"What's your name, pet?" he asked in a soft voice.

"Lindsey R—" Her mouth snapped shut as her eyes opened, and her body turned rigid. Color rushed into her face. "You bastard."

"Just wanted to know," he said mildly, eyeing her warily. Good thing the knife he gave her was still in the kitchen.

As she shoved to her feet, one hand came dangerously close to unmanning him. "I think it's time for you to head home, deVries. Thanks for the steak and all that."

"Fuck, you got a temper. I only asked your name."

"And you got that if I wanted you to know it, I would've told you. Hit the road."

"Are you in trouble?" He rose and stepped into her personal space.

Letting her understand he'd touch her even if she were furious, he pushed her hair over her shoulder. The purple colors gleamed under the brown locks. He liked that quirk of hers. "Can I help?"

"No." She shook her head vigorously and retreated out of his reach. Refusing his help. Refusing his touch. "My business is none of yours."

"Lindsey—"

"God, just go home. It was fun. We're done."

Oh no, we're not. All the same, he backed off. For now. After all, a submissive had the power to say no...until she gave it into his hands. And she would.

⋯⋯⋯

After deVries left, Lindsey finished cleaning up, even to the extent of running the dishwasher only half-full. She needed to eradicate his presence from her home.

She'd sure been fooled by his terse, tough-guy persona. Who'd think the Enforcer would be so clever and so snoopy.

But duh. She'd seen him in action at the club. A Dom who could play a submissive like deVries did was past intelligent. He was one of Simon's best investigators—and even worse, from the glint in his eyes, he was more intrigued than put off by her answers.

She wrapped her arms around herself and dropped down on the couch—then caught a hint of his scent on the pillow. Not aftershave. He used one of those woodsy guy soaps like Axe. With a huff of exasperation, she moved to the other side of the couch.

"Can I help?" His straightforward offer in his low sandpaper voice kept echoing in her head.

She'd so, so wanted to jump into his arms, blurt out everything, and let him fix her world.

Only no one could.

Trying, he could get killed—like Craig. It hadn't been her fault Parnell had ordered the young police officer killed. She still felt responsible.

If they hurt deVries, she'd never, ever forgive herself.

CHAPTER NINE

O n Saturday night, the dance floor at Dark Haven was butt-to-butt crowded, but Lindsey didn't care. She'd needed to dance and work off frustrations.

She'd firmly decided to avoid deVries...and spent her entire desk shift hoping he'd come in. Every time the door to the club had opened, her pulse had sent up fireworks. Sheesh.

Scowling, she spun around, trying to dislodge her foolish thoughts. "Go, sweet cheeks!" Dancing beside her, Dixon waggled his ass and gave her a hip-bump. "Shake them boobies."

Her handmade leather halter-top matched her butter-soft leather skirt—and made the most of her small breasts. "As you command." She tossed her hair back and shimmied.

Around her came whistles from men—and a couple of women.

Copying her moves, Dixon urged her on, getting himself a nice accumulation of cheers as well.

By the time the music died, she was panting and laughing and thoroughly warmed up.

Dixon laced his fingers with hers. "After our nice show, we should have Doms lined up, begging to scene."

She snorted. "You might, Mr. Prettier-than-a-girl. Not me. But hey, aren't you dating someone?"

"Not seriously. He only wants to fuck."

"Huh, I know the type."

Dixon pursed his lips. "Not that I mind the sex, but I want a

Dom. He's not—was putting on a show to get laid."

"Oh." Not like deVries, who wore his authority in every cell of his muscled...gorgeous...snoopy body. She squeezed Dixon's fingers. "You know, honeybunches, you're going to find someone who is perfect for you. Don't give up." Why *did* Dixon attract guys like that? "Hmmm."

"What?"

"Maybe you shouldn't be so cute." She frowned. "My mama would say when you flirt too much, you attract men who only want what you're...silently promising."

He gave her a disbelieving look. "Are you giving me advice from your *mother*?"

"Hey, she had some pretty good advice." As long as it wasn't about actual sex. Then it was like getting guidance from a nun. How had the woman ever managed to conceive?

"Uh-huh." Shaking his head, Dixon led the way across the room to a table filled with Doms and subs. On one side of the table was the blond masochist named HurtMe. Jacqueline, a newer submissive, sat beside him. She was older than Lindsey, maybe in her late thirties, and tended to safeword out of anything intense. Abby was near one end; Sir Ethan at the other.

"Hey, y'all." Lindsey dropped into an empty chair.

Dixon detoured to sit beside a gorgeous gay Dom. After giving the guy a completely flirtatious look and getting one back, Dixon winked at Lindsey.

So much for Mama's advice. Lindsey smothered a smile.

The conversation wandered from subject to subject as people watched a depersonalization scene on the raised left stage where a collared slave was being treated like a disobedient dog.

Lindsey heard the scrape of a chair, and she glanced to her right.

Clad in his usual worn leather pants and black T-shirt, deVries set his toy bag under the chair beside her and sat down.

She sighed. There were lots of other empty chairs, dammit. And she sure didn't need him setting her hormones to doing a Texas two-step.

His eyes, the color of a winter sea, swept over her. "Evening, girl."

Without even nodding, she turned away. Maybe Mr. Pushy-Pants would get the hint.

The rasp of his deep voice as he spoke to the other Doms sent goose bumps up her arms. Should she leave? What if he followed her? One on one. That would be worse. Because, if he really did push, she'd cave.

Why couldn't she have met him...before? Before marrying Victor. Before all the blood and death and horror? *I can't do this, deVries. Can't.*

Tucking her head down, she studied her bottle of water, turning it between her palms. If he'd only see reason. Or get bored and give up.

As the conversation turned to depersonalization and degradation scenes, she stayed unnaturally silent.

Rather than leaving, deVries put his arm along the back of her chair. She stiffened.

Near one end of the table, HurtMe gave her a narrow-eyed look. What was up with that?

Uneasy, she checked her friends. Abby's face held no expression. Dixon, of course, was grinning.

Lindsey could feel the heat of deVries's arm behind her shoulders. Just the brush of his skin sent tingles through her. Wanting to cuddle into him, instead, Lindsey leaned forward.

"I don't understand how some submissives like such ugly stuff," Jacqueline was saying. "Getting put down. Humiliated."

Rather than answering, the Doms around the table left the submissives to try to explain.

Not surprisingly, Abby spoke. The professor loved to teach. "Part of the appeal is showing your surrender," Abby said. "It's akin to taking more pain than you like, because it will please your Dom—which is giving up physical control. Humiliation play is giving up emotional control."

"Doms like to work on areas you're most uptight about." Dixon wrinkled his nose. "That said, I'm not so much into the ucky things like piss or serious depersonalization."

Abby nodded. "There can be a kind of humiliation play

that's beneficial and even erotic, when other types seem closer to emotional masochism." She smiled at Lindsey, and, professor-like, called on her. "What do you think, Lindsey?"

So much for staying silent. Put on the spot, Lindsey frowned. Honestly, her vote went with Jacqueline. "I don't think I understand the difference. It all looks creepy to me."

"Degradation stomps on a sub's feelings of self-worth. Not my thing. But humiliation play—like erotic embarrassment—works pretty well." DeVries's gaze lingered on Lindsey as his long lean fingers curved around his glass.

As she remembered how those fingers had curved around her breast, her nipples contracted—which everyone could probably see. Feeling her cheeks redden, she made a pfffing noise. "Bless your heart, how can a sadist like you understand anything about emotions?"

Indrawn breaths around the table told her what she already knew. She'd crossed the line.

DeVries's eyebrows lifted, and he pushed his chair back. "Good thing you're a receptionist. You can demonstrate what I meant by embarrassment."

Excuse me? Receptionists were expected to help with demos, but no way. Not with deVries. She shoved her chair back. An inch.

His knee barred her escape.

She blew out a slow breath, trying to think. "Listen, I'm not up to your speed. Sir. Getting beaten raw is a hard limit for me." And Xavier was death on people ignoring those limits.

"Guess that means I shouldn't beat on you." He took her chin, his hand tightening to the point of pain, letting her know she couldn't escape. No kindness or amusement or anger showed in his level eyes. Lordy, she'd just discovered exactly why submissives called him the Enforcer. "Every time you speak—unless it's your safeword—this show-and-tell will continue a minute longer." He removed a small bullet vibrator from the toy bag under his chair.

"No, waaaait!" Her words ended in a shriek when deVries plucked her up and onto his leather-clad thighs.

He clamped an arm around her, pinning her elbows to her

sides. With his other hand, he flicked the vibrator on and slid it under her leather skirt. It rested against her mound. Almost on her clit.

With relief, she realized she was too uptight to react to anything right now. She relaxed slightly. *Okay, this is embarrassing...but bearable.*

His cheek rubbed against hers as his husky voice whispered, "I remember the feel of you, little girl." He repositioned his grip on the vibe, and his warm, hard fingers slid over her folds and traced around her entrance, reminding her how he'd brought her to orgasm over and over.

"I remember your taste." His tongue ran over the curve of her ear. Hot and wet. He always knew exactly how to use his mouth, damn him.

Her body shot from no interest to a simmering desire.

He chuckled, his voice still low, only loud enough for her to hear. "I'd like to set you on my cock and make you ride me, feel that cunt of yours pulling me in. A shame that's not what we're here for."

She stiffened.

He moved the vibe closer to where she was throbbing. "I know how much you like toys, though."

As if she needed the reminder of that morning in bed. His grip on her clit. The way he'd forced her to endure the vibrator. Had hurt her. And had made her come so hard she'd almost died. "Don't," she whispered. "I don't want this."

"Ask me if I care," he murmured. "You got a safeword if you can't take it."

The vibrations seemed to suddenly take effect, and heat swept over her followed by hunger. Holy shit, she needed to come. She wiggled, trying to get the vibrator closer to her clit. If he stopped...

And he did. After dropping the vibe into its plastic bag, he half smiled at their audience around the table. "Lindsey doesn't like showing her genitals."

Goddamn, how had he known that?

He flipped her skirt up and tucked the hem into the

waistband, baring her.

"Don't—don't do—"

"Lindsey, don't make me tie you up and put you on the stage." The threat sliced through her struggles. One arm still around her waist, he spread her legs to dangle outside his, exposing her to everyone.

"No," she whispered as embarrassed heat blanketed her like the air in a sauna. She remembered Victor's disinterested stares, as if she were a mannequin rather than a woman.

She closed her eyes as deVries's hand separated her labia.

"I enjoyed looking at her pussy, once I finally got her to open her legs," deVries said to the others. "See how plump her lips are? And slick, fuck, she gets slick. Major turn-on when a sub gets drenched for you, isn't it?"

His words stunned her, and she froze. He liked her...down there? Seeing her? The chorus of agreement was even more astounding.

"Nice clit too," deVries continued, running his finger up and down, making the nub of nerves harden. "Sits right out where I can play with it."

Could she get any more humiliated? Yet the thrill of pleasure swept over her. He liked her pussy. Really?

He used her own wetness to slicken her. "To be honest, though, have you ever seen a clit you didn't like?"

More murmurs of agreement.

Maybe a woman's pussy was like her breasts—men went blind and dumb at the sight of breasts, right? Victor hadn't, but still... Yet Lindsey couldn't face them. Eyes closed, she felt their gazes on her intimate parts of her like scratches from jagged fingernails.

"More than the taste and sight, I got off on this..." His finger rubbed along her clit, building a fire inside her, sending her excitement spiraling upward. His arm immobilized her. She was almost there...

God, she didn't want to come now. *No, no, no.*

He took her hand, placing her fingers as he had before in bed, making her hold her folds apart. "Show yourself to them. If you don't, I'll dig out clamps to keep you open, and this will last a lot longer."

Need and anger and humiliation warred inside her. *Damn him.*

Her fingers stayed in place, and she heard his satisfied grunt.

She managed to glance at the table, at the fascinated audience. No one was making horrid comments about her being ugly down there. The interested gazes were...hot. Not scathing.

Admiring. Aroused.

Her fingers trembled.

She heard him say, "Jacqueline, embarrassment can not only be erotic but also bust apart defenses keeping a sub from fully living." He kissed Lindsey's cheek. "You're such a good girl. Now, stay like that."

The vibrator come down directly on her clit, held there by his determined hand, and she shot straight to climax, with not even a chance to say a word. Her body jerked inside the prison of his arm, and through the roaring in her head, she heard her own breathless cries.

Her heart hammered; she gasped for oxygen. As she sagged against him, sliding into a mindless satisfaction, a cracking noise from the demonstration behind them split the air. On the stage, the submissive shrieked. Screamed again and again. More cracks.

Lindsey's world blurred. *The pistol in her hands jerked, and the blast made her ears ring. Blood flowed between her fingers, sticky and hot and horrible as Victor convulsed. His eyes went blank and empty. Her screams went on and on, yet nothing escaped her frozen throat.*

Inch by inch, she sank into the quicksand of horror, finding no footing, no escape. The darkness closed over her.

WHAT THE FUCK. DeVries stared at the little submissive in surprise. She'd gone from a warm, squirming armful to a frozen, blank-faced puppet. Horror filled her face as she looked at...nothing.

Trigger. He'd hit a trigger, one he hadn't been prepared for because—because he was an idiot. "Lindsey," he said, his voice dropping into command mode. "Look at me, girl."

She didn't move.

He took her chin and turned her. "Look. At. Me." He added a snap to the last word.

One blink. Two. She shuddered, her haunted eyes meeting his. Jesus, he'd fucked this up. Holding her gaze with his, he yanked her skirt down, covering her and turning her so he could cradle her in his arms. He'd mindfucked her right into something he wasn't prepared for.

Sure, back before they'd first screwed, he'd checked through the records kept at the desk: her limit list, medical information, preferences. There had been nothing about past trauma or triggers. Nonetheless he should have gone over everything again with her. He'd gotten complacent.

Cuddling her against him, he glanced at the audience, seeing the appalled submissives. The more experienced Doms, including Ethan, wore frowns. They knew he'd stepped in it. He rose. "If you'll excuse us, I'm going to find somewhere quiet and deal with this."

"I think you better give her to someone who has a heart." Slender, short, defiant Dixon stood directly in deVries's path, showing that, no matter the popular opinion, male submissives weren't pushovers. "Another Dom can—"

"No." DeVries shouldered past.

"Fucking asshole," Dixon muttered and hurried away.

Hell. A few steps away from the group, deVries stopped and considered. Where could he take her? Maybe downstairs. The dungeon had quiet aftercare rooms. "Hang in there, babe," he said, rubbing his chin in the soft hair.

She didn't respond.

Carefully, he moved around the tables and chairs, past the clusters of members, working his way toward the back of the room.

"Hold up." Xavier's deep voice halted him at the top of the stairs. Obviously the mouthy Dixon had found him.

Great. If the owner of Dark Haven thought deVries had

overstepped with a submissive, their friendship would stand for nothing, which was the way it should be. "I fucked up. She did fine with a bit of erotic humiliation, but right after she came, she went into a meltdown. Damned if I know why."

Xavier gently tilted Lindsey's head. "Talk to me, pet. What's your name?"

"L-Lindsey." Despite being in deVries's arms, she struggled to sit up. "I'm sorry, my liege, I didn't—"

"You did nothing wrong," deVries muttered. No, he was the one who should apologize—once he figured out what he'd done.

Xavier's hand stayed on the little brunette's cheek, undoubtedly feeling the shivers coursing her body. "Use my office. Get her back into her own head."

"Thanks." The office had a couch. Was quiet. "I'm taking her home after."

Xavier considered him out of black eyes before nodding. "I know you'll take care of her."

The trust in his statement was one of the finest gifts deVries had ever received.

—⋘⋙—

Lindsey roused, hearing an even thudding sound and a low rumble. Blinking, she brought her mind into focus. Warmth surrounded her, and comforting...arms...were around her. Arms? Yes, she was on a lap, her cheek against a hard chest.

The rumbling was a man's voice talking to her. "It's okay, baby. You're safe."

She tipped her head back and...met deVries's concerned eyes.

"There she is," he murmured. "You know where you are?"

"On your lap."

"Right." The corners of his mouth tilted up. "How about the general location?"

"Um." Why was he holding her? Oh, she was in Xavier's office. "Dark Haven." She'd been talking with people. DeVries had grabbed her. She'd gotten off and... A tremor ran through her.

There had been gunfire and—no, that couldn't have happened.

Lordy, the top on the stage had been using a whip, and his bottom had screamed. And Lindsey had fallen right into a funk. *Good going, girl.* "I had kind of a panic attack, I guess, huh?"

"Something like that. Why?"

Oh, this was not good. Her brains weren't moving fast enough to deal with questions. "A-a childhood trauma." She swallowed at the disbelief in his eyes. "I don't want to talk about it."

"Uh-huh." He picked her up and stood her on her feet. "I'll let you get away with that—for now." He tugged a man's T-shirt over her head—from the size, she'd guess it was Xavier's. He put his leather jacket on her as well. "Let's go."

She was ushered into deVries's car without any chance of arguing. Why did this routine seem familiar? Lindsey frowned as he fastened her seat belt for her. "I'm perfectly capable of getting home."

"Maybe. Now you don't have to."

As he drove, she drifted. A few minutes later, she sat up straight. "Wait, this isn't Mill Valley."

"You're coming back to my place."

Wonderful, now he was being bossy again. He'd been so sweet in Xavier's office, holding her and murmuring to her. It was hard to believe he'd totally humiliated her minutes before.

Even worse, she'd gone all mental on him. How could she ever show her face there again? "You're such a jerk," she muttered.

"Yeah, I know." With the surprising agreement, he drove down a tree-lined street and into a parking garage under a small apartment building. Once parked, he helped her out of his SUV. If he'd only stop jumping between mean Dom and sweet guy, she wouldn't be so dizzy.

His apartment was on the second floor, and he kept a light grip on her arm as he escorted her inside, through a dimly lit kitchen, and into the living room. When he flicked on the lights, she saw walls colored a beautiful blue-green with white trim around French doors. The steeply angled ceiling beams were also white and matched the mantel over the dark granite fireplace. He led her across a sisal rug and sat her down on the L-shaped sectional.

"Settle in, babe." After tugging his coat off her, he took off her high-heeled pumps.

With a sigh, she curled into a corner of the couch, sinking into the warm suede fabric. "You have a pretty apartment," she said. The austere lines of the wooden coffee and end tables, and the wrought iron hanging lights kept it masculine. And, of course, being a guy, he had a huge wide-screen TV over the fireplace.

"Thanks."

He laid a fluffy quilt over her lap. "You want a hot drink or an alcoholic one?"

Something warm sounded wonderful. So did— "Both?"

With a snort of amusement, he circled to flip on the gas fire. Outside the bay windows, trees rustled in the light breeze.

The noise he made in the kitchen—cupboard doors opening and closing, the microwave running—was reassuring.

Normal.

Not normal enough. She felt the shakes starting anew. After pulling her legs up to her chest, she wrapped her arms around her knees and hung on.

Something thudded on the table beside her. DeVries cupped her chin, his hand warm and hard. "Damn." He picked her up and settled back down on the couch with her in his lap. She couldn't quite let go of her legs, and he patiently rearranged her until she leaned against him.

"Haven't we done this before?" she muttered through gritted teeth, remembering after the gang fight. "Sorry."

"You didn't get to this headspace by yourself, babe."

After a minute of silence, she squirmed. He couldn't sit here all night, doing nothing. That wasn't right. "This is boring—you can't—"

"Yeah, I can." He ran a finger down her nose. "It makes you uncomfortable, doesn't it? Little Miss Busy. Bet you never sit still for long."

Well, sometimes. If she was doing paperwork. She tried to think of other times...

His chest rumbled with his low laugh. Picking up the remote, he flipped through the channels and settled on *Casablanca*. "This should be girly enough for you and give you something to focus on."

At the sound of Bogie, she gradually relaxed. Her eyelids drooped, and she rubbed her cheek on the solid chest beneath her face. "Thanks."

"Mmmm." The amusement in his voice made her insides melt. "Now drink." He held a mug to her lips, and she took a sip.

Warm liquid, sweet and buttery. She got a taste of cinnamon before the expanding rush of alcohol. "What is that?"

"Hot buttered rum. Never had it before?" He lifted the mug and drank some before returning it to her. The casual sharing was...nice.

"Uh-uh." It was yummy. She took another sip before curling her fingers around the mug. "I've got it."

"So you do."

As he held her against him, occasionally lifting her hand so he could sip, she felt as if all her fantasies were being granted. She was enjoying a cozy evening at home on a Dom's lap, sharing a show, a couch, a drink. But a sadist? One who didn't want a relationship with anyone?

Pushing away the bittersweet knowledge, she reminded herself she couldn't afford a relationship either. *Live in the moment, girl.* As she laid her cheek on his soft T-shirt, she inhaled the piney scent of his soap. Soap and man—with deVries, you didn't get any additives.

As her muscles relaxed, she felt as if she were sinking into him.

"Babe." He took the mug and kissed the top of her head. "Bedtime for little Texans," he murmured.

Before she could find the energy to move, he stood, still holding her in his arms.

Her eyes opened. "Wait. No."

"Shut up, subbie," he said, and somehow, the bottomless

growl was affectionate.

He carried her up the stairs. OMG, up the *stairs*. She clutched at his shoulders, just waiting for him to trip, sending them plunging to their deaths.

A chuckle rumbled against her ear. "You're hyperventilating, Lindsey. Slow it down."

Easy for him to say.

Inside a bathroom, he bent and set her on her feet.

She muttered her gratitude for survival, not to him, though. "Thank you, little baby Jesus."

He burst out laughing and ruffled her hair. "Wash up and get into bed. There are spare toothbrushes, combs, and towels in the right cabinet."

"But—"

The door closed behind him. Well. Obviously she was staying the night. The empty quiver beneath her ribs said she didn't want to be alone. Fear wasn't far away.

So much for brave independence, huh?

She turned toward the sink, saw herself in the mirror, and almost screamed like a ten-year-old facing Freddie Kruger. Her un-runnable mascara had run in black streaks down her cheeks. Her hair was tangled on one side, limp on the other. Any thought of not cleaning up went right out the window.

By the time she finished scrubbing, brushing, and combing, she was exhausted but felt almost human.

Taking a deep breath, she pulled the lap blanket around her shoulders and opened the door. The light of a bedside lamp showed chocolate-colored walls with white wainscoting and window trim. The king-size bed had a wood-and-wrought-iron frame as beautiful as it was probably functional for a Dom. It left her breathless.

DeVries came into the room a second later and stopped to give her a focused survey and nod of approval. "You can wear the T-shirt. Lose the skirt." He tossed back the quilt of browns and tans. "In."

Without waiting for her response, he took her place in the bathroom.

She glanced at the door, unsure about sleeping with him again. And she really didn't want any sex—not when her emotions had been through a log chipper. Sure, she and deVries had already done the deed once, but it was all so much more complicated now.

Even worse, she knew the feel of his skin, drawn so tightly over the underlying rock-hard muscles. She knew his murmur when he was pleased with her. She knew—

"Do I need to repeat myself?" came from inside the bathroom.

Right. She remembered too, how he sounded when he was impatient with her slowness.

She wrinkled her nose at the door—the most defiant act she could dredge up—laid the blanket over the chair, and removed her leather skirt.

The sheets were soft and cool. His scent was on one pillow; she chose that one on which to lay her head.

Would he expect to have sex? She shivered. Being with him was like barely managing to halt halfway down a steep, rutted road, all jostled and scared. Should she keep going and hope for the best? Or back up to try to pick a safer path?

He came out of the bathroom, saw her staring at him, and a corner of his mouth edged up.

Why did he have to have a dimple?

After turning off the bedside lamp, he stripped and crawled under the covers. His weight tipped her toward him. Her body braced, waiting for him to come down on top.

Instead, he rolled her onto her side and spooned behind her. His chest rubbed her back. When his erection nestled against her bottom, she tensed.

"Go to sleep, babe."

Huh? "But—"

"Not going to fuck you now."

"But you're..." She wiggled against his erection.

"Teenage boys get a chubby half a dozen times a day. Doesn't take long to learn a hard-on won't kill you." He curled his hand over her breast, settled in more comfortably. "You'd make a nice teddy bear if you'd shut up and go to sleep."

Despite the hot drink, she had still felt chilled inside, as if her bones were carved out of ice. Now, with his living heat wrapped around her, the cold melted, leaving her limp. Warm.

CHAPTER TEN

DeVries came awake abruptly. Without moving, he checked his surroundings. Not yet dawn. The rumble of the garbage truck told him what had wakened him.

When Lindsey moved, he realized the noise had woken her as well.

He felt rested. The woman was better than any sleeping pill. Sometime during the night, he'd rolled onto his back, hauling her with him. Her head was on his shoulder, one leg lying over his, her elbow resting on his chest and her hand curled around the side of his neck.

"You really are a hell of a teddy bear," he murmured.

"Thanks, I think." She stroked her palm over the coarse stubble on his cheek. "Did you ever have a teddy bear?"

"Yeah." He'd never slept without it. "Present from a neighbor." For the pitiful kid.

"Mine came from my daddy." Her breath created a pool of warmth on his shoulder. "I still miss him. Is your dad around?"

"Died." His mouth twisted. "He survived Vietnam and returned to die stateside from a fucking helicopter malfunction."

"That's hard." She gave his chest a comforting stroke. "So you only had your mom?"

"Nosey little submissive." There was the difference between them. His curiosity was driven by the need to know how things worked—even humans. Hers was because she gave a damn.

What the fuck was he doing here, letting her...in? He

turned his head so he could breathe in the scent of her hair, rub his chin in the silky strands. That's what he wanted. More than her soft body, he wanted the sweetness of her spirit. Her warmth. Tex had the backbone to stand up to him—and the heart to care.

Yeah. He might just have to keep this one.

Which meant he owed her more of himself than anyone had gotten since he'd been a young, stupid man.

She didn't speak, didn't demand answers. Her silence was patient. No wonder people talked to her.

"Mom lost it when he died. Alcohol. Drugs." His mouth tightened as he remembered how his mother would hook up with a man to get rent and food. Eventually the guy'd tire of pricey nooky or catch her screwing around, and kick her—and her kid— back into the street. "Prostitution."

"I'm sorry," Lindsey murmured. Her fingers stroked his rigid jaw, down and over his chest.

The darkness seemed to enclose them in a bubble. Her touch was giving him a hard-on, and he caught her wrist. "Stop."

She froze for a second and pulled away.

"Shit." He turned to face her, side by side. In the dim light, he could see her gaze was lowered. Her expression was blank. He ran his knuckles over her cheek and let out a breath of relief when she looked at him. "If you kept touching me, I'd end up fucking you. Not a bad thing, but I wanted to talk."

She blinked and then her expression filled with understanding. Her lips turned up. Pleased.

"You know you turn me on, pet," he said softly. "Don't doubt that."

Her nod was short. Uncomfortable.

Yeah, they were going to talk some more. "Tell me about feeling unwanted. Was your last husband seeing someone else?"

Her breathing stuttered. Rather than answering, she pressed her mouth into a flat line. Stubborn Texan.

"Guess that's a yes. We're going to stay right here until you tell me about it."

"It's none of your business." Her defiance—in his bed—

reminded him of a scrappy terrier facing off against a Rottweiler. Not smart, but plenty ballsy.

"You're my business." The words belled through him with a resonance that said truth.

When she fought to sit up, to get out of bed, he tossed a leg over her to hold her down while he reached for the bedside-stand drawer. Damn he liked her wiggling.

After donning a condom, he rolled on top of her, flattening her with his weight. Her small breasts were crushed against his chest; her full hips cushioned him in softness. He set aside the need to simply take her and instead braced himself on an elbow and captured her chin.

She glared up at him, her soft lips set in a sulky expression.

Be fucking fun to kiss the attitude off her mouth. A shame it wouldn't help him get answers. "Tell me."

"Get off me. I need to leave. I have an appointment at nine."

"It'll suck if you miss it. Tell me."

"God, you're a pushy bastard."

"Yep. Keep squirming, and I'll fuck you after our talk. Make you even later." He grinned at the screech she made—like a whistling teakettle.

"How did you find out he was screwing around on you?" In his experience, a memory like that set off a cascade of others.

"I picked up the phone at the wrong time. Someone had called from the ranch to say he had a"—she struggled over the word—"*pretty boy* for my husband to check out."

"Fuck, seriously?"

"Y-yes." Her voice broke. "And Victor s-said it was about time, since if he had to keep fucking his old, fat wife without a break, he'd barf."

DeVries wanted to snap the bastard's neck. With an effort, he set his anger aside and concentrated on the rest. "A pretty boy? Sounds like you married a pedophile."

"He was," she whispered.

Most pedophiles weren't attracted to adult women. Braced on his elbow, DeVries stroked her arm. Her skin was chilled.

"There a reason why he married you?"

She nodded. "My ranch. He never wanted me." Her sigh was bitter. "He acted very loving, but...I got so I knew he didn't like the way I looked. Not sexually. I had breasts. And hips. And—"

"And now you don't think they're appealing." She made sense. Lindsey had a woman's body. He ran his thumb over her lower lip, felt the quiver. "You know, a man—unless he's gay or a pervert—likes breasts and hips."

"I know." She averted her face. Denying him control.

"Your head tells you that. Your subconscious won't believe it. Not easily." He put his hand over her breast and felt her flinch. Talking about the bastard had revived old memories. "We've got some more work to do."

"We?" She pushed at his shoulders with her small hands. Totally useless action, considering he probably outweighed her by about seventy-five pounds. "There is no we."

"Right," he said agreeably, using one knee to part her legs. "So I'll show you how I feel about breasts and hips and afterward let you leave."

"You—you weasel."

He kissed her neck. Her cheek. Her mouth.

She pressed her lips together, denying him a kiss.

Damn, he enjoyed her. His mouth feathered over hers as he fondled the breast in his hand. Mmmhmm, the combination of soft and firm could drive a man crazy. He pinched her nipple hard enough she gasped.

He took her mouth and surged in, plundering in the same way he planned to take her cunt.

Fuck, he loved the little purr he coaxed out of her. How she went boneless under him. Even when she was pissed off, her body responded. Wanted him. Made him feel like a god.

He gentled his touch, thumbed her nipple to a point as he considered. He'd fucked a hell of a lot of women—enough to know the difference between faking and real excitement. Lindsey hadn't had a wealth of lovers in her past, and when she was married to the asshole, her subconscious would have felt every slight and let them damage her sense of self-worth.

It'd be a pleasure showing her the effect she had on a real man. And was a relief to know the play they'd done yesterday had actually been on target. Even if it had ended badly.

He lifted his head. As she sputtered, he smiled down at her.

He considered flipping her so he could fondle all the parts he liked, but...face-to-face was better right now. "Since you have an appointment..." Deliberately, he fit his cock against her entrance and pressed. Slick and hot. "We'll have to be quick."

With one hard thrust, he buried himself to the hilt.

Her whole body arched. Her cunt pulsed around him.

Her gaze had gone slightly unfocused, and he waited until he was sure she could hear him. "Damn, I love the way you feel. Under me. Around me."

He could almost see her subconscious take his words in.

Yeah, there was going to be a lot of fucking in his future.

❖

Lindsey entered the battered women's shelter with two minutes to spare and headed toward the meeting room.

Her insides were still quivering. DeVries might be pushy about getting what he wanted, but he always made her come at least once—usually more—before he finished. Damn it. How could she yell at him properly when she was all flushed from coming?

He'd driven her back to her car, politely held the door, and kissed her so sweetly, so possessively, she could only stare at him when he closed the door. His smack on the roof of the car had made her jump. And he'd laughed when she'd glared at him.

God, his teasing sent tingles up her spine, and she was totally thrilled she could lighten his spirits. Especially after finding out how ugly his childhood had been. She held a hand to her chest, aching for what he'd endured. While she'd been playing with her sisters on the ranch, he'd been living with a hooker.

DeVries hadn't totally spilled his guts, though. More haunted him. But...she'd get it out of him and help him deal. She could. She wanted to share everything with him. Her feet stopped abruptly as she realized her total idiocy.

She couldn't. Absolutely couldn't.

And he was so damn persuasive, she almost had. At least she'd kept from blurting out the entire story of Victor's death and how she'd been stupid enough to go to the ranch to confront him.

Her stomach tightened. Victor had not only been raping the young Mexicans being smuggled across the border but was running a smuggling operation. Humans and drugs came from Mexico; weapons and ammunition went back.

She'd been unbelievably gullible. He hadn't loved her. Ever. He'd wanted her ranch because it sat right on the US-Mexico border.

Enough of that.

She pushed open the door to the room. "Hey."

At the table, Edna watched Lindsey with hope in her eyes and an uncertain set to her mouth. "I got the form filled out."

"Perfect. As it happens, I have some ideas on jobs. We can fill out applications if you find any you like." When Edna gave her a tentative smile, Lindsey felt more than rewarded for the extra time she'd taken.

"I appreciate you coming in on a Sunday," Edna said.

"Not to worry." Lindsey opened the folder up. "Your counseling and doctor appointments are more important. And my boss will let me take time back." Xavier had made it clear he appreciated flexibility and would give extra comp-time in return.

Within only a couple of hours, Lindsey was pleased with their decisions and even happier with the look on Edna's face. *Hope.* Fragile but present.

"We did good work today," she said to the older woman. "That was the last of the applications." And she was starving. The scent of bacon had drifted into the room, reminding her she hadn't had breakfast. Her stomach rumbled in complaint.

"Why don't you stay for brunch?" Edna said. "The cooks always make too much food."

"I-I..." Why not? The more she learned about how shelters operated, the better job she could do for the women. "I'd love to stay."

The residents were sitting down at the long tables in the

dining room.

Edna said, "Everyone, I've invited Lindsey to eat with us. Would you believe, she has a for-sure job for me as well as a couple more I might like. And she'll get me into a trade school when I'm ready."

As the chorus of congratulations made Edna beam, pleasure washed over Lindsey. This was why she'd gone into social work.

Jeremiah's mother waved her hand. "Can you sit by me? I have some questions."

"Of course." Lindsey joined the table, dispensing information about jobs, education, and finding daycare.

Almost silently, Jeremiah, Jenna, and another child ate their food. Lindsey and her sisters had never behaved so nicely when there were guests. In fact, they'd chattered away, delighted to have a new audience. Each visitor had been like a gift.

For these children here, she wasn't a treat but a possible threat. Only a man would be considered more menacing. Poor deVries. He really hadn't liked terrifying the kids.

And now that she'd thought of him... She smiled at the boy he'd befriended. "Jeremiah, did Mr. deVries return to work on the door?"

He nodded vigorously. "I helped him. With everything." The boy's eyes were shining. "He gave me ten dollars because he says a man gets paid for his work."

"You must have done a very good job," Lindsey said. Did deVries have any idea of the effect he'd had on this child? Sure, he did. His Dom talents didn't shut down when he left the club.

"He worked hard," Jenna piped up. "The man said Jeremiah was an *sellend* helper."

"Ex-cell-ent," her mother prompted.

"E-sellend." Jenna chewed on the end of her braid before offering, "Jeremiah spilled the things on the floor. The man laughed."

DeVries had *laughed* at the kid? What kind of a—

"He didn't hit me or yell," Jeremiah whispered. "He made a...a little huffy sound. An' said it was nothin'. He helped fix cars when he was eight, and he dumped a whole bucket of oil all over.

Cuz he tripped."

"Damn," she said under her breath. A perfect response.

One woman, sitting beside Lindsey, sighed sadly. "So many of us forget what a normal man is like." She patted her chest. "Even me. I actually had a good childhood. That's the kind of joke my father would have made."

Lindsey smiled. "Mine too."

"If Papa had still been alive, he'd have killed my husband," Jeremiah's mother said softly enough the children wouldn't hear.

Lindsey's smile faded. Yes, her father would have torn Victor apart.

DeVries was also the type of man who would defend a woman. Regrettably he couldn't protect her from the police. Getting him involved might get him killed.

Looking down, she pretended to concentrate on her food, seeing instead the officer who had responded to her 9-1-1 call that horrendous night. Craig had been a classmate of Melissa's. He'd been stunned at the sight of Victor's body. Even so, after viewing the boxes of weapons and the drugs and speaking with the boy, he'd been firmly on her side. After calling in the report, he'd let her go to shower off the blood.

And Parnell had killed him. His own officer...merely for knowing what had really happened.

No, she couldn't risk deVries. Mustn't.

CHAPTER ELEVEN

Friday evening was chill with a mist bordering on rain as deVries knocked on the door of Lindsey's house. Country-western music was playing softly enough he could hear the soft thud of her feet on the wooden floor. Over the past few days, he'd noticed she was often barefoot. One more habit showing who she was. He liked a woman who went for comfort at home.

When she opened the door, he had to grin. Yep, he was dead-on. Barefoot. Jeans and a loose T-shirt. A clamp held her brown hair on top of her head, showing the purple strands. Her face brightened for a second before she scowled. "What are you doing here?"

"We went out last night. Tonight we'll stay in." He motioned to the grocery sack at his feet. "Can you cook chicken? Southern fried chicken?"

"DeVries, have you been taking your meds?"

Fuck, he liked her sassy mouth. He bent down and sampled, feeling the way her lips softened. Her scent drifted upward, the fragrance like a flower garden in the spring. Bet she just got out of a bath. He deepened the kiss.

She took a step forward, her hands on his shoulders. Oh, she was into him whether she thought it was smart or not. Lifting his head, he whispered against her lips, "Answer my question, baby."

"Um..." She backed away and shook her head like a boxer after catching a hard punch.

"Can you cook chicken?" he repeated, curving a hand

around her bared nape. Tiny soft tendrils tickled his fingers.

"Of course. But what are—"

"Good." He picked up the grocery sack and his toy bag and walked through the door. "I brought food. And a movie."

"Excuse me." Her voice rose. "Stop!"

Almost to the kitchen, he turned. God, she was cute.

Hands on hips, she glared at him. "Polite people call first. They don't ask themselves right over." The Texas twang had definitely increased.

"Don't like talking on phones. You gotta eat supper; we can eat together." He strained to keep his face straight when the ire in her eyes burned. Be fun if she attacked him.

"You-you..." She caught up to him in the kitchen and grabbed his arm. "I'm not your damned cook!"

"Sure you are. I'll help." Chuckling, he set her on the counter beside his toy bag.

Her unexpected kick to his gut knocked him sideways a step. Her eyes rounded. "I'm sorry—I—"

"Not a bad defense, but you should have followed up." Pinning her lower legs with his body, he toppled her over onto her back on the counter. "Now you're going to pay."

"Damn you, don't you dare!" She struggled, but the gleam in her eyes, the way her nipples strained inside the T-shirt—fuck, she wasn't wearing a bra—he knew her objections weren't serious. Still, in case...

"Safeword still works." He met her wide-eyed gaze and smiled slowly. "Nothing else you say will." And he yanked her jeans down.

Lightly tanned legs. And one red lacy excuse for underwear, which barely covered her pussy. He removed her right pants leg, leaving her left leg encased. After shoving the loose end into a drawer, he leaned on it, trapping her leg with the caught fabric.

They'd played lightly a few times over the past week. She knew him fairly well. Time to push her a bit. And...well, how convenient...there was a knife rack.

When he drew the wood-handled butcher knife out, she

froze, staring at it, a rabbit cornered by a wolf.

He took an alcohol swab from his bag. As the sharp scent filled the air, he cleaned the blade and leisurely dragged the edge like a shaver down her stomach.

Her breathing stopped.

He slid it under the left side of the underwear, feeling the fibers part. Pretty damn sharp. "Guess I owe you new undies."

Her eyes couldn't get much bigger. Fuck, he loved this.

He did the other band of the thong and bared her pussy. "You're not going to kick me again, right?" he asked softly.

Her voice came out in a whisper. "N-no. DeVries—"

"I like being called Sir. Master works once in a while."

"Sir. You wouldn't really—"

"Shut up, babe." He touched the point of the knife to her nipple. Just so she could feel the point—not nearly enough to draw blood.

Her pounding pulse jiggled her little breasts, and she was hardly breathing. *Nice. Just right.*

He laid the hilt on her stomach and positioned the hefty bare blade between her breasts. "You planning to move?"

Her no was so low he barely heard it.

"Didn't think so. Gonna have some fun now... Warning, babe, you wiggle and I'll amuse myself with the blade instead." He kept his weight on the drawer, ensuring the jeans would keep her left leg anchored. With a firm grip, he pushed her right knee outward, opening her pussy. The folds glistened, assuring him she liked edge play as much as he did.

And he did; he was hard as a rock.

After giving her a warning look, he bent and licked from above her asshole to her clit. Under his palm, her leg muscles jumped. Be fun to see how long she could hold still. In fact...

Since his hip and left hand were keeping her open, he happened to have a free hand. With his right thumb and forefinger, he captured her nipple. Nothing felt as smooth as a nipple. Nothing tasted like a woman's cunt. He wiggled his tongue over her clit and pinched her nipple at the same time.

The sound she made, fear and passion. Yeah, he'd enjoy this. Working his way down, he pushed his tongue into her entrance, felt the first wiggle. Lifted his head. "Did you move?"

Her hands clenched again. "No. Please, no."

He released the jutting peak, smoothed over it, took the time to pinch the other, and felt her legs jerk. She was already nicely close to coming.

Spotting a dish towel, he arranged it over her eyes to block out her vision. Firmly, he took her hands and put them under her lower back in a token restraint. "Now, that's just pretty. All laid out for me."

She made a noise of frustration but was smart enough not to speak.

After unzipping his toy bag, he found a soft anal dildo, lubed it, and fitted it against the tight rim of muscle. "Let it in, babe," he cautioned. As it slid in, he saw the tremor run through her. Perfect. The pressure would keep her right on the edge while he played...with edges.

After quickly cleaning the blades of his two favorite knives, he lifted the butcher knife from her chest. With her eyes covered, she wouldn't know what he used—and he preferred his own where he knew their sharpness—they didn't have any burrs to catch flesh—and how hard he could press.

If she figured he was using the butcher knife, well, wouldn't that just break his heart?

"You played with knives before, pet?" He leaned forward, pinning her legs down again.

"N-no."

"This time, I'm not going to cut you, babe. Might welt you up a bit; not more. We clear on that?"

Her head moved up and down an infinitesimal amount, as if she were afraid to move.

Why did playing with knives and little females make him want to laugh? "Good. Safeword is red. You get too scared, and you let me know." This time around, he wouldn't push her further.

He dragged the knife over the flatter parts of her body—her tender stomach, tops of her thighs. Normally he'd start on her back, but he liked this position for her. Trapped by her own tight jeans.

"Let's see how pretty a line I can make," he whispered. Using his forearm to pin down her torso, he picked up his smaller knife. Tilting the blade so the flat side was toward her, his finger near the tip, he lightly drew the point across her stomach.

A fine line appeared. Good, her skin was his favorite kind. Not so thin as to tear; delicate enough to mark easily. She'd have a pretty red line there in a few hours. "Oh yeah, that's nice, Tex."

She swallowed. "DeVries, I—"

"Uh-uh." He took the butcher knife up and laid it between her breasts, so she could feel the weight of it. Recognize it. When he saw the tiny quiver of her muscles, he picked the knife up and rested the back of the blade against the side of her neck.

Her muscles all went tight. With no experience, she'd only note the coldness of the edge, not that it wasn't the sharp side.

"What'd I ask you to call me, Lindsey?"

"Sir." The cords in her throat stood out with her tension. "I'm sorry. Sir. Master."

"Very good."

HE WOULDN'T HURT her, she told herself that. Again. And Again. Every cell in her body seemed located in her neck where the cold steel lay over her carotid artery. Her breathing was so shallow, she could feel the tiny lift of her ribs with each fast breath.

Hours passed, years, eons, before he lifted the blade away. "Ready for another mark?"

"Yes, Sir," she whispered. Pressed down by her weight, her hands clenched. And despite the fear—maybe because of it—she had a desperate need for him to touch her. The heat of his hard thighs pressing on her and the scrape of his clothes made her head swim. The plug he'd inserted somchow seemed connected to her pussy.

He drew the knife down between her breasts, the scraping bite at the edge of pain, leaving a lingering burn in its wake.

Gradually, he made more marks, cross-hatching her stomach, going lower and lower, until he left one right above her mound—and the biting sensation gripped her clit with a pressure all its own. Her hips attempted to lift, but he had her so securely pinned she couldn't budge.

"Getting antsy, are you?" His rasping voice matched the rawness of her need.

"Yes, Sir," she tried to say. Only a grunt escaped her dry throat.

"Good to know." The scrape went back up her body and slowly circled her breast.

Pain burst in her nipple. *He cut me!*

She screamed, struggled to wrench away, and realized he hadn't used a knife. He'd applied a nipple clamp; she felt the points digging into her sensitive flesh. "Oh my effing *God*. You bastard."

"That's me." His voice was deep and satisfied.

Her left breast flowered with the thick heat of a clamp as well. The pain was so much easier to endure when she knew a blade hadn't been the cause.

She heard the zip of something, the sound of a condom wrapper. And his mouth came down on her. His tongue worked her clit until her leg muscles trembled, and her every breath held a low moan.

The tangle of welts added to the hot arousal pooling in her belly and the pressure building low in her pelvis.

God, she was going to come. *I mustn't.* If he picked up the knife again, she'd lose it. His tongue flickered over her, teasing. Everything inside her was boiling; the tiny button of nerves was consuming her whole lower half.

When he lifted his head, she groaned. Her pussy felt swollen to ten times normal size. She was a second away from coming.

He moved between her legs. She was no longer pinned by her clothing. "Put your legs around my waist."

The loose jeans weighted down her left calf as she locked

her ankles behind his back.

The dish towel covering her eyes was suddenly gone, and she blinked up at him.

Holding her gaze, he picked up the butcher knife, turned it so the light glinted off the shiny sharp metal, smiled at her low moan, and laid it aside.

"Up you come." She stared into his sage-gray eyes as he gripped her waist and lifted her up, face-to-face with him. He handled her so easily, as if she were a fragile doll. "Hang on, babe."

She felt his cock seeking entrance through her swollen folds. When he entered her slightly, she gasped at the feeling—even the tip was stretching her.

"Eyes on me," he said. He held her gaze as he ruthlessly lowered her. Penetrated her. Filled her completely.

She shuddered. The relentless need was too much, burning inside her with a dark hunger. "Oh please."

"Beg more," he whispered. He moved his hands to grip her ass, lifted her, and little by little let her sink down onto him. Far too slowly.

Her fingers dug into his shoulders. "DeVries...Sir...please. Faster. Do something. Please." She tried to wiggle on his cock.

"Do something? Anything?" He secured her with one hand under her butt. His other hand smacked her ass so hard the sound echoed in the kitchen.

The brutal, scorching pain burst inward, sizzling every nerve tip in its way to her core. Her fingernails dug into his shoulders. "Aaah!"

Hands gripping her hips, he lifted her up and down, hard and fast, pulling her in until her clit ground against his groin with each downward movement.

Another and another.

Her neck arched as the coiling pressure grew and grew and burst outward—a violent flash flood battering her senses and filling the rivers of her body with pleasure.

Gasping for air, she braced her head against his shoulder

and heard him murmur, "You really are gorgeous, babe."

The words soaked into the hollows in her heart, making her glow from the inside out.

"Hang on, now," he muttered.

She wrapped her arms around his neck. As he lifted and lowered her, her vagina pulsed with pleasure. He took his time, enjoying himself with powerful, driving strokes.

He buried his face in her hair with a harsh, almost silent exhale and pressed her down onto his thick, iron-hard shaft, holding her in place, and she felt him pulsing inside her as he came.

After a minute or two or three, she lifted his face. Kissed him—which, of course, he turned into something long and wet and deep. And then glared into his eyes. "Okay, fine. I'll cook you some damn chicken."

The sound of his laughter filled her so brightly she probably lit the kitchen with her happiness.

He rubbed his cheek against hers and looked at her with a serious expression. "Should have had this discussion before."

She wet her lips. "What discussion?" As anxiety quivered awake, her grip on his shoulders tightened.

"You're the only one I'm seeing, babe. You feel the same way?"

As her breath sighed out with relief, she nodded. "No one else."

"I know Dark Haven has test results, but we get tested again and lose the condoms. You good with that too?"

So deVries. An order, and yet giving her a chance to object. The thought of really feeling him, all of him, made her clench.

His dimple appeared. "Yeah, you like that."

"Uh-huh." Burying her face in his neck, she inhaled his clean scent. A thought struck her, and she started giggling so hard she couldn't stop.

He slapped her butt to get her attention. "What the hell is so funny?"

"You." She gasped for breath, her insides hurting as she fought to hold back her giggles. "I-I can't believe the *Enforcer* wants to go *steady*."

His eyes widened in disbelief, then narrowed. "Now I do have to hurt you."

CHAPTER TWELVE

Thanksgiving Day was cold, with a small glittering sun in the gray sky. Lindsey carefully carried her pies up to the Mediterranean-style mansion, shivering in the moist chill air. *Brrr.* Unhappily her black secondhand jacket didn't look sophisticated enough to wear today. Shoot, Xavier's Tiburon home would make Armani feel underdressed—let alone a Texas ranch girl.

But Abby had said the attire of the day was nice, not fancy, so Lindsey'd donned her favorite black jeans, heeled black boots, and a wide silver-encrusted belt. It wasn't as if she'd accumulated much of a wardrobe. She sighed, thinking of all her clothes back in Texas. So many of them had been gifts—like the Texas-themed T-shirts from Mandy. Or the western shirts from Daddy, which she'd worn until the material was almost threadbare. She never had nightmares when she wore one of Daddy's flannel shirts.

At least on a trip to the secondhand store, she'd found a nicely festive red, satin shirt. The neckline even dipped far enough to flash a bit of cleavage. Only a bit.

Mama had once lectured her sister, Melissa, saying holiday meals were intended to show off turkey breasts, not women's breasts.

Don't think of home, dummy. Missing what she couldn't have never helped anything. But...dammit, it was supposed to be her turn to have Thanksgiving dinner at her house this year. Instead they'd all be at Melissa's.

Melissa and Gary with little Emily, Amanda, and Mama. Lindsey smiled slightly. Mama was flighty as a hummingbird, but she had a ranch-size heart. Lindsey bit her lip, remembering lullabies sung to drive away night terrors, big squishy hugs for lost pets, huge productions for each girl's birthday, and special-made chocolate-chip cookies for when a best friend was mean.

There was something wonderful about being loved so completely. *I want to go home. Now.*

Before she could free a hand to ring the bell, Xavier opened the door. "Happy Thanks—" He used a finger under her chin to tilt her face up. "Are you all right, pet?"

"My liege—I mean, Xavier—I'm fine. Maybe a tad homesick." She curled her lips upward.

His frown indicated her attempt had failed to reassure him. "Abby said you had sisters. In Texas?" He motioned her into the house.

"Uh. Right." Lordy, what had she babbled to her friends? How much had they shared, not knowing better? "Who all is coming today?"

"Eight total. No children this year. Rona's sons are at their father's. Simon's son is with his ex." He smiled slightly. "Abby's parents are sailing in the Caribbean, and her good sister is skiing with a friend's family."

"Well, I'm glad you're having a dinner for all us strays," Lindsey said, her voice shakier than she liked.

"It's our pleasure. Now go drop the pies off and come out and talk." Xavier stepped back, releasing her, although the concerned expression on his face said he'd be keeping an eye on her.

In the kitchen, Abby gave her a hug and sent her off with a bottle of wine to join the others.

In the living room, the floor-to-ceiling windows overlooked the Bay, framing a view of fog-shrouded Angel Island. The fireplace held a cheerfully crackling fire. A Dom from Dark Haven occupied one of the white leather chairs. In tight jeans and a stretchy Henley shirt, Dixon sat on the chair arm, talking with Rona on the adjacent sofa.

Standing off to one side, Simon, in his usual white long-sleeved shirt and black slacks, broke off his conversation with

Xavier. "Lindsey."

When Lindsey stopped beside him, he touched her cheek with gentle fingers. "All healed up. Good."

She felt her homesickness recede. Her family was in Texas, but her friends were here. "Happy Thanksgiving, Simon."

"And to you, pet." He held out his glass, and she topped off his drink. "Thank you."

As he returned to Xavier, Lindsey walked across the room to the others.

Dixon bounced up to give her a hug. "Hey, girlfriend! Love the hair!" He tugged at her new red-and-green highlights.

"I'm getting ready for Christmas."

"Awesomesauce! Let's dress up for Dark Haven as Santa's elves."

"Oh sure." Lindsey grinned. "I'll consider it only if you talk Xavier into a Santa costume. With a big belly and a white beard and—"

Dixon doubled up at the idea.

"Lindsey." Her grin faded at the sound of Xavier's voice.

She turned to see his black unreadable gaze on her. Surely he hadn't heard her.

"No."

Oh God, she was dead meat.

As the men returned to their talk, Simon backhanded Xavier—in his awesomely flat belly.

Snickering, Dixon shoulder-bumped her. "Maybe you should avoid the club until after New Year's."

"No shit."

"Well, on to other topics," Dixon said and turned to the Dom next to him. "Have you met Tad?"

Brown-haired. Fairly muscular. Full lips. Was this the so-called Dom who only wanted sex?

"In passing." Hands occupied, Lindsey nodded at Tad. "Nice to meet you."

The man didn't stand—Lindsey's father would have frowned

at his lapse in manners—and held his glass out to be filled. "A pleasure, Lindsey."

Rona's expressionless face showed she wasn't impressed with the man. It just went to prove Dixon really did have crummy taste in boyfriends.

And this guy looked like he was all hat and no cattle. She'd definitely have to keep an eye on Dix. Quiz him a bit. Nudge him along to a better selection of man. Meanwhile, Lindsey poured wine and dropped down beside Rona on the sofa.

Carrying a platter of porcini mushroom tartlets, Abby came in. "Here's something to munch on, but don't ruin your appetites." As she set the plate on the coffee table, the doorbell chime sounded. "I've got this one," she told Xavier.

Sitting back, Lindsey glanced around, feeling like when her high school hosted a father-daughter night and she'd had no one to take. It sucked deVries's assignment to Seattle had run over, and he hadn't been able to return in time.

Yet, perhaps his absence was best. In her world, taking someone to a Thanksgiving dinner meant *serious*. What had she been thinking, agreeing to go steady with deVries? Sure, exclusiveness was logical to prevent disease and everything, but...what they had was far too much like a...a real relationship.

And she knew better.

It wasn't safe for him. And it wasn't safe for her because if—when—she had to run and leave him behind, her heart was going to bust into a million pieces.

Even worse, what would her leaving do to him?

Since she'd had the meltdown at Dark Haven two weeks ago, they'd been together each night—and she'd loved every minute.

She'd believed she wanted someone intellectual, refined, and aristocratic, into opera and fancy restaurants. But deVries enjoyed home cooking—which was what she actually preferred to cook. He was definitely super intelligent, but...also super blunt. He liked fun movies and grilling and going on long hikes. And so did she.

She'd begun to realize her dreams were something left over

from childhood—and not about finding a person who would match her likes. Who she could live with. When deVries wasn't in Dom mode and deliberately making her uneasy, she was comfortable with him, whether arguing over which television show to watch or trading him cookies for gardening work. He was surprisingly fun to be around.

And the sex was off the scales. Especially without a condom. The feel of his bare cock inside her... She shivered.

Okay, no more thinking like that. He'd probably come over tonight, so she'd save her carnal thoughts for the appropriate time.

And tell her heart to stay out of the game entirely.

When Xavier left the room, Simon walked over to the couch. "How are you doing with the new job, Lindsey?"

"I love it."

"That's excellent, although you're going to disappoint Mrs. Martinez. She hoped you'd return."

Warmth flooded Lindsey's heart. "Can you give her a hug from me?" However, a squeeze didn't seem nearly enough to pay the sweet woman back for all her help. Perhaps, since she had a good paycheck coming in, she could do something more tangible. Her Rayburn family was famous for their Christmas tins filled with homemade candy. This year, she wasn't known as a Rayburn, but her San Francisco friends deserved some treats, didn't they?

A guttural voice from beside Lindsey said, "What kind of a hug you want delivered? I'll see it done, Tex."

To her surprise, she looked up into deVries's face.

The corners of his mouth rose as he tugged her up and into a long embrace.

Resting her face against his wide chest, she inhaled the fragrance of his woodsy masculine soap. When his cheek rubbed her hair, the feeling of being treasured shook her. Even knowing she was heartsore and vulnerable, she melted right into his embrace.

With reluctance, she lifted her head. "DeVries. What are you doing here?"

"I finished early and caught a ride down with a friend." He brushed his mouth over hers in a light, affectionate greeting and whispered, "Each time you call me deVries from now on will be rewarded with something nasty. Got that, little girl?"

The threat in his voice sent goose bumps down her arms. "I—right." Her gaze dropped. He'd asked her to call him Zander more than once. But darn it, she didn't want to be sucked into caring for him. She mustn't.

"Good." As if they were a long-standing couple, he tucked her against his side as he walked over to greet Simon and Xavier.

As Simon glanced from her to de—Zander, his brows drew together. "Zander. Good to see you."

When Lindsey looked up, Zander only smiled slightly and squeezed her closer. Unlike a few previous boyfriends who'd tried to display ownership, he didn't grope or kiss her neck. He merely kept his arm around her, showing the others he considered her to be his date.

She shouldn't be his date. Shouldn't encourage him.

"Have you been shooting this week?" he asked Simon. "Got a new GLOCK you might like."

As the men talked, Lindsey stood stiffly and...the hell with it. She didn't want to think about the future or having to leave or dying or hurting her friends. Not now. Today, there was nothing more she wanted than to be right where she was. With a sigh, she slipped her arm around his waist and snuggled against his side.

He stopped midsentence, bent to kiss the top of her head, and continued with his conversation.

She'd surprised him, she realized, and pleased him. The knowledge set up a sweet glow inside her.

After a few minutes, she noticed Rona had disappeared—probably to help Abby. She pulled away slightly.

He looked down. "Babe?"

"I need to help in the kitchen."

He nodded. "Those pies yours?"

"Uh-huh."

"Any chance you saved one at your place?"

Criminy, did he know her so well? She had. Despite her attempt to smother her smile, she saw the knowledge in his eyes.

"Good girl."

When he let her go, she hesitated, wanting only to snuggle back up against him; however, both Xavier and Simon were watching her. Studying her.

Jeez.

In the kitchen, Abby was putting a pot of potatoes on the stove and talking with Rona.

"Hey, y'all. Need help?" Lindsey leaned on the creamy-colored granite-topped island. With ample windows and golden-oak cupboards, the high-ceilinged kitchen seemed filled with light despite the gray sky outside. She moved a bouquet of dark red roses off to one side and noticed they matched the hand-painted backsplash tiles.

"You can dish something up—and I'm talking information." Setting rolls on a baking sheet, Rona raised her brows at Lindsey. "Last I heard, you thought Zander was an asshole. Now Abby says I missed part of the story. I'd say a lot of the story. Like when did he get elevated to teddy bear status?"

"Teddy bear?"

"Huggable." Rona put the last roll on the pan, picked up her wine, and gestured with the glass. "Talk fast."

As heat filled Lindsey's cheeks, Abby gave her a sympathetic wink.

"Uh, okay. I ran into him when he was setting up security for a battered women's shelter where I was doing interviews, and we talked. Then he came to my house, but he pissed me off, so I picked on him at the club, only he...kind of gave me a lesson in manners...but that upset me, so he took me home with him."

Rona choked on her wine.

Giggling too hard to speak, Abby made a *continue* gesture with her hand.

"And he kept showing up at my place with food without calling first or anything. I have no clue why I even let him in the door."

From the way her friends were snickering, they were

jumping to all kinds of ideas.

Probably pretty accurate ones. She flushed.

"Oh right," Dixon said behind her. "Like anyone in their correct mind would close a door on the Enforcer." He fanned himself. "Ooo, BFF, that's megalicious hot!"

She pointed at him. "*You* are not helping." Unfortunately, he was right; Zander could simply look at her, and she got damp. "So, Dix, what's the story with you and Tad? I thought you said"— she dropped her voice—"he only wanted sex, and you were going to kick him to the curb."

Dixon's happy smile faded, making his face gaunt. "He does. I was."

Leaning across the island, Rona patted Dixon's hand. "Why did you bring him to the dinner?"

Dixon shrugged. "I'd asked him to Thanksgiving before, and he was looking forward to hanging out with the San Francisco big shots."

Simon and Xavier *were* rich and well-known. Lindsey wrinkled her nose. Tad was using Dixon; she knew exactly how the realization could hurt.

"Oh honey." Abby walked over to give Dixon a hug. "That really bites."

He sagged into her. "Kinda. But I saw we weren't going anywhere. He's not even a top, let alone a Dom."

And Dixon wanted—needed—a Dom, preferably one with a touch of sadism in his soul. "Honeybunches, don't you worry. You're going to find someone wonderful. This guy is just a li'l stepping stone on the way there."

Even as his face brightened, Lindsey was considering. They could rearrange the seating at the dinner table, so Tad would be seated at the other end from Simon and Xavier. Once there, she and Rona would draw the jerk out...and the Enforcer could flatten the smarmy piece of bull-pucky.

Leaving the men in front of the football game, deVries took his beer and went in search of Lindsey. Dinner had been great, the company—with the exception of Tad—lively and intelligent.

But his woman had seemed more sad than normal.

In the kitchen, Rona and Abby were seated at the island, quietly chatting and cleaning off the turkey bones.

With a yark of excitement, Abby's half-grown dog dashed toward deVries, floppy ears bouncing as it skidded on the smooth floor. The little body hit deVries's boots with a thump, and the pup gave an embarrassed whine.

"Sorry," Abby said. "Blackie hasn't grown into his feet yet."

"No problem." He bent and ruffled the soft curly fur. "You'll get there, buddy. Give it time."

Blackie's fluffy tail dusted the floor with the pup's enthusiastic agreement.

"Looking for Lindsey?" Rona asked.

"Yeah."

She pointed to the French doors leading outside.

"Thanks." As the pup returned to his job—cleaning up dropped tidbits—deVries went out onto the wide stone patio. After the warmth of the house, the cold briny air was a welcome wake-up call.

Leaning on a railing, Lindsey was looking out at the bay and talking on a black cell phone.

Black? Wasn't her cell phone red?

"I miss you too, sissie." Her voice broke, and she wiped her hand over her cheek. "Maybe someday I can come home. Until then, y'all have to be careful. Okay, honeybunches?"

Seeing her cry put an ache in his chest. Why hadn't she gone home? And what did "sissie" need to be careful about?

He and Lindsey needed to have a long talk—but not during a party. He silently backed a step to return to the house.

"Bye." Still sniffling, she pitched the cell phone in a high arc past the cliff and into the roiling water of the bay.

What the hell? DeVries stared. Why would she throw away her phone? No...wait...it hadn't been her red smartphone. Had she just tossed a *burner* phone? The cheap, cash-bought cells were often used to avoid being traced...by people who worried about being traced. Something wasn't right here.

He stepped forward, deliberately scraping his foot on the flat stones.

She jumped and spun around. "Oh! De—Zander!" As he walked over, she gave him such a fake smile he wanted to shake her. "Uh, hi." Her voice wavered before she firmed it up. "It's nice out here, isn't it? Xavier has a gorgeous view of the bridge."

"You missed a tear." With his thumb, deVries swiped away the dampness on her cheeks. "You running from the law, babe?"

Her eyes rounded. A second later, her chin came up. "Do I look like a criminal? Lordy, what a question."

Great nonanswer. If she wasn't a felon, who was she avoiding? Fake identity. Burner phone. Twitchy about being in the open. Definitely on the run. Forestalling her retreat, he put a hand on the railing on each side of her, trapping her.

She still smelled like the pumpkin pies she'd baked. Edible. With grunt of exasperation, he kissed her cheek, her soft hair with the new glints of red and green, and the curve of her neck.

"Don't," she whispered. "This isn't the time."

"There is only now." Unable to resist, he snuggled her against him. Despite her firm body and lush ass, she seemed far too fragile. "Wish you'd tell me what's going on. Let me help, Tex."

The stiffness melted from her, and she leaned her head against his chest. Finest feeling in the world, taking a woman's weight like that.

"I can't...Zander."

Hearing her say his name was good. Very good. Didn't make up for her refusal, though. "Why not?"

Her fingers clenched, wadding his shirt, before she pushed him away. "I can't." She looked into his face, shook her head, and walked toward the house.

Too pissed off to try to continue the non-discussion, he let her escape. *"Can't,"* huh? He was seriously regretting he'd stopped his computer search on her. At the time, he hadn't felt right about investigating a bedmate.

Now? Now, Miss Nonexistent Adair had just won herself a

free ticket to a full-blown background investigation. When he finished, he'd know the color of panties she'd worn in college.

His lips quirked. Probably a bright red.

Once he knew the story, he'd do what needed to be done to fix her life.

And if she didn't think he should get involved? Well, that would be a shame, since he had no intention of backing off.

Pacing the patio until his annoyance decreased, he felt his phone vibrate.

The display showed Blevins. "What?"

"Job came up. South America. Need you on a plane ASAP."

Through the French doors, he could see Lindsey talking with Rona. Smiling valiantly. He admired the little submissive's strength. Admired a lot about her. Wanted more from her.

Needed to know what trouble she was in.

"Iceman?" Blevins prompted.

But if he stayed the relationship course, it wasn't fair to offer her a body that might return home riddled with bullets. "I'm done, Blevins. Remove me from the list."

"Shit." After a brief silence. "I figured you were getting close to this point. I get it. All the same, can you take this one last job? It's a kidnapping, Iceman. The boy's not even ten."

Fuck. Blevins knew he wouldn't refuse. DeVries watched joy fill Lindsey's face as she played with the pup. He wanted her sweetness. "Last one. After this, I'm out. Completely. No calls; no contact. Agreed?"

"Your choice." Blevins hesitated. "Thanks."

"Yeah." Hopefully he wouldn't get blown away before he could come back and claim his woman.

⸻◈⸻

On Friday, Lindsey dropped into the chair at the small desk in a corner of her living room. Hanging out in the kitchen at the Thanksgiving dinner, she'd missed the football game, and after Zander got her all upset, she'd not even asked the guys about the score.

With high hopes, she called up an online newspaper. Scowled. Her fingers twitched with the urge to slap the numbers right off the monitor.

The Cowboys had lost to the Saints because of some stupid *fumble*. Seriously, what was with that? *C'mon, guys, you can do better.* Perhaps it was best she hadn't been able to watch the game yesterday; Zander had threatened to gag her last time.

And—the nerve of the jerk—he'd said since she lived in California now, she should follow the 49ers.

When hell freezes over.

With a frustrated grunt, she switched the papers to the *San Antonio Express-News*. Half breathing, she waded through the articles. Muggings. Drug busts. Immigrant woes. Murders. Nothing new.

That was good news. At least they hadn't announced her arrest—LINDSEY RAYBURN PARNELL CAPTURED IN SAN FRANCISCO. Visualizing the imaginary headline sent a chill up her arms.

If only something would go wrong for Parnell and Ricks. Why didn't someone catch them?

She shivered. Ricks's voice was always sliding into her nightmares. *"Be a while before Parnell can pick you up. Enough time to do you. He doesn't care if you're damaged."* He'd ripped her shirt, shoved her to the floor, and unbuckled her belt. She'd fought, but he was twice her size and weight. When his fist had slammed into her cheekbone, her face felt as if it had broken in half. Eyes blurring, she'd battled to scratch him, hit him—and he'd snickered. He'd been excited by her struggle. And then he'd punched her over and over until she was retching and crying as he'd unzipped her jeans.

God. She swallowed hard. It was in the past. Over. He hadn't succeeded, and she'd gotten away. Arms covered in blood from the window, but *free*.

If there was ever a next time, though—the upsurge of sickness made her swallow hard—if he caught her, her rape would be...ugly.

Unable to sit longer, she walked through the house, trying to lose the taste of fear. Ricks wasn't here; neither was Parnell.

She was in San Francisco, buried in a city, with a new name. Perfectly safe as long as she was careful. And she'd be careful.

And darn well watch her back more carefully.

How could she have let Zander sneak up on her? How long had he been listening? Even worse, he'd seen her throw away her disposable phone.

Damn man. Her life would be much easier if she could just brush him off.

However, he was so...so amazing. Like at Thanksgiving dinner with Dixon's jerky wanna-be Dom. She smiled. Tad had insisted a "real" submissive wouldn't safeword out, and Zander'd told him, *"I'm trying to see it from your point of view, but can't get my head that fucking far up my ass."* The silence afterward had been glorious.

And Zander wanted to help her. His offer made her all quivery inside—and terrified her. He couldn't fix her problems. If he tried, he could end up arrested or hurt.

If she only knew what was on those flash drives. If there were anything there to incriminate Parnell or Ricks, she'd take the risk of sending off the information. Everywhere. All the law enforcement agencies in Texas. The newspapers.

If only she could break the encryption.

Maybe she should contact a different law enforcement agency. Surely not all of them were corrupt.

And how did that work out for you last time, honeybunches? She rubbed the scars on her arms, remembering how the glass had ripped the skin away. *Hadn't worked so well, had it?*

Smuggling weapons and drugs meant the bad guys had money to buy off just about anyone. What was the life of one Texas woman when compared to hundreds of thousands of dollars?

Zander wouldn't sell her out.

She sat back at the computer. No, he wouldn't. He might be gruff and rude and pushy, but his muttered comments during action movies showed his inflexible opinions about what was right. He really was like a hero in a western—the lone sheriff ready to stand up to an entire gang of villains.

She took a sip of her coffee. Having seen him take on a gang, she knew he could do it too.

God, she loved him.

Her gasp drew coffee into the wrong pipe, and she burst out coughing.

No. Absolutely not. Bad, stupid, insane. Texas girls on the run do NOT fall for snoopy, controlling Doms. Especially sadist Doms. "I need my head examined. And to be fitted for a straitjacket. And to be put on some psychotropic medications."

Reality check, please.

Talking sternly to crazy people rarely worked—and it didn't this time with her. She wasn't listening to herself speaking reasonably. Nooo, all her insides were doing a squishy happy dance. *Love him, love him, love him.*

She was pretty darned sure he didn't feel the same.

On Thanksgiving, he'd left soon after their talk on the patio. He said he'd been called away. Yet if he worked for Simon, how could he be called away? And Xavier had told Zander, *"Be careful."*

Be careful of what? Where had Zander gone? Well, whatever he was up to apparently wasn't safe.

Her life wasn't safe either. So falling in love with him was doubly stupid.

Dump him. Dump him now.

No.

CHAPTER THIRTEEN

The mission had taken over a week, but the hostage was safely home with his family, and that felt damned good. The kid had shown more guts than many grown men.

Not a bad job either. One merc with a busted forearm, couple with knife wounds. Everyone—except the kidnappers—had returned. And deVries was now done with jobs for hire. Felt fucking good.

Anticipation rising, he walked onto the porch of Lindsey's duplex, carrying his toy bag and overnight bag. Only around midnight on a Friday. Maybe she'd still be awake.

He knocked on the door.

Her footsteps approached quickly, so she hadn't been upstairs in bed. The tiny light from the peephole darkened as she checked who was on her porch. Good habit.

But when the door opened, her cheeks were pale, her breathing shallow. "Zander," she half whispered.

Hell. "So late. I scared you?" Fuck, he should have called first.

"I—well, yes." As color seeped back into her face, she moved aside to let him in. When he stepped into the well-lit room, her eyes rounded. "Oh my God, are you all right?" Her hands closed over his forearms.

Crap, where were his brains this evening? He stank of sweat, blood, gunpowder, and oil. His face was scratched from branches, his jeans torn from hitting the ground and rolling. The kid's blood had stained his shirt. He should have swung home and showered.

He hadn't been able to wait. "Good enough once I shower. You mind?"

"Of course not." And, even as filthy as he was, she hugged him, pressing her clean little body against his. Jesus, she could break a man. "Zander, where have you been?"

An evasion rose to his lips. No. Truth now. "I took a job with a mercenary unit. Rescuing a kidnapping victim. A boy."

"Oh God." And, with her soft heart, she asked the right question. The only right question. "Did you get him back? Is he okay?"

"Affirmative. He'll probably have nightmares, but he's home. His big sister was making him a cheeseburger before we left."

Her smile could light up a room. It damned well lit up his heart. "Thank God." Her brows drew together. "How about you? Have you had anything to eat?"

"Later." The need was on him. On the plane as he'd catnapped, his dreams had been full of violence. Of pain...inflicting pain. Only...could she take it?

"Lindsey, I...need..." His fist bunched in the front of her shirt—and sweetness filled him when he realized she was wearing one of his old flannel shirts.

"Oh. Of course." She started to unbutton the shirt. "I want you too."

"Lindsey." He had to make her understand. "I'm looking for more than sex."

Her gaze fell to the toy bag on the floor beside him. "Right." She swallowed audibly. "Sure."

"I can go to the club, babe." Normally, that's what he'd do, but he and Lindsey had agreed to be exclusive.

"No." She lifted her chin. "You'll use me, not someone else."

So fucking stubborn. Dammit, as a submissive, she might try too hard to give him what he needed. Nonetheless they were a couple now; he wouldn't seek surcease elsewhere. He handed her the bag. "Strip completely. Put on the ankle and wrist cuffs. Kneel beside your bed and wait for me."

DeVries scrubbed off the physical stench of battle, wishing it were as easy to wash away the emotional residue. He considered jerking off, but his need wasn't for sex. He needed to mete out pain. He needed a willing masochist.

Instead, he had himself a willing submissive. Fuck. He'd have to be damned careful.

There were still ropes looped on the tall wooden posts of Lindsey's bed from his other visits. Kneeling as ordered, she was a beautiful sight with her pale golden skin, pink-brown nipples, hair a dark cascade over her shoulders.

Mine.

Tightening his control, he dragged the bed away from the wall and angled the headboard into the center of the room. "Up. Face the headboard."

"Yes, Sir."

Even standing, she was short enough her chest could rest against the heavy wood of the frame. Perfect. He clipped her wrist cuffs to the ropes on the carved posts. Felt the scars running up her forearms. He still needed to know what had caused them—but this wasn't the time.

After pulling her feet apart, he tied her ankle cuffs to the legs of the bed frame. Opening her. The musky fragrance of her arousal invited him to run his fingers over her pussy. Push inside to feel her squirm.

Not yet. He was hard already, but he needed more than a fuck tonight. "I'm going to hurt you, Lindsey." His voice almost guttural. "Red is your safeword. Yellow if you need it."

"Yes, Sir." She was breathy with an erotic mixture of anticipation and trepidation.

After dropping the toy bag beside her, he set out the impact toys he'd use. Warm up first.

After wakening her skin with a light flogging, gentle slaps, and massage, he upped the ante with a heavier flogger.

Her back and ass turned pink, and at length, a pleasing red. The occasional gasp from her was like liquid gold sliding into his gut. *More.*

Needing to remind her of who was the top, he leaned

against her from behind and rubbed his cock between her buttocks. Her shiver made him grin. Made him enjoy not having dressed for the scene.

Pulling her back from the wood of the headboard, he cupped her breasts. Kneaded them cruelly. Pinched the nipples until her breathing hitched and he could hear a protest deep in her throat.

With his other hand, he curved his palm over her mound, pressed down on her clit, and shoved a finger—two fingers—into her cunt. Slickly wet. She was enjoying everything he'd done so far.

He'd barely gotten started.

OH MY EFFING God. Lindsey bowed her head as blows rained down on her back. He was using a flogger with a multitude of thick, heavy falls. Each impact drove deep into her bones and set her skin on fire.

He'd put clamps on her nipples, tightening them until she couldn't keep from pulling away.

Every strike of the flogger shoved her forward to hit the nipple clamps against the headboard. And hurt. All of her hurt, and it wasn't fun anymore. But she could feel his need as if her own—and her own need was to give him everything.

Her face was wet with tears. With sweat. *Owwww.* She gritted her teeth to keep from using her safeword, from screaming, from crying. Instead, she braced her forehead against the wood so he wouldn't see how she felt. She'd take it—she'd endure *anything* if he got what he needed.

It took her a second to realize he'd stopped. A hand on her cheek turned her face to the heat of his gaze.

Dismay filled her as she realized his tight face held none of the peace he displayed when he flogged masochists at the club.

"You're done, babe," he muttered.

"No." Her voice wavered past the sobs stuck in her throat. "I didn't use my safeword."

His thumb stroked her wet cheek. "Think I'm blind? Scene's over."

"But you—" *You aren't done. Not even close.*

"Shhh. Let me get you free." He opened each Velcro cuff with a quick, frustrated yank.

More tears spilled over her lids as she realized she couldn't give him what he needed.

"Turn around." He steadied her, his palms warm on her upper arms. "Hold still now." With unnaturally controlled movements, he removed the clamp from her left nipple and, without waiting, did the right.

Like a one-two step, blood rushed back into the abused tissues, burning and engorging each nipple. She groaned, moved to cover her breasts.

"No." He held her wrists at her sides as he drank in her pain. Pleasure glinted in his eyes. "Nice."

Her gaze clung to his, as if he were reeling her in like a fish on a line. Everything in her pleaded to ease the strain in his face. "Take what you need, Sir. Please."

When his lean fingers touched her cheek, she saw the answer in his expression—she couldn't give him what he required.

"You're what I need, pet." Hand around her nape, he guided her to the side of the bed and bent her over the mattress. Under his firm touch and the suggestive position, her pain coalesced into something entirely different—into a raging need. She might hate really hurting, but rough sex lit her up like a fireworks display. And God, he knew that. Used it.

Running his hands over her back and butt, he fingered the slight welts, making her squirm. "Such a pretty ass. I'm going to admire my work while I fuck you." When he squeezed the tender, reddened buttocks, she sucked air through her teeth.

A small pleading sound escaped her.

"Oh yeah, you'll get what you need, Tex." As his callused hands spread her open, he dragged his cock against her entrance and pressed slightly inside.

Her clit throbbed in anticipation. Her pussy felt sensitive and needy—and very wet.

His laugh was harsh. His hard palm smacked her right buttock. *Ow, ow, ow.* As the burn seared through her, he gripped her hips and ruthlessly sheathed himself to the hilt.

Too big. Too fast. Her insides spasmed in protest, and lights burst in front of her eyes. "Aaaaa!" Mindlessly, she pushed up, trying to escape.

A hand fastened on her nape, holding her down on the bed. "Take it, babe."

His merciless grip turned her core molten. As her pussy pulsed around him in protest—and pleasure—he kicked her legs farther open, rendering her more helpless, and hammered into her. Each hard, inescapable thrust stretched her insides, pushed her deeper into the mattress, rubbed her hurting nipples and her clit on the coarse cotton spread.

Trapped. Her mind went blank as he forced her to take it, to feel it, to enjoy his use. A slap on her bottom sent more fire arcing through her. Her back arched—and he kept her pinned to the bed.

Abruptly, he withdrew and instead swirled his fingers in her wetness. Even as his cock drove in, he centered a slick finger against her asshole.

Instinctively, she fought to escape.

His grip tightened on her nape. His thick shaft pushed in deeply, pinioning her. "Don't. Move."

At the sound of the growling baritone, her insides clenched around him.

His hand moved from her neck to her hip, restraining her as he forced his finger past the rim of muscles, using only her own wetness as lubrication. The abrasion burned. Yet, like the thumping sound of massive lights coming on in a sports stadium, every nerve in her pelvis ignited.

He didn't move, his weight on her increasing, deliberately pointing out that she was pinned. That both her anus and vagina were penetrated. That she had no control

The sound she made was an animal's—a needy animal.

"Yeah, there we go," he muttered. His shaft slammed into her; his finger shoved into her anus. Cock withdrew. Then the finger. And again.

The ball of need inside her tightened, clamping down around him. Her legs trembled, her hands clenched on the bedspread. Her world narrowed to his finger. His cock, over and over.

More. Needed more. She wiggled, pushed up—

He slapped her bottom so hard the sound echoed in the room. Pain burst and burned into her like a wildfire of sensation sweeping everything before it. Uncontrollable pleasure ripped apart her senses, shaking her like branches in a wind, electrifying every nerve. *Oh God—too much.* She twisted under him, needing more, needing less, spasming, crying. Falling into a whirlpool of sensation.

Slap! His palm struck her buttocks, his cock slammed into her, his finger penetrated her. Again and again.

"Nooooo." The molten heat surged into her center, up her spine and belly, and she kept coming and coming, unable to stop.

With both hands, he gripped her hips, lifting her ass higher as he pounded into her and released with a growl.

—◈—

DeVries woke early with Lindsey's soft body cradled to his front. His arms were wrapped around her, holding her close. Sweetest teddy bear he'd ever known. Her breath was warm on his chest. Slowly, he inhaled her tangy sweet fragrance that mingled with the lingering scents of raw sex and the cream he'd rubbed into her skin.

After their session last night, he'd taken his time with aftercare, washing her, tending the marks he'd put on her—and enjoying her squirming—then rocking her as she fell asleep. Felt like he'd come home.

Considering his exhaustion, he should have slept longer. But, even though his body was sated, the knot of tension inside him hadn't subsided. Not the way a good S/M scene at the club would have accomplished.

Fuck, she'd tried.

Remorse scraped his already raw nerves. He'd satisfied her, he knew. Hell, she'd come as hard as any woman he'd ever seen and lavished him with grateful kisses when she recovered. His guilt was because he realized he'd flogged her longer and harder than he should have. Dammit, he'd known she'd try to take more than she really wanted. He just hadn't realized she'd attempt to disguise her pain from him.

She was going to get her butt walloped for not being honest with him...once he unwound to where he could deal. Fuck, his gut was tight. His emotions were a tangled mess, ready to snap.

After easing out of bed, he yanked on a pair of running shorts from his bag and headed out into a foggy San Francisco dawn.

—◦◦◦◦—

The biscuits were almost done. Hair damp on her shoulders, Lindsey finished cooking the scrambled eggs and bacon. Upstairs, the shower was still running. Back from his jog, Zander had found her in the kitchen, given her a quick kiss, and muttered he needed a scrub up.

Worry simmered under her happy mood. As late as they'd been up, he should have slept longer. Instead he'd gone running— and he never ran in the mornings. He always went to the gym after he got off work.

Taking her time, she set the table and poured juice and coffee. Her appetite kept decreasing.

Happily, as he came down the stairs, he was smiling. "Gotta admit, I missed your breakfasts last week."

The compliment sent her spirits soaring...but not enough. As he sat down across from her, she studied him. He'd had a night of sex. Gone running. He should look relaxed and satisfied. Instead the muscles around his mouth were tense, his body taut.

She hadn't given him what he needed. The knowledge lay like a granite boulder in her chest, weighting down her words, making her evaluate everything he said.

"You got plans for tonight?" he asked.

"Rona and Abby want to go shopping." For sexy underwear for the Yosemite trip. Unfortunately, Lindsey probably couldn't afford any. "Tonight I'm on the desk at Dark Haven until midnight."

He nodded. "Let one of them drive. I'll pick you up at midnight and bring you home. If I'm late, wait for me."

He still wanted to see her. Her heart lightened slightly. "Okay. But aren't we going to play at the club after I'm through working?" They hadn't yet done a scene together at Dark Haven.

He paused with his fork halfway to his mouth. Slowly, he lowered his hand. Stalling. "I'd rather fuck you senseless here again."

The warmth expanding outward from her core didn't succeed in melting the chill encased around her heart...because although his lips had curved up, none of the smile had shown in his eyes.

―――≪≫―――

"Hey, Lindsey. Look at this one."

Lindsey turned.

The Frederick's of Hollywood store was crowded with holiday shoppers, but Lindsey had no trouble spotting her friend's curly blonde hair. Abby held up a cami and thong. The lacy fabric wouldn't cover...anything. "What do you think?"

"Oh score," Lindsey said. "My liege would definitely like that one."

"Considering the price, he'd better."

Abandoning a rack of corsets, Rona quirked an eyebrow and said in a dry voice, "I think Xavier's budget might extend to the occasional lingerie purchase." Over her arm was a black lace teddy with garters and fishnet stockings. Tiny satin ribbons held the front closed. "How about this for the dungeon party at Serenity?"

"That's adorable," Lindsey said. "Only, tying all those bows while dressing would drive me nuts."

"Payback is watching Simon untie them. One by one. He loves unwrapping things." Rona smirked like a cat who'd found the *best* cream.

Lindsey rolled her eyes. "Thank the Lord I don't work for him anymore, or this would be such an inappropriate conversation."

With a giggling snort, Abby put Xavier's treat into her basket. "What about you, Lindsey? Aren't you getting anything?"

"Not today."

When Rona opened her mouth, Lindsey held up a hand. "Don't insult me by offering to buy something."

"Not to worry." Rona pointed to the rear of the store. "Everything there is 75 percent off. Will your finances cover that?"

"Seriously?" Hope rising, Lindsey led them to the rack. Most of the clothes were too big or too small. But... "Oh wow." She lifted out a virginal white satin negligee. The length went to midthigh. She held it up. The neckline dipped all the way to the waist. The lacing fastening the back together would end at a woman's ass. "I can afford this."

It would drive Zander crazy. Or would have. Her face fell. "But—"

"What is it, sweetie?" Rona squeezed her shoulder. "Money worries?"

"Uh-uh."

"I'd guess that means guy problems," Abby said.

Lindsey rubbed her fingers over the smooth fabric, envisioning Zander's big hands there. "More like sadist problems—as in, Zander likes handing out pain."

Rona frowned. "Is he going too far? He respects your safeword, doesn't he?"

"It's not that. It's that he's a real sadist and..."

"And you're not a masochist," Abby said softly. "I've seen those intense scenes he does at the club."

"That's it. He wants—needs—more than I can tolerate. I can see his internal battle."

"Mmmhmm. He usually plays with masochists who like a lot of pain." Rona's gaze was troubled.

"I know," Lindsey whispered. "I can't give him that. I tried, and I couldn't."

"No. And you shouldn't try. Taking a little extra pain for your Dom's pleasure is different from trying to satisfy a sadist," Rona said.

"Did you talk to him about it?" Abby asked.

"Kind of. He says he's fine, like it's not something I should worry about." How dumb was that? "If he doesn't get to... Do a sadist's needs go away?" Lindsey asked. Surely she could figure a way to fix this. She had to.

Abby bit her lip. "I don't think so. Not even if the sadist tries to ignore them."

"Oh." The acknowledgment was like a cholla plant, the thorns painfully ripping into her heart.

She hung the garment back on the rack—she wouldn't need something pretty after all.

Near midnight, Lindsey was working the reception desk at Dark Haven. Her shift was almost over, and the number of incoming members had decreased to a trickle. With a sigh, she slumped in the chair. Her heart hurt and somehow was making all the rest of her hurt too. Ever since she'd talked with Abby and Rona, the world had seemed to darken, as if someone had drawn the curtains in a house.

The door squeaked open and thudded shut, and she looked up to see the masochist named HurtMe. He sauntered up to the desk and handed her his membership card. "Lindsey."

"Hey." She nodded at his PVC chaps and matching chest harness that showed off his lean muscles. "I like the look."

"You should get some cowgirl gear. You have the accent to make it work." He leaned a hip against the counter. "So...have you seen deVries today?"

She felt her face heat up. "Um..."

"Fuck, is he still screwing with you?" He sighed and patted her hand. "I'm sorry, Lindsey. I'd hoped he was over his snit."

"Snit?" Seriously? She lifted her eyebrows. Did the word "snit" and the man named the Enforcer even exist in the same zip code?

"Like how he was using you to make me jealous."

"What?" She swiped his card through the reader and slapped it on the counter. "Why would he do that?"

"I thought you knew. We were together—before you came

along. The trouble was he didn't want me playing with other guys." He rubbed his hand over his lean, shaved chest. "I don't think it's right he'd use you to get me upset, you know?"

Zander had used her? Lindsey flattened her hands on her leather skirt. "I don't get you. We are together."

"Oh please." HurtMe gave her a pitying look. "He's punished a female off and on, but do you see him actually have a *real* scene with females? Seriously? No."

"Whatever." She forced her back to stay straight. "It's none of your business what he does with me anyway, now is it?"

"Well, I guess not. Fine." His mouth went flat. "I liked you, you know, and I thought you'd want to hear this before you made yourself into more of an idiot over him. Before everyone in Dark Haven finds out how you were played." He snatched his card off the desk and stalked through the club entrance.

Used. Played. She stared at the wall, seeing scenes unfolding. Zander with Dixon. With HurtMe. With johnboy. All men. Sure, Zander would flog or paddle a woman, but usually because Xavier had asked him to.

His intense sessions were always with guys, and rumors said Zander was bisexual. If he was serious about HurtMe, maybe Zander *had* used her to make the guy jealous. From the snipe in HurtMe's voice, the maneuver was successful.

Feet in the chair, she curled her arms around her ankles, and laid her face on her knees. *Used.* The thought was like a fingernail digging into the unhealed sores inside her.

All the same, HurtMe's assertions didn't matter. Not really.

Breaking up with Zander was simply the right thing to do. They were getting too involved, and if Parnell or Ricks found her, there was a chance Zander might get hurt.

So...she was a danger to him, and she didn't satisfy his needs. Couldn't get much more straightforward than that, right? She stared down at her hands, watching her knuckles blur as grief welled up and filled her eyes with tears.

I can do this. I have to do this.

Nonetheless, when Zander walked in a few minutes later, she still wasn't prepared.

"Ready to go, Lindsey?" he asked.

"Um... Hey." She attempted to smile at him.

Eyes narrowed, he leaned over the counter. His fingers—so familiar a touch—curved to cup her chin. "You've been crying. Why?"

The authoritative demand of a Dom sent a shiver up her spine. She swallowed. *Do it now. Here.* If she left with him and tried to argue—face it, he could make her change her mind in a heartbeat. "Because I'm sad."

The words kept sticking in her throat. *Get it out now.* "Because I'm not going to see you again."

His fingers tightened on her face. "What the fuck are you talking about?"

DESPITE FEELING SCRAPED raw all day, deVries had looked forward to seeing his little Texan. Her sense of humor, her caring, her warmth—being around her was like stepping into springtime. But what was this shit? He let go of her. As short-tempered as he was today, he needed to be careful. Patient.

Her face was pale, eyes haunted and wet with tears. She really was upset.

Gentling his voice, he rested his hands palm-down on the desk. "Okay, babe. Tell me what's going on."

"There are reasons why we're...breaking up." Actual grief shadowed her face. "Several, actually. Only there's one difficulty we can't get past. It's impossible."

"Go on." Impossible rarely was.

"You're a s-sadist," she whispered.

"You knew that when we met. I'd never go beyond what you wanted. Not if you're honest with me." Unlike the way she'd been last night. One more thing they'd talk about.

"Yesterday, you stopped long before you were ready to. B-before you were satisfied." Her raised chin defied him to deny her statement. Her quivering lower lip tugged at his heart.

Hell...this he hadn't been prepared for. Perceptive, wasn't she? And...hurting. She must feel as if she'd failed him. He softened his voice. "Satisfaction isn't everything."

"It is to me—when it comes to you. I'm not comfortable if you're suffering. If you need something I can't provide." She reached out to touch him. Drew back.

Fucking submissive who wanted to give him...everything. Dammit, this wasn't her choice to make. "We're good. I'm good."

"You're not. I can see it."

He growled. Wasn't as if he couldn't function without handing out heavy pain. S/M was a craving, not an addiction. Wasn't like going hungry... More like giving up pizza or steak. Sucked to cut back, but other things were more important. "I fucking care for you." The words sounded ugly. Harsh. Not how he'd figured on telling her.

The tears in her eyes overflowed. "And I care for you."

He saw her lips firm. His gut registered the loss even before she whispered, "I won't let you live handicapped because of me. I can't. We're done, Zander. Please... If you care, honor that."

What the fuck? He straightened, staring at her. Just like that? *It was fun. We're done?*

If she'd really cared, she'd stick. She wouldn't walk away for such a fucked-up reason. Anger flared, burning apart his shaky control. "Might have known. A relationship takes work. Aren't many women willing to put out the effort."

"Zander..."

"It's *deVries*." He leaned forward into her face, gritting out the words. "You got your honor, Tex. Hope it helps you sleep good in your empty bed."

The ashes inside him settled over everything, turning his world gray.

"I'm so—"

He moved toward the exit and stopped at the sight of fucking-richer-than-God Ethan Worthington. Had she arranged to meet the other Dom there?

Even as he told himself he was being an ass, deVries glanced over his shoulder at Lindsey. Hand over her mouth, tears rolling down her cheeks. *Right.* His wife had done silent crying; hadn't meant shit. Tamara had dumped him for a rich man who'd keep her in style without any *effort* on her part.

He glanced at Worthington, then Lindsey. "Looks like you won't have an empty bed for long."

He took little pleasure in slamming the door behind him.

On the street, the cold air slapped him in the face. Brought him up short, playing over his asshole words. *Fuck.* He suppressed the need to head back in and apologize. Fix things. Lindsey wasn't Tamara—she wouldn't play him that way.

She'd just dump him and cry. Would give up without even a fight. *"We're done."*

Not fair. Not right.

Now what? He stopped, feeling the frustration growing inside him, needing an outlet more than before.

He couldn't do a scene. His control was shot.

A bar fight, though... He studied the rowdy tavern down the street. Full of city boys. No challenge there. But he could visit some of the places by the docks.

He glanced back at Dark Haven—a haven no longer. Big brown eyes, trembling mouth, sweet words. She'd gutted him worse than a KA-BAR.

Yeah, he'd make the rounds of the dock bars. See if he couldn't get his outsides battered up enough to disguise the pain inside.

⋯⋈⋯

The slamming of Dark Haven's door shattered Lindsey's control. He wasn't supposed to be mad at her. He should have been relieved.

"I can't say I've seen deVries upset before," Sir Ethan said. He walked around the desk and leaned his hip on the edge. Even with her vision blurry, she saw the concern in his clear blue eyes. He handed her a tissue from the box beside the computer. "What happened?"

Tears flooded her eyes faster than she could wipe them away. "H-he... I-I..." She made herself stop. Zander—DeVries—wouldn't want to be talked about.

Why should she care? He'd been cruel...but only because she'd upset him. God, she'd really hurt him. Her lip trembled. He'd cared for her...more than she'd realized.

I changed my mind—come back.

No. She couldn't waver. This was for the best. It was. She pulled in a shuddering breath, wanting to hit her hands on the desk, to throw things, to scream to heaven. *Why—why is life so unfair?* Sobs boiled up inside her, impossible to subdue.

When Sir Ethan put his arm around her, she buried her face against his chest and cried.

With a low rumble of approval, he wrapped her closer, holding her firmly. As he rubbed her shoulder, he murmured soft words she couldn't hear. Zander had done the same before, his hands rougher, his voice harsher, and God, she wanted him.

Can't have him.

After a minute, Lindsey regained control and struggled to pull away.

Sir Ethan's arms tightened for a moment before he let her go.

"Thank you," she whispered.

His aristocratic expression was gentle as he used a tissue to clean her face. "You are very welcome, sweetheart. You can have my shoulder anytime. Or anything else you need."

The warmth in his gaze said he meant the invitation exactly as it sounded.

The Dom was a walking, talking definition of gorgeous. Skilled, powerful, caring. She should want him.

And yet, her heart was set on Zander. Why had she ever wanted to be in love? It hurt—hurt far more than any whip a sadist could wield.

⬥⬥⬥

Sitting at her small patio table the next day, Lindsey heard a knock on the duplex's front door. A salesman? Probably not on a Sunday. Likely Rona and Abby. She didn't care. Talking wasn't what she had in mind.

Silence.

Good. She dumped more light rum from the bottle into her glass and studied the color. Paler than it was dark meant more alcohol than Coke. Excellent proportions.

Something rattled, and Lindsey jerked around to see the wooden side gate swing open.

Abby and Rona walked through as if they owned the place.

Jeez. "I thought this state had rules about rentals. Like giving twenty-four hours' notice before using a key." She glared at her landlady.

Abby smiled. "Oh, it does. Sadly there aren't any laws governing the behavior of BFFs. Sorry."

Shit, that was hard to answer. She scowled at Rona. "What's your excuse for trespassing?"

"Same one. BFF—only I'm BFF number one since I'm older." Rona sank down into a chair. "God. Joint Commission was here for the hospital survey. I think my feet are three sizes bigger."

"Poor baby." Abby checked the label on the bottle. "Rum sounds good. Have you got more Coke, and are you going to share?"

"Y'all are damn stubborn." Lindsey considered getting up. Unhappily the door looked awfully far away. "Glasses are in the kitchen."

Abby grinned. "I know where they are."

"So you're here because..." Lindsey prompted.

Abby reappeared with the glasses as Rona answered, "Because we were worried about you."

"But..." She hadn't called them, and Zander—deVries—sure wouldn't. "How..."

"Sir Ethan talked with Xavier last night. Xavier talked with Simon," Abby said. "Afterward, Simon talked with Zander."

Uh-oh.

"Zander was...less than polite, I gathered. So Simon shipped him to Montana this morning to work on a security system." Rona chortled under her breath as she poured a strong drink. "A blizzard is supposed to hit Montana tonight."

"Serves him right." Abby mixed herself a drink and topped off Lindsey's with Coke. "Maybe his penis will freeze off and drop into the snow alongside his testicles."

Oh God, they were blaming deVries for everything. Guilt pushed the alcohol aside. "He didn't do anything. I...I was the one who broke up with him."

"Because of what we'd talked about? Him being a sadist?" Rona asked softly.

Lindsey nodded miserably and gulped more of her drink.

"Sir Ethan said Zander was rude." Abby set her glass down with a thump.

"Zander was furious with me." A sob hitched Lindsey's voice as she remembered his shocked expression. "God, I hurt him so bad. He didn't w-want to break up. Acted as if it was something we could fix. But it wouldn't work." She looked at her friends. "It *wouldn't*."

"A relationship doesn't change your basic personality," Rona remarked carefully. "Did he think it would?"

"He only said he could handle it." Lindsey pulled in a breath. "Except when he was relaxed, his face was all tight. He wasn't the same. He looked like he was being rubbed raw from the inside out."

Abby leaned back in her chair. "So he was angry and blasted you verbally."

"Kind of." She bit her lip. "First he said I wasn't willing to put any effort into a relationship. And that—I could see his point. But when he saw Sir Ethan, he made a crack about me not having an empty bed. As if we broke up because I wanted Ethan. I don't get it."

"Huh." Abby glanced at Rona. "Does Zander have a money hang-up or something?"

"Money?" Lindsey asked. "His ex left him for a rich guy. Still, what's that got to do with Ethan?"

Rona blinked. "Zander was married before? I hadn't heard that."

"Yes. And Xavier told me Ethan's really wealthy," Abby

said. "He doesn't act like a snob, so most people don't even know."

"DeVries thinks I dumped him to get Sir Ethan's money?" Insult set up an acid burn in her chest. "Did I tell you that was why he was so mean after the first night? He figured I'd divorced my ex and taken him for all he had." *Oh Zander.*

She'd bet he didn't really think that—had spewed something out in the heat of the moment.

"He's got a skewed idea of women, sounds like," Rona said. "No wonder he never gets serious. But he treated you differently."

"I thought he did." Lindsey frowned and blurted out, "I heard he was using me to make his boyfriend jealous."

Rona and Abby stared and broke into laughter.

Lindsey glared. "Thanks, y'all." With an effort, she shoved back from the table, walked into the kitchen—with only an occasional misstep—and fetched her second cure for heartsickness—a plateful of brownies with extra fudge frosting.

"Oh hey, let me help you with that." Abby rose to take the goodies. "Look at all that chocolate. You really are feeling crappy, aren't you?" She helped herself to one and moaned.

Rona motioned with a brownie at Lindsey. "Nice attempt at a diversion, sweetie. Now tell us why you'd think Zander has a boyfriend?"

"I'm kinda thinking it's not my secret. And actually, I don't believe it." Last night, she'd decided HurtMe hadn't been totally honest. Zander had wanted a relationship with her—he hadn't even had a hissy fit when she'd called it *going steady.*

Regrettably HurtMe was right about one thing—he could offer Zander more than Lindsey. HurtMe loved pain.

Abby's gaze had unfocused, and Lindsey could almost hear the professor's mind buzzing. "Zander wouldn't have told you that. Someone else did. Maybe someone who wasn't being totally truthful."

Lindsey straightened. "I—"

Rona clinked her glass against Abby's. "You're such a sociologist. Good call."

"Hey, I've got a degree in psychology, you know. However, I didn't figure it out until about 4:00 a.m." Lindsey stared at the table.

Rona laid her hand over Lindsey's. "That's because you're involved with him. We look at our lovers with our hearts, not our minds."

"However, Lindsey, the man is going to return—if he doesn't freeze. Maybe you should talk with him. Try to work something out."

"I was fixin' to do that, only I think it would hurt us both. Nothing gets past the fact that his need and my tolerance don't match. And never will."

The two women stayed silent, visibly upset and feeling for her. Lindsey gave them a twisted smile. They'd come to take care of her despite her attempt to ignore them. So wonderfully caring. As she picked up her drink, her shirtsleeve inched back to reveal the white scar running up her forearm. The one she'd gotten when she'd escaped from Ricks.

As Abby poured more rum into Rona's glass, Lindsey had to wonder. Would her friends be here if they knew she was wanted by the law?

A second later, she realized they were both looking at her in concern. She blinked hard, realizing...yes, they'd be here. "I love you guys."

Rona patted her shoulder. "And we love you too. Which is why we're going to go in, watch some schmaltzy movie, eat popcorn, and talk trash about asshole men."

When Lindsey burst into tears, Abby just snickered and hauled her out of the chair.

CHAPTER FOURTEEN

O n Saturday, DeVries stalked into Dark Haven in a pisser of a mood. Knowing how much he hated cold weather, Simon had deliberately sent him to install a security system in the iciest fucking part of the country. It had taken an entire week to finish the job. Even the daytime temperatures had been below zero.

"You need some time to cool off," Simon had said.

DeVries growled. He was gonna gut his boss.

In the entry, he saw Dixon, not Lindsey, behind the desk. Probably for the best. DeVries held out his membership card. Behind him, several other members entered, forming a quiet line.

Dixon took the card by the corner in a blatant show of reluctance, swiped it through the machine, and shoved it back.

Ignoring the insolence, deVries pocketed the card and walked away.

"Have a nice night," Dixon said and added under his breath, "You bastard."

Hell. He couldn't ignore the deliberate rudeness. He grabbed the young man's chain harness and yanked him over the desk.

The submissive yelped.

With one hand, deVries lifted him by the harness, holding him up like a puppy being punished. "You get to wear a gag in your insolent mouth until your time at reception is done."

He dropped the white-faced submissive to the ground hard

enough to hear his bones rattle. "Am I clear?"

Dixon went to his knees. "Yes, Sir. I'm sorry, Sir."

DeVries took a ball-gag from his toy bag and tossed it at the sub. Still pissed off, he glanced at the line of members waiting to enter. Three submissives hit their knees. Two Doms nodded approval. One guffawed.

From behind deVries, Xavier said, "Is there a problem here?"

DeVries turned.

In his usual black jeans, vest, boots, and white shirt, Xavier studied Dixon, who made an I'm-screwed-so-bad whimper.

Mood lightened slightly, deVries answered Xavier. "Nah, no problem." He nudged Dixon with his boot. "Get back to work, boy. You have people waiting."

The submissive scrambled up. Fastening the gag straps behind his head, he hurried behind the desk.

Xavier watched him for a moment and motioned toward the main clubroom. As deVries fell into step, Xavier said, "You look a bit battered."

DeVries shrugged. The bar fight last week had been fairly satisfying, well worth the bruises, which were mostly healed now. "I'm good."

"How was Montana?"

"Fucking cold." His irritation returned. "I'm going to murder Demakis and toss his body in the gutter."

"Simon overreacted." Xavier's smile faded, and he gave deVries a level look. "As did you. The girl only did what she thought was right." Lindsey must have shared with Abby. The Dark Haven community gossiped worse than people on a naval base.

Stopping at a table, DeVries put a foot on a chair and rested his forearms on his thigh. "I know. Took a while to realize it, though." Maybe he wouldn't kill Simon after all. Being halfway across the country had kept deVries from showing up on Lindsey's doorstep and yelling at her...more than he already had. Fuck, he was a dumbass sometimes. "Given she lied about her identity, I figured she'd lied about our relationship too. But—she's a crap liar."

"She is." Xavier leaned a hip against the table. "She's hurting, Zander."

Lindsey hurting. At the sudden stab deep in his chest, deVries looked down, half expecting to see a blade jammed between his ribs. He drew in a measured breath. "She has some righteous concerns. I am a sadist; she's not a masochist."

Ever since returning from the merc job, his sleep had been filled with gory, violent nightmares. Sure, he could cope, but he also knew a good S/M session would relieve the feeling. It was why he'd come to Dark Haven this evening. "I can live without, but—"

"But Lindsey sees your need. A submissive's greatest desire is to fulfill your wants. If she can't, she'll feel like a failure."

DeVries ran his hand over his short hair. "She already does."

"Did you determine what you can do?"

"No." He scowled. "Or my ass would have been here, no matter what Simon wanted." The thought of losing Lindsey was a twisting ache in his gut. He missed her sweet body beside him. And how she strained to be polite in the mornings, despite her grumpiness. Her need to feed him. Her ability to listen so hard everything else apparently faded away. Her easy laughter that could turn into the cutest uncontrollable giggles.

Yeah, he fucking missed her.

"I can see her point of view as well as yours." Xavier didn't say anything further; the sympathy in his gaze was enough.

"Is she here?"

"No. She hasn't been in since that night."

Hell. Dark Haven was the source of most of her friends. "I should never have touched her," he muttered.

"At one time, I thought that. Now"—Xavier frowned—"I'm not so certain."

As DeVries jerked up his chin in acknowledgment, he spotted a submissive kneeling a few feet away. "HurtMe, you here for a reason?"

The blond man lifted his head. "For you, Master." His

almost purring voice was an invitation.

"I'm in the mood to push. To make you scream."

HurtMe bounced in place. "I can take it. Please use me, Master."

"Don't call me Master. Go find a cross downstairs."

"Yes, Sir." HurtMe rose. Hesitated. "The Victorian nook is empty."

What was wrong with the man? "People who want privacy use theme rooms. I got no need for privacy."

HurtMe's face fell. And he ran downstairs.

"What got into him?" deVries wondered.

Xavier frowned after the masochist. "Later, maybe we should talk about him and his assumptions."

⋯⋯

A man's screams drew Lindsey across Dark Haven's dungeon.

A couple of steps behind, Rona followed, having insisted on accompanying her to the club. After finishing his meetings, Simon planned to join them later.

"Crom. Someone is sure having a time tonight," Rona muttered.

The sound of the masculine howls of anguish sent goose bumps down Lindsey's arms.

Surrounded by observers, the St. Andrew's cross at the foot of the stairs held the poor victim. HurtMe was getting his wish all right. His entire back was reddened from a heavy flogging. Diagonal cane welts ran down the backs of his thighs. In a few spots, the skin was torn, with blood dotting the long lines. His balls were clamped, and weights hung from them.

Rona frowned. "Surely the top didn't leave him hanging there. Xavier would have a fit."

"I don't see him, though." Dark Haven had strict rules about never leaving a bound submissive alone. A few seconds later, she realized the standing observers had concealed a man who was taking something from his bag.

The top was deVries. Every blood cell in her vein jumped with yearning.

She took a step back. *No. He's not mine.* As the joy drained away, she sagged slightly, feeling the heaviness return. She needed to leave. Lindsey turned to Rona and found someone had tugged her off for a private conversation.

As deVries shook out a heavy flogger and took his position, Lindsey's mouth went dry. *Just look at him.* Sweat darkened his faded black T-shirt around the arms and neck. Pumped-up from the exercise, his biceps and shoulders strained against the fabric.

Oh God. Lust tangled with longing. He'd held her with those hard arms. She knew the salty taste of his skin, the growling sound of his voice, the scent of him from the fresh soapy fragrance on his chest to the intoxicating musk of his groin. Her craving for him wrenched her insides.

But he—he didn't need her. He wanted a masochist. And maybe HurtMe *had* told her the truth. The minute deVries returned from Montana, there he was with HurtMe. The pain was a knife sliding beneath her skin and gouging right to the bone.

As if to show what she couldn't possibly give him, the scene continued. When deVries struck, the thick strands of the flogger hit HurtMe's shoulders with a bone-shaking force, and the masochist whimpered.

"Yell for me, you bastard," deVries said, his voice rough with enjoyment.

The flogger struck again, and HurtMe screamed.

Lindsey cringed. She could never, ever take that kind of pain. *Leave, stupid. Leave.*

Her legs wouldn't move, as if clamps held her feet to the floor. She had to watch. To see the way deVries moved from side to side, striking new areas, easing the blows, changing floggers.

HurtMe slid into subspace; deVries drew him back out. Steadily, the sadist worked the scene into an inevitable climax.

Lindsey's heart thudded in time to the rising and falling of deVries's arm. Watching the expressions on his face—the enjoyment, the power, the cruelty—she felt the wetness between her legs increase. The air itself thickened and heated until each breath was a struggle.

After delivering the final blows, deVries removed the clamps on HurtMe's balls and nipples. Even as the masochist moaned at the influx of blood, the sadist picked up a cane.

God, he wouldn't. Lindsey couldn't help crossing her arms over her breasts in sympathy.

With a light in his eyes, deVries smacked the cane over HurtMe's abused nipples and testicles and finally his straining cock.

Giving a high-wrenching groan, HurtMe came, shaking so hard the cross itself moved, and Lindsey couldn't tell if his orgasm was from pain or pleasure.

As HurtMe sagged on the cross, Lindsey realized deVries was standing several feet from the man, smiling faintly…but not touching. That seemed odd. When Lindsey came—every time she climaxed—deVries had crushed himself against her as if to let his body absorb every shake and quiver. She licked her dry lips and shifted her thoughts away.

Working methodically, deVries released the masochist and helped him sit on the floor with a blanket around his shoulders. Talking in a soft voice, he handed HurtMe a bottle of water and made sure he drank.

Lindsey frowned as she watched deVries clean the equipment and pack his bag while tending HurtMe with a firm kindness, much as her father had cared for a horse in labor.

HurtMe's face showed open desire. Despite his hard-on, deVries showed nothing of the sort.

"Are you okay?" Rona asked. A Dark Haven staff member stood beside her.

"I'm confused," Lindsey whispered.

"Not surprising." Rona squeezed her shoulder. "Come on. Show's over."

"Right." Her body still burned. Needing…needing something and someone it wasn't going to receive.

"Lindsey," Rona prompted, "Xavier sent MaryAnn down to get me. He wants me to check out a submissive who's bleeding."

"Go on. I'll meet you in a bit." *As soon as I can get my body to move.* As Rona hurried off after the staff member, Lindsey looked back at the scene.

Having helped HurtMe to his feet, deVries motioned for two of the masochist's friends to approach.

HurtMe shook his head, set his palms on the sadist's chest, and leaned forward to whisper.

Lindsey flinched, wanting to smack the masochist and rip his hands away.

No. Not mine. DeVries isn't mine.

When deVries got a you've-got-to-be-kidding scowl, HurtMe lifted his hands, whining, "But, but Master. I want—"

"No, boy. That's not going to happen." As deVries turned his back, HurtMe's friends escorted him away.

Stunned, Lindsey stared. What was that about?

Slinging his bag over his shoulder, deVries glanced over the dispersing audience.

Oh shit. Lindsey edged sideways to retreat.

Too late. His potent stare trapped her, held her in place. His regard traveled from her face down her body and back up. His eyes narrowed.

Then his lips curved...as if he'd won a prize.

Oh, that's bad. Lindsey sucked in a breath and forced her feet to move. *I've got to get out of here. I can't do this again.*

She dodged a Master attaching a harness to his pony-slave and had to stop for a submissive kneeling before her Mistress. Finally the way was clear.

A powerful hand closed on her shoulder. "Going somewhere, pet?"

He turned her, forcing her to face her most wonderful dream, most savage heartache. Heather-gray eyes bored right into her soul and twisted every aching emotion.

"I—I was just watching." When she strove to ease away, his grip tightened. "I'm sorry if my presence bothered you."

He brushed his knuckles over her cheek. "Nope. Bothered you, though. I could feel the heat from over there. All excited are you?"

The blood rushed into her face with an almost audible whoosh. "I'm not—"

"Oh baby," he murmured. "You are." He slid his hand under her chin, tilting her head for a leisurely perusal. "Seems like watching me hurt someone arouses you." His voice deepened and dug holes through the barriers she'd raised. "Yeah?"

Couldn't run. Couldn't breathe. Couldn't lie. Not to him. Even the abject humiliation she felt didn't prevent her nod.

His hand dropped, the gray in his eyes lightened to green, and the harsh lines bracketing his mouth smoothed into a smile. Hellfire, her heart could resist his irritation, his scowls—not his smiles. With merely his expression, he'd hobbled her like a horse prevented from straying, keeping her where she could be touched. Used.

When he took her hand, she instinctively struggled to pull away. He snorted. "Oh Tex, you know better than that." With his eyes holding the heat of the previous scene, he wrapped her hair around his fist. "Come with me."

"No," she whispered. He kept moving. "Damn you!" She dug in her heels. "Stop."

To her surprise, he did. Still controlling her hair, he put his other hand on her cheek, and the juxtaposition of control and tenderness wrenched her heart. "Let's talk. A few minutes. Can you give me that?"

Why did she long to offer him anything he asked for? Knowing her agreement would only lead to more pain, she still nodded.

"Thank you, pet, for the trust." He touched his mouth to hers—a gentle graze of lips.

To her horror, he steered her into a theme room and closed the door before releasing her.

Lordy, the harem room. She'd looked in a few times, yet never entered. Breathing in the heady fragrance of sandalwood, she turned in a circle. Over her head, dark blue silk draperies angled from the center point of the ceiling to high on the walls and dropped straight down to give the illusion of an opulent tent. A wrought iron screen attached to one wall held ready-to-use wrist and ankle cuffs. "How about we talk upstairs instead?" Where the atmosphere didn't whisper decadence.

Although his lips twitched, his gaze stayed serious. He took a seat on an ornately carved wooden bench and pulled her between his outstretched legs, holding her hands in his. "You saw the scene with HurtMe?"

She nodded.

"I know you don't like that level of pain, Lindsey, but, when you watched, what were you thinking?"

"I—" She looked away, trying to think.

"Look at me." When she met his intense gaze, he said, "Now tell me. All of it. I won't be angry, but I need to know, pet."

"I was glad it wasn't me under your flogger." She started with the easy answer.

His gaze never left her face as he nodded. And waited.

"Um. I was a little"— *a lot*—"jealous he and you could share that."

"All right. Go on."

"I was…" She didn't want to confess more. Her throat dried, making the words stick and jumble.

Silence.

"It…it was hot. What you did."

One side of his mouth tilted up.

Did he think she was silly? Stupid? Anger slid into the unhappiness welling inside her. "You walked away from him. Shouldn't you be with him now? To finish…" Maybe even to fuck him. The thought made her throat close.

A vertical crease appeared on his forehead. She remembered how she would trace her finger up the tiny valley between his brows.

"Finish what?" he asked. "The scene was over. He doesn't require much aftercare; he got what he needed."

"But he wants more. And HurtMe said you were…" She flushed. Aw heck, she'd known. HurtMe hadn't told her the truth. Or—even worse—he had told her *his* truth. Maybe that was why she'd been confused—because he actually thought he and deVries had something going on. Regrettably deVries didn't have a clue.

"What...exactly...did HurtMe say?" His eyes hardened.

Oh spit. "He thought you used me to make him jealous."

"Why the fuck would I want to do that?" The expression on deVries's face went from blank to comprehension to irritation.

She wet her lips and spoke carefully. Time for really, really clear speech. "You're not—weren't—in a relationship with HurtMe?"

DeVries snorted. "I don't do guys." He let her hands go, catching her hips before she could retreat. "If I wanted to fuck men, I would, babe. My dick prefers women."

"You had an erection during your scene."

He dug his fingers into her buttocks, pulling her closer. "I'm a sadist, and dishing out pain makes me hard." He shook his head. "When I was younger, I tried reaming a guy or two. Doesn't do it for me."

"But..."

With one big hand curved around her thigh, he used the other to unzip her latex shirt. A hum of enjoyment came from him. "I like breasts," he murmured, taking one in his hand, weighing it, stroking his thumb over her nipple, sending random flares lighting up her body. "I like cunt. The way you smell. The softness. The sound of a woman's voice when she gets off."

He wasn't upset. Not trying to prove something. Just stating the facts with an undeniable conviction. This was deVries. He knew himself. Knew what he liked.

"I think you should talk with HurtMe." No matter how much he'd added to her upset, normally the masochist was a nice guy. Perhaps confused. "I know emotions can get muddled when two people scene together and make such a connection. He believes there's more between you than there is."

"I'll give Xavier a heads-up, and I'll talk to HurtMe." His lips quirked. "Can't beat on him—he'd enjoy it too much."

She rolled her eyes. "Thank you."

"Softhearted baby." DeVries's mouth went firm. "So, you were confused, but you didn't come to me for the truth. Even worse, you didn't give us a chance to talk about the problems of me being a sadist. That's going to change in the future."

What future? She nodded.

His expression said he wasn't buying her silent concession. "And you're figuring there's no future because you can't fill my needs."

"I can't."

"Lindsey." His hands stroked her waist under the shirt. "How do you define being exclusive?" His mouth twitched. "Or, as you put it, *going steady.*"

"I don't understand."

"Exclusive means you don't fuck anyone else, right?"

"Of course."

He slid his hands under her matching latex skirt to cup her bottom before moving higher to tease the sensitive hollow above her buttocks.

Her toes curled under.

He asked, "Does doing an S/M scene with someone else violate those terms—if there's no fucking involved?"

Flustered by the intimate knowledge he displayed of exactly where to touch her, she tried to think. "I…don't know."

He smiled.

"I didn't agree."

"No, but, pet, you're thinking about it." He drew her closer and nuzzled between her breasts. "If you get hot and bothered while you watch me whip a guy, I'd consider it a win all around."

"You want me to watch?"

His eyes glinted. "Baby, if you're in the building when I'm doing a session, I'm going to tie you up in the corner so I can keep an eye on you."

She started to say he was insane, only remembered the caning and wand scene he'd done with johnboy. How Master Rock had been delighted deVries had given his slave what he couldn't— and afterward had reaped the benefits.

Could she do that? "I… We can try."

"Good." His strong fingers massaged her bottom as a corner of his mouth tipped up. "We'll start now."

FUCK, HE'D MISSED having his hands on her. DeVries felt his control shredding inch by inch. But little Tex was all female, so she probably wanted to talk shit over for another hour. Had good reason, really since she'd had, hell, almost as bad a week as he'd had...though, at least, she hadn't frozen her damned balls off.

He wasn't going to talk now.

She'd get a lengthy chat...later. He closed his thighs to trap her between his legs long enough to yank her shirt off. Unzipped her skirt and let it drop. Sat back to enjoy the sight. "Damn, you have a gorgeous body." And he watched her blush from her pretty little tits to her face with the compliment.

But taking her without thought to what had happened would set a bad precedent. "Now you're dressed appropriately, kneel in front of me. Eyes down."

Indecision wrinkled her brow. Yeah, the lack of talking had done damage. Nonetheless when he straightened slightly, she went to her knees. There it was. As a submissive, she wanted control—his control. When she'd broken them apart, they'd lost that instinctive balance.

Before clouding the issue with sex, he needed to set their D/s relationship straight. He studied her face as he considered.

She'd made decisions. He didn't want a submissive who didn't think for herself. Hell, no. Neither would he let one choose for them both without talking it over. She'd misstepped, and in a way he couldn't ignore. Her arbitrary actions had almost cost them each other...and she had to know down deep he wouldn't tolerate that again.

She had to be punished. Right now. For future mishaps, he'd have the time to figure out more appropriate punishments, but here, they needed the intimacy of sex to reforge their bonds.

First, pain to break down the barriers, followed by pleasure to bring them back together.

"I don't want to do this," he said resolutely. "But when you ended our relationship without discussion, you disrespected our partnership, my authority, everything we were building."

She nodded, her lower lip between her teeth.

"To start with a clean slate, I'm going to punish you. Got any questions about why?"

Her shoulders tensed, and yet she shook her head. Her quick glance at his bag made him smile. Newer submissives worried about impact toys, never realizing a spanking could sting even worse.

"No toys, pet." He patted his thighs. "Right here; right now."

Her arms closed around her waist in a telling fashion. Breaking up had hurt her badly, even if she'd been the one to do it. Now her subconscious was trying to keep a distance between them.

Too bad. He wouldn't permit any distance...which was why he wanted the intimacy of a bare-ass, bare-hand spanking. "Now."

He'd seen snails move faster. Finally she draped herself over his knees. Hands flat on the floor, toes on the other side. Damn, she had the sweetest ass. Soft and heart shaped. "I'm sorry to have to do this, Lindsey," he said. "I hate hurting you when you don't enjoy it...and you're not going to like this."

No warm-up. No fun. He simply gripped her shoulder and started smacking her ass. Hard and fast, one cheek followed by the other. It only took a few slaps to have her squirming and kicking. She rose up, trying to use her hand to protect her butt—so he captured her wrist, pinned it in the small of her back, and continued.

She struggled harder. "Dammit, stop. I don't like you anymore. Let me go!"

No safeword. He stopped to rub her buttocks briefly, letting her hope he was done, letting the nerves recover. And he started again. *Slap, slap, slap.*

She fought to kick him. "You fucking asshole. I h-hate you!"

He closed his eyes, breathing through the pain of her words. Didn't mean them; he knew it. Still hurt. "I'm unhappy you feel that way, babe." He spanked her, not harder. Not softer. Seemed like forever.

She broke, her sobs filling the room, shaking her shoulders. "I'm s-s-sorry, Zander. I'm sorry."

Thank fucking God. He stopped, pulling in air through his

nose. After a minute, he managed to unclench his jaw. "God, baby, I don't like this. Don't make me do this again." Why the hell had it been so hard to punish her? He was fucking known as the Enforcer in Dark Haven. Jesus, hopefully someone would shoot him before he ever had to discipline her again.

Her crying didn't stop, but she nodded her agreement.

Eventually, his guts settled. "Tell me what you learned, Lindsey."

She sniffled. "I-I-if I hear something, I talk to you about it. And we discuss what's wrong between us."

He considered. "Yeah, that covers it." With a feeling of relief, he boosted her up and set her in his lap. She didn't pull away but buried her face in his shoulder and cried. Yet even as she did, she relied on him to hold her. Comfort her.

Jesus, yes. He wrapped his arms around her and rested his cheek on the top of her head, feeling his world return to normal.

When her sobbing had moved to hitched breathing, she lifted her face. "I'm sorry I didn't talk to you first."

Fuck, she was going to unman him with her sweetness. "It's past." He used his fingers to wipe away her tears. "I fucked up too. Said shit." Guilt lodged in his chest. "You want to hit me, I'll take it. I deserve it."

"Like I could even dent those muscles of yours?" She rubbed her cheek against his hand and was silent a moment. "I just won't make you cookies for a week."

Hell, he'd looked forward to her cooking. "You got a mean side in you, babe." He kissed her damp face. "We'll both do better next time." Next time. Had a good sound. A future.

"Next time." She bit her lip. "I didn't ask you before...because you looked unhappy. But—"

"Go on."

"The mercenary stuff. How—isn't the work awfully dangerous?"

She was worried about him. Damn. Damn, he liked that. "It's risky." He tipped her face up and kissed her slowly. "And last week was my final mission as a merc. I told them I was quitting on Thanksgiving." Iceman was now retired. *Damn straight.*

"But…" Her eyes softened. "You took the job because it was a child." She read the answer in his face. "You have a big ol' mushy heart, Sir."

"You *want* another spanking?"

She giggled and twisted in his arms. "Nope. I have something else I think you should do." Gripping the hem of his shirt, she yanked it off.

"Bossy, aren't you?" Lifting her with her round, red ass in his hands, he carried her to the pile of cushions filling one quarter of the room. By the time he got there, his cock was straining against his leathers.

He went to his knee, shoved her back onto the pillows, and stopped for a moment to enjoy the sight. A hanging wrought iron light illuminated her golden body surrounded by the rich blues and dark red cushions. Her streaky brown hair waved over her breasts, leaving the pink-brown peaks jutting up. Her legs were open, her cunt wet with her arousal.

And the scent was…captivating.

Kneeling between her thighs, he ran his hands over her curvy shape, teased her nipples to even tighter points, and smiled as her hips wiggled. Fuck he loved making her squirm. Making her eyes glaze over. And this time, he was going to let her move as much as she wanted.

"C-can I touch you?" she whispered, trying so hard to be a good submissive it warmed his heart.

"Sure, baby, touch me."

Eyes lighting, she pulled him down onto her and kissed him. Her soft hands stroked his face, his shoulders, his back.

Yeah, here was home. He reveled in the welcome, simply enjoying the anticipation…until it became too much.

Back on his knees, he inhaled, smelling the musky fragrance of a woman in need. He bent, licked around her clit, entertained by her sharp gasp. The pink nub was swollen, exposed, easy to tease…and from the way her breathing changed, she'd get off like a rocket if he continued.

He hesitated, wanting to feel her come from his mouth. And yet…for this first time in what seemed like forever—what could easily have *been* forever—he needed to be inside her. He wrapped her legs around his waist and undid his leathers, letting his dick out to play.

When he fit himself to her entrance, she clenched his shoulders, trying to tug him closer. Oh yeah, that too—he had a need to see the yielding look in her eyes when he exerted his control. "Hands over your head."

THE DEEP GROWL seemed to stroke over every nerve in her body. Lindsey looked up into Zander's face, saw the determination in his jaw, the authority in his gaze, and everything inside her did a shimmy. She put her arms over her head, crossing her wrists as she'd been taught.

He restrained her wrists with one big hand, pressing down enough her back arched. Looking into her eyes, he whispered, "I'm gonna take you so hard you'll feel me for a week...and now you can't do a thing to stop me."

The shiver running down her spine turned to a molten heat at the base.

He pressed his cock against her, slid inside a fraction of an inch, and took her in one long, forceful thrust, not stopping until he was sheathed completely.

Oh God. From empty to shockingly, uncomfortably full. Her head tilted back as she gasped for air. Her pussy spasmed around the intrusion in protest that transformed into need.

"Fuck, I like that look on your face," he muttered. His eyes were ruthless, dangerous. "Give me more." He drew out steadily and plunged home again. And again. His gaze never wavered from hers as he increased the pace. The force.

The hammering set up an overwhelming sensation sweeping her away. With his heavy weight on her, his unyielding hold on her wrists, every merciless stroke took her higher, pushed her toward the inevitable.

And then she crested—plunging headlong as brilliant spasms shook her, surging outward until her whole body trembled with the climax. The darkness behind her closed eyelids sheeted to white. Her hips bucked uncontrollably, seeking more, more, more.

As the waves receded, she managed to open her eyes.

His gaze was still on her face. His smile tight. Not satisfied. "Nice. Now give me another one."

Unable to move, she stared at him. "What? I can't."

"Babe, you know that's not true," he chided and released her hands. After tucking his elbow behind her knee, he planted that hand beside her shoulder, forcing her bent leg up in the air. Tilting her hips upward so his cock went even deeper. He kissed her lightly, nipped her chin. "I like being this far inside you," he whispered. "Now, let's see how you feel around me when you come this way."

"Zander…I—"

His other hand settled over her mound. After slicking a finger in the wetness, he slid it over her clit.

At the exquisite surge of pleasure, her insides clamped down around him, making him laugh. "Oh yeah." His gaze focused on her face, like an inescapable light showcasing her very soul. "Hands on my shoulders—and keep them there."

As she obeyed the verbal restraint, she felt even more helpless than before. His arm held her leg up, his weight held her pinned to the bed, and his shaft was filling her so, so full. Instead of pounding her, he gradually withdrew only to bury himself in stages, rotating his hips to hit new places.

His finger slid over the tiny ball of nerves, around, on top, relentlessly rubbing one side, before bringing the other side up. Between his cock and his touch, every nerve swelled until she couldn't tell if sensations were coming from her clit or from within. Her legs quivered as her thighs tensed, her stomach tensed, her arms…

Sweat dampened her temples. "I'm going to come," she whispered, straining upward toward his teasing.

"Yeah, baby, you are."

"You come too."

His gaze was tender. "Right after, pet." He kissed her lips lightly, and his finger slid from one side of her clit to the other, sending her up, up, up.

As she hovered on the pinnacle for the most perfect

moment, she heard him murmur, "I like to watch you get off."

And ever so slowly he pulled back, until only the tip of his erection pulsed at her entrance. Staring into her eyes, he slammed in, hard and deep.

Oh, oh, oh. Everything inside her clenched around the intrusion, stopping the entire world before spasming over and over. The overwhelming pleasure seized her, engulfed her until her nipples tingled and her skin shimmered with sensation.

"Sweet," he murmured, and as he'd promised, his cock pistoned into her hard enough to hit the edge of pain, the edge of helplessness, before he set his forehead against hers. The cords stood out on his neck, his jaw was tight, as he let himself go, filling her with his heat.

CHAPTER FIFTEEN

In the gathering twilight, deVries surveyed the outside of Lindsey's duplex. Golden Christmas "icicle" lights hung from the roofline; red ones bordered the windows and door. The trees were outlined in blue. Multicolored lights ran up each side of the walkway. "Not bad."

Next to him, Xavier brushed dirt off his hands. "Agreed. The ladies should be pleased."

"You're not doing your place?" deVries asked as he picked up the tools.

"Abby requested some decorations outside; however, since you can't see the house from the street, we didn't do much. Thanks for using Abby's trimmings from last year—you made her very happy." Xavier glanced at the trees. "I did happen to notice there are more lights than she mentioned."

DeVries ignored the comment, because, yeah, he'd bought a few extra strands. He had a fondness for blue. And the trees looked fucking good. The whole place did. He'd never put up Christmas lights before—never had a house to decorate. It was surprisingly satisfying. "Let's get this stuff put away. Want a beer?"

"I do."

⸺◈⸺

In her kitchen, Lindsey poured a measure of vanilla into the fudge, inhaling the fragrance of chocolate. The sound of the candy bubbling blended with the strains of "O Holy Night" drifting in from the living room. "Now we have to stir—and stir—and stir."

"No problem." Finished chopping up walnuts, Abby took a sip of wine and gestured toward the hearth, where Blackie slept next to a Santa doll. "I love the decorations."

"I've been having fun." Scavenging and crafting required ingenuity. Keeping Zander from buying her anything she wanted took even more. She'd relented and let him buy a Christmas tree, drawing the line at decorations. Paper ornaments would look just fine. "Somehow I wasn't in the mood last week. Now..."

Humor lit Abby's face. "Amazing how a relationship can affect a person's spirits. You're looking pretty settled in, though. Are you feeling like San Francisco is becoming home?"

"Home? No, Texas is where I belong and always will be." She regretted her lapse when Abby frowned.

"Your ex is keeping you out of the entire state?"

"For now." Until certain people are behind bars. I hope. "You know, when I was little, I used to dream about living on a big ranch filled with cattle and horses and children. And a gorgeous husband, of course."

"Of course," Abby said in a dry voice. She took the bowl from Lindsey. "My turn to stir. It sounds as if your dream changed..."

"A bit." Lindsey poured more wine in Abby's glass and her own. The buzz of the sweet ice wine hummed in her veins. "I found I don't like cattle so much, let alone the fencing, culling, feeding, vaccinating and deworming and delousing, pasturing, and breeding." She frowned. "Same with the horses. I enjoy riding, but I don't want to do the work."

"That makes sense." Abby's face pinkened as she worked at stirring. "How about living in the country?"

"I did love that." Lindsey popped a walnut in her mouth. "Still, I love the city too. And how tolerant everyone here is."

"Mmm, I bet that's different, all right." Abby smiled. "I'm glad—I'd miss you if you left San Francisco."

"Me too." She really would; however, it didn't matter. "But Texas is home."

DEVRIES STOPPED OUTSIDE the kitchen feeling as if he'd

spotted an IED in front of his speeding Hummer. How had he not realized she still considered Texas to be home?

Maybe because he didn't think of anyplace as "home"— something he needed to return to.

She had family in Texas.

She hadn't talked about her people. Or her plans. Neither had he, but damned if he hadn't just realized he'd been making some.

Unsettled, he walked into the kitchen, followed by Xavier and the black pup. "Lights are up." He grabbed a couple of beers from the fridge and handed one to Xavier.

"All right!" Lindsey pumped her fist in the air in victory. "I need to see. But we have to finish the fudge first. Want to take a turn stirring?"

"Sure." He swallowed some beer before accepting the bowl from Abby. "I only have to stir, right?"

"Right." Lindsey gave the candy a glance. "It'll be a while. The shine has to go away."

"The shine? It's a liquid, babe. It will stay shiny."

"It's fudge, and it will change. Trust me, Oh-Enforcer-Man."

Knowing her ass was probably still tender, he swatted her and got a cute squeak. "Watch it, Tex." He drank in her giggle. He fucking loved her laugh.

"That reminds me, Enforcer-man." Xavier removed his jacket and set it on a chair. "Do you want me to stop drafting you to discipline submissives?"

DeVries stopped stirring for a second. "I'm not sure. We've never discussed it." *We.* Had a nice sound to it. He'd always figured being part of a couple would strangle him. Instead, the time with Lindsey was comfortable. Calming. Fun. He glanced over at her. "You got a choice in this too, babe."

She bit her lip. "Well…" Face flushed from the heat in the room, long hair tied up in a ponytail, wearing a flannel shirt over a tank top, jeans, and bright-red-and-green fluffy socks. Seriously cute.

"Spill it."

"I feel small-minded, but it would bother me seeing you touch other women."

Good. At least that was mutual, since anyone touching *her* would end up with busted fingers. "I'm okay with that. And men?"

Her lips curved. "I'd probably enjoy watching you beat on guys."

"All right," Xavier said. "Zander, I'll save you for male discipline and give Ethan or Mitchell the females. Ethan might be a bit too soft-hearted, though."

"Worthington is a nice guy," deVries said, able to acknowledge it now.

"I had a chat with HurtMe," Xavier continued. "And I referred him to one of the kink-friendly counselors in town. Apparently he wants a Master so badly he's misinterpreting what happens during a scene."

Abby nodded. "I think, now he sees it, he'll be able to get straightened out."

"That's good." Lindsey gave deVries an unhappy look. "In his case, I'd rather you—"

"I won't." Unable to resist, he handed Xavier the bowl and pulled her close. Her small body fit against his, and after a second of surprise, she snuggled into him.

Living in the moment was all very good. Nonetheless they were going to have a long chat about her future plans and Texas.

—◇◇◇—

Midweek, Lindsey stared in horror at the video playing out on her laptop. A younger Victor walked across the screen toward a barely pubescent Hispanic boy, like the one who had escaped from the ranch building. The child was blindfolded and tied facedown over a stack of crates. Crying, then screaming in pain as—

Lindsey's skin went clammy, too hot, too cold. As roaring filled her head, she swallowed convulsively, trying to watch, to finish, to—

Her stomach revolted, and she ran into the bathroom. And vomited again and again, endlessly, draining her strength, her sight, everything.

When the sickness finally eased, her clothes were damp with sweat, and her belly muscles ached. With a trembling hand, she closed the toilet seat and rested her cheek on her forearms.

How could she possibly have lived with the monster and been so blind to his evil? She swallowed again.

God, she was glad he was dead. She'd never get over the ghastliness of having shot him, but...she was glad he'd never hurt another child.

He couldn't—both the others still could. Rubbing her face, she attempted to set aside her wrenching disappointment. She'd figured out a password, opened one flash drive, and found only nightmare. She needed incriminating documents showing Ricks and Parnell were bad cops. A film of Victor raping a boy, no matter how horrendous, wouldn't help, except to show she had motivation to kill him. People would believe she'd murdered the police officer to escape arrest.

It would be her word against Parnell's, and he'd been police chief for a decade now. If she testified against the border patrol agent, she'd have the same problem. Agent Ricks was well established.

If only she could tell Zander. Keeping things from him—anything—bothered her more and more. Filled her with regrets for what they might have had if she wasn't in such a mess. But she was.

With a moan of exhaustion, she pushed herself to her feet. Maybe the other flash drives contained evidence she could use. *Please, God, let them not have more rape footage.*

Now that she'd hacked into a file, she knew how Victor had created one password, at least. He'd used his birthdate along with his middle name and a few random numbers. So she could restart the software to try variations on that theme. Unhappily the next success might take a long time.

Meanwhile, although Victor was dead, the smuggling of children into the United States wouldn't stop. Ricks and Parnell were still using her ranch for those crimes. How could she let them continue? Fear slithered like an icy touch over her skin. *I can't fix that—I can't.*

She had to try.

With wobbly legs, she regained her feet. The video didn't incriminate Victor's brother or Ricks; however, maybe someone watching would realize the crates were boxes of smuggled weapons and see more than the perversion.

If she visited an Internet café and e-mailed copies to the various Homeland Security offices in Texas—customs and border security and ATF, surely some official would pay attention.

Hopefully, not so much attention they'd trace her back to San Francisco.

She held her hands out, watched them shake, and heard John Wayne, *"Well, there are some things a man just can't run away from."*

There really were.

DeVries unlocked the front door of the duplex. Every time he used the key Lindsey had given him, his mood lifted.

Trust. Hell of a thing. They both had suffered shit in their lives, and trust didn't come easily. Nonetheless she'd started to let him in.

He smiled. And she was worming his secrets out of him in return. Sneaky little brat.

After tossing his jacket on the old-fashioned coatrack, he looked around. The house was silent. She wasn't upstairs or in the kitchen. He headed out to the backyard.

And there she was, kneeling on a blanket next to a flowerbed. The sunlight streamed around her, glinting off the cute green-and-red streaks in her rich brown hair. As a breeze swirled dry leaves on the patio, the wind chime swayed and tinkled peacefully.

He started across the grass. Stopped. The little Texan was jumpier than a merc who'd blundered into a kill zone. So, staying put, he cleared his throat.

She startled, and the fear filling her face infuriated him...until she really saw him and relaxed. "Hey." Her brows drew together. "Is it that late?"

"'Fraid so." He crossed the small lawn and squatted beside her.

With an oddly unreadable expression, she laid her palm against his cheek. "I'm glad you're here."

The naked emotion in the sentiment shook him slightly. She looked whiter than normal, he realized. He put his hand over hers and kissed her fingers. "I am too, baby." A seed packet lay on the grass. "Planting?"

"I thought I'd see how lettuce would do—it can pretend to be an edging plant and still give us salads." She'd tilled a line in front of the taller plants behind. "It's so pretty out, I wanted to get my hands in the soil again."

He ran his finger over her cheek, brushing off the dirt. "Not used to being a city girl, are you?"

A flash of sadness crossed her face before she smiled. "Actually, I like living here. At least while I'm young enough to enjoy it." She finished planting the seeds. "Having a backyard helps a lot. I hadn't realized how closed in I felt in my condo."

"Got that. I grew up in apartment buildings." He sat beside her on a corner of the blanket. Tipping his head back, he looked up into the sky. Light blue with a few misty clouds. Pleasant day for the bay area, and he wouldn't have enjoyed it without this backyard patch. "I didn't know what I was missing." A house and a bighearted, sociable, energetic, submissive woman to share it with.

"Really?" Her expression brightened. "You can share it anytime you want."

"Thanks, babe." Was that a timid way of inviting him to move in? Not her usual straightforward manner, but she hadn't quite returned to her previous easiness level with him either. Needing more contact, he bracketed her with his legs. Time for the first assault. "You get lonely, being so far from Texas?"

"From home? Yes." Her open joy faded slightly. Still, rather than pulling away, she put her elbows on his knees. Pleased the hell out of him she liked to touch and be touched.

So what was his competition back there? "Your mother still

in Texas?"

"Yep. Mama and Melis—" She broke off to correct herself, "and my sisters." With his body touching hers, he could feel her tense, a contrast to her light answer. "We don't have anyone else."

No one else. So, Melis-something. Melissa? Not many variations on the combination. Another item to include in his search. Tex answered to "Lindsey" so readily, he figured it must be her given name. Melissa and Lindsey. Tonight, he'd add the combo to the program.

Doing a search on a lover went against his personal credo. A pity she hadn't given him a choice. Dammit, wouldn't she ever let him in? "Who got your ranch in the divorce? Is one of your family running it for you?" And if she had property, why was she broke? Or here?

"It's complicated." With the noncommunicative answer, she tensed further before smiling. "No one would let Mama run a ranch. She has trouble managing a two-bedroom house. She loves us—God, she really does—but she's not exactly practical."

"At least she loves you," he muttered. Even though he'd been married before, he'd never experienced true loving. In a myriad of small ways, Lindsey had been showing what he missed. Like doing his laundry with hers. Turning on the front door light for him if he was late. Buying the brands of groceries he liked and adding in other "treats" she thought he might enjoy. Cooking his favorite foods. Always having his favorite beer in the refrigerator. Saving up news tidbits to discuss.

His mother had done those things for him...before his father died.

"Your mama must have loved you," Lindsey protested. Her fingers closed around his.

"She did." He looked away, watching how the wind chime glinted in the sunlight. "And then she didn't." Her love had disappeared into the vacuum of a drug-driven life. "I knew she'd stopped when I was ten, and she sold me to get money for a fix."

Lindsey's mouth dropped open, and she snarled, "That *bitch*." When her hand fisted, damned if he didn't smile. Given the chance, his little submissive would probably start a knockdown fight.

Only Lindsey could make him smile when talking about his mother. "Easy, Tex." He pried her fingers open. "I ran. Ended up in foster care, which wasn't fun but was better than that."

When he heard her growl under her breath, he couldn't help but lean back, pull her on top, and kiss her until she forgot his past, her past, and they could both think about the present. The future would have to wait for a little while.

⋘⋙

Where the hell did Lindsey keep her stamps? Friday afternoon, DeVries glanced at his watch and scowled. Simon would arrive any minute.

DeVries sure wasn't pleased with the crazy transportation arrangements the women had arranged for the weekend at Serenity. That morning, Lindsey had picked up Dixon and Rona at the Demakis offices. The three had wanted to leave early to sightsee in Yosemite Park. Since deVries and Simon had work to finish up, they'd ride together.

He'd left the office thinking he was finished. Unfortunately, once home, he remembered paperwork he'd worked on here last night. It needed to go out today. If he could find a fucking stamp.

He detoured to the kitchen to open a red candy tin and grab a hunk of Lindsey's fudge. He'd never understand women and their addiction to chocolate, but this shit was damn good. A shame she'd given most of it away to her favorite shelters. She'd taken another big tin to drop off for Mrs. Martinez when she picked up Rona and Dixon.

The girl liked her holidays. She'd talked him into helping decorate the pine tree. He'd managed to win the Christmas music war, so it was Ella Fitzgerald instead of Willie Nelson. Papier-mâché angels dangled in front of the kitchen window. The fireplace boasted the red felt stockings she'd sewn, and handmade cards from women and children at the shelters the mantel. The rooms smelled of pine and chocolate.

The delight she took in creating a holiday atmosphere made him feel odd. Maybe because he was enjoying it.

She'd giggled like a maniac when he gave her a fleecy tan

hoodie with teddy bear ears on the hood. Later, she'd rewarded him by wearing only the hoodie while they'd watched TV.

Focus. He was supposed to be looking for stamps. He frowned. Probably in her desk. He went through the top drawer. Pens, pencils, scissors, brightly colored paper clips. The next drawer looked as if she'd locked it, but the wood was so warped a firm jiggle opened it. He found envelopes and stationary. Getting close. Beneath them were...printouts of newspaper clippings? He frowned at the heading for a San Antonio daily. Wasn't she from Dallas?

Expecting to see graduation, wedding, or birth announcements, he realized the first article was about a woman who shot her husband. The responding officer was murdered by Lindsey Rayburn Parnell, the rancher's wife.

Fuck. Yesterday, his search program had returned a hit for sisters named Lindsey and Melissa. Both born with the surname *Rayburn*.

A cop murdered? Feeling as if he'd been punched in the gut, he sank down into the desk chair. This was the secret Lindsey had been hiding? "No," he muttered. No fucking way would she have killed anyone.

He dug through more of the clippings. One article insinuated the wife had been screwing a ranch hand. She and her husband fought, and she killed him. Maybe...maybe that scenario was possible. Not that she'd cheat. However if this was the pedophile husband, he deserved to die. So maybe she'd killed him.

He couldn't visualize any circumstance where she'd murder a cop.

One clipping showed the murdered officer. Uniform bright and shiny. Idealistic. Probably younger than Lindsey. The girl couldn't have hurt someone like that.

Piece by piece he went through the papers and found she had extensive background information about the police force in a small Texas town, the border patrol, and an agent named Ricks. She had e-mail addresses for ICE—Immigrations and Customs. What the fuck was she doing?

At the bottom, he found articles on password recovery and breaking into encrypted files. No reason for a little social worker to be reading those—not unless she wanted to hack into something.

His jaw was clenched tight as he shoved the clippings back in the drawer and shut it with a frustrated slam. She was in some seriously bad shit. And she'd damned well have to accept his help.

Babe, we're going to have a chat. About everything.

The next drawer yielded a stamp. And he heard a car stop outside. Simon had arrived.

At the Hunt brothers' Serenity Lodge in the mountains near Yosemite National Park, Lindsey stepped out of her rustic cabin and stopped to stare. After living in the misty bay area, the starkness here was visually astonishing. She was surrounded by a forest of black tree trunks and snow. Above them, the gray granite tops of the lower mountain ranges worked up to pristine white peaks.

"Brrrr." Pulling her coat more tightly around her, she headed down the narrow footpath toward the main lodge. Hopefully Zander would be here soon. There wasn't anything planned for tonight, and she looked forward to a quiet evening beside the fire with their friends. Tomorrow would be more exciting—a dungeon party.

She spotted Simon going into the adjacent cabin. "You're here already?"

In the room behind him, Rona was shaking out a pair of pants from his suitcase.

He turned. "We're just arrived. Did you get settled in?"

"Yep." How many men could wear tailored clothing and still look perfectly at home in the wilderness? Only Simon. "I'm fixin' to get something to eat in the lodge and talk Rebecca into letting me hold Ansel."

Lindsey hadn't seen the baby since he was born. Being the overprotective type, Xavier had insisted Rebecca have her baby in San Francisco where hospitals were available. To Rebecca's annoyance, her husband, Logan, had heartily agreed. "Did you lose Zander on the way here?"

"He stopped down at the lodge to use Logan's landline for a call."

"Oh. Okay." She'd already discovered her cell phone had no signal, and only a few of the cabins had a landline. "See y'all in a bit." Lifting a mittened hand, Lindsey trudged her way down the mostly cleared path. Although the light snow from earlier in the day crunched under her boots, her feet stayed warm. Thank goodness secondhand stores could provide footwear, a hooded jacket, and mittens. To her delight, the knife sheath Zander had given her fit inside the snow boots.

Even better, with such good deals, she'd had enough money left to visit the mall and purchase the virgin-slut nightgown she'd wanted so badly. Zander would have a treat one night, especially since he'd gotten used to her wearing his flannel shirts.

The forest trail opened into a wide clearing. To the left was the two-story lodge, on the right was the road leading in, and at the far end, the parking area was half-concealed behind evergreen bushes. She detoured there to give her car a quick glance. Crime in such an isolated place was doubtful, but she still felt nervous.

Being uneasy at getting too far from evidence that might save her skin, she'd taken the flash drives from the fake smoke detector and hid half behind the car stereo, the other half inside the taillight area.

She gave the parking lot a careful scrutinizing. Everything looked fine, so she retraced her steps back to the log building.

In the lodge, Zander was standing beside the reception desk, talking on the phone. When she moved toward him, his eyes narrowed, and he gave her a long, somewhat uncomfortable perusal—almost as if he'd never seen her before. At last he smiled and held out his hand.

Lindsey went up on tiptoe to press a kiss to his jaw before nodding at the man sitting behind the desk.

Logan Hunt owned Serenity Lodge with his brother. Steel-blue eyes, small scar below his left cheekbone, face wind-and-sun darkened. Over six feet and all muscle, he had the same military bearing and indomitable aura as Zander.

Logan's gaze ran down her body in an impersonal assessment and with enough power to remind her he was a well-known Dom in the area. "You dressed for cold. Good job."

"Thank you." She looked around. The room held several sitting areas with leather couches, dark red upholstered armchairs, and colorful rag rugs. A stone fireplace contained a roaring fire. On the mantel were carvings of wolves so realistic she could almost hear them howl. The far end had card tables in front of a wall of books and games. "Is Becca here?"

"She hoped you'd come over early. She's in the kitchen." He nodded toward a door on the left near the back.

"Got it."

The country-size kitchen was fragrant with the scent of baking bread. Like Lindsey, Rebecca liked to bake, and last summer, they'd spent time exchanging their favorite old-fashioned recipes.

"Hey, you." Rebecca held up a wooden spoon in welcome. She was browning hamburger in a skillet on the stove. "I'm making shepherd's pie for your first night here."

"Sounds perfect." She spotted colorful Christmas cookies on a plate and, when Becca nodded, helped herself to one. Santa with sprinkles—who could resist? "I haven't seen Jake or Kallie yet. Aren't they here?" Logan's brother and his wife had a house behind the lodge.

"Kallie lost a bet to her cousins and had to make a supply run to Modesto. Jake went too, since he's giving her a surprise night on the town." Becca grinned. "He likes to remind her she's a pretty woman, so he had me pack her a suitcase of hot-night-out sexy clothes."

"Now there's a Dom for you," Lindsey said. Since Kallie had been raised with boys, she tended to dress like them.

"Oh, he so is. They'll be back tomorrow in time for the dungeon party."

"Good." Lindsey swallowed the last of the cookie and brushed her hands off. "Now, please tell me you have the baby here. I need some cuddles."

"He's always up for cuddles." Rebecca tilted her head toward a corner. A cradle swing held a black-haired baby with a battered-looking German shepherd nearby.

As Lindsey approached, the dog rose to his feet. No wagging tail. No doggie smile. Someone took his guard duties seriously.

"Thor, right?" She held out her hand for him to sniff. "Becca says I can hold Ansel. S'okay with you, buddy?"

After a minute, Thor relaxed. The tail waved back and forth in permission.

"Good." Lindsey lifted the baby out of his cradle. *Look at those dark blue eyes.* "You are totally going to break hearts when you get older, Master Ansel."

A tiny fist tapped her chin as the baby gurgled back.

"Isn't that the truth?" Rebecca said. "At least he will be able to have girlfriends. Can you imagine being Logan's daughter? She wouldn't be allowed to date until she was thirty."

"Ha. First she'd have to find a guy brave enough to ask her out." Lindsey cuddled the warm weight against her breasts, breathing in the fragrance of baby, and felt tears prickle her eyes.

"You okay?" Becca asked softly.

Lindsey bit the inside of her cheek to keep from crying. "My niece was this size when I left Texas." Emily was turning one in a couple of months. *I missed it all.* Homesickness felt like someone had carved hollows into her chest, leaving it echoing with emptiness.

Becca frowned. "I'm sure Xavier would let you go home."

Hell, betrayed by her own emotions. "I'm...staying away for now. Things were a bit riled up when I left."

"Your ex-husband?"

Lindsey kept her gaze on the baby and nodded. Guilt tightened her mouth. In her world, friends didn't lie to each other.

But her world had never included being accused of murder. Worlds change. She wouldn't give her friends the dilemma of obeying the law or betraying a friend.

"I want to meet that ex of yours." Zander's rasping voice cut across the warm kitchen like a chainsaw.

Lindsey turned. "Hey. Business done for the day?"

"Yeah." Mouth tight, he crossed the room with his predatory gait. He gave her a brief kiss...and stepped away.

Unease ran cold fingers up her spine at the way he studied her. What was with the odd stares today?

In her arms, Ansel kicked and chortled, obviously liking the newcomer. Maybe he too noticed Logan and Zander gave off the same dangerous vibrations.

Zander's face gentled. "Cute little mite, Becca," he said. "You do good work."

"I'd say Logan put more effort into it than I did. Ansel's nose looks like mine; everything else is pure Hunt."

Zander ran a finger down the baby's cheek—and the tiny fingers caught and held. "Tough bugger, aren't you?"

"He really is." Lindsey rocked back and forth. "What should I get a macho boy for his first Christmas? Maybe a rattle shaped like a hatchet or a baby bonnet Stetson?"

Becca laughed.

Ansel's fingers still clung, and Zander hadn't moved. What was there about seeing a big, powerful man with a helpless infant? Lindsey felt as if hands were squeezing her heart.

But Zander looked at her with an unreadable expression. "You're gonna miss your family next week. For Christmas, maybe I should take you back to Texas. I can keep your ex from bothering you."

"Hey, that's a great idea," Becca said, busily stirring the meat.

The hands squeezing Lindsey's heart clenched, flattening it like roadkill. No blood was reaching her brain. Go back to Texas with Zander? Lindsey forced a snicker. "Nah, I'm not sure Texas is ready for the war you might start."

"You think?" Zander said. "I guess, even in Texas, they'd frown if I murdered your ex."

His comment was like a dash of cold water in her face, and she barely kept from gasping.

With the baby still holding his fingers, Zander stared at Lindsey. "I'd hate to have the cops after me."

She couldn't control her flinch.

His eyes narrowed. "Babe, it's time for you to—"

"Here, Ansel, let's see how you do with a rattle." Her hands shook as she put Ansel in his crib. Were Zander's comments offhand, or did he know something? Did she want him to know anything? Half of her wanted to run, the other half to bury herself in his arms and blurt everything out.

"DeVries, ready for some shooting practice?" Logan asked from the doorway. "Simon's bringing your range bag."

"Lindsey and I are—"

"Lindsey, you're going to come?" Logan asked, jumping to conclusions.

Ugh. But if she went, she might avoid a discussion with Zander. She wasn't prepared to lay everything out. Somehow, she couldn't see him calling the cops on her. Unluckily that meant he could be arrested for *not* turning her in. *God.* Okay, go with, and once Zander was occupied, she'd break away. She wanted to talk to him—she did—however, she needed to think first. Somehow. "I don't have a gun, but sure, I'd love to join you."

"I'll grab Becca's revolver for you, sugar," Logan said.

Zander lifted an eyebrow before nodding. "Let's go."

Already in the clearing outside the lodge, Simon handed deVries a dark bag. "Joining us, Lindsey? Good enough."

A couple of minutes later, Logan returned and led the way up a trail.

Lindsey felt as if an internal blizzard had arrived, filling her bloodstream with ice. What was she thinking? She hated guns. *Hated, hated, hated.*

CHAPTER SIXTEEN

eVries studied the shooting range. Fenced-off and backed
up to a dirt cliff. Probably to prevent people and animals
from wandering into the field of fire. Inside the fencing,
various posts held range markers and were topped with head-size
metal plates. Along the firing line, waist-high stumps served as
tables. "Nice setup," he said to Logan.

"It works for small arms. We have a rifle range farther out."
Logan handed him a revolver, box of bullets, and earmuffs. "You
can start her with the .38s, and I have .357s if she gets
enthusiastic." Choosing a stump, Logan set his range bag down
next to it and pulled out a box of bullets.

Simon followed suit.

DeVries motioned for Lindsey to join him at the far end.

Well, his comments about murder had definitely shaken
her. Her face was still pale. He should have dragged her back to
her cabin, but...dammit, he wanted her to tell him voluntarily.

Think hard, girl. Make the right decision.

"Okay. What am I doing?" She straightened her shoulders,
looking sick.

"You know how to shoot at all?" She didn't like firearms, he
remembered, as he put the earmuffs on her.

"Uh-uh." She stared at Becca's Smith & Wesson lying on the
stump top as if it were a snake.

"Right. You watch me load and shoot this. I'll walk you
through it for your turn."

Becca's pistol should do well for her, he thought. She might find the pistol's six-inch barrel heavy, but the longer length decreased the recoil.

After loading and donning earmuffs and eye protection, he took his stance, feet apart, double-handed grip, sighting, breathing, moving precisely so she could absorb without him having to say anything. Slowly he squeezed the trigger. A high metallic sound gave auditory indication he'd struck the target. When the post swayed slightly, he realized the Hunts had used a car spring as part of the target construction. He glanced over at Logan and raised his voice to be heard. "I like the feedback."

"Me too. We put the springs in when we taught Becca to shoot. Instant gratification works a treat."

No shit. Enjoying the dinging and shaking of the targets, he emptied the S&W.

"You didn't miss once." Lindsey was wide-eyed.

Her admiration felt good—and made him feel like a fucking teenager. What was he, twelve? "Get killed if you miss." He wanted to take back the words when she flinched. What the fuck had happened there in Texas? Had she really murdered her husband? He wouldn't think a cold-blooded killer would cringe at the word.

Tell me, baby, so I can fix it.

"Here." After giving her the safety glasses, he handed her the pistol and showed her how to eject the spent shells and reload. The revolver was a good choice for a beginner—almost idiotproof when it came to loading. His S&W 1911 semiautomatic was his preferred weapon, but he did enjoy the heft of a revolver at times.

As she stepped up to the line, he adjusted her stance, enjoying the feel of her. Her sweetness. Dammit, if she'd murdered her husband, the bastard must have had it coming. And yet, there was the dead cop. "Ready?"

She nodded and took aim. Squeezed the trigger.

THE GUN BUCKED in Lindsey's hand, and her world fell in. Even as the muted noise hit her ears and the acrid stench of gunpowder filled her lungs, darkness closed, turning even the snow to black.

She could feel Victor's body landing on top of her. Hear his screaming. The gun bucked in her hands, the bullet hitting him with a horrible punching sound. Screaming and screaming. Her vision filled with red. Hot and sticky, Victor's blood soaked into her clothing.

His body pinned her down as he convulsed. His feet hammered the floor, and then nothing. There was liquid on her face. She pushed, pushed, smothering under his weight, under the terror.

Couldn't breathe.

Something stung her left cheek. Her right. Powerful hands held her shoulders and shook her. "Lindsey."

She grabbed the arm, holding on as the world disintegrated around her. "He's—" Her voice cracked. "He's dead. Oh God, Victor's dead."

"Open your eyes, babe. Look at me."

The hard-edged tone ruthlessly sliced through the blackness. She still felt the lifeless weight of her husband's body. She'd waited and waited for him to take a breath.

"Look. At. *Me.*"

She blinked.

Sea-gray eyes bored into hers.

"Zander?" She was on her knees, pushing him away from her.

His painful hold on her shoulders loosened. "Fuck, baby." He yanked her forward, hauling her into his arms, squeezing the breath out of her. They were sitting on the ground. Earmuffs and safety glasses lay nearby in the snow.

Snow.

This was California, not Texas. Not her ranch. She swallowed, trying to keep her breakfast down.

"What the fuck happened?" She knew the voice. Logan.

"Guessing a flashback." Zander drew her closer on his lap, enfolding her in strength.

"That sounded as if she saw a murder," Simon said.

She burrowed her head against Zander's shoulder. Red still hazed the edges of her vision, and shudders shook her until her bones hurt.

"More than just *saw*. She didn't react to us shooting. Didn't react till she used the S&W herself." His callused palm cupped her chin and lifted, forcing her to look at him. "You shoot your husband, Lindsey?"

She quivered under his hard words, his merciless stare, his unbreakable grip on her face—yet he held her to his chest. Relentless and gentle. A Dom's paradoxical traits.

Around them, the tree branches creaked in the light wind. The world was so still she could hear the thudding of her heart.

"Lindsey, answer me."

"I killed him," she whispered, turning her gaze away. But Victor's eyes stared back at her from a dark tree; red started to pool in the snow. A scream built up inside her, filling her ears, erasing the silence.

"Stay with me, pet." Zander shook her lightly. "Why'd you kill him?"

"I—*Why?* "He..." She saw the rifles along the side of the metal walls. "There were guns." She hadn't meant to shoot him. *The boy. Screaming. The pistol bucking in her hands. Blood hot, covering her chest.* "He wanted..."

"Fuck, she's lost in it." A stinging smack on her cheek. "Girl, look at me." Zander's sharp gaze pinned her in the present.

"I'm sorry. Sorry. Sorry. I didn't—"

His eyes turned soft as a morning fog over the bay. "You're doing good. Now, step by step."

She nodded.

"Back me up, Simon," he muttered.

"I ask and push; you comfort." Simon went down on one knee, facing her. His olive complexion and black hair stood out against the whiteness of the snowdrift behind him. "Lindsey, where did this happen?"

"My ranch." While Zander stroked her shoulders, soothing her, she said, "I told you—remember the phone call about a pretty boy? I went to the ranch. To see." As her shaking eased, as she did her best to think, she froze. What was she doing? She'd—oh *God*—she'd told them about Victor. Told them—

"Too late now, babe," Zander whispered into her ear. His stubbled cheek rubbed hers. "Get it out."

Simon was crouched in front of her, expressionless. She looked to her right. Logan leaned on a stump, arms crossed on his chest, gunmetal-blue gaze on her. She heard her voice saying the words, *"I killed him."* She'd dug her own grave; might as well finish burying herself.

They'd turn her in—they'd have to. A tremor ran through her.

Zander squeezed, reminding her she was on his lap. In his arms. "Spit it out. Afterward, we'll figure out how to fix it."

How to fix it. "You can't. I tried." Misery drained her hopes into the ground. Down and down and down. "They'll kill me."

He shoved her face into his chest, and she inhaled the wild clean scent of him, as if he'd been born in a pine forest. "Nobody is going to kill you," he grated out.

She clung for a moment, unable to let go.

"Let's go through this step by step, pet," Simon said quietly, and she raised her head. "You went to the ranch. What happened?"

"I drove there at dark, only I wasn't sure exactly where to look. *'Hey, Parnell, got a pretty boy for you. I'll stash him in the usual spot at your ranch.'"*

Like a book on tape, her voice kept going, reciting the movie in her head. "Victor's car wasn't at the main house. I found it at the old one." Knowing she was stalling, she tried to explain how the original ranch house was used occasionally for guests during hunting season. Victor hadn't been there or at the broken-down stable.

She walked across the flattened ground toward voices coming from the aged metal shed used to store broken machinery.

There was a high, muffled scream.

"You little bastard, hold still!" Victor's voice.

The door opened under her hand...and she froze. An unshaded bulb cast light over a young boy, barely past puberty,

206 | CHERISE SINCLAIR

lying on the concrete floor. Wrists and ankles tied together in front. Gagged. Jeans pulled down.

Victor stood there, unbuckling his belt.

"What are you doing?" *Her voice emerged shocked. Stupid.*

Somehow, Simon's black gaze came into focus—she was still talking, wasn't she? She said to him, "I should have run. Should have—"

"Tell us," Simon prompted.

His face dissolved as she felt Victor's hands grab her and throw her. "I hit the crates..." Her voice didn't sound real as she kept talking...

She'd slammed into a pile of wooden crates a few feet away from the boy. *Blinking, half-dazed, she stared around her. Ranch machinery had been shoved against the metal walls to make room for heaps of small boxes and the stacks of long cases. One crate lid was pried off, showing gleaming rifles.* "Guns? What are you—"

"Jesus, you're a stupid cunt. Why would I want a cunt like you when I can fuck sweeter meat? Like him?" He nudged the terrified boy with his shiny dress shoe and buckled his belt as he walked over.

Cold grew inside her. "Why?" *Her numb lips had trouble forming the word.*

"This place. Miles of emptiness right along the border."

My ranch? He married me to get the ranch?

He had. He smirked at her, so smug, his chest puffed up with pride. She'd kissed that chest. Kissed him.

Sickness twisted her stomach—and as she breathed in the snowy mountain air, she heard herself whimper. Zander's arms tightened around her. "I got you, baby. I got you." Warmth. Safety. Caring. She folded it in, made it her own.

"Go on, pet," Simon said. "Let's get through this."

"Okay," she whispered. "I said to him—to Victor— 'You're smuggling.' He jeered at me." Word by word, she continued, tracing the path of the nightmare she'd walked so many times before.

"You're smuggling." Somehow she had to get up. Free the

child. Find help. She couldn't. Her head spun like a dust devil when she strained to move.

Victor sneered. "Aren't you so smart when it's all laid out?" He reached behind him where his coat was draped over a crate stack and pulled out a pistol. "Drugs and fresh meat in, weapons and ammo out. Rake in the cash."

Her land had been in her family since Texas was settled. The Rayburn honor was polluted by this bastard. Anger flared inside her; fear clogged her throat.

He waved the pistol. "Guess I'm going to be a widower sooner than I figured. Travis'll find your body eventually. Your family's heard me tell you not to take long rides by yourself."

They had. And now she knew it hadn't been because he cared, but to keep her from blundering into the men doing the smuggling. She felt as if she were drowning in filth.

He never loved me. And she'd made love with the monster, let him inside her. "You bastard."

"Hell, you married me for my money," Victor snapped. "You just didn't realize I married you for your ranch."

As her words echoed in the air, beneath her, holding her in the snow, Zander went rigid. "Jesus, you *did* marry him for his fucking money."

She turned and saw his face.

Cynicism twisted his expression, filled his gaze with ice. Even while she sat on his lap, he was...distant. Gone. He blamed her. He actually thought she was as greedy as his wife. *Again.* His rejection seemed to burn through her, crisping every support beam to ash, letting the last few timbers fall around her.

"Lindsey." Simon directed her attention back. "How did you get away from your husband?"

She wanted Zander's arms—no, no, she didn't. She didn't want him anymore anyway. Not if he could think that. Yet losing him...hurt far more bitterly than losing her ranch, even her life.

As her skin chilled, she wrapped her arms around her waist. She was the sole support and comforter for her own self. Why did she keep forgetting that? "No more questions."

No more help. No more friends. And now, she had to leave.

Run. Start over…again. Another strange city. Buy a different name. Find a new job.

Don't ever try to find friends or lovers again. The future had turned dark, not from clouds on the horizon but from an engulfing blackness.

Zander wasn't holding her anymore. He was so distant, he could have been in a whole different county. She pushed to her feet.

Her legs trembled, but she could walk. Their old tracks would lead her back to the lodge.

"Lindsey." Simon had risen to his feet. "We need to hear the rest and figure out how to fix this."

She couldn't keep from looking at Zander. His face was expressionless, his eyes flat and cold, as if he'd never met her before. She wanted to kick him.

To cry.

The deadness inside her grew, a black hole sucking away all warmth. She'd move on again…to nothing. Why hadn't she just let Ricks kill her? "No need. I'll be gone within a half hour."

Zander didn't speak.

"Hey, *deVries*, thanks for believing in me." She burned to say more, to scream at him, but her throat closed with sobs instead, and she walked away.

The trail down kept tripping her as her blurry eyes missed seeing logs and rocks. Eventually she realized footsteps trailed behind her. Hopes rising, she turned.

Not Zander. Logan.

"Go away."

"Sorry, sugar. I'm walking you down." He didn't look as if he'd listen to reason or sentiment. In fact, he looked about as tractable as the granite mountaintop behind him.

Fine. Without speaking, she spun and kept going. At least anger burned the tears away for the moment.

"HEY, DEVRIES, THANKS for believing in me." The bitterness in her voice was a knife to deVries's skin. His heart.

Dammit, she'd killed her husband. Whom she'd married for money. DeVries felt as if he had blundered into a firefight. The thunder still hung in the air. He shook his head hard, trying to cast off the fucked-up shit in his skull. Forcing himself to not run after her was one of the hardest things he'd ever done.

He had to get his act together first.

He realized Logan had gone with her. That was good. Should have been him. Jesus, someone better shoot him for real. Guilt twisted the blade already stuck in his chest. How could he have fucked her up like that?

He couldn't hold back any longer; he needed to get to her. He pushed to his feet. His snow-crusted, wet jeans stuck to his skin, hindering his balance for a second. He started after her.

"You leave her alone," Simon snapped, grabbing deVries's arm, spinning him around. "You've done enough damage."

DeVries staggered back a step.

"What the hell is wrong with you?" Simon shoved him another foot.

"She got me by surprise—and I'm a fucking asshole." Unwilling to fight, deVries caught the next blow and held.

Eyes black with fury, Simon slapped deVries's fingers from his wrist. "She needed your support."

The blade dug deeper into his soul. "I know. I fucked up." Turning away, deVries unloaded the revolver and tucked it, bullets, and gear into his range bag. "I got to get down there."

"I'll bring Logan's bag. Head out."

Simon caught up to him a few minutes later on the trail. "Would you mind telling me what happened there?"

DeVries worked his jaw and forced the words out. "My wife dumped me to marry a rich dude. For his money. Hearing Lindsey did the same..."

"You don't know that. She told us what the bastard said."

"Simon, I think she did." The first morning, he'd asked, *"What did you do—marry for money?"* and her guilt had been obvious. After stepping over a half-buried log, he ducked a snow-covered branch hanging over the trail. "But dammit, money doesn't mean much to her."

"No. It doesn't."

DeVries sucked in a breath. "I had a brain-dead moment." From the very beginning, he'd found she didn't care about getting rich. In fact, rather than conning him out of grocery funds, she'd tried to convince him she loved mac 'n' cheese. Had told him the best accommodations came with pets—like the mouse in her kitchen. She hadn't wanted to accept a lower rent from her friend. Never asked him for anything. Hell, she had more pride than sense sometimes. "If Lindsey married the bastard for money, she had a hell of a good reason—and it probably wasn't for her."

"I'm pleased to see you're not a total moron," Simon said in a dry voice.

He deserved the reprimand. "Since the killing was self-defense, why's she running and using a fake name?" Why was she wanted in Texas for murdering a cop?

"Let's find out."

"Yeah."

The trail emerged from the forest and into the lodge clearing. DeVries headed down the winding path leading to the cabin.

They met Logan halfway there. "Here." He tossed Lindsey's keys to Simon—rather than deVries.

Ignoring the unspoken insult, deVries asked, "She see you take them?"

"Nope." Logan gave him a hard look. "Your head on straight yet?"

DeVries suppressed the urge to bury his fist in the man's gut. He'd earned Logan's question. "Got bit by shit in the past. I fucked up."

The muscles in Logan's jaw eased as he shrugged. "I can't bust you for something I've done myself. Thank fuck women are forgiving creatures."

"Is she packing?" Simon asked, handing Logan his bag.

"Not yet." A glimmer of a smile lit Logan's eyes. "I told her if she didn't get in the shower and warm up, I'd strip her down and put her there."

"If you manhandled Lindsey, Becca will poison your

supper," Simon said. "And Rona will help."

Logan chuckled. "I know. But it made a fine threat." He led the way back to Lindsey and deVries's cabin. "Do you want me there or not?"

DeVries considered. "She's been running for months. You block the door—let her know that's over. And you'll be one more ally when she realizes she's got to stop." He looked at Simon. "I lead. Step in if I overlook something."

Both men nodded agreement.

"You want a minute to apologize before we come in?" Simon asked.

He did—but he didn't deserve it. "I fucked up in front of you; I can man up and grovel there too."

Logan barked a laugh.

Simon used the keys to open the door and handed them to deVries.

Lindsey stood in the center of the room. Still dressed. Shivering slightly. He'd bet she turned on the shower to fool Logan and never undressed. She saw deVries and took a step back. "Get out!"

He set his range bag down. When he walked forward, the speed with which she retreated hurt his heart. God, he was an asshole.

Her back bumped into the wall. "Go away."

"No." He braced his palms on the logs on each side of her shoulders, trapping her and hopefully ensuring she'd listen. "Lindsey, I'm sorry. I fucked up."

"Get—what?" Her brown eyes flickered up to his before she looked away.

"I heard the 'married for money' business, and my own shit buggered my mind. But"—he leaned his forehead against hers, his lips almost touching—"I know you. If you married him for money, you had a fucking good reason."

Her breathing hitched. "You don't think I'm a...a whore?"

God, he should be horsewhipped for giving her any cause to believe he wasn't in her corner. "Not even close. Can you forgive me for taking a minute to get my head out of my ass?"

Tears swam in her brown eyes.

"Fuck, don't cry." She was going to bust his heart open.

She swiped her arm over her eyes and huffed. "You're a sadist. You like tears."

He kissed her damp cheek, tasting the salt. "Not this kind. Never this kind." The tightness in his chest loosened when she let him gather her in. He molded her against him, feeling as if he'd climbed out of the fog into the sunlight. Soft and sweet. Logan was right. Thank fucking God good women were forgiving.

Unable to release her for long minutes, he cuddled her. Her breathing hitched a few times as if she held back sobs—tough Texan—and finally, he felt the stiffness ease from her small frame.

With a feeling of loss, he pulled away. Jesus, he didn't want to do this, to drag her into reliving a nightmare. A man fought to keep his woman from unhappiness. And he couldn't this time. He inhaled a measured breath and checked his control. "Now, let's finish this, baby."

She went stiff, brittle as glass. "I don't think so."

Stubborn little submissive. "I do."

With a shove hard enough to knock him away, she ran, then realized Logan blocked the door. She skidded to a halt. Her eyes widened at the sight of Simon in a chair beside the small wood stove.

She spun to face deVries. "This is none of your business. I won't talk about it."

"Yeah, it is. Yeah, you will." His toy bag was still on the bed, so he took out two short lengths of rope. When he walked toward her, she retreated...right into Simon.

Simon pulled her onto his lap and held her forearms out to deVries.

"No!" She struggled...halfheartedly. Her fear was obvious, but she needed help and deep down, she knew it.

"No more running, pet. That option is gone," he said gently. With one segment of rope, he tied her wrists together and used the second length on her ankles. The ropes would drive home that escape wasn't possible. "You're going to let us help you."

He scooped her up, holding her firmly. Mercilessly.

Surrounded by Doms, restrained, choices gone. Showing her subconscious had surrendered, she sagged against him. Right where he wanted her.

Cradling her gently, he sat on the low bed. "He—Victor—was going to kill you. What happened?"

Her level gaze met his. She'd lived a nightmare but wasn't trapped in it now.

"I've got you, baby. Share with me." *Trust me. Please.*

When she started to speak, he felt his eyes burn with tears. He'd stretched the bond between them, and yet it hadn't broken.

"Victor took a step forward, and the boy kind of rolled into him." She looked down at her bound wrists. "I don't know why—trying to save me or panicking. Victor stumbled back into the crates and dropped the pistol, and it slid a little ways. I was still on the floor, and I jumped for it."

Her hands fisted. "I grabbed the gun and rolled over. Victor lunged too, and he hit my foot and landed on me."

Her face drained of color.

"THE GUN WENT off." Her finger had been on the trigger, and Lindsey bit her lip at the memory, feeling the sickness return. The recoil of the pistol and the jerk of Victor's chest had been almost simultaneous. The blood splattered on her, even her face. His body had been half on top of hers, pinning her down. She shuddered.

Zander clasped her tighter. God, she loved him.

"I—" She regulated her breathing and found a smidgen of courage when her gaze met Simon's compassionate eyes.

"It was an accident," she whispered, "but...even if it hadn't been, I think I would have shot him anyway."

"Good to know you're not an idiot," Zander muttered.

Her gaze went to him. "What?"

"He'd have killed you and the boy. What part of that didn't you understand?"

"I—yes." His matter-of-fact statement smoothed the jagged

214 | CHERISE SINCLAIR

edges of guilt. "I called 9-1-1."

"So far, so good. And?"

"I untied the boy, and we...we kind of had hysterics together. Finally the police came—well, one. He'd been in high school with me. After checking things, Craig believed us. He let me go up to the house because I...needed...to clean up." Victor's blood had covered her face, her clothes. She swallowed hard.

"Easy, babe. I'm here." Her fingernails were digging into her palms. Zander uncurled her fingers and wrapped them around his.

"Okay." She concentrated. "I was cleaning up when I heard the chief of police talking outside the bathroom window. Victor is—was—Chief Parnell's brother. Travis had been to the shed and seen Victor's body. He was crazy mad. Wanted to kill me—to cut me up, he said." She felt the cold slide up her spine. *"...cut her so bad that even in hell, Victor will hear her screams. I'll see how many pieces I can chop off before she dies."*

"He was talking to Craig?" Simon asked.

She shook her head. "Another officer. They said Victor's death was a p-problem. Chief—Travis—is in charge of the smuggling. Victor worked with him."

"Oh hell," came a low comment from Logan. She'd actually forgotten he was there.

"He told the detective with him to kill Craig and make it look like I did it. They could dump my body in the river and tell people that I'd run."

Zander made a noise, a growl deep in his throat, and she stopped. "Go on, babe," he said.

"They'd say I killed Victor and later shot Craig, trying to get away. The ranch would be tied up in legal stuff, and they could keep using it."

"I stood there." She'd been numb. "Craig was yelling that the boy had run, and I ran to the front door and screamed for Craig to watch out. I heard the gunshots." *Too late. Too, too late.* Grief and guilt churned inside her. "If I'd moved faster. Yelled sooner."

"Wouldn't have mattered, pet," Simon said gently. "They

were his comrades. He'd never have believed you in time."

"How'd you escape?" Zander asked. His jaw was tight, his eyes furious. For her.

He was on her side. The relief drained the strength out of her.

"Babe?" Zander prompted.

"I hid." She managed a weak chuckle. "My grandpa was crazy. Paranoid. During the Cold War stuff, he made a hidden room off the basement to prepare for a nuclear war and Commie invasion. It gets ventilated through an outside pipe, has an old chemical toilet, and was stocked with ancient civil defense cans of drinking water and food. I hid there for a week."

"No shit." Zander cupped her head against his hard chest. "That took balls."

"I guess." She'd bitten her knuckles raw to keep from screaming. Not knowing who was around, she couldn't afford to make any noise. Day after day. Alone. Sometimes it'd seemed as if the floor was covered with blood. Sometimes she'd wake to see Victor over her or Chief Parnell with a knife. Each night, the walls would move in closer.

She managed a smile. "If I ever smell another can of canned lunch meat, I'll puke."

Simon shook his head, his expression holding only respect. "How did you decide when to get out?"

"My sisters came." The thought of them was like sunshine in the murk. "My car was still at the house. The police said I'd escaped—hitchhiked out or died somewhere on the ranch, but when I didn't turn up or call, my sisters thought maybe I was hiding."

When the door had opened, they'd scared her so bad she'd screamed. And had hysterics. "I told them what had happened and they…they believed me."

Simon said, "Anyone who knows you would, Lindsey."

Zander kissed the top of her head with a growl of agreement.

As tears filled her eyes, she blinked furiously. "I knew I'd have to run. And I hoped—I'd told Victor about the hidden safe once, and since he was using the place for illegal stuff, I hoped maybe he'd left something I could use. I found lots of cash in it and a case with flash drives." She shrugged. "I wasn't sure what the drives contained. I figured maybe evidence, so I took them."

"What was on them?" Simon asked.

"I couldn't read them. They're—"

"Encrypted," Zander finished for her. He half smiled at her startled look. "I'll explain later about my stamp hunt." He looked at Simon. "She's been trying to find the password."

She nodded. "With the money, I bought a fake ID in San Antonio, bought a second one in Chicago. And another in San Francisco."

Silence hung heavy in the room, like a snowfall, muffling all sound.

Without speaking, Zander untied her wrists, rubbing the dents out of the reddened skin.

Simon was frowning. "Why didn't you go to a different law enforcement agency to tell your story?"

She blinked, realizing she'd left a part out. "I did. I called the border patrol and talked to an agent—Orrin Ricks. But he worked for—with—the chief. It wasn't good." Tears rose again. "I—I don't want to discuss it."

As Lindsey stared at the three men, pressure landed on her chest, a massive boulder of realization. *What have I done?* By telling them about her crime, she'd made them...whatevers. Accessories. Knowing a murderer and not turning her in was against the law. "God, I shouldn't have said anything."

"What?" Zander snapped.

She wrenched around in his arms, taking his face between her hands. "You could be arrested for knowing me, for aiding and abetting a criminal."

His eyes narrowed. "You're worrying about us?"

"Yes, you dummy. They'll arrest you." She fumbled at the ropes still around her ankles, her heart rate increasing. "I'll just... I can disappear. No one needs to know I told you anything. I bam-bamboozled you and Simon and Logan. You thought I was a nice person." Her attempt to jump off his lap got her nothing except his grunt of exasperation.

"Babe, you *are* a nice person. And I'll turn your ass red if you try to run away again."

Tears rose in her eyes. She grabbed his shirt and shook him. "Don't you get it? They'll kill you!" She turned to glare at Simon and Logan. "And you two as well."

A deep chuckle came from Logan. "She's no bigger than a minute and trying to save our asses. I like her, deVries."

"Hands off," Zander said in a half growl. He drew her against his chest, arms over hers, trapping her in his lap. "Sit still, or I'll tie you up again."

A sob caught in her throat. They didn't understand the danger.

"Shhh," Zander said. "We get your worry. Now let us see what we can do about this mess."

"You shouldn't do anything; don't you understand?"

"That's not an option. But—"

"But," Simon interrupted, "we won't take any action without talking it over with you first. And giving you time to run, if that's what you need."

Zander's arms tightened until she couldn't breathe. At last, he relaxed. "Better not come to that, but all right."

Logan gave a brief nod.

"You agree not to run before we talk?" Simon asked.

Lindsey kept her gaze down as she rubbed at her wrists. "Agreed." What was one more lie?

"Good enough." Zander kissed the top of her head. "Why don't you finish the shower you didn't take? I'm going to talk to Simon and Logan, but I'll be right back."

"Okay."

She watched as the men left. Waited a full minute—and grabbed her purse.

Her keys were gone.

⋙∘◇∘⋘

DeVries approached the cabin—warily—because fifteen minutes before, they'd all heard Lindsey's scream of fury. Logan had shoved his hands in his jacket pockets. "Sounds like your pet discovered her car keys are gone."

At the moment, it had seemed funny.

Now, deVries was remembering how long the girl could hold on to a grudge. Prepared to dodge, he opened the door and stepped inside.

She didn't throw anything at him. With a quilt around her, she was sitting on the bed. Her face was flushed, and steam from the shower hung in the air. She gave him a look filled with misery before staring at the floor. "You should have let me leave."

"Not gonna happen." He sat beside her and laced his fingers with hers. She still didn't look at him.

Hell, she'd had a crap time of it. DeVries had been fucked over by a greedy wife; at least she hadn't destroyed his life or tried to kill him. After what Lindsey had endured, he was amazed she'd trusted him at all...let alone wanted to protect him.

He put a hand on each side of her face, forcing her to see only him. "Lindsey, we're going...steady." His lips twitched at the word. "Remember?"

Her head dipped up and down.

"That means you're mine. Mine to care for." He ran his thumb over her full lower lip. "Mine to fuck." He leaned forward, his mouth an inch from hers. "And *mine* to *protect*. Don't forget again."

"Zander."

Damn, the way she whispered his name tugged at his heart. "You're not in this alone anymore." He rested his forehead against hers. "In the military, you learn there's nothing like a team, having someone at your side, someone guarding your back. Let me help, Lindsey. Let *us* help."

A tremor ran through her...and finally she heaved a breath. "Okay."

Thank fuck. He saw the acceptance in her face. She wouldn't try to run again. "Good."

"But what am I"—she halted and amended—"what can we

do?"

"Simon, Logan, and I know a lot of people. Simon's taking point on making calls." He pulled her closer, pleased when she snuggled into him. "Did you ever crack the password for the jump drives?"

"Only one so far. And it was..." Her voice held revulsion. "Sick. Victor raping... Nothing incriminating for the bad cops."

Jesus, she'd been through hell. "You willing to give us the drives?"

"I...yes. They're hidden in my car."

"Good. Simon and I have access to stronger software-cracking programs than you used."

"I forgot to tell you. I already sent copies of the one drive to a bunch of Homeland Security offices in Texas."

"Good job. I like the way you think." Tilting her head up, he kissed her. "I got another question for you."

"Shoot," she said with a wry smile.

"In your fancy-ass condo, I asked if you'd married for money. You nodded. Turned red." He shifted his weight. "Kinda led to my knee-jerk reaction to what your asshole ex said to you."

Her mouth dropped open and understanding lit her eyes.

"So, Tex, mind telling me why you married Victor?"

She bit her lip before nodding. "That's fair. My sister, Mandy, had cancer. Her doctor thought a different treatment might work—only it wasn't approved by Mom's insurance company. None of us had much money—I worked part-time so I could be home with her. I was dating Victor, and he said if we were man and wife, she'd be his sister, and of course, he'd be happy to cover her treatment."

The asshole. "Got you married and indebted to him before you had time to think, huh?"

"Actually, he was making me uneasy, and I'd backed off. I usually have pretty good instincts, but when he said that, he seemed like a dream come true." Her eyes reddened. "I wasn't thinking too clearly at the time. The d-doctors didn't think Mandy would survive another year."

He tucked his arm around her shoulders, hoping to hell he was asking the right question. "How's your sister now?"

"Just fine. She starts college next month." Her smile turned radiant. "God, Zander, she's so happy and excited."

He'd asked the right question. And here was that Texas-size heart of hers. Fuck, she was something. He gave her a light kiss and studied her. "Is this the end of the secrets between us?"

She nodded.

"If so, seems like we should enjoy ourselves." Ignoring the way she clutched at her quilt, he yanked it off and tossed it across the room.

Her mouth dropped open. "Now?" Her nipples were bunching in the cool air.

"Hell, yeah." He started to push her down and changed his mind. She'd been pushed around all afternoon. Instead, he coaxed her lips open, teasing her, drawing her into the kiss. By degrees, enjoying every second, he kissed her until she responded, until her arms wrapped around his neck, and her firm breasts flattened against his chest.

Finally he fell back onto the bed, pulling her on top of him.

"Zander?" She straddled him, her palms braced on his chest.

"Your turn, pet," he said. "Take what you want."

She stared at him a minute, flushed with arousal, and delight filled her face. "Me?"

He nodded.

"All right!" When she tugged at his shirt, he lifted up so she could pull it over his head. His boots and jeans followed. Her lips, softer than flower petals, brushed over his chin, his neck. She varied tiny nips of her teeth with caresses of her tongue.

Fuck, he was going to die. He put his hands behind his head to keep from grabbing her hips and impaling her on his dick.

She licked around his nipples. Nibbled. Kissed the ridges of his stomach muscles, tracing them with her lips. Detoured down his arms and sucked on his fingers.

Her pussy dragged over his straining erection as she moved...downward...torturous inch by inch. When she licked the top of his cock, he barely kept from groaning. Mischief brightened her eyes. "Does *take what you want* mean I get to tie the big, bad Enforcer up?"

"Don't push your luck, Tex."

She actually giggled, and then her mouth closed over his cock, surrounding him in wet velvety heat. *Fuck.*

CHAPTER SEVENTEEN

As the crackling fire in the huge lodge fireplace exuded welcome heat, Lindsey curled against the couch arm and listened to Simon and Dixon talk. She couldn't seem to come up with the energy to join in. Ever since yesterday when she'd confessed her past, time had moved like a drunken armadillo.

Last night, the hours had flown by as she'd teased Zander until he cursed and took control. Completely. After they both got off, he'd exacted his revenge, bringing her to the brink of orgasm over and over, until she was begging mindlessly. When he'd finally taken her to their mutual satisfaction, he'd stayed inside her, watching over her as she fell asleep. She'd never felt so close to anyone. So protected.

But today had dragged interminably. After breakfast, Zander had taken the memory drives and disappeared into Logan's office to try to break the code. Simon had been on the phone all morning. Rona had slept late. Logan had been doing lodge-keeper duties. An elderly couple had needed to be checked in, a single lodger later.

Lindsey had wanted to run errands with Becca or go with Kallie to help with chores at the Masterson place. However, with Zander's overprotectiveness in full flood, he demanded she stay close, and she hadn't had the willpower to say no. Not after yesterday. She sighed. Another week and she'd be back to her normal stubborn self.

Thank goodness, Dixon had shown up, and the women had returned. Between him, the women, and the baby, conversation had been lively. Distracting.

After lunch, she'd started worrying again and had retreated into the main lodge to think. To *stew,* her daddy would have said. A few minutes ago, Dixon and Simon had joined her, talking around her, keeping her company.

How had she won such wonderful friends?

With a mild squeak of hinges, the door of the lodge swung open, and Lindsey opened her eyes to look.

A tall, absolutely stunning man in a sheepskin coat, jeans, and boots stepped in, paused, and crossed the room directly to their small group.

"Simon." The man held out his hand as Simon rose. "Good to see you again."

Simon shook his hand. "Stanfeld. It's been a while." He turned. "Lindsey, Dixon, this is Homeland Security Investigations, Special Agent Jameson Stanfeld." He smiled at Lindsey. "He's a recent transfer to California from Texas."

Keen gray eyes in a tanned face surveyed Lindsey. "It's good to meet you, Ms. Parnell."

Parnell. He knew her *real name.* Sheer terror impacted her chest, stealing her breath. He stood between her and the door…too close.

The man took a step forward. "Lindsey—"

Instinctively, she cringed.

"Uh-uh." Dixon jumped up and blocked his path. "Back off, sweet cheeks."

"No, Dixon," Lindsey hissed. The big man could crush him with one hand. *Shoot* him. "No, don't. He'll hurt you." Her legs shook as she stood. Seizing Dixon's wiry arm, she tried to jerk him back. Tried to step in front of him.

He stubbornly stayed put.

"Christ Jesus," the agent muttered to Simon. "They're both cute enough to die for and braver than many a soldier I've known."

"That they are," Simon said. "Dixon, listen. You don't—"

"Stand down, buddy." Stanfeld held his hands up. "I have no

intention of hurting or arresting your friend. Simon asked me to come."

All the strength drained out of Lindsey's legs, and she sank back onto the couch, pulling Dixon down with her.

"What the fuck?" From nowhere, Zander appeared—and stepped right into Dixon's place between her and the agent. His hand was under his jacket, on the pistol he wore in a shoulder harness.

"Zander, this is a good guy," Simon said, his voice relaxed and calming as he went through the introductions again. "Lindsey was a bit..."

"Lindsey overreacted." She managed to stand up. Leaning slightly on Zander, she held her hand out. "I'm pleased to meet you, Special Agent Stanfeld."

"Likewise—and make it Stan." He took her hand gently and undoubtedly felt the way her fingers trembled.

The minute Stan released her, Zander tucked her against his side. And she'd never been so happy to be under an overprotective Dom's care.

Simon resumed his seat. "I met Stan when Demakis Security provided protection to a model threatened by a serial killer. We've been friends for years now." He leaned forward. "I called him yesterday. Having come from Texas recently, he has contacts we need. This morning, he and I had a conference call with one of his Texas friends, a special agent in charge—name of Bonner. Bonner has quite an interest in you, Lindsey."

Riiight. I'm the woman who murdered her husband and a police officer. Bitterness filled her mouth. "I'm sure."

Zander gently pushed Lindsey down on the couch beside Dixon and set his hip on the armrest beside her. Staying close and staying mobile, she knew.

Stan took an empty chair directly across from Lindsey and leaned forward, resting his forearms on his knees. "You sent Bonner an e-mail attachment of Victor Parnell raping a boy."

The thought was enough to make her sick, but she nodded.

"Bonner had already been looking into your husband's and the young officer's murders. He'd noticed the investigation was somewhat…irregular, and after talking with Simon, he's very interested in knowing more. Since I'm stationed in San Francisco, I volunteered to drive here this morning and talk to you."

And arrest me too. Her hands closed into fists as despair started to weigh her down.

His gray eyes met hers. "Lindsey, did you kill the police officer?"

"What? *No.*"

"Didn't think so." He leaned back.

Wait. Wait. "You believe me?"

"I'm good at detecting liars." His smile transformed his face from stern to gorgeous, and she heard Dixon give a small sigh.

To her surprise, Stan's gaze shifted to Dixon with sufficient appreciation to send her gaydar dinging. The agent liked her Dixon? *Hold on one cotton-picking minute.* Dix had been through enough. Lindsey put her hand on top of Dixon's and gave the man a narrow-eyed stare as a warning.

He tilted his head in acknowledgment, and she had to give him props for picking up on her unspoken threat. He continued, "Bonner plans to interview your sisters, by the way."

Oh God, would he arrest Melissa and Mandy for aiding and abetting or something? "They don't know anything. They *don't.*"

He gave Simon an amused glance. "Like I said…"

When Zander chuckled, she looked up at him in surprise.

"You really are a lousy liar," Zander said.

She frowned. Should she take his comment as an insult or a compliment? "Well. Now what?"

"Simon told me the encryption on the jump drives from your husband's safe has been broken. I'd like permission to go through the information. Do I have it?"

Her heart skipped a beat. The last time an agent wanted those drives, she'd almost died. If he confiscated them… They were her only proof Victor had been a criminal. "I—"

He studied her for a minute before rubbing his forehead wearily. "Let's take a step back. Simon says you talked with a border patrol agent who worked for Parnell. Tell me about it."

She pulled her legs up onto the couch, huddling into herself. "I—"*I don't know you.*

"Lindsey, I can't reassure you unless I hear everything," he said quietly. His eyes were level.

Simon nodded at her.

Zander set his hand on her shoulder, holding her to the course and steadying her at the same time. She wasn't alone. "In San Antonio, I called the border patrol and got Agent Orrin Ricks."

Stan took out a pad and started making notes.

"He sounded like he believed me. And he was worried I'd get ambushed if I came to his office, so he told me to meet him at a safe house. The place was in a nice neighborhood, but I was so paranoid, I parked a few houses down. Agent Ricks let me into the house."

Stan frowned. "You didn't give him the drives?"

"I didn't have them. When I got out of my car, there were a bunch of men on the sidewalk—all in suits and ties and stuff." She attempted a smile. "I was so nervous, I left my purse in the car and ran to the house before I realized they were Mormons or Jehovah's Witnesses or something."

"Got it. So Agent Ricks talked to you?"

"He seemed nice at first. Professional." Tall, bullishly muscular like a weight lifter. He had narrow eyes, straight red-brown hair in a conservative style. Polite. Her mother would have considered him adequate son-in-law material. "He asked me about everything. Then he pulled his gun."

"Jesus," Zander muttered. His hand tightened on her shoulder.

She swallowed, remembering how the pistol had seemed so huge. How her skin had flinched away. "He called Travis to report he had me and that Victor had probably put incriminating recordings on the flash drives. During their arguing, he said he'd collect the drives from me, but it was Travis's job to dispose of me." She halted, unable to face the next part. So she wouldn't. "When I got away, I—"

"No, pet." Zander shook her shoulder lightly. "Yesterday,

you refused to talk about this. Today we need to hear it."

"But..."

His expression held the frightening combination of a Dom's sympathy...and determination. "All of it, Lindsey."

Even as she pushed at his hand, his command helped. She wanted to tell someone—needed to—if only it hadn't been so difficult. Staring at her fingers, she forced the words out. "Agent Ricks said since Travis would kill me, he might as well have fun first. He knocked me down. Kicked me so I couldn't breathe." Couldn't scream.

She had to stop and swallow back the sickness. "I fought." *But he hit me and hit me.* "He unzipped my jeans and..." The words wouldn't come.

"Go on, pet," Simon said softly. Yet when she managed to look up at him, she saw his expression was filled with rage.

"Before he could—the doorbell rang, and I could hear voices. It was the people who'd been in the van." She realized she was rubbing the scar on the back of her right hand. The big one. "When he put his hand over my mouth, I poked my fingers at his eyes, and he let me go, and I dove through the front window and ran."

Zander took her arm and pushed her sweater sleeve up, showing the scars. "Did glass cause these?"

"Uh-huh. When I covered my face, the glass ripped my arms instead." She paused. "I terrified the religious people. They were calling and running toward me. Probably to help, but I panicked. I ran and didn't realize till I got to the car that I was all bloody."

The sound Zander made was sheer fury. "Did you go to a hospital?"

She shook her head. "I was too scared. I used socks to stop the bleeding and went to a drugstore. Got a ton of butterfly strips and gauze and antibiotic ointment." She frowned at the scars. Did they bother him?

He ruffled her hair. "Smart girl. He'd have found you otherwise."

"Did Ricks give chase at all?" Stan asked.

"Uh-uh. He didn't even open the door. The religious guys

didn't even know he was there. Heck, they probably figured I was some druggie burglarizing the house."

"You've provided a pretty damning statement of Ricks's involvement with smuggling." Stan sighed. "I'll tell Bonner. And I can see why you're wary about agents." He stared at the fire for a moment before looking at her. "How about this—Simon will stay with me while I go through the evidence. Once I know what's there, we'll talk some more."

"I want to see what these guys look like." Zander stroked her hair. "Will you be comfortable if Dixon stays with you?"

"I'll let you beat me at pool if you make me a margarita afterward." Dixon bumped his shoulder into hers.

Dix was a terrible pool player. She gave a tiny laugh. "You're on."

—◇◇◇—

After beating Dixon at pool and mixing him a couple of drinks—and having some herself—Lindsey pushed all her worries into a corner of her mind. This might be her last chance to hang out with friends; damned if she'd spend it huddled in her cabin.

In the kitchen, Rona was sitting with Jake's wife, Kallie, at the long center table. Standing at the counter, mixing something, Becca said, "I heard an awful lot of moaning. Did Dixon lose the game?"

"He is one whiny loser." And he'd gone out of his way to keep her spirits up, bless his heart. A ton of alcohol was bubbling in her bloodstream. "What can I help with?"

"How about cutting up carrots for the salad." Becca started to hand over a knife and had it plucked away by Rona.

"I don't think so." When Rona pointed to a chair, Lindsey obediently sat. "Alcohol and knives—not a good combination."

"Maybe not for cooking." Kallie patted her shoulder. "However, from what Logan said you went through, I think you deserve all the liquor you can get."

"And we'll keep you company," Becca said, her eyes warm with sympathy. She held up her spoon. "Since we'll be playing in Jake's dungeon, make sure it will wear off by tonight. Perhaps a glass of Bailey's for now?" Receiving assenting nods, she poured three hefty drinks, and a smaller one for herself.

When Lindsey looked surprised, Becca nodded to the baby monitor. "Can't indulge much these days; probably not until he goes to college."

"It definitely puts a crimp in ever getting drunken sex," Rona said, amused.

"Logan mentioned you weren't playing in the main lodge anymore." Before Becca got pregnant, the Serenity Lodge had specialized in "special" parties where a swing or BDSM or leather club might rent all the cabins and take over the place. And last summer, Lindsey had enjoyed the dungeon party held in the lodge.

"Nope. With Ansel here, we're going mainstream." Becca grinned. "We can't use the lodge for play parties if there are non-BDSM people renting cabins. Like this weekend, besides the Dark Haven group, we have an older couple and two single men who've rented cabins—all vanilla-straight."

"The guests are why Jake designed a good-size underground dungeon when we built our house." Kallie waggled her eyebrows. "It's really well soundproofed."

"The parties are smaller, but at least we still can play," Becca said.

"It's a shame Abby and Xavier couldn't come today," Rona said. "I know they were looking forward to seeing the new dungeon."

"Lindsey." Logan stuck his head in the kitchen. "Got a call for you. Use the phone on the reception desk."

"Oh. Okay." Lindsey followed him out.

Sprawled next to the reception desk, Logan's dog thumped his tail on the hardwood floor twice to express his overwhelming pleasure at her arrival.

"Hey, Thor." She ruffled his fur and stepped past him. The desk held an old-fashioned landline with a spiral cord connecting the receiver to the phone. Logan turned the phone around so she could use it easily.

She picked up the receiver. "This is Lindsey."

"*Mija*," Mrs. Martinez said, her voice unhappy.

"Mrs. Martinez?" As Lindsey frowned, she saw Zander come through the door leading to Logan's private quarters upstairs. Logan stepped to his side, talking. Turning slightly, Lindsey returned her attention to her call. "What's wrong?"

"I got a call from your neighbors. They still had our office phone as your contact number."

Oops. She'd never updated her information, had she? "Is there a problem?"

"The police were at your duplex."

"*Police?*" At her raised voice, Logan and Zander looked up.

Putting his arm around Lindsey, Zander squeezed her closer, his ear next to hers so he could hear.

"Yes. Someone broke in," Mrs. Martinez said. "They went through your belongings and damaged some things."

"Burglars? I don't have valuables..."

"Waldo and Ernesto weren't sure. They didn't think anything was stolen except for your laptop—unless you took it with you. Not the television or your jewelry."

"No, I left the laptop there." A chill swept over Lindsey although the lodge door was closed. Her pretty little duplex damaged. Her home. A cold knot grew in her belly as the realization slammed into her. She'd been found. Her lips were numb as she forced herself to stand, to talk. "Do the police want me to go in?"

"Waldo talked with them. I talked with them. So the police say you can call them when you return."

"Okay." She couldn't go back to San Francisco. She made her lips curve into a smile. "Good thing I bribed you with Christmas candy, huh?"

"And excellent candy it was. I barely managed to keep my new son-in-law from eating it all. I'll talk with you Monday, mija."

She was a rabbit, wolves closing in, trapping her. Ready to rip her to shreds. Parnell and Ricks knew she lived in San Francisco. Her hand shook uncontrollably as she hung up the phone. *God, what am I going to do?* She stared at the desk, fighting the desperate urge to run to her car and just...drive.

Inside, a voice was shrieking *run, run, run.*

When she tried to flee, an arm tightened around her waist. "No!" She spun and shoved—Zander. "Oh God, I'm sorry. What am I doing?"

"Panicking, I'd say." He held his arms out, and she buried herself in his embrace.

"They found me." Shivers coursed through her as she whispered, "I'm so scared."

"I'm here, babe." He kept her tucked to his side as he turned toward the door behind the desk. "Meeting's already started. Let's give them a briefing."

Upstairs in Logan's kitchen, Lindsey filled a glass of water while Zander updated the others on the phone call. By the time she'd emptied the glass, she felt steadier. Quietly, she took a seat between Simon and Zander. Jake, who apparently had been briefed, sat on the other side with Special Agent Stanfeld. Logan leaned against a counter.

"So they discovered you're living in San Francisco," Stan said.

"Guess so." Lindsey worked to make her voice firm. "I don't know how they found me."

"Probably me," Zander said. "I ran searches on you when you started working for Simon." His mouth tightened. "I set off another a few days ago—for Lindsey and Melissa combinations—and found Lindsey Rayburn."

"Oh my God, seriously?"

"Yeah."

"Where's my favorite castration knife when I need it," she muttered.

A dimple appeared in his cheek. "Ouch." He set one hand over hers—over the fist she'd made—and squeezed her shoulder. "I wasn't worried about protecting your identity, so I didn't hide my tracks. Sorry, Tex."

After a second, she sighed. She *had* been lying, after all. He'd been upfront that he intended to protect Simon from her scheming ways. It might be a tad bit unfair to geld him when he was there supporting her. "S'okay."

Moving on. She looked at Stan. "Now what?"

He shifted in his chair, looking uncomfortable. "The flash drives contain enough evidence to arrest Ricks and Parnell for smuggling. Unfortunately, nothing there connects them to the two murders." He frowned. "It will be your word against theirs, and I daresay they cleaned up after themselves. The coroner in your town isn't particularly competent, and when he released the bodies, both were cremated. We're trying to find the boy, but…either Parnell got him or he joined the thousands of illegals in the area."

"What are you saying?"

"I'm saying nothing completely clears *you* of the murder charges. The police chief, especially, can muddy the water enough to leave you hanging for quite a while."

Lindsey felt the blood drain from her face. He meant they'd arrest and jail her. She'd have to go to trial.

Zander slung his arm around her shoulders.

"What can I do?" she asked.

"They didn't find the drives when they searched your duplex." Stan rubbed his cheek, frowning. "So once you're home, one of them is going to come after you. Probably both. They'll have your place staked out in hopes of grabbing you."

"You don't think they'd hire someone?" Jake asked. His lean face was hard, blue eyes angry. "Contract her murder out?"

"Doubtful," Stan said. "Ricks knows about the flash drives. Neither of them will rest easy until the evidence is destroyed— and I doubt they'll trust the other guy to do it. They'll have to be here in person to get her to hand over the drives. They won't kill her until they have it."

"You want me to be your bait," Lindsey said steadily. This felt like a really, really bad television show. "To wear a wire so they can incriminate themselves."

"Exactly."

"No," Zander said flatly.

Stan stared. "What?"

"Not fucking happening. We're not going to use her. Find another way to get the evidence." Zander's jaw looked like granite.

"We're not going to use her." Did he just say that? Lindsey stared at him, a shivery sense of wonder filling her.

"This is the best way," Stan said. "We can protect her."

"Fuck, you can't keep that promise for sure." Zander crossed his arms over his chest. "They'll know I've been with her. I can contact them. Blackmail them so they'll come after me."

"We're not going to use her." He wanted to risk his life to keep her safe. Her heart felt as if he'd enclosed it in his strong hands. Her eyes filled with tears as she turned and put her fingers on that hard, hard jaw.

He looked down at her. "Don't bother to argue with me, girl. This is—"

"I love you." The words spilled from her like a river spilling over a dam. "I love you so much."

His face went blank. Oh God, what had she said? But the damage had been done. Now he'd run. He'd…

With a groan, he lifted her into his lap, holding her so tightly she couldn't draw a full breath. As she buried her face in his neck, his chest rose and fell. "Fuck, I love you too," he muttered into her hair.

Around her, the men spoke in low tones. A door opened and closed, and there was only silence in the kitchen and only Zander's arms loosening far enough so he could kiss her senseless.

CHAPTER EIGHTEEN

"*I love you so much.*" Over the past few hours, through the end of the meeting, to the dinner with everyone gradually relaxing, to showering and getting ready for the dungeon, deVries had held those words close.

After locking the cabin, he joined Lindsey on the path. The moonlight shone on her face—and didn't come close to the glow she radiated.

Fuck, he'd never felt this way about anyone before, and he could almost be grateful to his ex-wife for leaving him. For letting him be free to discover how different love felt if trust was there. If the caring went both ways.

When Lindsey smiled at him, he bent to take another kiss before setting off with her down the path.

Jake's two-story cabin was well back into the forest behind the lodge. Jake had mentioned that he'd planned to build closer, but he and Kallie had opted for privacy instead.

On the covered porch, deVries tapped on the door.

Kallie opened the door, already dressed in a corset and short red skirt. "Hey, guys. Right on time." She took their coats and hung them in the entry closet. "So...the rules are pretty much the same as at Dark Haven. The dungeon safeword is red." She stepped around the massive cat sitting beside the basement door.

"Wow," Lindsey said. "If people don't obey the rules, the cat gets them, right?"

DeVries eyed the beast warily. The damn thing looked almost like a bobcat.

"Absolutely. Mufasa has no pity, trust me." Grinning, Kallie led the way down the flight of stairs. "Jake and Logan are the dungeon monitors—whichever of them isn't busy at the time."

The staircase opened up into a basement dungeon, where Nine Inch Nails was playing on the sound system. Was rather nice that the Hunt brothers preferred the old BDSM classics.

Jake had done some good work on the place. The walls were constructed of stone with matching pillars running down the center of the room. The iron wall sconces held candle-shaped lights, and a fire burned in a river-rock fireplace so the lighting was pleasantly ominous.

St. Andrew's crosses stood at either end of the floor. The low exposed beams boasted heavy bolts with conveniently placed chains. The rest of the equipment included a leather-covered spanking bench and a bondage table.

"It's exactly the way I'd think a real dungeon would be," Lindsey whispered, stepping closer to him. "Scary."

Fuck, she was cute. He slid an arm around her shoulders and whispered, "It's going to get scarier, pet."

Her eyes rounded.

Oh yeah, this would be a good night. He intended to drive her out of her head and give her a break from worrying.

Across the room, Jake laid out implements beside the spanking horse while Logan talked to Virgil Masterson, Simon, and Rona.

"Where are Summer and Becca?" Lindsey asked, looking around for the rest of the submissives.

"They're taking care of Ansel upstairs. Becca will be down soon, and I'll trade places with Summer later." Kallie wrinkled her nose at Masterson.

"Damn right you will, little bit," Masterson said.

DeVries kept his mouth straight with an effort. Since Masterson considered Kallie like a sister, he refused to stay in the same room when Jake was doing a scene with her. Good decision. It'd suck if the linebacker-size cop flattened Jake for making his little sis cry. Might be fun to watch, though. Both men were over six feet, in mountain-country shape, both ex-military. Be a hell of a match.

Over in a corner, Dixon was studying a human-size birdcage. DeVries gave Lindsey a nudge in that direction. "Can you keep Dixon company while I talk to the others for a minute?"

"But—"

At his frown, she quieted immediately. He kept his gaze on her, silently reminding her the evening had begun. The reins were in his hands. "Your task is to follow directions. To hear only my voice," he told her softly. "Everything else is my job."

Her gaze dropped, and a flush warmed her cheeks. Even better, the tenseness eased from her face as she gave control over to him.

Watching her relax to his will set up a fire inside him. They hadn't been in a dungeon since getting back together. This'd test if their new dynamic would work. Damned if he wasn't going to bust balls to see it did.

"Before you talk to Dixon, strip down." He pointed to shelves in a corner of the room. "Leave only your thong on."

Her expression held her protest; she'd be the only person baring so much. Too bad. If he liked seeing her exposed—and he fucking well did—she'd be naked. And after reliving all the crap her husband had put her through, she needed the reinforcement he found her pussy and tits as gorgeous as they were.

"Yes, Sir." Reluctance in every step, she obeyed.

He smiled. Odd how adorable a submissive was when she complied despite her own inclinations.

Once in the corner, she tugged off her boots and unstrapped the sheathed knife he'd given her. He hadn't realized she was wearing it, but...hell, he liked her armed, even though it pissed him off that anything, ever, should make her afraid.

When she removed her shirt and bra and glanced at him, he let his enjoyment show. Her hair was tied back, so he had a good view of her round, high, very sweet breasts.

Face flushed, she frowned at him, but after glancing at his crotch, the corners of her lips tipped up. Someday she'd accept how much the sight of her turned him on.

Joining the other men and Rona, he asked Logan, "Is this it

for the crew tonight?"

"Yep. We'd expected Ware with a play partner. A pity he ended up having to work."

Simon added, "The other two Dark Haven couples were unwilling to risk the storm. Last newscast said the blizzard has shifted, and it'll hit us tomorrow."

Hearing, Jake looked over his shoulder. "New snow will be fun. If you're up for it, I'll take you cross-country skiing after the winds die down."

"You're on." DeVries checked Lindsey. Had the Texan ever skied? He'd enjoy sharing with her. "You're keeping the lodge open this winter?" The Hunt brothers normally closed Serenity to spend winters in the tropics.

"We didn't want to take Ansel away from home his first year or two," Logan said.

"Gives Kallie and me more time to play with him—and start our own." Jake smiled. "And I can join her winter tours. Been a while since I went ice fishing."

DeVries glanced at Kallie. Amazing someone so tiny worked as a wilderness guide.

Jake's gaze settled on his wife, and his expression turned stern. "Tonight we're going to discuss you making all-male bookings without arranging to have me along." He dropped a flogger next to the cane.

"Jake," she said, taking a step back. "This is my job and—"

"Good plan, Hunt, but don't beat on her too hard. She has to feed the stock tomorrow." Catching a glare from both Dom and sub, Masterson smirked. "Yep, I'm out of here." The cop ruffled his cousin's hair and headed up the stairs.

Kallie's hands were on her hips as she confronted her husband. "I don't know why you—"

Jake put his palm over her mouth and calmly accepted the gag Logan handed him. "Gonna be a long night, isn't it? For you, at least, sprite."

Amused at the muffled cursing, deVries joined Lindsey and Dixon.

As a concession to the rustic atmosphere, Dixon had

foregone his normal flashy fetwear and instead wore a red flannel shirt tied at the waist, red latex shorts, and matching Velcro wrist cuffs. "Sir," he said with a dip of his head.

"That's more polite than when you called me a *'fucking asshole.'* The worry that appeared on the young man's face was satisfying. Good start to a scene. "I'm in the mood to beat on you. You up for it?"

"Yes, Sir!" Dixon bounced on his toes.

DeVries studied him. The boy was moving easily. Expression open. Since they'd scened together before, negotiation was a snap. "Anything new I should know? Sore spots, triggers, places to avoid? Additional needs or requests?"

"Nothing new, Sir."

"Strip." He pointed to a spot beneath two dangling chains. "Both of you, kneel there."

Anticipation was rising inside him. His plan was simple: dominate the two of them, inflict pain on the boy, tease his own little subbie, hand the boy over, play with his woman.

His cock went rigid as he tugged Lindsey to her feet and ran his fingers through her silken dark hair. After kissing her velvety lips, he molded her against him for a sheer erotic rush.

As he fastened wrist cuffs on her, he stroked her arms. Sturdy wrists—for a woman; compared to his thick bones, hers seemed incredibly fragile. The white scars on each arm pissed him the hell off. Ricks was a dead man.

No. He pushed away the thought. Tonight was for now. Nothing else. He crouched and buckled the ankle cuffs on her legs before nuzzling her soft stomach. She wore a light floral fragrance that didn't overpower the scent of her delicate musky arousal.

"Where do you want me to kneel?" The eagerness in Lindsey's eyes had increased with the addition of ankle cuffs. Recently, he'd discovered having her legs restrained flipped a nice little switch in her.

He smiled slowly. "Get in the cage."

"What?" The oval birdcage was constructed of black rebar rather than wire and hung freely from a ceiling chain. "In there?"

"Oh yeah. In you go." He braced the birdcage as she

reluctantly climbed inside the hip-high door. After she had knelt on the doughnut-holed leather pad, facing him, he said, "Arms up."

He hooked her cuffs together and clipped them to the cage top. "Spread your knees, pretty bird. And get comfortable. You're gonna be here for a while." He closed the door. Didn't lock it or chain it shut.

Designed for BDSM play, the frame had clamps attached to accommodate the two-foot-long steel stakes waiting in a container. He inserted a stake through a clamp and inward until the dull point touched her upper back, then secured it. He set another stake to press on the other side of her back. Now she couldn't move backward in the cage.

Two more stakes grazed each ass cheek. Her eyes widened when he slid the next thick stake in to dimple the outside of her right breast. He did the same on the left. "I recommend you don't do much wiggling, right?"

She shook her head.

"You've never seen a birdcage before?" He angled two more stakes to the insides of her thighs, ensuring her knees stayed apart.

"N-no."

He stepped back and studied her. Lips still swollen from earlier, cheeks slightly flushed, arms over her head so her breasts were lifted, showing the tight, jutting peaks. The dim light of the dungeon was enough to see how wet her thong already was.

Made him want to yank her out and take her immediately.

Soon. And by then he'd have her squirming mindlessly. *Yeah.*

"You start getting muscle cramps or get scared, you sing out, pet." To extract her from the cage, he'd have to flip the quick-releases of the four stakes in front and remove them. More stakes were in the container, but this was plenty until he knew how she'd react. Some submissives loved this kind of immobilization. Some got terrified.

That wouldn't be good. Problem was that with impact play, his focus needed to be completely on the bottom, so he might not catch it right away if Lindsey started to panic.

He walked over to Logan, who stood in the center of the room. "You monitoring now?"

Logan nodded.

"I'm going to flog Dixon with Lindsey in the cage. It's her first time there and being restrained with stakes. Could use some eyes on her while I'm occupied."

"You're splitting your attention?" Logan studied the two submissives and the area. The birdcage was within a few feet of the dangling chains. "I'll have Simon monitor the rest of the room so I can stick close."

"Appreciate it."

Problem solved.

He glanced at Lindsey, pleased to see the tenseness of her body. For the time she'd be watching, the stakes would serve as a constant reminder she was still under his control. Would give her small amounts of pain—which he'd enjoy—especially once he upped the stimulus for her to move.

He joined Dixon. "Now you, boy." Fisting the bottom's pretty blond hair, deVries yanked him to his feet. The boy gave a tantalizing yelp. "Arms up."

After lowering the chains secured to the rafter beams, deVries used panic snaps to secure Dixon's wrist cuffs to the chains. He considered adding a spreader-bar for his legs, but...nah, he was in the mood to watch some dancing feet. This setup looked good.

He stepped back and assessed Dixon. Too cocky.

Fuck that shit. DeVries blindfolded the boy's eyes.

Dixon's muscles tensed, but he took a calming breath and relaxed.

Good control, deVries thought...and waited.

As nothing happened and the seconds ticked by, Dixon started to tense up again.

Much better. How far could he wind the submissive up? DeVries leaned forward and growled in his ear, "Got all of your body to use for my target, boy. Best you hope I don't flog those fat balls of yours to ribbons."

Swallowing, Dixon edged his legs together, hiding his vulnerable parts; yet, as if dissociated from fear, his dick strained upward.

Very nice. This boy wasn't the type of masochist who found any and all pain enjoyable. No, Dixon felt actual pain at first and had to endure the discomfort to reach his goal of subspace. Was a hell of a lot of fun to push this kind of masochist up the brutally painful slope to pleasure. "Your safeword still the same, boy?"

"Frank-N-Furter."

"Might be amusing to hear you squeal that." DeVries ran his hands down the leanly muscled arms, over narrow shoulders, down his back. Sensitizing his skin. "Party safeword is red. Use one or the other if you need it."

"Yes, Sir."

DeVries stepped over to the birdcage. Lindsey hadn't moved. None of the stakes were digging into her skin too far. He studied her face. Her head was right here with him, nothing else on her mind. Perfect. Fitting his arm through the bars, he laid his palm along Lindsey's cheek. "All right?"

Her eyes were the melting chocolate color of the fudge she'd made. Fucking sweet. "Yes, Sir."

"Good." He jerked his chin at Logan, who was leaning against a stone pillar, gaze on them. "I get that you're not one to want to interrupt a scene, so Logan is there if you need him. He'll stay till I'm with you."

The relaxation of the muscles in her neck and around her mouth told him she'd worried. "Thank you, Zander."

Good. On second thought, damned if he wanted her too relaxed. He ran his knuckles over her firm little breasts and rolled her nipples between his fingers, increasing the pressure until she started making pleasing squeaks and squirming uncontrollably. Her movements pushed her into the stakes, reminding her of their presence. Reminding her she was trapped for his pleasure.

He could actually see her grow wetter. Fuck, he loved the way she responded.

Nonetheless, her turn was over. "Hang tight, babe. Next

time I'll pick on that pretty pussy of yours."

Her instinctive movement drove her knees into the stakes, and the luscious helpless sound she made kicked up his own hunger. Oh yeah. He wanted more of that.

As he returned to Dixon, the fire of need simmered under his skin. "I got an itch to hear you yell, boy," he said. "First I'll give you a bit of a warm-up so I can draw this out until you're sweating." He started in.

The sound of the flogger striking skin—no matter how lightly—increased his pulse and steadied his focus. Pinken that patch of skin. Avoid there. Make the sides match. Study the results.

Dixon's muscles were relaxed, breathing steady.

Gradually, deVries found a good rhythm. He snorted, realizing Dixon's ass was swaying to Combichrist's "Get Your Body Beat."

After a while, he moved to a heavier flogger. Added some caning for variety.

"Brace yourself, boy," he said. And he finished—for the moment—with three much harder throws with no break between.

The sheer force rocked Dixon forward each time. Hands fisted, neck bowed, Dixon breathed through the pain. His forehead and shoulders were damp with sweat, but the change in his expression, the glow, said he was moving into subspace. *Nice. Very nice.*

"Don't move now, boy. You stay still."

Dixon received the instructions with a submissive shiver.

While the boy finished processing the pain, deVries went over to the birdcage. "Pretty little canary. Gonna listen to you sing next."

Lindsey's gaze was fixed on him like a bird watching a cat approach. While he'd flogged Dixon, her breathing had increased, her cheeks had flushed. She was getting nice and toasty with excitement.

"How are you doing, babe? Can you last longer?"

Her chin came up. "I'm fine, Sir."

Well, hell, a submissive shouldn't say that to a sadist. Might as well shout *nah-nah, ni-nah-nah,* right? "Good to know."

He didn't intend to draw out Dixon's scene—he had other plans for the boy in mind—so he might as well fuck Lindsey's head up a bit now. He pinched her pretty nipples back to a dark red and stopped before she got too squirmy. "You're going to need to remember to stay still."

"Sure. Sir."

"Good for you." He smiled into her eyes and saw worry appear. She knew him well.

His favorite wand was in his toy bag. He added the nubby attachment. Plugged into the wall, the device fit through the space under the birdcage door. He clamped the wand in position so it barely…barely vibrated the thong covering Lindsey's pussy.

"What are you doing?"

"Making sure you don't get bored, baby."

Her hands fisted as the vibrations registered. She was already aroused, and it took only a few seconds before she wanted more. Her hips tried to move forward…and were stopped by the stakes. When she persisted despite the undoubted discomfort, he tsk-tsked and withdrew the vibrator far enough so she couldn't quite touch it. So she wouldn't be able to get off.

Her glare made him laugh.

As he returned to Dixon, he could hear the hum of the wand and her low moan. *Nice.*

He grabbed Dixon's hair and yanked his head back. "You sleeping there?"

The boy gasped. "No, Sir!"

"Good. Maybe you need some noise to keep you lively." He'd brought one of his single-tails—a medium-length one. Stepping back, he picked it up and gave it a quick snap.

As the crack echoed in the room, Dixon straightened so quickly his spine almost shattered.

"Got a problem with whips, boy?" Nothing had been on his limits list at Dark Haven.

"No, Sir." When deVries didn't respond, Dixon swallowed

244 | CHERISE SINCLAIR

and added, "They make me…nervous."

"Shows you're not stupid." The harsh sting would center the bottom's attention after the small break and steer him into the mind space where he needed to be. Afterward a hard flogging should take him up and over.

He flicked the tail over the young man's ass, his shoulders, down to his ass, and grinned when the bottom's feet started moving, his ass twisting, trying to avoid the startling burn.

"Good luck with that." He settled into an even rhythm, knowing it was counterbalanced by the erratic nature of the stinging impacts.

As the whipping continued, Dixon's shoulders relaxed, his hands opened. Heading into subspace.

DeVries checked Lindsey. Her face was flushed. The wand had done the job, and her muscles were taut with the need to get off. She was sweating, her face showing she'd reached her limit of frustration.

He met Logan's eyes, looked at Lindsey, and made a cutting motion. *Pull the plug.*

Logan nodded.

DeVries walked forward, grasped Dixon's chin, and lifted. "You holding up, boy?"

The simple touch and question made Dixon's mouth curve up sluggishly. Oh yeah, he was nicely into la-la land. "Sir," he breathed. "Yes, Sir."

"Good boy." As deVries returned to his work, he heard the hum of the wand die and the whine of Lindsey's response.

Crack. Crack. Crack. Dixon's back displayed a gratifying pattern of thin red lines. No blood.

Time for the flogger. A medium weight, deVries decided, with enough sting to remind the boy of the whip, enough weight to be thuddy, not so heavy as to break open the stripes.

Smiling, he moved into a nice figure-eight pattern, melding in the music, his heartbeat, Dixon's swaying with the *slap, slap, slap* of the flogger. He was sweating, enjoying the weight, the sounds of the blows, the sucking of air as the bottom processed each blow. Nothing felt like swinging a flogger.

In the corner of his eye, he saw Stanfeld. Right on time as agreed.

DeVries flicked the strands, pulling back enough that only the tips struck Dixon, giving him a new sensation.

Stanfeld seemed like a decent guy. Honorable. Honest. And Simon considered him a damn good Dom. Xavier and Simon had been concerned about the crappy Doms Dixon kept choosing. Tonight, deVries figured on handing the boy over to someone who was all Dom.

DeVries paused and jerked his chin up at Stanfeld.

Arms crossed, the agent had taken a position near the wall to watch. Stanfeld smiled slightly…and nodded.

IN THE BIRDCAGE, Lindsey couldn't take her gaze off Zander. *"Fuck, I love you too,"* he'd said. Over the past few hours, those words had run through her mind like an ever-spinning carousel of joy. After hearing of the burglary of her duplex and realizing Ricks and Parnell had found her, she'd hit rock bottom. Yet, this evening, she was ready to soar upward and dance like a happy star in the night sky.

"Fuck, I love you too." Zander never said things he didn't mean. His devastating bluntness did have a benefit. *He loves me.*

And I really, really love him.

Maybe a little less right now, though. *Damn Enforcer.* After the vibrator, her clit was so engorged and throbbed so intensely she wanted to scream. Trying to shift her weight, she only succeeded in making the birdcage rock. His stakes—like giant needles on steroids—poked her bottom and her back and her poor breasts.

The way Zander had reduced Dixon to a glassy-eyed, subspaced body seriously turned her on. Every time Dix hissed with pain, Zander's focus grew more intent, as if he was drinking in the sounds her friend made. If Dixon tried to shift his weight to avoid a blow, the next hit of the flogger would thwart him.

She couldn't help seeing poor Dixon had an impossibly hard erection. He was suffering as badly as she was.

Again Zander walked around in front of Dixon to study him.

"Yep, you're done." He flicked the flogger at the young man's genitals.

The yelp Dixon made was terrifying.

God, how could he pick on a person's privates—especially when all swollen up? Lindsey squirmed in sympathy. "Friggin' sadist."

Obviously hearing her, Logan gave an amused snort.

Zander gripped Dixon's jaw and removed his blindfold. "Look at me, pup."

Dixon's eyes opened and focused. "Yessir."

"You're about at your limit—but I could play with the flogger and whip for another hour." Zander's lips curved when Dixon strained to inch back. "We can continue…or I can hand you off to a Dominant who'll take the scene in a different direction. Simon vouches for him, by the way." He looked to the right.

Lindsey followed his gaze. Whoa, the Homeland Security guy was in the dungeon. He wore black jeans and a black skintight body shirt that showed off a leanly muscular body. He was looking at Dixon in appreciation.

But she hadn't had a chance to talk with him—not enough to decide if she trusted him with her friend. She frowned. Still, if Simon said Stan was okay…maybe it was all right.

Dixon blinked, stared at Stan, and blinked again. "I—I—I."

Sneaky sadist, Lindsey thought. Dixon sure didn't want that whip again. Since *Zander* had suggested the change in Doms, Dixon wouldn't look as if he were chasing after man-candy. She glanced at the agent. The Dom was definitely a gay boy's dream.

"Do you want Stanfeld to take over?" Zander asked.

Dixon's expression held both desire and worry.

I so understand. Lindsey'd been in that position. The first scene or two with someone unknown was awfully scary.

"Boy," Zander said in his grating voice. "Your play stays in here, nowhere else. Tex and I won't leave before you do. And Logan will keep an eye on you as well." He raised his eyebrows at the two Doms.

"Agreed," Stan said.

Logan nodded.

"Okay." Dixon went starry-eyed. Lindsey could understand why, since Stan was not only gay but also very, very dominant.

"All yours," Zander said to the agent and moved his bag to the other side of the birdcage.

Stan stalked across the room and stopped in front of—

Zander's body blocked her view. After opening the cage door, he curved his hand around her jaw. "You going to watch them or me?" Zander asked.

Oops. "Um, you, Sir." She could barely hear them talking—going over limits, she thought.

"Yeah, what I figured." He considered the blindfold he held and tossed it onto the bag. His gaze was level and serious. He was so close she could smell him—light musk and sweat, soap and leather. "They aren't your concern now. Keep your eyes on me, babe, or I'll be unhappy."

Oh. At the thought of letting him down, she wanted to curl up like a repentant puppy. "I won't disappoint you. I won't." *Never. Ever.*

The smile softened his hard features. "No, you won't."

His gaze on her face, he teased her breasts, pinching her nipples to attention and more, until she was squirming at the arousing pain.

As the stakes poked her, the added bites made her thoughts swirl like falling leaves before the approaching winter. It felt as if she'd been stirred up all night...because she had. "Zander, pleeeze." *Touch me, take me...hard.*

"Feeling needy, are you?" As he gave an ominous laugh, he retracted the stakes, one by one. Nothing sharp was pressing on her skin any longer, and she took a relieved breath. *Free!*

He didn't unfasten her wrists, though, and she tugged at the restraints in a silent reminder.

"'Bout time to torture those little tits of yours. See how sensitive they can get."

Torture? *Wait.* Her jaw dropped. Her wrist cuffs were still clipped to the top of the cage—and prevented her from plastering herself on the opposite side from him.

When the corners of his mouth tipped up, she knew she'd reacted as he figured. And knowing didn't help. Her skin felt so sensitive already, her nipples still ached from his pinching, and now...more? She barely kept from whimpering, and yet, seeing the merciless light in his gaze sent a dark hunger through her.

As he bent to his toy bag, she shifted position, rubbing her thighs together to ease the ache.

He noticed—of course—and his chin lifted slightly. *Open.*

God. It felt as if heat were streaming off her body as she parted her legs, opening to him.

Unhurriedly, he wrapped scratchy rope around her, above and under her breasts, creating a kind of harness. Soon the rope circled the base of each breast, squeezing and constricting the skin. By the time he stopped, her breasts felt too, too full, as if being pressed outward. Her already tender nipples filled with blood until every beat of her heart made them throb.

She was panting, unable to do anything. Her breasts had never felt like this—exquisitely sensitive to the point of pain.

"Nice." His voice was sandpaper harsh, his gaze piercing as he firmly rolled the peaks.

Too much. Even as she gasped at the sharp, painful pleasure, uncontrollable need swept over her like a wind off the desert, turning the air scorching hot.

His callused fingers on her moved deliberately, wringing more from her, as his smoke-green eyes watched her intently. Pushing her. She whimpered.

"Yeah," he rasped, "there's the sound I like."

The pull of his fingers sent a current of need arrowing straight to her core. And, as if he could follow the line of tension, he ground the heel of his hand against her mound and slid his finger inside her. Making a low helpless sound, she clenched around him, wiggling. Needing more.

"I'll give you more." The masculine threat sent shivers racing over her skin. He unclipped her wrist cuffs. "Ankles, please."

Awkwardly, she maneuvered until she sat with her butt on the cushion. She could feel the slickness between her thighs as she extended her legs toward him. God, what was he going to do?

"Lie back."

As she tipped backward, he guided her legs out the birdcage door until half her bottom was outside. She swallowed hard and stared up at the metal frame around her, feeling the cage swing slightly.

She could hear the music change to something softer. Darker. A sharp cry came from a woman down the room. Nearby, Stan was talking to Dixon, low and soft.

Zander's powerful hands closed on her left leg, lifting up and out. He clipped the ankle cuff high on the outside of the birdcage before doing the right. Her bottom was so far through the door her legs were angled toward her head, elevated enough to tilt her ass upward. Blood rushed to her head—and her bound breasts swelled, erotically painful.

He smiled and tore the sides of her thong, ripping it right off. The coolness of air touched the hot flesh between her thighs. She was extremely wet.

And God, she wanted him inside her. But... A quiver of anxiety ran up her spine. Who knew what the Enforcer would do?

In answer, he leaned in and hooked her wrist cuffs to the frame behind her head. "I don't want you interfering when I hurt you," he said in such a level voice that he sounded reasonable until she took in the meaning.

"B-but, I'm not—"*Not a masochist, remember?* At his stare, she didn't finish. Just bit her lip. The swinging of the birdcage seemed to make her helplessness even more apparent. She wasn't even on the ground.

His hands ran down the backs of her legs, and she realized the cage put her bottom right at the height of a man's groin. Good—she wanted him inside her.

"I think I should examine that gorgeous pussy of yours," he said. He pushed a button on the control device hooked on the frame. The cage rose to the level of his chest.

Her eyes widened when his gaze settled between her legs. God, her pussy was right out there, totally on display. He ran his fingers down her mound, opened her labia, and just...looked at her.

"Zander..." A glance made her swallow and try again. "Master, don't. Please."

"Please is a great word—and I intend to please. Me, for sure. Maybe even you." He pressed a rough finger inside her, his smoldering eyes on her as she sucked in a breath at the light scrape against sensitized nerves. One corner of his mouth tilted up. When he rubbed on a certain place, her hips jerked violently.

A dark hunger rose in her core.

"Guess you like this spot."

He continued until she could feel the strands of an orgasm start to gather. *Finally.*

And he removed his hand.

Leaving her empty inside, he caressed her clit for a wonderful few seconds before tugging the hood up off it. She stiffened, realizing he was looking right at her pussy. Her face felt as if she were turning the color of a beet with embarrassment, even as need surged high and fast.

One finger of his other hand circled the nub of nerves, making her shake uncontrollably. "You're gonna have to get used to this, babe," he said. The considering look he gave her was disconcerting. "I'm a visual sort of guy—and I like looking at your cunt."

Oh my God, did he really say that? She stared at him.

He watched his finger circle her clit, and his pitiless eyes stabbed at her again. "Before I fuck you, I'm going to have myself a cunt show. Watch you get puffy. And red. And hurting."

Hurting? The look she gave him must have been horrified, because his dimple flashed with his amusement.

He slicked up her asshole with cold lube and picked up a...thing from his toy bag. The length of his hand, the flexible stick was constructed of glass balls that started about the size of a grape and increased in diameter. Without any hesitation, he pushed the first small one into her anus.

She felt the tiny stretch before her rim of muscles closed around the narrow part. But he kept *going.* The next ball was slightly bigger. Each one stretched her more until she was panting, feeling far too full inside. Her legs up over the sides of the cage prevented her from escaping the discomfort—and she didn't want to disappoint him, so she panted and gasped.

"Next one's really big," he said.

Oh God, bigger would hurt...really hurt, past what she could take. She started to grit her teeth and hesitated. He'd been unhappy with her when she'd covered up her pain during the flogging. Had said he needed to trust her to be honest.

But where was the line between taking the pain to please a Dom and going too far? "Yellow," she whispered.

"Now that's a fucking good girl," he said, his voice deeper than normal, approval warming her like a hot bath. "Saved yourself from a timeout in a corner." The lines fanning out from the corners of his eyes deepened with amusement.

Damn Dom. He'd wanted her to speak up—and had deliberately pushed her into it. Her anger died under the sweet reassurance that he cared.

A sensual flame glowed in his eyes as he laid his hand between her legs, over her mound and pussy. Why did the casual caress seem even more intimate than what he'd already done? Maybe because he did it in the same way he'd squeeze her shoulder or tug on her hair, as if all parts of her were his to touch. The realization she wanted him to possess her burrowed into her heart along with the knowledge he'd do exactly that.

"Now I'm going to hurt you," he said gravely.

What? She licked her lips and said carefully, "But-but you hurt Dixon already."

"I kept it light...so I'd have enough energy for you too."

A shiver shook her as he picked up a cane in his left hand and an eight-inch flogger with narrow rubber strands. So short. He tapped the cane along the backs of her thighs, lightly. When he reached her ass...*Smack.*

Ow! The stinging pain blasted up through her body, squeezed her center, and swelled her aching breasts. When he struck her other cheek, she realized the aching fullness from the balls increased her sensitivity. Each swat of the cane made her clench, made the burn worse, and yet she could feel the hunger filling her. She needed him inside her so, so badly. Her breathing changed to hard pants as she fought to stay still.

He slicked a finger around her clit, inserted it into her entrance, and her blood turned to fire, racing through her veins. "Ready for more, aren't you?"

The tiny flogger rose and came straight down on her pussy.

"*Shit!*" At the brutal bliss, her entire body arced upward. Her hands fought the restraints.

"That's it." And he gripped her right thigh, flicked the strands to hit her labia from below, then struck her clit from above.

Oh God, oh God, oh God.

"Yeah, nice." He leaned in and pinched her nipples cruelly, yet under his hot gaze the pain slid downward to her core, reverberating through her like the low ringing of a bell. Before she could process anything, he struck her buttocks with the cane and her labia with the flogger.

Too many sensations crashed in on her, transforming to dark, molten heat pooling in her pelvis. She clenched around the thing inside her, drowning in the monstrous need.

"Oh please." Her fingers clamped on the cage bars. *Don't move, don't move.* But she couldn't take more. Couldn't. Everything hurt and pulsated with the strangest mixture of pleasure and pain and needs. "I want—"

"No, pet. This is about what you need," he said, the iron in his tone merciless. The flogger hit her again, right between her legs.

Her whole body spasmed, surging toward the peak. Not reaching it, and as she slid backward, the cage itself seemed to sink. All she could feel were the sensations shivering over her skin, boiling inside her. She started to shake.

And his gaze was on her again, on her pussy. "Fuck, you're gorgeous." He traced a finger around her clit. "Slick and so red you're almost glowing."

With a hum of the winch, he lowered the birdcage to groin level. He opened his jeans, and his cock pressed against her entrance.

Her vagina felt too empty, and yet the anal balls were very big, and her mind wavered back and forth between fear and desire. *Please, please, please.* Her begging made no sound.

"Take me, babe." His shaft pressed into her, slick and hot and so very thick. Her anus was already stuffed with the round objects, and he filled her far too full. "Fuck, you feel good."

She wasn't sure it was true in reverse. And yet as he forged deeper, the pleasure seemed to fill her until her body sang with it.

"All in. Look at me, Lindsey."

Sweat dampened her temples as she managed to lift her heavy eyelids.

He studied her for a long moment, heart-squeezing tenderness and amusement—and lust—in his expression. "Yeah, you're good." He curved his fingers around her thighs, close to her pelvis, and pushed. As his cock slid out without his hips shifting, she realized he was standing still and moving the birdcage. With his gaze on her face, he yanked it toward him, impaling her.

The ferocious thrill arched her neck. Her breasts jiggled and ached with need. Her whole lower half felt as if it were overstuffed on the inside, swollen and throbbing on the outside.

She stared at him as he pushed the cage away, emptying her, brought it back and filled her. Over and over. Hard and ruthless and her body gloried in it. Her hips struggled to move. She yanked at her restraints, every thought gone except the ones of need churning her blood. The need to take more, to come, to—

And gradually, he withdrew all the way, stepped back—and the flogger came down on her clit. *One. Two. Three.* Not as hard as before, but relentless stings directly on the exquisitely sensitive ball of nerves.

"Nooooo." Incredible pain and the most supreme pleasure whipped through her.

He didn't stop. *Whap, whap, whap*, and the rocketing sensations kept soaring upward. It *hurt*, yet, a devastating pleasure crescendoed outward like an overload of electricity, sending every nerve into ecstasy until she couldn't stay still.

"Fuck, you're beautiful."

She could barely hear his baritone rasp over the roaring in

her head. He thrust into her rhythmically, his hold on her hips merciless. She loved it. Loved him. Loved being taken until she was mindless.

He slowed. "After all your complaining, you'd better get off one more time."

Another? She'd die. "Uh-uh." Her protest was hoarse. "Done. I'm done."

"Sure you are, babe." Although she heard the strain in his voice as he kept himself under control, his cock made lovely sweet circles and measured thrusts as if he could last for eternity.

She might never move again.

He stopped moving. "Look at me, Lindsey." His soft tone was encased in iron.

Her eyes opened.

His expression was demanding, his face absolutely masculine as he watched her with the sternness of a master. "Time for more."

As if she was completely under his control, her body quivered awake around the cock impaling her. The other thing in her ass was still there—and not comfortable when she moved.

He bent slightly forward into the birdcage, holding her thigh, keeping himself in her. His other hand reached toward where her breasts strained beneath the binding ropes.

"No!"

Ignoring her protest and wiggling, he kneaded the taut flesh.

The huge wave of heat was indescribable. She gasped—and then he pinched her engorged nipples.

"Oh my *God*." The sensation wasn't...quite...pain, more a pressure blooming deep inside her, like a purposeful rise of molten rock in a volcano.

He laughed as her world dropped away from her, as if she were engulfed in his control. His cock slowly slid in and out of her, deeper than before, driving her body into arousal again. Her clit wakened, sending bursts of *need, need, need* messages along her nerve endings.

"That's it, babe. Better grab hold now." The warning came none too soon. Even as he slid out of her, he pulled on the thing in her ass. One glass ball bumped out, and he thrust it back in—and his cock as well. *Out.* She felt the coldness as he added more lube, and the anal bead toy slid in through the ring of muscles, stimulating everything in the area. *Out. In.*

Her whole lower half had turned to an overloaded, rawly sensitive nerve, and each breath she took was a moan. The pressure coiled and coiled within her center. "I can't," she moaned, her fingers clasping the metal frame, searching for something to anchor her.

"Let go, Lindsey." He squeezed her bottom gently as if to let her know he had her. "Now." His cock slid out first and a second later, he yanked the anal beads out—*all* of them.

"Aaaaah!" Her back arched; her nails dug into her palms as her insides contracted, expanded, clenched harder. When his cock forced its way back inside her slick pussy, every nerve in her body lit up like a galaxy of sparklers, expanding outward until her skin tingled, her hair tingled, her toes tingled.

Oh my God, oh my God.

"Mmmhmm, baby. Beautiful."

Before she'd managed to stop gasping, before her heart rate had slackened, he gripped her hips and pistoned into her, fast and forceful, until he released in a series of hard jerks.

God, he was going to be the death of her. The heavy satisfaction had dissolved her bones. Under her, the cage rocked slightly. Maybe she'd simply lie right here for a millennium or so.

Still deep inside her, he caressed her hips and bottom as she gathered her senses and reacquired the art of breathing rather than gasping. When his fingers brushed over several tender, stinging areas, she flinched. *Whoa, baby.* He'd definitely tanned her hide—and more besides. Her asshole and other intimate places burned.

A second later, he slid out of her, leaving her insides doing tiny spasms of loss. "Don't move for a second, Tex," he said. A second later, he cut through the ropes binding her breasts.

She felt as if her whole body stilled in relief...until the blood started surging in and out, painfully equalizing. "Ow, ow, ow!

You're such a sadist," she said, half under her breath—not softly enough.

"Got a good eye, babe." He chuckled and, as if to confirm her belief, swatted her sore butt.

"Ouch!" She glared at him, making his lips curl up.

At length, the sadist released her restraints and helped her out of the cage as gently as if she were a baby. When Logan tossed over a blanket, he wrapped it around her and guided her to a place on the floor.

Her head was too heavy for her neck, all her muscles felt like overstretched rubber bands, and, without the wall at her back, she'd probably have fallen over.

Crouching in front of her, Zander gave her a thoughtful study and nodded. "You look better."

Better. She snorted. Her hair and skin were damp with sweat, her face probably purple, and she still quivered with little aftershocks. "I'm sure."

He caressed her cheek. "Relaxed, not worrying about things you can't prevent, well pleasured. Yeah, better."

Oh. She sighed. "Well, if your plan was to drive me out of my mind, it worked."

His smile made her glow inside. Damn, she loved him.

"Now, tell me how you felt watching me with Dixon."

Dixon. She turned her head, looking for her friend—Zander was right between her and the room.

The amusement in his gaze said it was deliberate. "Asked you a question, babe."

How did I feel about watching? When she hesitated, he curled his hand around her nape, sending shivers down her spine at the heat of his hand—at the power of his grip. "I'll ask again in a few days after you've had time to process everything. Give me your gut feelings now."

"I—it was weird because he's a friend. And he likes you— *likes* you." His gaze never left her face as she searched for the right words. "But after a bit, friendship and attraction didn't seem to matter. You weren't interested in him sexually. All your focus was on taking him where you wanted him to go. And watching you…kind of…sucked me in." She bit her lip.

His dimple appeared a second before he pulled her forward and kissed her. Sweet and powerful and possessive. "I love you, Tex," he whispered.

Oh jeez. She rubbed her cheek on his and inhaled through her nose. "D-don't be nice now. I'll cry."

He snorted. "Babe, when this shit is over, we're going to talk about the future." Before she could respond, he set a bottle of water in her hand. "Drink up. All of it."

"Yes, Sir." She took a sip, felt the upheaval in her emotions settle, leaving her feeling as if she'd sucked down a couple of shots of rum mixed with liquor of hope. She smiled at him. "And I love you too."

"Good deal." He rose, watched her take another drink, and went to clean up the equipment.

Letting out a long sigh, she sagged against the wall. Darned if every nerve in her body wasn't still glowing with satiation. Mmmhmm, that was a nice time. And now, with Zander out of the way, she spotted Dixon off to one side, bending over.

Sometime while she and Zander had been busy, Stan had unchained Dixon and instead, hooked his wrist cuffs to a wide leather belt. He'd also put a play collar around Dixon's neck. Clasping the collar, the Dom had bent him over and was inserting a well-lubed anal plug—not cruelly, not particularly gently either.

Lindsey's newly tender asshole puckered in sympathy.

When Stan directed Dixon back upright, she saw her poor friend's balls were wrapped in a leather harness with a testicle stretcher and divider and a cock ring as well. Looked painful as all get-out.

After inserting the anal plug, the Dom snapped a leash onto Dixon's collar. He didn't even look back at Dixon as he tugged him through the room.

Zander squatted down beside her, his gaze on the two men as well. "You're frowning."

"The agent doesn't seem to be very nice."

"Nice isn't what Dixon needs." Zander tugged her hair lightly. "The boy won't submit without some work. Erotic control is a straightforward path there."

"Stan isn't even paying attention to him."

Zander snorted. "You notice the mirrors?"

"Huh?" Lindsey blinked and looked around. Son of a gun, small mirrors were embedded in the rocks here and there...and she saw Stan was checking them without Dixon even realizing.

"The boy's got a bad habit of using his pretty face to get his way. A Dom who wants more than a quick fuck won't tolerate that kind of behavior."

"Oh." She pursed her lips. "And how many sneaky Dom-manipulative tricks have you used on me? What are my lessons?"

To her surprise, he didn't shrug off the question. "We're starting with the basics. Trust. Honesty. Transparency." He ran his finger over her lower lip and added, "Remember, little Tex, a Dom's got lessons too. You're not the only one learning to trust."

Oh. The sweep of sweetness took her by surprise. "God, I love you. I really, really do."

"Well." He tapped her nose. "For that, you get chocolate."

CHAPTER NINETEEN

T he next day, Lindsey stepped out of the cabin into a quiet realm filled with glittering falling snow. The untouched white powder carpeted the ground, making the world seem fresh and clean. The air was so cold, her lungs seemed to clench.

After a long stretch, she started down the path to the main cabin. Heck of a night, last night. First the dungeon party, afterward the hot tub.

She still had tender spots—especially her bottom. However, poor Dixon might be even worse off.

Before they'd left the dungeon, Stan had removed all the various devices from Dixon's body and blindfolded him, stood him in the middle of the room while he went to the fridge. He'd brought back an icy ridged dildo, bent Dixon over, and shoved it up his ass. Dixon had come, screaming as if he was being murdered.

It was a wonder he hadn't had a heart attack.

After slapping his ass, Stan had hugged him lightly and said the scene was over. *"You can join me in the hot tub if you want, boy."* Dixon had spent the entire time staring at the Dom, undoubtedly trying to understand why the man hadn't even tried to get off. Stan had retired soon afterward, leaving Dixon looking confused—and forlorn.

Poor Dix.

While Lindsey walked, snowflakes tickled her cheeks and hung on her eyelashes. From the looks of it, snow had been falling all morning. And she'd sure slept late, which was Zander's fault.

He'd worn her out.

Around dawn, he'd noticed her new virginal-slut nightgown and woken her up to show his energetic appreciation. *God.* Three orgasms later... When he finished, he'd gotten dressed, leaving her facedown and boneless in the bed.

As she crossed the clearing to the lodge, the door opened. Jake, one bare foot raised, supported by Simon and Zander, hopped out. "Morning, Lindsey."

"What happened? Are you okay?"

"I slipped on a fuc—ah, a rock when I was checking the hot tub."

She frowned at his very swollen, purpling ankle. "Is it broken?"

"Probably not," Simon said. "We'll get it X-rayed to be sure."

"We're hauling his ass to the clinic in town," Zander said before his jaw hardened. "I'm keeping Simon's car and stopping at the police station after. Seems Stanfeld took off to talk with Masterson."

"Hokay." Sounded like Stan was going to get a *teamwork* lecture. Lindsey smiled, amazed at how the mere sight of Zander lifted her heart. Well, aside from the fact a bulky jacket made him look as if he could wrestle grizzly bears. *Be still my heart.* "Y'all drive safe, okay?"

Jake nodded. Simon winked at her. Zander gave her a macho man snort.

Right. How could she forget that alpha male Enforcers simply laughed at snow?

After watching them navigate the slick ground, she crossed the porch and read the sign posted on the lodge door. LUNCH WILL BE LATE TODAY. BECCA.

Inside, the main room was quiet, with only Logan present. He was sweeping the fireplace hearth, treating the sleeping dog as if Thor were a piece of furniture. "Morning, sugar."

"Good morning to you. Is Becca around?"

"Nope." He nodded at the snow plastering the glass window. "It's getting nasty out there. When the blizzard really hits, we might get over a foot of snow, so Becca drove into town for groceries. She and Ansel should be back soon."

"Kallie?"

"At the Masterson place. Her cousins haven't returned from a guide trip, so she's over there feeding the livestock. Rona and Dixon went along with her to visit Summer."

"Oh. Right." Rona had invited her, but Lindsey didn't know Summer very well. Sometimes old friends needed time to catch up on gossip. "I guess the place is pretty empty. Did your other guests flee in the face of the storm?"

"We're emptying out. One man and an older couple left early—they didn't want to chance the road closing. Stanfeld'll be here another day. He went into town to talk with Virgil Masterson. Got one cabin rented out through Sunday, but I haven't seen him this morning. Don't know if he'll stay or not."

"Since you've been abandoned by your staff, is there anything I can do to help?"

His rare smile was her reward. "If you'd answer the phone while I clean and restock a couple of cabins, I'd appreciate it. Be about an hour or so."

"Let me grab a cup of coffee, and I'm your girl."

Time went by in a lovely quiet as she drank her coffee and flipped through old *Field & Stream* magazines. Outside the lodge, the wind picked up, spattering the windows with snow, covering the world in white. With a sigh, she leaned back in the comfortable chair.

She'd had a harsh few months, but now peace wrapped around her like the warmth from the crackling fire. There was an end in sight. Someday soon, she might have her life back.

Or a better life, even.

He loves me. Smiling, she said it aloud, just to hear the unbelievable words. "He loves me." She'd never dreamed to hope for that—not with Zander.

Every time she remembered the determination in his voice as he'd argued to keep her from being "used," her insides fluttered as if she'd swallowed butterflies.

God, she loved him so much her poor heart hurt. She'd sure never felt this way about either of her husbands. She'd *thought* she loved them. Had thought they were friends. Had enjoyed the sex. But her feelings for them hadn't made her shiver and hurt and...yearn.

Looking into the future, she knew—*knew*—she wanted Zander beside her forever. Even if they were dumped in wheelchairs in a nursing home, she'd still reach for his hand—and giggle when he growled at a nurse. Which he would so totally do.

And hey, he'd need her there to keep him from getting his aged bony butt tossed out, right? Really, with his unsociable manners, he needed her far more than she needed him. It was her...duty...to love him and cherish him and keep him out of trouble.

And wear slutty-virginal nightgowns to tempt him, and to tease him, and to—her eyes burned—to love him so, so well he'd never remember that his mother hadn't.

"My mama will like you, Zander," she whispered. After she got past how scary he could be. She bit her lip at the surge of longing. Never before had she not been home for Christmas with her family.

Hearing the stomping of boots on the porch, she scrubbed her face with her hands and sat up straight.

A man entered and stopped to brush snow off his head and shoulders. His hair was black, eyes dark under heavy eyebrows. Thick stubble blackened his cheeks and jaw. "Good morning. You are the receptionist?"

"I'm filling in for a bit. Can I help you?"

"Possibly. I have a question for one of the staff—I'm in Cabin Five. Is anyone around?" He had a slight Spanish accent.

"Becca will return from town soon. Logan's cleaning cabins."

"Guess it's just you and me?"

She stiffened at the assessing look. "Logan should be back any minute."

"I only need a minute...Lindsey." With an ugly sneer, he moved closer. "Chief Parnell has Mrs. Hunt and her baby. You come with me quietly, or he slits the brat's throat."

Becca and Ansel? Lindsey's lungs felt as if he'd stomped on her ribs; she struggled to inhale. "No. Y'all wouldn't dare."

The indifference in his expression showed he could care less if a baby died.

She shoved her chair away from the desk. Could she reach her knife before he grabbed her? "I don't believe you."

He took a satellite phone from under his coat and punched in a number. "Need proof of life. Let's hear it." A second later he held the phone toward her.

Becca was yelling, "Don't—don't touch him. Don't you—"

The sound of a baby crying drowned out everything.

"No! Stop!" Lindsey jumped to her feet. "Don't hurt them. I'll go with you. Stop it!"

"Now wasn't that easy?" As he tucked the phone inside his coat, she saw he had a pistol as well. "Move fast, *puta*. If Hunt stops us, I'll put a bullet in his head, and we'll have a mess."

―◦≫◦◦―

Jake Hunt made a piss-poor patient, deVries thought, but at least the man's ankle wasn't busted. After helping Hunt into the lodge truck, which Simon was driving, deVries continued down the slick boardwalk and into the Bear Flat police station.

Small place. Desks around the walls. A table in the center served as an intake area. Damn quiet for a cop station. Seated at one of the desks was a uniformed officer who looked barely old enough to shave. "Can I help you?"

"Masterson here?"

The boy stiffened. "Lieutenant Masterson is in his office. Give me your name, and I'll—"

"I see him." Spotting the glass-fronted room with a LIEUTENANT placard, deVries headed in, leaving the pup gaping behind him.

In the office, Masterson was seated behind an oversize desk while Stanfeld and another man sat at a table off to one side. Masterson looked up from the paper he was studying. "DeVries. Didn't think I'd see you in town today."

"Unscheduled trip—we took Jake to the clinic for a sprained ankle." He ran a hand through his hair, still damp from the snow.

264 | CHERISE SINCLAIR

"Kallie wants him at your place for a couple of nights. Guess she figures having Summer on hand might help." Masterson's wife was a registered nurse.

"Sprained, huh? Bet he's in a shit mood." Masterson snorted. "You need assistance transporting him?"

"Nah. Simon is delivering him. I stayed to talk with you and Stanfeld." DeVries gave the Homeland Security agent a cold stare and colder warning. "You make any plans about Lindsey, you make me part of them."

Stanfeld frowned. "I can see how—"

Much like a wolf when faced with another male, the other man in the room rose to his feet. Six-one, muscular build, white shirt, badge on his belt, shoulder harness for his pistol. Dark brown hair reached his collar. Trim goatee. Hard blue eyes in a tanned face. "I don't recall being introduced."

Interfering bastard. "DeVries. Lindsey's mine." He didn't bother holding out his hand to shake.

The cop snorted. "You're clear enough." He did hold out his hand. "Atticus Ware. Detective."

Ware's handshake was strong, and he didn't resort to using it for a pissing contest. The cop might be likeable if he refrained from being an obstacle. "I prefer being clear."

"I haven't met your lady," Ware said. "A Texan?"

DeVries nodded.

"Bet she's enjoying the snow."

Masterson grinned. "Coming from Idaho, Ware doesn't panic at a few snowflakes—unlike the new grad we had from San Diego."

San Diego. Palm trees. DeVries snorted at the vision of a southern California cop in a blizzard.

"After the fourth time we towed his patrol car out of a ditch, we sent him home," said Ware.

Stanfeld shook his head. "If you ladies are finished chatting, we might move on?"

Ware resumed his seat.

Now what would have dragged an Idaho cop to California?

Odd.

As deVries leaned against the wall, Stanfeld told him, "I came in to talk with the local law enforcement about luring Parnell and Ricks here, where there are limited ways in."

"And fewer people to fuck things up," deVries said.

"Exactly." Stanfeld nodded. "I know you don't want Lindsey as bait, but—"

The phone on the desk rang.

"Lieutenant Masterson." Virgil listened and glanced at deVries. "You seen Lindsey here?"

DeVries straightened. "No. Why?"

Masterson's jaw hardened. "We'll check around town. What's she driving?"

He hung up and looked at the others. "She'd told Logan she'd answer the desk phone while he cleaned cabins. He came back, and she wasn't there. Her car's gone."

"Maybe she went to join Rona and Dixon," Stanfeld said.

DeVries's gut clenched. "If she said she'd watch something, she wouldn't leave until relieved. She's solid like that."

Masterson was on the phone to his wife. Seconds later, he hung up. "No Lindsey. And Summer says it's getting to be a whiteout up there."

"That's bad," Ware said to deVries. "What are the chances your coyotes have already grabbed the bait?"

He answered Ware through a dry throat. "Too fucking good."

⸺◦◦◦⸺

The snow was falling so thickly the forest looked as if it were draped in gauze. The car fishtailed with every corner, almost sending them over the side of the mountain. By the time Parnell's hireling turned off onto a barely visible road, Lindsey's jaw was clenched to an aching tightness.

And she was freezing. The man had shoved her out the door, not letting her get her jacket. Shivers racked her body as her old car finally started to put out some heat.

The car hit a patch of ice and slid toward a tree as the man frantically fought to regain control.

"You've never driven in snow, have you?" she said, forcing the words out.

"Shut up."

Biting her lip, she worked her fingers. Even though she'd accompanied him without fighting, the man had tied her wrists together in front of her so tightly her fingers were half numb. Still, she needed to be able to move when—if—rescue came. It *must* come.

Logan would finish his chores eventually and notice she was missing or realize Becca was late. But how soon would they begin to search? And could rescuers even find them in the storm? When the man had seen her cell phone attached to the car charger, he'd thrown it out the window to remove any chance of tracking the GPS.

No one would arrive in time—if anyone arrived at all.

As her breathing sped up, she bit down on her tongue sharply. *No panicking.* She had to believe Zander and the men had a chance of finding her and Becca and the baby.

Oh God, I'm scared.

Her fingernails dug into her thighs. Parnell would hurt her. Kill her. Hurt Ansel.

Ansel. Cold determination smothered the roaring fear. She had to save the baby.

Branches scraped and squealed along the sides of the car as the tiny dirt road narrowed. She stared out at the snow, thinking she could have walked faster than the car was moving. "Can I ask how you found me? I mean, how you found me in Yosemite?"

"Traced you to Demakis Security. Staked out the building. I followed you." He glanced at her. "Parnell broke into your duplex before he drove here."

So they'd been watching Simon's building when she picked up Rona and Dixon. And she'd been oblivious. Now Becca and Ansel would pay for her mistake. Despair clogged her throat, weighted her chest. *God, I'm so sorry.* "My friends will be looking for you. They'll find you."

"Doubt it. By the time they notice you're missing, they'll figure you decided to go into town. That's why we took your car and left my junker rental." He showed badly rotting teeth as he grinned. "And nobody knows nothing about you—doubt you told your boyfriend you're wanted for murder."

Zander did know. And so all the men would start looking for her right away. They'd look for Parnell too. *I have to hold on. Stall.*

In the swirling snow, the dark outline of a small cabin suddenly materialized. The man parked behind the low wooden rail, which blocked the way to the house.

Without waiting for her to get her footing, he dragged her across the uneven ground and shoved her through the front door so hard she fell to her knees.

Pulling in a deliberate breath, she shook her hair from her face and looked around. The one-room cabin had a woodstove in the far corner, bunk beds on the right. In the middle, Becca sat in a wooden chair, ankles secured to the legs. Her wrists were bound, forcing her to hold Ansel awkwardly in the circle of her arms. Her red-gold hair hung in tangles down her green sweater. Bruising showed on her white, strained face. Tears filled her eyes when she recognized Lindsey.

"Good job, Morales." The voice was familiar.

Lindsey turned her head. At a battered kitchen table, a man the size of a bear rose to his feet, and her hopes dropped like a rock breaking through ice. She'd known Parnell was here but had hoped Ricks wasn't. Stan had been right about Parnell and Ricks not trusting each other.

Ricks looked down at her. Although his eyes were shadowed by dark brows, the lust in them showed too clearly. "Guess I'm going to get some playtime."

Lindsey forced herself not to look away. *You tangle with me, I'll have your hide,* John Wayne would have said. If only she could.

"Playtime? Maybe." Police Chief Parnell sat at the other end of the table. Victor's brother had brown hair shaved to military shortness, a medium height, lean body, and deep-set eyes holding cold rage. A knife was sheathed at his hip, a pistol on the other. "Nice of you to join us, dear sister-in-law."

The way he looked at her chilled her to the bone. She'd shot his brother. He'd killed Craig without a second thought—what would he do to her?

Parnell set his coffee down, picked up his chair, and carried it the few feet across the room to place it beside Becca.

Becca's gaze met Lindsey's, desperation in their depths. A mother whose child was at risk.

My fault. God, I'm sorry, Becca.

"Question-and-answer time." Ricks yanked Lindsey to her feet and burrowed his face into the crook of her neck and shoulder.

Gritting her teeth, she struggled, tried to elbow him. He wrapped a thick arm around her waist and groped her breasts.

"Ricks, give it a rest. Put her in the chair," Parnell snapped and turned to Morales. "Go make sure no one followed you in."

"Got it." As Morales left, Parnell grabbed the front of Lindsey's flannel shirt, wrenched her away from Ricks, and shoved her into the chair beside Becca. His mouth twisted with impatience. "Where'd you put the memory drives?"

"Well..." She'd known this was what they'd ask, and unhappily hadn't come up with a response. If she said Stan now had the drives, they'd cut their losses and kill her, Becca, and Ansel. Even if she bargained the location in exchange for the other two's freedom, Parnell wouldn't honor his word. Becca could identify them; they wouldn't leave her alive.

Did they think Lindsey was stupid?

The only hope was an escape or rescue, no matter how unlikely. *Stall.* "I hid the stuff really well. You'll never find a thing." She gave Parnell a slight smirk.

He backhanded her so hard the chair rocked. Pain blasted into her cheek, tears springing to her eyes.

Becca made a sound, a low whining, "Nooo."

Blinking, Lindsey shook her head to clear her vision, to hide her tears. *I can't do this.*

"Don't give me shit," Parnell said.

Her voice came out shaky. "The flash drives are hidden."

"Stupid bitch." Ricks stepped outside. "Morales, did you find anything when you searched her cabin?"

"What the fuck you think?"

Ricks slammed the door. "Asshole."

The chief snorted. "He's reliable enough. I don't care if he lacks manners." From his pocket, he drew out long plastic zip ties and anchored Lindsey's left ankle to the chair leg, wrapping it over her boot below her jeans hem. He did the same on the right.

"Why bother?" Ricks moved closer. "She gave herself up."

"When I interrogate someone, I don't want them moving. Especially this cunt who killed my brother." His attention turned back to Lindsey. "Tell me the hiding place."

"Fuck, I figure the struggle is the best part." From behind her chair, Ricks reached around to grab her breasts painfully. She tried to jerk away as he squeezed and pinched. "Fight me, bitch. I don't mind."

"I do mind." With his open hand, Parnell slapped her, knocking her head back. "Where?"

The entire world pulsed with red-edged pain. A sob twisted in her chest. Her whole face felt scalded. As she sucked air in small pants, the sweat stench from Ricks roiled her stomach.

Startled by the shout, Ansel had woken and was crying. His little hands waved helplessly. Tears rolled down Becca's cheeks. With her son in her lap, she could do nothing to help.

Ansel needs me. Think. Please, think. Lindsey swallowed down sickness and forced herself to look at Parnell. "If you let Becca and the baby go, I'll take you to the memory drives."

If only one man took Becca from the cabin, Becca would do her best to escape him.

"Tell me now, or I'll slit Mama's throat." Parnell's thin lips tipped up. "This close, her blood will spray all over you before she dies."

Ice formed splinters in her heart, hurting and tearing. Chilling her. "I don't—"*have the drives.* No, he mustn't find out she'd given them to Stan.

Ricks squeezed her breasts, making her grunt with the pain. Nauseating her. She let the retching sound escape. "Please, I'm gonna—" She gagged, started to heave.

Both men stepped back.

"S-sorry." Pretending she was trying to regain control, she looked around. Parnell's pistol was strapped down. Ricks wasn't wearing one. Couldn't make a grab and succeed.

Beside the woodstove was the bathroom. The open door let her see a book-size window. Too small. No back door. In the yard, she'd seen the two front windows had bars on the outside. No easy escape.

"Can we just...just make a deal?" she asked.

Parnell unsheathed his knife. "No deals. Talk fast." Setting the blade under Becca's chin, he pricked her skin. A drop of blood appeared.

Becca closed her eyes, holding her son so, so carefully. Ansel stared up at Parnell, blue eyes full of tears, little chest hitching with his crying.

Despair welled up in Lindsey. There was no way out. *Lie.* If it didn't get her killed immediately, it might buy some time. "The jump drives are at the lodge, but—"

With a rattle, the door opened, and Morales stuck his head in. "Hey, snow's getting deep. We're going to need chains on the tires to get out of here. If we want to leave in a hurry, should put them on now."

"Well, do it," Parnell snapped.

"Don't know how."

Parnell stared at the guy. "Fuck."

Off to one side, Ricks shook his head. "I don't know either."

With a scowl of disbelief, Parnell said, "Leave the bitches alone. You'll get your chance later." He grabbed his jacket and stepped outside.

Only one person remained inside. Hope rose within Lindsey.

"Fucking dick," Ricks muttered. Crouching down, he ripped open her shirt. His face flushed. "When Parnell's done, I get you."

Her chest tightened. The thought of him touching her, inside her... *Let me go, please. Oh please.* She kept her gaze on him and clenched her teeth to keep the words from escaping.

His color darkened, and he squeezed her cheek roughly

enough to bring tears to her eyes. "I'll fuck your mouth, fuck your ass. Finish off with my knife in your cunt. Bet you don't stare at me then, bitch." He shoved her face to the side and rose.

She blinked rapidly, choking on the sobs in her chest.

He took a can of beer from the fridge. Other cans scattered the counter. How much had they been drinking? Would it matter?

Over the howling of the wind, she heard Parnell yell at Morales, "Lay the chain out like this."

Finishing off the can, Ricks walked into the bathroom. The door closed.

Now now now! Despite her lashed-together wrists, she managed to tug her pants leg up above the top of her boot. With numb fingers, she dragged Zander's knife from the sheath.

A sharp gasp came from Becca.

Twisting in her chair, Lindsey extended the knife toward Becca, blade up, and mouthed, *Hurry.*

Becca moved her arms from around Ansel and offered her wrists.

With a hard tug, the sharp blade severed the plastic zip tie. *I love you, Zander.* Taking the knife, Becca cut Lindsey's ropes and handed the blade back.

Lindsey sawed through the zip ties around her ankles and stood—for a second. Her knees buckled, and she hit the wood floor with a painful thud. *Don't have heard me, please.* Heart thundering in her chest, she slid closer to Becca. Ansel was kicking and squirming.

If she could get Becca freed and—

The toilet flushed.

Shit, shit, shit. Her hammering heart was shutting off her breathing. Couldn't run with Becca still tied to a chair. Couldn't fight the huge border patrol agent. Not with such a small blade. *Need...something.*

After dropping the knife beside Becca, Lindsey lunged for the woodstove to snatch up a heavy chunk of firewood.

Working on cutting her leg ties, Becca was watching. After giving Lindsey a sharp nod, she burst into pseudo-sobbing and pleading. "You have to tell them. Please. They'll kill my baby. Please, Lindsey." Ansel started wailing again.

Lindsey couldn't hear her footsteps as she crossed to the bathroom. Raising the log over her head, she flattened herself against the wall.

The door opened inward. Ricks's boot appeared. Stopped. "What the—"

He wasn't far enough out. Frantically, Lindsey swung in a sideways curve around the door frame, aiming blindly. The log hit his forehead with a horrible noise like thumping a watermelon.

Boneless, he fell backward, and the back of his skull struck the small toilet. Blood ran from his forehead in rivers of red.

Roaring sounded in Lindsey's head, getting louder and louder. She saw Victor's body, his chest covered in red. Eyes open. Not moving.

Black danced at the edges of her field of vision.

"No fainting, girlfriend." A hand grasped her shoulder and dragged her from the bathroom door. "Got to move," Becca whispered.

A shudder shook Lindsey, and she swallowed convulsively. "Okay. Okay."

Outside the cabin, Parnell was shouting to Morales, "Back up a few more inches." They weren't done. Yet.

She looked at Becca. Ansel had quieted, happy to be carried again. He had a lock of Becca's hair in his little hand.

No matter what happened, Ansel must live. Becca too. Their escape first. "Listen, Becca. You're going to sneak out the door. Stay by the wall, go around the side. The car is a ways out; they won't see you." *I hope, I hope.*

"They'll find us. Track us," Becca protested. Nonetheless she handed Lindsey the baby and donned her coat.

"They're gonna be chasing *me*. Your job is to keep Ansel safe." She put the squirming baby into Becca's arms. "He's what matters."

"I can't let you—"

"You must." Zander hadn't wanted Lindsey to be bait. To be

used. And here she was, using herself as bait now—and it was okay. This was right. "No time to argue."

Conflict warred in Becca's face until Lindsey touched Ansel's soft, pink cheek and whispered, "You have to, Becca."

"Okay," Becca whispered back. "Good luck."

"And to you." Lindsey opened the door a crack, hoping the light didn't show through the snowfall. She heard the men's voices but saw only snow. "Go."

Becca slipped out and disappeared around the side of the cabin.

Give her a minute to get away. Lindsey yanked on Ricks's giant parka and snatched her knife off the floor. Her mouth was so dry she couldn't swallow. She could sneak out like Becca. Not be seen.

Except...Becca's tracks were obvious in the fresh snow. Parnell would catch her and Ansel within minutes.

I don't want to die.

Her daddy whispered in his pretend John Wayne voice, *All battles are fought by scared men who'd rather be someplace else.*

He'd expect her to do what was right; she wouldn't let him down. This was her battle. Pulling in a breath, she shoved the door wide open. It hit the back wall loudly.

"Shit, she's loose!"

Grateful the two men were blocked by the car, she dashed straight down the road. *Please God, let help be coming.*

"Goddamn cunt."

"Puta."

Two voices cursing. Her plan had worked—both men were after her. *Run, Becca. Get away.*

The powdery snow was almost silent under her feet as she tore down the barely visible road, trying to stay in the half-filled tire tracks. She slipped and staggered back into a run.

When she went around a curve, she dared a glance over her shoulder. Nothing but falling snow.

Now. She jumped sideways onto a downed tree trunk and launched herself into the forest. She landed hard and rolled behind a tree. Why the heck couldn't there be more underbrush? Who ever heard of a neat and tidy woods, all tree trunks and snow?

Harsh breathing. Low cursing. She heard them despite the muffling effect of the falling snow.

As she held her breath, they ran past on the road. They hadn't seen where she'd jumped from the tire tracks to the tree trunk.

She lay for a moment, gasping in the thin mountain air. It was a reprieve—a short one. When they didn't overtake her in the next few minutes, they'd retrace their steps, watching for where she left the road.

Her tracks would be there, easy to spot once they'd slowed down.

Still—they were focused on her. *Please, God, let Becca and the baby get to safety.*

CHAPTER TWENTY

Peering through the windshield into white and more white, deVries cursed the snow.

Hands on the steering wheel, Stanfeld gave a grunt of agreement. "Good thing my sedan's got all-wheel drive or we'd be really screwed."

No, they'd be in a fucking ditch, deVries thought.

A Jeep approached from ahead, flashed its lights, and stopped. Logan stepped out.

Even before Stanfeld had finished braking, deVries was opening his door.

"No news. Got a missing renter—his car's still there. He isn't," Logan said, his voice tight and controlled. "DeVries, drive the Jeep. I'll spot for Stanfeld, and we'll check the east side roads."

His face was strained with worry. Soon after they'd started the search for Lindsey, Logan had called, asking if anyone had seen Becca and Ansel.

An officer had found Becca's car abandoned in town. Children building a snowman had noticed an unfamiliar car on the road toward the lodge. Becca had been crying and in the backseat next to a strange man.

Masterson said there were hunting cabins scattered all over and had stayed in town to question the rental management firms about recent activity.

DeVries and Stanfeld had hoped to locate any recently used dirt drives. It sucked that they could barely spot *any* roads through the thickly falling snow.

"I need someone to watch for me," deVries protested as he slid into the Jeep.

"That's my job," Dixon said from the backseat.

"And mine," Kallie said from the passenger side.

DeVries stared at Kallie. Bundled in a thick parka, she looked like a child, dammit. "What the fuck are you doing here?"

"I know where the cabins are and the roads and what fresh tracks look like even when they're half-covered with snow." She gave him a scowl. "Now drive. Slow."

He opened his mouth, thought better of it, and put the car into gear. Wasn't she supposed to be at the Masterson's place with her husband? "How'd you get here?"

She rolled down the glass and hung out the window like a dog. Her answer came back to him distorted by the snow. "Rona and I took Jake up to the lodge so Logan could search. But my Jeep's better on icy surfaces than Logan's truck, and I figured I'd better help."

"Jake okay with this?"

"Hell, no. He cursed up a blue streak. He doesn't want me here and thought he should come himself."

DeVries heard her snort and had a moment's sympathy for her husband.

In the sedan, Logan had taken the backseat behind Stanfeld.

"He wants you to make a U-turn and go in front. They'll bring up the rear," Kallie said.

"Got it." DeVries turned the Jeep around and took the lead. He understood the arrangement when the sedan followed on the wrong side of the road, giving Logan a closer look at the left bank.

Foot by foot, they moved forward. Once the sedan slid back behind deVries's to let a car pass. A couple of miles later, a truck came from the other direction, and the driver reduced speed long enough to exchange waves.

"That's the vet," Kallie commented. "Probably making a house call. He sure cut it close. The roads are going to be impassable soon."

"Fuck," deVries muttered. *Where are you, Lindsey?* Worry and fury roiled inside his chest. He'd kill them when he found them. If they hurt her, hurt Becca. Jesus, the baby was out in this shit somewhere.

"Why isn't Virgil here?" Kallie asked.

"Masterson and Ware stayed in town to make calls. They're looking for new rentals."

"Got it." She leaned out so far he grabbed the back of her coat to ensure she didn't fall out. "Slow down. There's a road around here."

"There." Dixon pointed, and deVries braked.

Kallie jumped out.

Before he could get out, she'd popped back in. "Hasn't been used today."

Seeing her shiver, he turned the heater to high and drove on.

Mile after mile. Stop after stop. How many damned cabins were in these mountains? Fucking hunters. He growled under his breath, stared at the side of the road until his eyes burned, and forced his impatience down. *Hang on, Lindsey.*

"Stop." Kallie got out to check another tiny road. She knelt and ran her hands over the lumpy snow. From where he was, deVries saw no difference in the blanket of white.

She waved him in.

After flashing his brakes to get Stanfeld's attention, he shut his lights off and turned onto the small single-lane road.

Stanfeld drove in behind him.

Logan jogged past and crouched down beside Kallie, sweeping snow away with his gloved hand.

As deVries stood by the car, Stanfeld and Dixon joined him.

"What do you see?" Stanfeld asked Kallie.

She looked up. "Older ruts are iced over from the melt and freeze we had a couple of days ago."

Logan patted the uncovered tire tracks. "This track was made on top of fresh powder today."

"Know who lives here?" Stanfeld asked.

"It's a rental. One-room log cabin." Logan continued to brush at the snow. "Two different cars came through. One more recently."

"Means at least two perps," Stanfeld said. "What do we do with our vehicles and...?" He motioned to Kallie.

Her chin lifted in defiance for a second before she gave in. "I'll flag the road and take my Jeep back to the lodge. From there, I can phone Virgil and give him your location."

"Thanks, sugar," Logan said.

After deVries tossed her the Jeep keys, she trotted away.

Stanfeld removed his coat and opened the sedan's trunk. He took out two bulletproof vests and handed one to deVries before donning the other. "Sorry, Logan. I only carry two."

Logan jerked up his chin in acknowledgment.

Stanfeld glanced at Dixon. "You go with Kallie. This isn't—"

"Stuff it, sweet cheeks." Dixon braced himself. "I have paramedic training."

"Don't have time for this." DeVries saw the red lettering on a small pack and slapped it against Dixon's chest. "First aid stuff. Stay in the rear."

"Yes, Sir."

Stanfeld frowned and nodded, falling in after Logan, who'd already headed down the snow-covered road.

DeVries followed. *Be strong, Tex. We're coming.*

Lindsey's lungs felt seared from the bite of the icy air. She'd fallen so many times her jeans were soaked from her knees to her ankles, and the wet skin burned. Her fingers, face, and ears were growing numb.

The road had disappeared.

Lost. Hopelessly lost. The snow was falling so thickly, she couldn't see anything past a few feet. She tripped and fell again, barely catching herself. Her arms shook with weariness as she pushed upright.

After turning in a circle, seeing only the shadowy darkness of tree trunks—*I really hate snow*—she put her hands on her thighs, trying to catch her breath. Sweat trickled down her back. Hot inside the parka, freezing outside.

"Here!" The shout came from nowhere and everywhere, bouncing off the trees. *Morales.*

Shit, they'd found where she left the road. They could follow her tracks now.

She ran.

And ran.

They were closing on her. Both of them, the bastards. Her knife was in her right hand. With her left, she snatched up a fallen branch. Too big to swing. The next was a better size and as thick as her wrist.

She stepped behind a tree, forcing her mind away from the memory of hitting Ricks. Of the blood. She strained to tighten her grip on the knife, but her fingers were agonizingly cold.

"She can't be very far ahead." Parnell's voice was low and out of breath.

"Gonna break her neck." Morales sounded closer. His footsteps neared. Almost on her.

She jumped out and swung the branch into his face as hard as she could.

"Fuck!" He staggered back, nose streaming blood. She hit him again alongside his forehead, and the wood broke.

He dropped to his knees.

"Bitch." With a sweep of his arm, Parnell knocked her off her feet and onto her back. "Fucking cunt." He lifted her by the front of her coat and drew his fist back.

Screaming between gritted teeth, she thrust the knife at him.

He jerked aside so the blade barely cut him and backhanded her into the snow again. As she landed with a grunt, he kicked her in the side so hard even the coat didn't shield her. The brutal pain tore through her ribs. She couldn't breathe, could only curl around herself.

"Jesus, she did a number on you, Morales."

"Gonna break every bone, bust her up..."

The sound of Morales's cursing, of what he would do to her, got her moving. She rolled over...and saw her knife lying within a few feet. *C'mon. Sit up.*

Parnell wiped his cheek and examined the blood. "You're really going to regret that," he whispered and kicked her again.

At the blast of pain, the world wavered out of sight.

Even as her vision refocused, she saw Parnell scoop up her knife from the snow. Despairing tears burned against her icy face when he hefted her to her feet and shoved her in front of him. "Move."

—◇✕◇—

DeVries heard erratic footsteps approaching and hissed to get Logan's attention.

In the lead, Logan held up a hand to halt.

A dark shadow came through the forest from the side. Staggering. *Rebecca.* Her face was dead white. She had her arms in front—damn, she had the baby.

"Jesus." Logan sprang forward.

Without speaking, deVries and Stanfeld spread apart to guard the perimeter in case she'd been followed.

Rebecca stared in disbelief. "Logan?" Her knees buckled.

He caught her awkwardly, handicapped by the baby between them.

Dixon dashed over. "Let me, Becca." He carefully took Ansel. A high wail showed the baby was still alive and displeased at the jostling.

"Fuck, little rebel." Wrapping his arms around her, Logan buried his face in her hair as she took a death grip on the back of his jacket.

Eyes burning, deVries turned away to watch the forest. The need for Lindsey was a hard ache in his guts.

Logan hadn't forgotten. He lifted his head. "Where's

Lindsey, sugar?"

"I don't know." Tears filled Rebecca's eyes. "She drew them away while I hid with the baby. I didn't want to, but with Ansel, I couldn't let them... All I could think of was to find help."

"You did right," Logan said, his cheek against hers.

"No. I should have—"

"Babies come first," deVries said forcefully. He wanted to yell at her for leaving Lindsey; however, she'd made the right choice. Had to save the kid.

But Jesus, Tex. His woman had more guts than some mercs he'd known. Only, if... His jaw clenched. "Becca, you got any idea where the men are? Where she is?"

"I heard them yell. I think they caught her and took her back." She seized Logan's arms and shook him. "Please. Go save her."

"Not you, Logan," Dixon said in a quiet voice. "Ansel's shivering. You need to get them both to warmth."

Logan froze. "You can take—"

"I'm not used to driving in snow. You're their best bet."

Logan looked torn. After a second, he sighed and kissed the top of Becca's head. "Hell, sugar, now I know how you felt leaving Lindsey." He motioned for Dixon to give the baby to Becca. "I need to be able to move freely."

Exhaustion plain in her features, she held Ansel against her chest, mouth determined.

Logan glanced at deVries. "I'll be back once they're safe."

"Go." DeVries handed Logan his car keys and waved the others toward him. He needed to move. Get to Lindsey. Adrenaline surging, he led the way forward down the drift-covered road.

Did the damn thing ever end?

A few minutes later, he heard someone running toward them from the main road where Logan and Becca had headed. What the hell?

Two bulky figures appeared—too big for Logan and Becca. Stanfeld mirroring his movements, deVries pulled his GLOCK and waited.

Through the white curtain of snow, Virgil Masterson emerged, followed by the Bear Flat detective, Ware. Masterson glanced at the two pistols pointed at him. "Mind finding someone else to target, boys?"

"Let's go." DeVries turned and jogged down the fucking road again.

Behind him, Stanfeld said to the others, "You got here fast."

"Discovered this cabin had been rented yesterday," Masterson said.

"We passed Logan and family," Ware said quietly. "That's a stand-up woman he's got there."

"Damn straight. Hey." DeVries stopped and pointed. The snow was marred by fresh boot tracks.

Ware knelt. "Two men. Came this far and turned around. Becca thought they went after Lindsey?"

"Yeah. Maybe they didn't find her?" Hope rose inside him.

"Maybe. Wide strides—running. I'd guess they were chasing blindly, not watching for her tracks." Worry creased the cop's forehead. "Bet they remedied that."

"Becca thinks they caught her," Dixon said quietly from the rear.

"I have more men coming," Masterson said. "And two will remain on the road, in case they bypass us."

"Good enough." DeVries moved faster, his instincts clamoring at him to find Lindsey now. She'd escaped, made the bastards chase her. They'd want to make her pay. And then they'd kill her.

⋖⋗

By the time the cabin appeared, Lindsey was shivering with cold and pain and fear. Her legs kept buckling.

"What the fuck has Ricks been doing?" Morales grumbled. "He let her get away and sits on his ass?"

"Probably fucking the other one." Parnell made a disgusted sound. "Moron can't see farther than the end of his dick." He shoved Lindsey into the cabin.

Unable to catch herself, she landed on the floor, her cold knees screaming in pain.

Morales said sharply, "Where's the other bitch?" He picked up the ropes Lindsey had cut off.

"Jesus, he'd better find her." Parnell kicked the door shut. "Christ, how could he lose them both? I should never have let him come along."

Watching silently, Lindsey didn't move. No point in getting up. Her legs were so weak, she couldn't run again.

"Why did you bring him?" Morales asked.

"He insisted. Doesn't trust me to destroy everything." Parnell smirked. "And I wouldn't, if it was only his ass at risk."

Even if Lindsey could have grabbed a knife, her fingers had gone so numb, she wouldn't be able to hold it. Her hopes were disappearing into a black hole. No way out. But…if Becca got Ansel home safe, it was worth it.

It was. *Only…* Slow as molasses, grief trickled into her heart. For those few hours yesterday, she'd been…happy. Zander loved her—she'd never expected that gift. She'd never seen him so content, so open.

Now, now she was going to die; what would her murder do to him? A tear ran down her cheek. *God, Zander, I'm sorry.*

"Oh, look, the puta is crying." Morales rolled her over, dragged her coat off her, and yanked her to her feet. "Puta. I'm gonna hear you beg before you die."

As she sagged in his grip, he braced his legs apart to hold her up.

Without thinking, she jerked her knee up, right into his balls.

The sound he made as he dropped to his knees was incredibly satisfying. She staggered back, knowing she'd suffer, but—

Parnell's fist caught her on the cheekbone and knocked her to the floor.

Again.

This hitting-the-ground-shit was getting old. And she hurt. *Hurt, hurt, hurt.* It would get worse.

She could feel her spirit retreating from the pain even as she sniffled and wept. Deep inside, she retreated into a tight core of separateness. *I'm going to die now.* She knew it. Accepted it. No matter what she said or did, they'd kill her as painfully as they could.

A thin voice inside her was wailing *I want to live.* But she clung to the calm, unbreachable center in her soul. Her daddy seemed to be telling her *be a rock, Linnie. Be like granite.*

Cruel hands ripped her flannel shirt off, leaving her in only her bra. "Time for our chat, bitch," Parnell said. "Time to pay for what you did to my brother." His knee pinned her left arm to the floor. As he looked down at her, his eyes held her death.

He unsheathed his knife and raised it so the narrow blade flashed in the light from the unshielded overhead bulb. "Where'd you hide my brother's flash drives?"

If he made her speak, he'd learn Stanfeld had the evidence, and he might manage to escape. She didn't want him to go free. *Make him kill me before I can talk.* Push him and get it over with.

She had to try twice to get her voice to work. "Fuck you."

"Jesus, you're dumb." He flicked the knife across the soft flesh of her stomach, and she felt only an icy burn.

When he lifted the blade, she saw blood...and the pain blossomed into a line of fire.

"Gonna carve you up like a Sunday roast."

"What about me?" Morales growled. "I want some of that." He pulled his pistol and pointed it at her. "Kneecap her, and she'd talk."

"She'd bleed out too fast, asshole." Parnell drew the edge over her stomach again. Another line of pain.

She gritted her teeth, clinging to her refuge as the pain grew, unendurable, flattening her mind, her soul.

By the fourth line, she was screaming.

⟶⟨∞⟩⟵

DeVries forced himself not to charge into the cabin. But…the sounds. His jaw muscles grated his teeth together. Fuck knew, he'd heard screams before.

Not like this. Not his Lindsey in agony.

The cabin's drapes were drawn. Bear-proofing bars were on the windows. Silently, deVries checked the door. No visible hinges meant it opened inward, probably so drifting snow couldn't block the door from opening. Thank fucking God.

Pistol pointed up, he positioned himself.

Masterson moved beside him and said under his breath, "Let me—"

Cops. "My woman." DeVries ground his left heel through the snow until he hit dirt. Got stable. Lifted his right leg and slammed his boot beside the lock. The thick door splintered, didn't budge. *Shit.* He kicked again. It burst open, and he dove through.

A bullet punched into his vest, taking his breath, another hit beside it.

Enemy upright with pistol. Another kneeling beside Lindsey with a blade. Ignoring the gunman, deVries put two headshots into the knife wielder.

Gunfire filled the room as the cops took up the slack. The guy standing dropped, his face gone.

Ears ringing, deVries moved. *Fuck.* His ribs felt like a semi had plowed into him. A burning line of pain ran up the inside of his upper arm. He holstered his SW1911, jammed his elbow against his side, and slid over to Lindsey.

Fresh fear clawed into him. Her blood was everywhere. Her eyes were closed, her color ashen. *No. Fuck, no.* He put two fingers against her carotid and…felt a pulse. Way too fast, yet strong. The breath he was holding escaped.

She stirred and whimpered, her brows drawing together. Jesus, he wanted to shoot the bastard again. She blinked. When she saw him, her eyes filled with tears. "You came." Her voice was rusty.

"Hell, yeah." He barely kept from grabbing her up. But her stomach had a series of bleeding lines, some deep enough to gape open. "She's bleeding," he shouted. "Dixon, get over—"

"I'm here." Dixon dropped to his knees beside them, already pulling supplies out of the emergency pack. "Damn, girlfriend, you know how I hate blood play." He pulled on latex gloves, covered the cuts with gauze, and pressed down.

Lindsey sucked in a pained breath and whispered a halfhearted, "Ow."

Fuck, I love this woman.

On the other side of her, Ware yanked away Parnell's body. "Good shot, hoss." He crouched down and smiled at Lindsey. "Hey there."

DeVries scowled at him. "Mine."

"Mebbe." Ware smirked before asking, "Lindsey, how many bad guys are here?"

"Three." Her brow creased, and she said carefully, "Parnell, Ricks, and Morales."

"Got it." Ware raised his voice. "Yo, Stanfeld. There's another perp somewhere."

A low acknowledgment came from the agent.

Dixon stripped off his gloves and patted Lindsey's arm. "Okay, BFF, you're all dressed up and ready to party."

"The lieutenant is calling for an ambulance." Ware's body language turned dangerous as he looked at Lindsey's stomach. But when he took her hand, his smile was teasing. "If you change your mind about this bastard..."

"I won't," she whispered before looking at deVries. The love in her gaze was a river of warmth, filling him to the brim. She smiled and said softly, *"Mine."*

Would it be safe to pick her up and hold her now? DeVries reached for her—and pain ripped through his arm. "Fuck!"

"No kidding. You're bleeding like a stuck piggy." Dixon grabbed deVries's wrist, pulling his arm away from his side.

Looking down, deVries realized he was covered in blood. The bullet had nailed the inside of his biceps. Bad.

Dixon applied gauze. Held it. The white immediately turned red. "Shit, you're really bleeding. Get the ambulance here stat, Ware! He's going shocky."

DeVries felt the room waver, and he shivered. Odd how the pulse in his ears was louder than anything else.

"Found Ricks," Stanfeld called from what sounded like a mile or so away.

Stanfeld was suddenly in his face, pushing him onto his back. "Stay down, boy."

DeVries hadn't enough energy to punch him for the insult. Not good. They were a hell of a long way from any hospital. Ambulance probably couldn't get here.

He saw Lindsey struggle to move closer. Her hand curled around his. "Zander." Even drawn with worry, she had the most beautiful face he'd ever seen.

She loved him. Such a fucking unexpected gift. And as the blackness closed in over him, he grieved. So many times he'd expected to die and had lived. Now, when he had someone to live for, now he was gonna buy the farm.

Damn, he didn't want to leave her.

Chapter Twenty-One

The next morning, Lindsey sat beside Zander's hospital bed. The nurse had pushed the chair next to the bed so Lindsey could reassure herself of his survival by holding his hand. His warm, warm hand.

God. She'd come too close to losing him. By the time the ambulance had arrived, his tanned face had been gray-white and his skin terrifyingly cold.

All because he'd had to be a darned hero. Virgil said Zander hadn't waited, had busted open the door and jumped through. And, sheesh, instead of aiming at Morales, who had a gun, Zander had shot Parnell because his knife had threatened *her*.

Dammit. Morales's bullet had almost killed him. "Stubborn, bullheaded idiot," she whispered to him. She attempted to smile as she remembered how he'd told the detective *"mine"* in that possessive tone of voice.

She really was his—and wouldn't want to belong to anyone else. As her eyes filled, she glanced upward, where her father undoubtedly leaned on heaven's fence, one boot up on a rail, watching the goings-on of his children. *Hey, Daddy, are you there? I have a man you'd be proud to call son.*

She could swear she saw his approving nod.

Blinking happily, she toyed with Zander's fingers. Scars on the knuckles, calluses on the palm and fingers. Short, broken fingernails. A man's hand—the Enforcer's hand. Able to deal out punishment as well as pleasure. Someone she could lean on, and in turn, her love would make him stronger.

From the hallway, Dixon's raised voice drew her attention. After a minute of listening, she giggled. Were Dixon's flirtations finally going to come to an end? Feeling unrepentantly snoopy, she pushed her chair a few inches over so she could watch the show through the partially open door.

"Listen, sweet cheeks, you don't have any say over me," Dixon was saying. Hands on hips, he glared up at Stan.

Stan's low voice was very direct. "Wrong, boy. We're going to explore this—all the way." He curled his hand around Dixon's neck and pulled him closer. "I've been looking for someone like you."

"Someone to fuck..." The bitterness in Dixon's voice made Lindsey's heart hurt. And worried her. He'd been burned enough times he was getting cynical. On the other hand, Stan seemed pretty special. *C'mon, Dix, take the leap.*

"Do I look like a man who has trouble finding fuck-buddies? Seriously?"

Lindsey half grinned. A real-life agent, drop-dead handsome, tall, and built. Right—Stan probably got more offers than Zander.

As realization dawned in Dixon's face, he shook his head. "Then what do you want?"

Stan gave a low laugh. "I want a submissive. With a big heart. And loyalty. I hadn't expected courage, but damn, you have that to spare."

Dixon stared up into Stan's face as if he'd found a hero— and he had. Even better, he'd found a Dominant who would appreciate him for who he was. Would give him the control he wanted. Would take care of him.

As Dixon wrapped his arms around Stan, Lindsey let out a happy sigh.

The fingers she was clasping moved. Zander opened his eyes and tilted his chin toward the hallway. "I'm drowning in bleeding hearts. Can you close the door?"

As she rose, the stitches in her stomach protested. *Ow, ow, ow.* Her jeans were only half-zipped and still felt as if the waist was rubbing open her wounds.

Zander's gaze darkened. "Babe." When he reached for her, she evaded him and walked across the room.

As she closed the door, Dixon lifted his head from Stan's shoulder and smiled at her, his eyes filled with joy.

Stan winked at her.

She returned to her chair and settled carefully.

"When was your last pain med?" Zander asked.

She laughed lightly. "I'm supposed to ask you that."

"Hurts like fuck, but I'm alive." He held his hand out. "How about you?"

"Same." Nothing felt as good as having his hand around hers. "I love you."

"I know." His lips twitched when she glared.

"That's not how you're supposed to answer." A tap on the door prevented her from smothering him with his own pillows. "Come in!" One painful trip across the room was enough for a while.

Dixon and Stan entered, followed by Virgil with his wife, Summer. Jake maneuvered in, using crutches.

Right behind him was Kallie, swearing under her breath at his stubbornness. She winked at Lindsey. "Hey, we heard this was where we were supposed to store the cripples."

"Somebody fetch me a quirt," Jake muttered, frowning at her.

"This is the place. Got a spot for you, Jake." Lindsey pointed to the other chair in the room and said to Kallie, "I hope he didn't punish you too badly for helping find the road."

"Hell, no." Kallie wrinkled her nose at her husband as he lowered himself into the chair. "He moves like a moose on stilts; he's sure not going to catch me."

"My mobility, sprite"—he swatted her butt—"will change. And be warned, I'm counting your insults."

Somehow she didn't look very worried.

Simon and Rona came in, followed by Becca and Logan, who held his son in one arm. Ansel saw all the people and gave a baby squeal, kicking to show his approval.

Lindsey's heart lifted. "He doesn't look any the worse for wear. I need cuddles from him, please?" Her attempt to hold her arms up for the baby was abruptly halted by the pull on her stomach. She winced. "Never mind."

Beside her, Zander made a low growling noise. Logan's eyes turned a steely blue, and Simon's jaw tightened.

Doms. "Jeez, guys, lighten up. It's only a few cuts." Lindsey looked to the women for support.

Instead, Rona enfolded her in a gentle hug. "You... *Crom*, girlfriend, don't you *ever*..." Unable to finish, Rona huffed out a breath and kissed Lindsey's cheek, before returning to Simon and pushing her face against his shoulder.

Becca's eyes were filled with tears.

Lindsey heaved a sigh. The women were as bad as the men, and they were going to make her cry. "Get a grip, y'all. Everybody survived, mostly intact. And I'll make Zander hold me if I have nightmares."

The tightness eased from Logan's face. "It helps to have someone." He wrapped an arm around his wife and nuzzled her temple.

Lindsey smiled at him before glancing at Simon. "I want to thank y'all for your *extremely* bossy behavior in making me talk about Victor's death. Parnell figured I'd never reveal being wanted for murder, so he didn't expect anyone to come looking for me." But they had. *God.* She blinked hard and looked around the room. "And thank you all for the rescue."

"Ah, speaking of which, I almost forgot your toy." Stan dug in his pocket and handed over her knife in a new sheath. "This is yours, right?"

"Hey, thanks." Lindsey checked it, slipped it into her own pocket, then squeezed Zander's arm. She'd told him how it had saved her and Becca and Ansel.

His eyes darkened with memories, but after a second, his dimple appeared. "Every cowgirl should have a knife."

"Lindsey." Stan's voice was serious. "Time for less enjoyable topics."

Her heart sank despite the fact that she'd known what was

coming. "I need to go back to Texas, right?"

"You do. Immediately. I doubt you'll end up being charged once all is said and done. All the same, you have warrants stacked up that must be cleared."

"Will I have to go to jail?"

A shadow darkened his face. "It's not my decision or jurisdiction, and—"

"No. You won't," Simon said firmly. "As it happens, Xavier was quite annoyed at being left out of the fighting." His lips quirked. "So he and Abby are flying to San Antonio today. They—and your new lawyer—will meet you at the airport when you arrive. Your lawyer doesn't think you'll need bail; nonetheless, you're covered if it's necessary. No jail, Lindsey."

"Xavier can't up and simply leave." She stared at him. "He has a business and—"

"And a very bossy wife who loves you like a sister," Rona said.

Zander squeezed Lindsey's fingers. "Thank Xavier for us both. I didn't want her there alone, but the doctor won't discharge me for a couple of days."

As relief relaxed her muscles, Lindsey sagged in her chair. She wouldn't have to spend Christmas in jail.

She was going home. To Texas.

⋅◇✕◇⋅

On Christmas Eve, Lindsey settled down with her niece in front of the fireplace. How many hours as a little girl had she spent on this hearth, watching the fire and daydreaming about her future?

The path to her future sure had gotten derailed, hadn't it?

She shook her head, enjoying the piney fragrance from the massive Christmas tree in the corner. Angels lined the mantel, a knee-high Santa Claus at the door held umbrellas, and the antique nativity scene was set up in the dining room. All so familiar.

It was reassuring to return and see Melissa continuing the old traditions. Since only Melissa had an interest in ranching, she'd taken the central ranch and her two sisters the outer areas.

Her mouth twisted. If Mandy had drawn the high card, she'd have gotten the border property, and Victor would have gone after her. Thank God that hadn't happened.

Clattering noises came from the kitchen where Mama and Mandy were preparing a stew. Rather than cooking, Lindsey had been assigned the Emily-sitting chore—which wasn't a hardship in the least. She nuzzled the baby's soft blonde curls. "Did you know you're my favorite niece?"

Lindsey looked up as Melissa came in. "Hey."

"Hey, sissie."

As Melissa hung up her coat, Lindsey returned her attention to Emily. "You are definitely the smartest baby in the whole world." Big brown eyes looked up as Lindsey nodded solemnly. "And the bravest. And prettiest."

"And going to be the most conceited," Melissa added in a wry voice. She came over to kiss her daughter's head and give Lindsey a gentle hug before dropping into a chair. "You're spoiling her, you know."

"Yep. I can't help it if you and Gary created a superior child." As she made a buzzing noise against the little arm, Emily giggled.

"Her daddy totally agrees with you." Melissa held her palms out to the fire. "Lordy, I hate mucking out stalls." At Lindsey's raised eyebrows, she muttered, "We gave the hands some holiday time."

"Soft touch." Lindsey pointed her finger at her sister. "Mama warned you ranching was a twenty-four/seven job."

"I should have listened. She's usually right…as long as she isn't talking about sex." Melissa rolled her eyes. "Remember when she told me I could get pregnant from kissing? How old was I? Seven?"

Lindsey snickered. "Well, sheesh, what kind of a tramp were you, smooching with Danny in first grade?"

"He gave me a Pokémon card," Melissa said with dignity. "Of course, I kissed him."

"Those were the days. You know, when I started dating

Peter, she delivered the never-let-a-guy-past-first-base lecture."

"Did I hear that spiel? Oh wait, I remember—you can't get him excited because blue balls can be fatal."

"Yep, that's it. So then Peter gropes my boobs, and I worry all damn night if I should have told his mother—you know, in case she needed to call an ambulance."

Melissa let out of scream of laughter.

"It's not funny." She scowled. "I thought I'd killed the poor boy with my slutty behavior."

"Lordy, I've missed you." Dragging in a breath, Melissa wiped her eyes. "I'm so glad you're back. Have you been here all afternoon?"

The last few days had been hectic, and although her mother and sisters had come to San Antonio for a quick welcome home, Lindsey hadn't had any time to talk. "Nah, only for an hour or so." She grinned at her niece. "Enough time to get acquainted with your little flirt."

"Ma-ma-da-da-aaa," Emily responded happily and yanked Lindsey's hair.

Melissa frowned. "Do you have to go back to San Antonio?"

The sound of Amanda gossiping about school came from the kitchen, and the scent of venison stew filled the air. Lindsey felt wrapped in the sounds and smells of home. "Nope. All the briefing stuff is done. I might have to testify at Ricks's trial, but Stanfeld thought he'll try to cut a deal instead." She remembered the best news. "They located the Mexican boy who escaped. He was at a Catholic mission, and the priest figured out who he was. Juan backed up what I said, and he'll be back with his family this week."

"Excellent." Melissa sipped her drink and frowned. "Seriously, though, are you safe now? Will Ricks come after you?"

"Agent Bonner says doubtful. The judge denied bail, and they've impounded all his criminal gains. Since he's a cop, he'll be occupied with trying to survive prison."

"Oh. Right. You know, I don't have a problem at all with him having to fight for his life."

Her sister's voice was too grim. Needing to change the

subject, Lindsey nodded at the side window, where a low table displayed a wealth of African violet plants. "Thank you for rescuing my babies, by the way."

"My pleasure. Nonetheless you owe me twenty dollars for bribing the housekeeper to fetch them out. Mandy is tending the snake and spider plants from your ranch house." Melissa rolled her eyes. "She talks to them the same way you did. *'And how are my snakes and spiders today?'* You two really are warped."

"Hey, plants are sensitive," Lindsey said in a self-righteous tone. "You have to be nice to them."

"Did I hear Melissa come in?" Their mother appeared in the doorway. Her perfectly colored hair was clipped on top of her head, and she wore a trim slacks-and-sweater outfit.

Lindsey smiled as love surged through her. All Southern gentility and fussiness, and yet there wasn't a sweeter woman in the world.

"Dinner will be in another hour. Lindsey, honey, I made you a margarita." Her mother set the drink down on the coffee table. "Where's Gary?"

"He'd started feeding the stock when I came in." Melissa glanced at the darkening front windows. "He should be done soon."

"Good timing. Mandy ran upstairs to have a quick shower." Their mother beamed around the room. "It's nice to have my babies all in one house again." She patted Melissa's head. "And even nicer someone else is stuck cleaning this monstrosity."

It had all worked out wonderfully too. When their mother took a place in town, Melissa and Gary had chosen to live in the Rayburn house instead of his adjoining ranch. There was nothing like marrying the boy next door and merging ranches. And even though her sister had fallen for Gary way back in high school, their love had lasted.

Lindsey felt her pleasure waver. She hadn't heard from Zander after leaving him at the hospital three days ago. Nothing. Of course, he couldn't call her, since her cell phone was in a ditch somewhere on a snowy mountain. The problem was that the times she'd tried to reach him, he hadn't answered his phone. Everything went to voice mail.

The hospital said they'd discharged him yesterday.

Maybe he'd managed to get the number here, though. "Did you check your messages today?"

Melissa rolled her eyes. "I started, but I can't tolerate those: ' *This is so-and-so from the such-and-such paper.'* They filled my voice mail."

"Right. Sorry. Give it another week, and I'll be old news." Tonight she'd listen to the messages.

The anxiety had her squeezing Emily so tightly her little niece giggled. Maybe Zander wasn't interested any longer. No, that was silly. He'd almost died for her. *Jeez, girl, stop being so vulnerable.* There was an explanation why he didn't answer his phone. Probably the battery'd died or something.

And hey, if he didn't want her, he'd face her and tell her it was over.

The thought made her feel as if her heart had been trampled under a cattle stampede. Had been ripped and flattened.

No. That wasn't it. They had something between them. It hadn't disappeared because a half-a-continent and a few days separated them. She sighed. God, she'd be happy when her emotions weren't bouncing around like grasshoppers on drugs.

Outside, the two ranch dogs set up a clamor. Melissa tilted her head. "Guess Gary finished already."

A tap sounded on the door.

"He must have his hands full. Did you ask him to gather eggs, Mama?" Melissa opened the front door. "Hey, did you— Um, hi. Can I help you?"

Uneasy at the alarm in her sister's tone, Lindsey handed Emily to her mother and hurried over. What if there were still bad cops around?

"Is Lindsey here?" The voice held more gravel than the road out front. Deep. Hard. Raw. Zander was here.

Oh my effing God. The shock was followed by such surging joy she felt the air around her sparkle. She flew the last few feet.

And there he was. Standing politely on the porch, waiting for Melissa's answer. He saw Lindsey, and his expression lightened. Heated. "Seems she is."

Melissa turned far enough to look at Lindsey. Her eyes narrowed. "And seems there's a tale or two someone missed telling."

Uh-oh.

When Melissa glanced at Zander, uneasiness filled her face, but she moved away.

Lindsey managed a step forward before Zander's steady gray-green gaze made her hesitate. She stalled, unable to more. "You're here." Her words were only a whisper. "You came."

Satisfaction filled his gaze; nonetheless, he hesitated. "Maybe this isn't a good time…"

She threw herself at him.

He caught her easily, only a grunt betraying his injuries.

"Oh shit." She froze and started to step back. "I'm sorry—I forgot about your ribs."

"Fuck my ribs," he muttered and yanked her closer, holding her carefully enough he didn't hurt her stomach—and so firmly she knew she'd never escape. *Thank you, God.*

Each breath she took was filled with his clean masculine scent, and when he buried his face in the curve of her shoulder, she burrowed even closer. "I missed you so, so much."

"You might not feel so friendly"—the voice was that of Dark Haven's sadistic Enforcer—"after I whip your ass for disappearing." Then he sighed and added, "I missed you too." He kissed her, slowly and thoroughly, before looking over her head. And stiffening.

Lindsey glanced back and smiled at her stunned mother and sisters. Mandy stood behind Melissa.

Zander cleared his throat. "I'm Zander deVries." He studied her family for a moment and accurately pegged them. "Mrs. Rayburn. Melissa." He turned to her littlest sister. "And Amanda?"

"You and your damn search programs," Lindsey muttered. "That's right."

"It's good to meet you, Zander." Melissa gave Lindsey another of the sisters-who-hold-out-on-the-good-stuff-get-hurt stares. "Obviously, you know more than we do. I'm not sure why

298 | CHERISE SINCLAIR

Lindsey hasn't told us anything about you."

He raised an eyebrow, and Lindsey flushed. "I didn't because—" She smacked him hard on his uninjured shoulder. "You bastard. I've been calling you. Why aren't you returning my calls?"

One corner of his lips tipped up. "Busted my cell diving into a hunting cabin. I called you; you're not answering your phone. Left messages here you didn't return."

"Oh jeez." She leaned her forehead against his chest. "The ranch voice mail is full of reporters. And my phone is in a snowbank somewhere down the road from Serenity. Morales didn't want the GPS around."

He snorted and lifted her chin. "I see we still have a bit of a trust issue here."

"I...was worried. A little." *A lot.* Her lips curved. "And you weren't?"

"Hell, yeah. Difference is I know I'm not letting you go."

"Doms," she said under her breath.

Little Tex had a crazy family, deVries thought a few hours later as they sat in the great room and chatted. They'd been cautious around him at first...until after supper. While the women were cleaning up, Lindsey had dumped the baby girl into his lap. Almost scared the piss out of him. Melissa had started over to fetch her child—although her husband, Gary, hadn't made a move.

But Emily had chortled, grabbed his T-shirt, and pulled herself to her feet so she could pat his face and explore his mouth and beard stubble with her tiny fingers. And laugh. The kid had Lindsey's infectious laugh in a baby-size portion.

Fucking adorable.

Melissa had resumed her work.

Lindsey had winked at him. Yeah, he was going to beat on her for that one.

The evening was getting late; however, no one seemed to

care—probably because they'd all shared a pitcher of margaritas, the Rayburn household drink. Melissa was regaling everyone with tales of Lindsey's younger days—his Tex had been a hellion—and stories of sisterly catfights.

Catfights. Be a hell of a thing to watch. He and Gary grinned at each other.

"Well, I need to retire for the night." Tammy rose and kissed her daughters. "Y'all go ahead and party."

"I should be going," deVries said, wondering how to get out from under the sleeping baby on his lap.

With a snort, Gary claimed his child. "She needs to be put to bed anyway, but I thought you were staying."

"He is." Melissa gave him a happy smile. "Mom and I made you up a room upstairs."

"Yes, we put you next to Lindsey's bedroom." Tammy frowned at her daughter. "However, don't you get him...excited. We don't need any fatalities on Christmas Eve."

Fatalities? DeVries gave the woman a puzzled look before hilarity burst out from the three sisters.

Lindsey was giggling so hard her face had turned purple. She was wearing the fuzzy hoodie he'd bought her, and the teddy bear ears were bouncing up and down. Damn, some women couldn't handle alcohol well at all.

With a grin, he scooped her off the floor and settled her onto his lap.

Fucking A, this was where she belonged. He rubbed his chin on her hair, feeling her giggles like tiny vibrations against his chest.

"I almost forgot. We're going to need more milk, honeybunches," Tammy said to Lindsey. "Can you make a quick trip to the store in the morning?"

"Sure, Mama," Lindsey wheezed. "I can—"

"Not without me," deVries said.

"What?" Laughter slowing, she frowned up at him. "Agent Bonner said I should be safe now. And—"

"No." The thought of her in danger again sent an icy dagger

into his gut. "Bonner can't guarantee they got everyone. Could be a cop or two—or anyone—who might resent your involvement."

"But—"

"Argue all you want. You don't go anywhere alone. Not in Texas."

Gary winked at his wife before nodding at deVries. "You'll do, partner. You'll do."

"That could be argued," Lindsey muttered grumpily. But she huffed a laugh, leaned in, and whispered, "Stubborn Dom," before kissing his cheek.

He hugged her closer, feeling that odd warmth in the center of his chest. *My woman.*

Was she? It was damned well time to nail her down and find out where they stood. As Mandy and Melissa argued about a Cowboys' play, deVries leaned back and repositioned Lindsey so she straddled his legs. So he could see her face.

She wrinkled her nose at him. "You look awfully serious."

"Yeah." He stroked his knuckles over her cheek and watched her brown eyes go soft. "Now things are settled here, are you staying in Texas or coming back to San Francisco?"

LINDSEY HAD BEEN listening to her sisters bickering, and Zander's question came as a surprise. She blinked and stared at him. "Um."

His jaw was tight, and the lines fanning out from the corners of his eyes had deepened. "Gotta do better than *um.*"

He had a point. Everything had been too unstable for the past few months to make real decisions about her future. Still, she'd had dreams and longings. Wanting to come home. And building castles in the air around a life with Zander.

Her brows drew together. "What would you do if I said Texas?"

"Find a job down here."

Her mouth dropped open. "Really? B-but you love San Francisco. You told me that."

"Babe, I didn't even like being a couple of miles from you. I might miss California, but I'm sure as hell not going to live all the way across the country from you."

"Oh," she said, the word almost a sigh. He'd let her decide. She could stay here where her family was. Where she'd grown up. Texas was her home. *Isn't it?*

Yet Mandy would be going off to college. And, no matter how much she loved Melissa, she didn't want to live on a ranch. Or work in a small town. The kind of career she wanted was more suited to a city. She bit her lip.

Silently, Zander curled his hands around her hips, holding her steady...and letting her think.

What was her other choice? She could return to San Francisco, where her two best friends lived—ones who would drop everything to support her.

Return to where she had an awesome job and a fantastic boss.

Return to where she had a club to play in and a duplex she loved. And where she could watch the ongoing saga of Dixon and Stan. Her lips curled up. How could she resist?

"Isn't this strange? I've wanted to come back to Texas and take up my life again, and somehow, without realizing it, I made a new life. New friends. New family."

His hands tightened painfully on her hips. "Go on," he said softly.

"I want to live in San Francisco. With you." She put her hand on her chest, feeling breathless. God, she was insane—nonetheless, it was true.

He nodded as if he hadn't cared one way or the other; slowly his fingers relaxed.

She narrowed her eyes at him. "You really were willing to live here in Texas?"

"Yeah. I came close to buying the farm last week—but I wasn't fucking about to leave you. I figure you dragged me back to the living." He curled his hand around her nape. His grip hadn't changed a bit—unbreakable and determined—just like his words. "I go where you go, Tex."

"Same here."

Whatever he saw in her face made him smile. He drew closer, rubbed his cheek against hers, then took her lips in a kiss so deep and wet that she heard her sisters cheering—before the roaring in her ears washed them away.

No, home wasn't a state—not California or Texas. Instead, her home was one damn big Dom. Rough-hewn, and deadly when crossed. Blunt, grumpy at times, dominating and possessive.

Yep, right here, wrapped in the Enforcer's arms, was where she belonged.

The End

CHERISE SINCLAIR

Now everyone thinks summer romances never go anywhere, right? Well...that's not always true.

I met my dearheart when vacationing in the Caribbean. Now I won't say it was love at first sight. Actually, since he was standing over me, enjoying the view down my swimsuit top, I might even have been a tad peeved—as well as attracted. But although our time together there was less than two days, and although we lived in opposite sides of the country, love can't be corralled by time or space.

We've now been married for many, many years. (And he still looks down my swimsuit tops.)

Nowadays, I live in the west with my beloved husband, two children, and various animals, including three cats who rule the household. I'm a gardener, and I love nurturing small plants until they're big and healthy and productive...and ripping defenseless weeds out by the roots when I'm angry. I enjoy thunderstorms, playing Scrabble and Risk, and being a soccer mom. My favorite way to spend an evening is curled up on a couch next to the master of my heart, watching the fire, reading, and...well...if you're reading this book, you obviously know what else happens in front of fires. :)

—*Cherise*

Visit http://www.cherisesinclair.com to find out more about Cherise and her books.

Loose Id® Titles by Cherise Sinclair

Available in digital format and print at your favorite retailer

Edge of the Enforcer
My Liege of Dark Haven

———✦———

The MASTERS OF THE SHADOWLANDS Series
Make Me, Sir
To Command and Collar
This Is Who I Am
If Only

———✦———

"Simon Says: Mine"
Part of the anthology *Doms of Dark Haven*
With Sierra Cartwright and Belinda McBride

———✦———

"Welcome to the Dark Side"
Part of the anthology *Doms of Dark Haven 2:*
Western Night
With Sierra Cartwright and Belinda McBride

CPSIA information can be obtained at www.ICGtesting.com
Printed in the USA
BVOW02s0710110614

356045BV00002B/272/P